# BEST
# EUROPEAN
# FICTION

# 2017

Partially funded by the Illinois Arts Council, a state agency

Please see Acknowledgments on pages 307 for additional information
on the support received for this volume.

www.dalkeyarchive.com
Victoria, TX / McLean, IL / Dublin

Dalkey Archive Press publications are, in part, made possible through the support of the University
of Houston-Victoria and its program in creative writing, publishing, and translation.

Cover design by Gail Doobinin
Printed on permanent/durable acid-free paper

# BEST EUROPEAN FICTION

# 2017

### PREFACE BY
### EILEEN BATTERSBY

DALKEY ARCHIVE PRESS

# Contents

# PREFACE

THE WORLD IS growing smaller, ever smaller. The speed of travel, communication, headline-breaking news – much of it grim – is creating a universal language of celebrity and shared symbols or points of reference, such as those contained in a TV show or a broadcaster's familiar catch cry. We all watch the same movies, listen to the same music, and increasingly, read the same books.

Everything seems immediate, more accessible - because it is. The world of story is equally on the move, in fact it is moving even more quickly and is ever evolving; writers, traditionalists as well as innovators, continue to work, explore new themes. Other voices will emerge, develop, and mature. Crucial to this ceaseless expansion are translators, skilled linguists, who are themselves artists, alert to language and the wonders of nuance. This point must be made because new fiction is about far more than the latest big publishing deal that is mooted between New York and London; it is about the fiction writers across the world are shaping in a multitude of tongues.

Nowhere is this explosion quite as diverse and exciting and as freewheeling as in Europe, where the tradition was shaped in the nineteenth century by literary masters from Russia and France and from the nation-states of what would become modern Germany. A casual observer asked for the one word which dictated writing in Europe would, probably, immediately reply "war." It is true; territories ceded, cultures repressed, identities left reeling in chaotic self-doubt. European fiction retained a correct, measured intelligence; history, society and tradition dominated as did a prevailing sense of melancholy which tended to conceal the very anger that had caused so much conflict in the first place. Lamentation became a shared, subtle communal response, as Joseph Roth suggested in his defining novel, *The Radetzky March* (1932). To hail from Europe was to be somehow denied the freedom which North Americans and Australians if ever eager to assimilate took for granted while Africans and Asians looked on, wondering at what it was like to lose something successive colonializations had denied them. Original fiction written in languages other than English was simply not receiving the priority it deserved.

It had to change. And it has.

*Best European Fiction*, spanning Scandinavia, Western and Central Europe, the Balkans and the Baltic, Iberia, the islands of Great Britain and Ireland, is the most cohesive bulletin one could hope to find. Since its inception in 2010 it has proven to be a vibrant and informed literary gazette; daring in its selections. Now in its eighth year it continues to present new voices, new trends; both the preoccupations of the moment and the broader way in which the individual has come to supplant the public.

Over these years of change, Europe has not only begun to look more outward, it has taken over much of the energy and anarchic self-absorption which had made fiction from North America and Australia appear to be saying something that was new, more fresh. *Uppsala Woods* (2009) by Spaniard Alvaro Colomer, translated by Jonathan Dunne, is a numbingly funny and tragic study of a mosquito expert's collapse in the face of daily living. It is ironic and also worth noting that the dysfunctional family and marriage breakdown, so long thematic domains of US writers and filmmakers, have been adopted astutely by Europeans. The Austro-German Daniel Kehlmann proved, with his sharp, witty and poignant domestic drama, *F.* (2013, translated by the late Carol Brown Janeway, 2014) that he was far better at working Jonathan Franzen's chosen territory than Franzen could ever hope to be.

Visionaries such as Jon Fosse, Julian Rios, Peter Stamm, Christine Montalbetti, Jean-Philippe Toussaint, Jean Echenoz, Drago Jancar, Clemens Meyer, Ingo Schulze, David Albahari, Peter Terrin, George Konrad and his fellow Hungarian, the magus himself, Laszlo Krasznahorkai, have featured in Best European Fiction's pages. English writers have also been included. I first encountered British originals Tom McCarthy and Nicholas Mosley in previous editions. Why 'visionaries'? Why not simply 'writers'? Because each of those mentioned succeeds in looking at the ordinary in a different way. Their individual responses to life and the world in its internal and external forms do amount to visions of perception.

Publishing moves in mysterious ways and while readers enjoy discovering new writers, publishing giants tend to play safe and permit market forces to run advertising campaigns promoting obvious blockbusters that have already been secured by Hollywood. It takes the courage of independent publishers to consider writing as art and not as a commercial venture. Passion plays a part, as do perception and instinct. The independent publisher is alert to ideas, not fads; there is a valuable awareness of the individual response of a writer when exploring that most impossible of subjects: what it is to be human. It can be complicated – even abstract; human and alone, human and lost, human and angry. Most of all there is cohesion; little more than a century separates, or links, *Knut Hamsun's Hunger* (1890) with his fellow Norwegian Stig Saeterbakken's *Self-Control* (1998) and both are about responses to inner turmoil and both share that immediacy which great fiction achieves and retains.

For too long contemporary international fiction in translation seemed to inhabit a rarefied position, that of little more than minority reading for literary specialists and academics. How often have you groaned on hearing someone loftily announcing, "I only read originals." If so, does that mean that unless he or she reads Russian, they will not have experienced Turgenev and Chekhov? Much has been made of the small percentage of readers who will consider a novel or short story collection which has been translated from the original language. How many times has the coverage of the Nobel Prize in Literature been determined by the nationality, or more importantly the language in which the recipient writes and whether or not their work is available in English? But again, this has changed. It is a fact that the establishment of a competition such as the International Dublin Literary Award in 1995, then under the sponsorship of IMPAC, dramatically increased the readership of international fiction in translation. To date the winners have included Romanian Herta Müller and Turk Orhan Pamuk who both were later awarded the Nobel Prize, while Norwegian Per Petterson's international reputation was consolidated by winning in 2007 for his third novel, *Out Stealing Horses*.

Prizes help and yes, independent publishers, often lone champions, have enabled this to happen. We the readers have benefited and the rest is literary history in the making. Readers alert to independent publishers rather than publishing giants and hype have been seeking, identifying and supporting interesting writing. It sounds simple but this is exactly what has been happening, assisted by word of mouth and that most effective of opinion makers – book clubs. And all made possible by the efforts of literary translators. This year, 2016, witnessed the revamping of the Man International Booker Prize. It is now about far more than an award, it is an expression of confidence in the marketability of quality fiction in translation. If writers, readers, critics and publishers are pleased so too are booksellers.

Instead of being awarded to an author for a body of work, the Man International Booker Prize is now presented to a single book. Most importantly, the prize is shared equally between author and translator. It could be argued that the author should have a larger share of the prize money but the point has been made; translation is understanding and understanding is power. Translated fiction is also winning a growing share of readership, which has been proven to have increased almost one hundred percent since 2001. It sounds unbelievable. But why should it be all that surprising when one considers that many classic works of literature over the centuries have been translated into English from their original languages?

Literary translation is not elitist, it is essential, a vital transition; looking at a view through a window, the glass may be slightly misted by rain, but the view is still emphatically visible. Literary translation is of course a huge subject and Western readers are now discovering major Japanese, Chinese, Korean and Vietnamese writing. Yet our subject here is the diversity of contemporary European fiction. The Balkan region continues to intrigue with writers such as Albania's Ismail Kadare, who, by the way, was awarded the inaugural Man Booker International Prize in 2005. "At dusk the city [his birthplace Gjirokastë], which through the centuries had appeared on maps as possessions of the Romans, the Normans, the Byzantines, the Turks, the Greeks and the Italians, now watched darkness fall as part of the German empire" writes Kadare in his finest work, *Chronicle in Stone* (1971). The passage could be addressing the plight of many European peoples as their borders, rulers, and at times even their languages changed in the aftermath of each new war.

The Balkan wars of the 1990s have inspired a younger generation of writers such as Bosnian Selvedin Avdic: "Whoever ends up reading this text will not be my choice, as I have no say in the matter. Maybe that's a good thing, because I've never managed to choose the best option in my life . . ." (from *Seven Terrors*, 2012; translated by Coral Petkovich, also 2012). In common with many writers from the Balkans, Avdic not only has his own rich cultural heritage to draw from, in his everyman fiction he has also cracked Western culture. His depressed narrator, still suffering in the wake of his failed marriage has spent about nine months attempting to recover, largely in bed. Reading fashion magazines helps pass the time: ". . . I found out that something called Clinque exists – a new dramatically different gel: and another page brought a Tiffany broach, magical like the arch of a mosque in Isfahan, which I had seen in a photograph. The 'In Vogue' column presented me with compelling news from the latest fashion line and informed me that hysteria was ruling the world – the cause was a red dress in which every woman would become provocative." Aside from humour though there is the sense of having been present at dangerous times. Translation can and does soar. Also from *Seven Terrors*: "Silence. But it was not normal silence. This was inhabited. Something was living in it. It had composed itself and was holding its breath . . . something full of anger and hatred."

French and Spanish are the two European and international languages which are proving vehicles for much of the most exciting fiction being written in our sad, angry, exciting era. Siberian writer Andrei Makine has written all of his thirteen novels to date in French, not in Russian, and has said writing in French makes him think "with more exactness." Many of Ismail Kadare's books have been translated into English from Albanian via French. And to Spanish must be added Galician as spearheaded by Manuel Rivas (translated by Jonathan Dunne), Bernardo Atxaga who writes in

Spanish and Basque, and Catalan Eduard Marquez, whose novella, *Brandes' Decision* (2006; translation by Mara Faye Lethem, 2016), both celebrates and deconstructs the power of memory.

Intellectualism has always dogged fiction, preoccupied as it has been with the cerebral and the sleight of hand, demonstrated so magisterially by Alain Robbe-Grillet. Unique among his peers in this respect is the mercurial Jean Echenoz, who delights in tricks yet also engages with humanity through a candid generosity of spirit, as his novels based respectively on the composer Ravel and the long distance, Olympic hero Emil Zatopek, testify. Echenoz's profundity, as evidenced in his war novel *1914*, is countered by his lightness of touch and a balancing of pop culture with high art. Marie Darrieussecq's *Pig Tales* (1996; translated by Linda Coverdale, 1997) displays this peculiarly French flair for juxtaposing the profound with the profane. If Echenoz has a kindred spirit it is most probably the Spanish writer Enrique Vila-Matas, whose magpie flair suggests that he is aware of what writers all over the world are doing.

Considering a volume such as this new selection of work by European writers, many of whose names are unfamiliar, is not daunting. Instead it entices. The influences are present, Kundera and his compatriot Josef Skvorecky still shape the voices of younger writers. Equally can a translator draw a reader to a work. The veteran Celia Hawkesworth's lively rendition of young Croatian Olja Savicevic's debut *Adios, Cowboy*, extracted in an earlier selection, draws one on to Vedrana Rudan's forthcoming *Love at Last Sight*. Hawkesworth has also translated Rudan's *Night* and the Croatian Vladimir Arsenijevic's debut, *In the Hold – A Soap Opera* (1994), which remains an urgent, eye-witness account of what it was like for the post-Tito generation coming to age in a Yugoslavia that would no longer exist.

Why read European fiction in translation? Because it consistently proves to be among the finest literature of ideas, emotion and sensation in the world; thrilling, profound and heartfelt, it has created writers such as the metaphysical Berliner Jenny Erpenbeck who explores her country's fractured past in order to understand its present. Why read *Best European Fiction 2017*? It is the surest way of following the path forward.

# BEST
# EUROPEAN
# FICTION

# 2017

# TERESA PRÄAUER

## FROM *Johnny and Jean*

I PICTURE MYSELF as a young boy living in the countryside.

It's summertime, and we're sitting together in the grass, a group of girls and—yes, we already call them "guys." Some talk about going away, others talk about staying here. Then someone runs to the edge of the pool and everyone chases after him, some jump from the one-meter springboard, most do what we call a cannon-ball: splashing into the water with your knees tucked in, trying to be the loudest.

I dive in head first and almost lose my trunks. I quickly pull them up underwater, resurface, and see if anyone saw. Everyone claps and cheers, because someone's done a somersault from the three-meter board; he's the one they call Jean.

Then the summer is over and each of us goes his separate way, as the saying goes.

I don't see Jean again until I show up in the city with my work under my arm. I didn't go to the largest city, but the second-largest. Jean was here before me, he managed to take the earlier train, and already knows his way around. He's laid out his work and taken his shoes off under the table. He lays his portfolio on the table—no, he doesn't even have a portfolio, his pictures are gigantic, and he's made a handsome roll out of them, which he now spreads out on the floor. I turn around and see everyone staring at Jean and his roll, see him cut the cord and unfurl the individual leaves: each as big as the entire room all of us are standing in, where we've been waiting for half the day to be called up one by one.

I'm sitting now with Jean and the others underneath Jean's canopy of pictures, and we all scoot closer together, Jean sits in the middle and is pelted with questions. Having sat down next to Jean before, I'm almost sitting far away from him now, another three people have squeezed in to the narrow gap between us because they want to be close to Jean. I think what a dope Jean was when he cannonballed into that pool in the countryside, just a few weeks ago actually, and how magnificent he is now. I also think that his name isn't Jean, because no one's really called Jean where we come from, but I decide not to say anything for now. Then let it be that way, Jean, nobody knows how to pronounce it here anyway.

Jean is called up and they take him right away. He doesn't have to go through any more interviews or hand in any sample work. Jean can simply go home and pick up his *oeuvre* where he left off. When they call me up and I lay my portfolio on the table and pull out my studies of little fish in a water glass, I notice that something's not right. I notice it at precisely that moment.

They're correct, they're accurate, they're true-to-life, and I was still very proud of them when I mounted them in passe-partouts and sorted them into a portfolio. A homemade portfolio! I told myself, yep, that's just what a fish looks like, as my father slapped me on the back appreciatively. We even chose the colors of the passe-partouts together. I'd just learned the word for them.

In the city I realize, almost too late, that no one here paints little detailed reproductions of fish on paper in pastel colors. I stand before my pictures, and the school of fish looks at me from its hundred eyes, and he, too, like all the others, shakes his head in disappointment: Boy, wake up!

For one whole year, I walk the streets of the city crestfallen. When I look up to the sky, I see Jean's unfurled picture above me, covering up the sun, for an entire year. I'm ashamed of my fish, that I didn't have the presence of mind to leave them at home in my boyhood room. What I'm capable of is not what they want anymore. I look at the streets and the paths before me, thinking: I'll never catch up to Jean. His lead is just too big.

The following year I join him. In the months of waiting I've prepared myself, I've painted my pictures on rolls of paper and gotten rid of the fish—actually, I gave them to my neighbors. I attend every class I can now, I want to learn everything. I have twelve new arms and a hand on each one, each of which is doing something different. I want to make up for the year I missed, and I see Jean way ahead of me.

Jean has made a lot of progress. He even has a space with his name on it. Everyone calls him Jean here, and if there's something someone doesn't know, everyone just says: Ask Jean.

I knew nothing, so I looked for him, was planning to ask him everything, but Jean wasn't there. I took my thermos and sleeping bag and camped one day and night outside his door, waiting for him to come. Everyone passing by had something to say about Jean, but still Jean never showed up.

He was already the talk of the town. I think I said something about Jean too, in order to be a part of it; I called out his name, waved to him, then cupped my hand like a telephone, as if he were standing on the other side of the street, barely visible, and we'd call each other later.

I imagine making an important date with Jean.

We meet at the lake, at the hotel bar of Eden au Lac—no, wrong direction, we stay in our town and go to the seediest dive on the wharf. At Eden au Lac with Jean, that would come later, when we're older and money is no longer an issue.

For now, I imagine, we sit at the dive on the wharf and Jean tells me about his adventures. Jean has affairs befitting his name, or he claims to have had them, and I hide the fact that I never so much as kissed someone, back when there were girls, when they hadn't yet turned into women like now. Still, I do my best to keep up the conversation with Jean.

We order something alcoholic, and I imagine Jean is the one who decides what we're worthy of at this point in time. Pastis maybe, if a little sip weren't so expensive. But with a jug of water it's enough for a feast. Two more pastis, and then another two. Staggering home drunk together, Jean sees me off with an embrace and says: You're *mon ami*.

Now I'm his friend and Yankee. I imagine my name is Johnny.

Surely no one here is called Johnny, and back in the country-side, too, no one went by the name of Johnny, but I use the name to make a start in the city. Johnny, the quiet one, is not the best of roles, but it's better than no name or no face at all. It would certainly suit Jean to have a pallid admirer running behind him with a portfolio full of fish pictures, all of which he's given away.

Jean is working on his *oeuvre*.

Whenever there are dumpsters on the street, he climbs inside and digs through the bulky refuse. For several weeks straight, wherever you look, you see Jean climbing and digging all over the place. I see him by chance, several times a day, at distant parts of town. He's always at it, heart and soul. I don't even dare approach him, not wanting to distract him from his work.

I'm sure that Jean has multiplied himself, there must be four of him at least. A whole gang of Jeans is climbing and digging in time, second by second: tock-tock-tock-tock-tock-tock-tock.

Sometimes they drive Jean away, and sometimes the passersby shout something at him; but other times people even let him into their homes, and Jean is allowed to climb up to their attics to see if he can find something usable.

Those young people with their ripped jeans, the older home-owning ladies say, and sometimes one of them serves up coffee and cake to Jean.

No one knows what Jean does with all the things he finds. I can't get any work done myself, because I'm always asking myself what Jean must be up to.

We all wait for Jean and gradually get to know each other. I'm Johnny, I say to the others, and they call me Johnny.

Sometimes they talk about Jean. He's very busy, they say, and they talk about the places he hasn't been; they say that Jean is only a phantom.

When I go to sleep at night, Jean appears to me as a phantom.

He yanks me out of bed and wants to repeat our pastis evening. We go back to the dive on the wharf, I'm wearing my black-and-white-striped pajamas, Jean orders two glasses and a jug of water, we smoke and Jean tells me about a young woman. It's Denise, or by her Indian name: Denise-who-broke-your-heart. Jean draws his heart on a napkin and shows me where it's broken. We call it the predetermined breaking point and patch it up with pastis. Pastis-that-patches-up-your-heart. Temporarily, says Jean.

I decide to buy three dictionaries for my nightly rendezvous with Jean. The first one will be Native American. I would have loved to have told him something else. Me, I don't like anise.

Then the day comes when Jean puts up a poster. We should all come to his place, it says; it's taking place in his room, same day next week.

*L'art, c'est une chaise*, Jean wrote on it, from Deleuze.

One week later we ring Jean's bell, but no one answers. We wait, then go up the stairs to the apartment where Jean's room is.

The door of the apartment is barricaded. We stand in front of it and no one says a word. All we do is look. It's completely blocked. Then finally somebody takes away the first board, someone else tears through the barrier tape.

But we don't make any progress. We deliberate what to do next. Some just want to go home. Some don't want to destroy Jean's work. Some say we should just stick to it and fight our way through the barrier.

They pull out their pocket knives, saws, screwdrivers, scissors, whatever they can get their hands on. One of us sets his laptop up—maybe there's a digital solution.

I sit down on the stairs and watch. Johnny, you're such a good ciga-rette roller, they say, and I've found my task, as long as the tobacco lasts. Johnny-who-rolls-the-cigarettes.

None of us has been watching the clock, everyone just keeps digging. The city's bulky refuse has all found its way into Jean's apartment.

He's screwed and nailed together furniture, boards, car tires, everything. Everything is spray-painted, everything is polished. At first they carefully pried each piece from the next, but now they break out the electric saws.

A cloud of sawdust and a new pile of debris has formed behind the sawers, and I have to dig my way though it to get closer. I keep on rolling cigarettes, and sometimes a few of them sit down with me, drink a beer or eat a bologna sandwich to help them regain their strength. As long as our cigarettes don't set the sawdust on fire, we say, keeping an eye on each other. Joyful hours pass, and it's funny how everyone here is busy trying to get to Jean's room.

And at some point we actually make it. Jean needed six whole days to set up his collection, from the apartment door to his room. He did it all: glued, welded, soldered, painted—colossal! On the seventh day he seated himself on a giant plywood throne, had the last barricades erected and painted, said it was good, then he waited for us.

Hello Jean, the people call out to him from below, and the only thing they can see up there are his feet dangling in stylish shoes. Jean looks down and smiles. Did you film it?

What do you mean, film it? We saved you! they shout.

What a bunch of morons, says Jean, spits at them from his throne, and doesn't move till everyone is gone.

I thought you were all gone, says Jean to me at daybreak, when he climbs down from his throne. Only now do I notice that he's wearing a costume. He climbs down to me dressed as a faun in platform shoes, slow and proud, stripped to the waist, face painted white, and with a giant wig. Then he opens his left hand and produces a bright, slimy substance, a mass of pellets made of glue or cream. It's as if his hand were a blossom, opening fresh and dewy, lusting for the new day.

All for nothing, says Jean, and smears his moist pollen on his tartan kilt. If you didn't film it, it's useless. *Tant pis*, you assholes.

I'm not really one of them, I say softly.

He leaves without even asking for my name. I dreamed about

you a couple of times, I could say, but he's already gone. Not even a thank-you for not torching him along with his sawdust.

Jean doesn't know me. But still I like to imagine that, along with all the old furniture, he also found my pictures in the trash, the ones I gave the neighbors. They threw them away, but Jean salvaged them from the rubble: Jean-who-fishes-for-fish.

When I moved to the city from the countryside a year ago, it was supposed to be a glorious new beginning. I was counting the years, oh yeah! until this new beginning. Every New Year's I made an X on the calendar with a silver paint pen—discreet fireworks is what I call it. Later I started counting the months, and finally I even allowed myself to count the last 365 days. One X at a time.

On day 365 I packed my suitcase early in the morning and painted a whole calendar page in the colors of the rainbow. If I'd had it my way, I would have had my breakfast in an anorak and cap, just so there's no mistake about it: I'm leaving.

My suitcase contains the pictures, my leather jacket and boots, cigarettes and the usual paraphernalia.

The suitcase is opened one last time. A pair of pajamas is smuggled inside. The boots are taken out and polished, oh crap. When I'm gone I'll have to try and make them dirty again. The side pockets of the suitcase are searched:

Good heavens, child, you look at this kind of smut?!

Merely for research purposes.

It's the first time I don't turn red but stay pale. I'll be out of here before long.

Just one last hurdle left to go. Before I leave, they want me to run across the yard to the neighbors. Then I'm supposed to run to the neighbors' neighbors. They want me to let the next village know. They want me to down a farewell schnapps at the county office too. I have to take the train after the next, because the stationmaster wants to sell me an annual ticket so I can come back home any time. When the train after the next pulls in, a brass band marches past and plays me a farewell song.

I finally board the train, and the musicians wave their

handkerchiefs in a well-rehearsed choreography. Oh, Johnny! If only back in those days I'd had a way with words, like a rapper! And if only I'd told the cornet player to stuff it! And if only I didn't let people hold me up all the time!

Or maybe my obstacle course was like this. They force me to put on my gym clothes one last time: a pair of red short shorts and a white undershirt. A headband and knee socks. I run and jump, do the floor, beam, and pommel horse. Then the high bar: upswing, backswing, up and over. Land on both feet, arms outstretched. I almost lose my balance. The judges blow the whistle.

My father holds up a three, my mother a six, my sister a five. I don't know how, but I managed to get away. Almost for good.


We'll meet again, what a stupid song, says Jean in my head, just so you don't feel the pain of departure.

How was it, I ask him, when you packed your bags at the end of the summer and said your good-byes?

Ah, pouf, says Jean, no one really cared. We were so many kids they didn't even know my name.

Hmm, I say. When we run into each other in town in the day-time, you don't know my name either. I would have liked to ask you if you also dream at night that we're friends.

Johnny, Jean says in my dream, I don't have stupid dreams like that.

Then Jean talks about Angélique, whom he met after his barri-cade project, when they put him on an IV for an hour, dehydrated and sticky-fingered.

Huh? One more time: Jean had worked a whole week on his throne made of shelves and boards. He'd wanted us to videotape our attempts to reach him, and then he'd descend from his throne, dressed as a faun and in slow motion. Logical, in retrospect, I sup-pose. But when it didn't work out the way he'd imagined, Jean had reached his breaking point. That's how he ended up in the hospital with Angélique. How the heck does Jean always manage to meet women with French names in a town like ours, I wonder. That's what I call luck.

And that gave me ideas for my next project, says Jean.

The nurse, Angélique?

No, the IV.

Drip painting, Jean?

No, no, no, shouts Jean, it's got to be something new! As Franz always says: timelessly brilliant. Anyway, I'm opposed to the Americans and their painting.

I'm an American, Jean.

I don't count you, Johnny.

Angélique was supposed to assist me, because that's the way to do things. And everyone knows that the female assistants of great masters of the avant-garde always run around naked. Angélique didn't want to at first—but she'd do it for my *oeuvre*, she said.

Or was it like this: Angélique herself said it's not an *oeuvre* if she's not naked? Of course that's what she said. She tore the white gown from her body and the buttons began to fly, shooting at me like a hail of bullets; with her left hand she pressed the blood bag against her chest, and with a sweeping gesture of the right, she stabbed it right in the middle with a scalpel. Explosion of color! Yves Klein blue, adds Jean, would have been more appealing to me than blood, but I took her the way she came.

Right there in the hospital? I asked.

In the hospital, says Jean: in the nurses' lounge, in the emergency room, and in the cafeteria. We left a red trail on light-green linoleum through all the corridors. Red on green, Jean repeats: complementary colors! Of course, when I saw it, I had to leave Angélique on the spot in order to get my camera. She took it the wrong way, and stuck the knife right in my chest. Missed the heart by an inch, the surgeons said.

Jean unbuttons his shirt even more—it's already wide open—and shows me the bandage.

It suits him well. A subtle contrast between the white gauze bandage and the ivory tone of his skin.

Ivory Jean, I say.

Are you crazy, Johnny? It's chamois. Or a kind of very light beige. Off-white with a touch of yellow, sandy, seashell, eggshell. Okay, I say, baby powder, corn silk, not too much cream. And this Angélique has no clue about art?!

White is not only the color of Angélique's gown before it became a splatter painting. White is the color of paper and canvas.

White, titanium white, is what Angélique's gown became again once she put it in the washing machine.

White is a so-called achromatic color, but no less popular with artists because of it. All the galleries have been white, for example, ever since someone painted a black square. Because of the light-dark contrast, says Jean.

And that's why the employees in galleries are always dressed in black, and sit behind those white lecterns, right when you enter the room. The lecterns are tall so the gallery employees disappear behind them, since the color of their faces wouldn't fit the black-and-white principle. If an employee is too tall or his lectern too low, he has to open a laptop—white, black, or silver-gray—in front of his rosy-cheeked face.

Makes perfect sense, I say.

Absolutely, says Jean.

I'm drawing a blank, don't know where to start.

Does anyone know that song? Don't know where to start: that's the beginning of a song. And then?

I go to all the classes Jean never attends in the daytime and still there's a blank sheet of paper staring at me. I distract myself by learning how to prime a canvas with bone glue. The end result after three days of work: blank. Stinky and white as a sheet.

How do you make a canvas? You nail together the stretcher, crouch down on the floor, and stretch the canvas over the frame, always starting to staple in the middle of each stretcher bar: center top, center bottom, center right, center left. You practice, or so I've read, the politics of proper stretching. You work the staple gun from the center to the corners, always tugging firmly on the cloth to make it as taut as possible.

And then? You heat up the dried bone-glue pellets in a water bath and dissolve them until you get a bright, slimy substance. You add gypsum and mix it up, dilute it with the right amount of water, then you apply it to the canvas. Let it dry, coat it again. Let it dry, coat it again. This tightens the canvas even more, and the pores of the fabric are sealed for the subsequent application of paint.

Six white-primed canvases, six white squares: that's as far as I get. No further.

Jean doesn't give a damn about the politics of proper stretching. He throws himself in bushes, hugs trees, sticks his head into garbage cans, lies down on the street, opens sewer grates and climbs in up to his belly. He holds each pose for a couple of seconds and calls it sculpture.

We're still his only audience, but they'll notice him soon enough. This is neither presentiment nor omniscience. It's simple logic: the resultant sum of expected events.

Maybe those days in the swimming pool, when Jean wasn't called Jean yet, were all preparation for what he's doing now? I think of how he jumped in the water, a real show-off, and how muscular and tan he was. His hair was bleached by the sun, and he spoke in a completely different way, yelled more than he spoke. He fit so well in the countryside, and now he fits so well in the city. Now he's tall and slim, his skin is white—no, *blanche*—and the way he speaks, well, anyone can hear it. What a dope he was in the country, and now he's a freak in the city, and I envy him both—no, even more: I envy him no end.

Maybe it was even a good thing that his father was such an asshole. It's tough growing up the first eighteen years of your life, but maybe it helps when you want to leave home, helps you avoid making detours. Just up and leave, no niceties, and no pajamas either. I think of my nice little fish, what a contrast they are. Damn it all.

We'll think of something to do with the fish, says Jean, dressed up as Poseidon and rushing to my aid. Knees tucked in, he jumps into my stream of thoughts and rescues me from my sinking ship. This is not a metaphor, but exactly the way I picture it. He tromps through the water with his trident, yes. Maybe, says Jean, you need to stick to the fish, and from there, Johnny, take a stab in the dark, or jump into the ocean blue. Navy, cyan, indigo, calls Jean, reigning over the seas.

Or blue like swimming pools?

Yeah, like Hockney, hot like Hockney, cries Jean. Do it like Hockney, but different. Or *Quappi in Blue*! I love that title, says Jean: *Quappi in Blue in a Boat*. Beckmann, the painter, was pretty hot for his Quappi: *Quappi with a Parrot, Quappi in Pink*, Quappi here and Quappi there. And Jean repeats it a few more times: Quappi. But Beckmann also did a painting called *The Little Fish*. And *Journey on the Fish. Sleeping Woman with Fish Bowl*. Fish aren't so bad, says Jean, and Beckmann isn't bad either, any comic-strip artist nowadays will tell you that. *Sleeping Woman with Fish Bowl*, Jean shouts, oh, how I'd love to sleep with a woman right now! Maybe there's one somewhere who's hot for Poseidon?

And with that, Jean swims away. And sure enough, he encounters a water nymph, beautiful and willing—but, alas, it's common knowledge that there's not a lot you can do with a nymph.

Can Jean have your canvases?

Somebody from the group shakes me by the shoulder. Johnny, were you sleeping?

No, I was dreaming about water nymphs, I say.

Can Jean have your six primed canvases?

How come? I ask.

He said I should tell the guy they belong to that he used them already.

What, I ask, he took them already?

Yeah, Jean piled them on his bike this morning and rode off with them.

Oh, okay, I say, and sit down on the stairs in front of the entrance and think: At some point I'll have to tell this Jean that he can't just go and do that. I'll talk to him: You probably remember me, I'll say loud and clear, I'm the one who saw you climb down from your throne at the end of your barricade performance.

Wasn't everyone gone by then? Jean will ask.

Exactly, you said you thought that everyone was gone, and I wanted to tell you: I'm here, my name is Johnny.

That morning? Impossible, Jean will say, I was fooling around with Véronique. You mean Angélique, I say.

Yeah! Angélique, the nurse, Jean yells, you know her?

Hmm. Should I even try to explain to him—while trying to imagine at all what it's like to have a conversation with Jean—that of course I don't know his Angélique? That I only dream that he's my friend, who tells me about his affairs?

And would I, should I tell him he can't take my six white canvases without asking? Should I mention that if he'd asked me I would have gladly given them to him anyway, and probably even helped him carry them? That, anyhow, they'd been lying around far too long without my knowing what to do with them?

And that it was Jean himself who told me in my dreams how he walked out on Angélique, the nurse, once he'd finished his work.

Should I tell him that I talk to myself and imagine we're friends, Jean et Johnny, Johnny and Jean?

Ha! yells Jean. That's perfect. Then we can do it like Jules et Jim. Which one do you want to be? The quiet one with the faithful eyes, who's difficult but loves so intensely? Huh? Or the dark-haired one, who's the better lover, hmm? Take your pick, Johnny! We can scratch the bicycle scene. Your little fish won't fill you up, though, neither you nor her. Hey! Pale Johnny snatches my Angélique, just like that. Well, says Jean, I would have preferred Jeanne Moreau anyway. If I'd lived in Paris as a young artist, I definitely would have taken Jeanne Moreau; I understand every Austrian poet who did.

Jean, I say, there was nothing between Angélique and me. Really? Why didn't you say so! Angélique, Véronique, Quappique! Jean laughs. Quappique is my muse, Quappi is my musique!

Oh, Jean, you're crazy.

Nude drawing class is once a week. It's not as thrilling as everyone thinks. No, it's even more thrilling than that! I sweat, and my hands tremble—which isn't so bad for drawing, actually. Because anything is good for drawing. You just have to get started. The fact is, I've never seen a human being completely naked. Without a swimsuit. Neither man nor woman. In magazines, sure, but not in real life. The problem is, I don't dare look a nude model between the legs. Even if I dared, I couldn't draw what I saw there.

Just imagining that the others would see my trembling hands and think: Aha, now he's drawing the penis. Or imagining our female instructor, peering over my shoulder and saying: Johnny, when drawing the vagina you need to use more red.

I'm very pleased when a fat Thai lady shows up one day and refuses to strip all the way; she keeps on her big-flowered silken underwear.

I concentrate on the floral pattern—and come up with a nice series of charcoal drawings, green and red, very bright with dark, angular contours. There's a little bit of Quappi in my pictures too.

I group the drawings on the floor in front of me so they form a giant frieze. Ah, you're grouping your pictures in front of you to form a giant frieze, says the instructor when she gets to me. Come here, everyone, and see what Johnny's doing!

I'm very proud of myself, but try to keep my cool. The others gather around me—ah, if only Jean could see me now!

Georgia O'Keefe, our instructor begins, who's familiar with her work? A long, detailed, and enthusiastic talk ensues, about the symbolic use of fruits and flowers in the history of painting from antiquity to the present. The instructor calls a spade a spade, she says vagina, vagina, vagina, and at the end she even says genital panic.

Of course it's pathetic not to attend nude drawing class anymore after that, but the following week I couldn't bring myself to go; the week after that I figured everyone knew I didn't come because the whole thing is still too awkward for me; and the week after that I realized that after a three-week break, I can't show up just like that.

And I can't tell Jean it's because I've never slept with anybody, after months of imagining how I give him advice about his affairs. Love is probably just like nude drawing: first you don't go at all, then you think it's too late to start, and finally you give up altogether.

16

I imagine a group of young art students, standing before my life's work at the Museum of Modern Art in New York. An art historian, maybe Professor Mary Schoenblum, busily talks into her microphone with that typical biographical approach of the Americans:

Johnny was a tremendous artist, but never had any luck with women. The whole of his creative powers went into his work, and we, the future generations, thank him with dutiful admiration.

Then the young art students applaud, say their good-byes in the sculpture garden, sit in the sun and cuddle with their girlfriends. And the female art students cuddle with their boyfriends. And sometimes two men cuddle with each other, and sometimes two women, too. Professor Mary Schoenblum heads home, recalling the events of the day: Did I really say with dutiful admiration? Oh, boy!

TRANSLATED FROM THE GERMAN BY DAVID BURNETT

# STÉPHANE LAMBERT

## *The Two Writers*

I SHOULD HAVE KISSED Tom at the top of the observatory tower at Vilnius University. But I was the king of missed opportunities. And Tom was married. In a few weeks he would be the father of a baby whose sex he still didn't know. And I dared not let the moment belong to us. An agreeable uneasiness had come over us when the guide had abandoned us at the base of the tower; we had then briskly ascended the old wooden staircase. Hearing the steps creak beneath our feet, I had realized how much these minutes would count. As always, my emotion had provoked the first stirrings of an erection that I tried to conceal. At the top—Tom knew it, I had no doubt—we were expecting more than a panoramic view. We found ourselves in a dizzying proximity, and in our isolation above the city a sense of the erotic was palpable. At first we had clumsily tried to take an interest in the view. The space inside the tower was so cramped that we had to take extreme care to avoid standing shoulder to shoulder. Each of us was forced to orient himself toward his own side until the exercise came to seem too absurd, and we began then to share our vantage points and exclaim to each other insincerely as we pointed out one or another site that we had already visited. I perceived immediately that this playacting would soon exhaust our resources. Vilnius was a medium-sized city; I could foresee the precise instant when we would arrive at the end of it. Down there, beyond the former city hall, was the Gate of Dawn with its Black Virgin—it was also the neighborhood where we were staying; in another direction, the opera house, a typical Soviet-era performance hall, where on the first evening together we had seen an antiquated production of *Romeo and Juliet* that Tom nonetheless seemed to like—this was our first disagreement; behind the opera house flowed the Neris, and slightly more distant still, near several

18

looming spires, was the magnificent recreation center where I went swimming. At that point we could have taken a break from our viewing, let the silence get the better of our awkwardness, look at each other with light smiles, half-embarrassed, half-conspiratorial, feel our heartbeats quicken, and in any case not avert our eyes as I had stupidly done, pointing out the Church of St. Francis and St. Bernard—I who ordinarily took so little interest in churches—and reciting like an imbecile what was said about it in the guidebook, which I clutched in order to hide my discomfort. "Napoleon," I heard myself proclaim, "would have liked to transport it to France in the palm of his hand." When I mentioned the imperial name that still resonated through the city like a sinister memory, Tom moved toward me, and as he tried with one hand to indicate the direction of a cemetery he hadn't yet visited, he nonchalantly laid the other on my shoulder. That was obviously enough to arouse me again. "Soldiers . . . ," he said in French, "are buried . . . there . . . in a pit . . ." When he spoke French, Tom would lose the qua-si-aristocratic assurance that his cultivated British accent gave to his English, and then he would become like a small child who stam-mered while discovering the patterns of speech, and it was irresist-ible. "I wanted . . . ," he ventured, "to know . . . where . . . where it was . . . because . . . there are . . . several . . ." Tom got tangled up in his explanations, he had taken it into his head to inventory all of the city's cemeteries in order to create a kind of literary alma-nac. The previous evening, we had meandered across the hills of the Rasos Cemetery, both of us under the charm of the old grave-stones in such a natural setting, a romantic atmosphere in which death seemed as peaceful as the trees and the vegetation, and we had talked, we had not stopped talking, as we strolled along the narrow paths of the cemetery, between the rusted crosses and the timeworn slabs. With the passage of time, the tombs had become as humble as the ground they occupied, and we were so excited by the idea of knowing each other that we had never stopped convers-ing. I had tried in my rudimentary English to convey the emotion that this kind of place evoked in me, and Tom had approved in his spasmodic French. "I like . . . also . . . very much . . ." Throughout the afternoon, we had exchanged remarks darting in all directions, having no other motive than to bind us together. And there, at the top of the observatory tower at Vilnius University, we had arrived at the end of speech, the instant where our circumstances were about to change dramatically. We had exhausted all the sights, the horizon barred any further recourse. And it was going to be necessary—the thought frightened me—going to be necessary for me to be equal to his desire. The sensuality of the situation had pervaded the whole of the confined space where we were standing side by side. The city had closed in around us. There was no more than a second left. Tom had finished his sentence. I felt his hand on my shoulder. And our minds seized up, tense, awaiting a sign. And when he turned toward me, much as I would have wanted to reciprocate his gesture, I instead backed away. Despite the turmoil this aroused in me, I stepped away from him and moved brusquely toward the staircase. Then, already regretting my action, I stopped dead, and after pausing for a second or two, I turned back toward him. Tom had an embarrassed expression, yet with a composure that stupefied me he removed a camera from the inside pocket of his sport jacket and immortalized this moment that had escaped us through my fault. Fortunately, I told myself as we descended the old wooden staircase of the observatory tower of Vilnius University, fortunately, these lost opportunities are a godsend for novelists like me.

The autumnal coolness and the throb of traffic were entering my Parisian studio apartment next to the Gare de l'Est, I pictured again that moment with Tom, and my mind went back to Jude, and everything became mixed up, the real and the imaginary, the present and the remembered, fresh air and pollution. A century after Rilke, I experienced the same lonely isolation he had felt in the midst of the city; more and more bewildered by the emptiness of the world, I heard a buzzing in my ears. From time to time I observed two pigeon chicks quivering on the window ledge. Their mother had built her nest in the gutter, she returned there every day around noon to feed her offspring, they battled for first place, and then they would both plunge their beaks into the maternal craw.

The afternoon of the day I bungled the encounter with Tom, I learned of Jude's death in the crash of an Airbus A330 en route from Paris to Los Angeles. It was a few hours after I had come down from the observatory tower at the university. The first news was a bulletin on Radio France Internationale. A plane had disappeared from the controllers' screens while it was crossing an area of bad weather. Several minutes later I received a message on my cellphone from North, the only friend we had kept in common, telling me that Jude was on the plane. It took me several seconds to connect the two reports: Jude was aboard the Airbus A330 bound for Los Angeles that had dropped off the controllers' radar screens. This was a blurry reality, difficult to work out. I was in Vilnius for a colloquium on European identity in literature. Here, two days earlier, I had met Tom, a Welsh writer with whom I had felt an immediate rapport. I thought back on the minutes spent with him late that morning at the top of the tower, and the episode already seemed distant. Missed opportunities, I repeated to myself, are excellent starting points for novelists. Wasn't that the way someone became a writer, I reasoned. First you developed the habit of missing opportunities, then you took the attitude of celebrating the misses, because you could make them a subject for your writing. Inevitably, you finished by absolving yourself beforehand for your cowardly inaction. Frustration became a way of life, literature would be victorious. In the evening, Radio France Internationale confirmed that the A330, missing from the controllers' screens for several hours, had indeed gone down in the Atlantic, aircraft debris had just been spotted off the American coast, the hypothesis of terrorism seemed to have been dismissed, for the moment nothing more was known. And suddenly, while aeronautical experts were putting forth theories regarding the causes of such an accident, the news of it seized me in a whole different manner than it had in the afternoon; this piece of information that had fluttered around somewhere within my consciousness without knowing where to land assumed a new solidity, and I felt a shock stinging inside my abdomen, as if something knotted was violently disintegrating. It was almost six years since we had lived together, Jude had gone to live in Paris with someone else. She and Jude may have been flying together—that thought might have consoled me if my jealousy at not being next to him at the moment of his death had not immediately triumphed. We had sold our Brussels apartment, and I had stayed in that city without quite resolving whether I liked it or not. This small shade of difference would vary from one day to the next, and in this vacillation I came to suspect that it was not really the city that was causing the problem. I tried to imagine what Jude's last moments in the aircraft might have been like, but it was impossible—had there really been a last moment? The violence of such a death was inconceivable outside of its own reality, and in the confusion in which I found myself, incapable of thinking concretely about his death, I understood how much the accident that had just happened was a logical sequel to the one that had separated us. Jude no longer had a body, it had vaporized. In essence, he had returned to the state in which I had always known him: in my eyes our relationship had remained improbable, never did I believe that this had really happened between us, that his presence beside me was authentic, for seven years I had been living on an unsteady cloud, I had tried to get closer to him, but Jude was aloof, that was his very nature—or mine was formed in such a way that this was how I perceived him—and his death, in separating him definitively from me, his death was merely situating him in his natural place. In his inaccessible kingdom. And the sorrow I felt that evening in Vilnius as I contemplated his death did not arise from losing him again, instead it was a matter of never having known how to win him. And if I must express the nub of my thought, it was that I could not mourn his death, because his death and life alike were remote, belonging only to him, there was nothing sad in this event. Whatever happened to him, Jude would always be on the side of those who emerged victorious. And he had no need to conquer in order to shine, he had the makeup of those solitary heroes of old who would advance unscathed through everything. Their mere existence was fully adequate. And yet there was also this: one never gives up completely on a broken love affair. The possibility of its revival remains lodged somewhere. And it is this remnant that enables you to survive its end. And in fact there is no end. The love continues to live disguised beneath the present. And when the other person dies, this tacit hope that kept you going perishes at the same time—and that was the cause of the pangs I felt that evening in Vilnius. If I had kissed Tom in the observatory tower that very morning, perhaps I would have returned with him to Wales, we would have lived there in the mountains on next to nothing, rather like recluses, we would have fixed up an old house together, we would have bathed naked together in the cool water of the stream, as Tom had told me that he often did, yes, if I had kissed Tom I would not have chosen Paris. But I had not kissed Tom, and Paris had worked its will on me.

TRANSLATED BY PAUL CURTIS DAW

# IANA BOUKOVA

## FROM *A as in Anything*

"The Teacher Came Back Drunk"

*In memory of Krum Atsev*

The Teacher came back drunk. He had lost one of his sandals. The sharp gravel forced him to step with his bare foot in the grass and with his shod foot on the path, leaving a one-footed track. "Funny," the Student would have thought, had he seen it the following day, "how a shortcoming can unexpectedly turn into an advantage." His missing sandal even helped him to keep himself in check, to follow the line of the path without swerving and without staggering. "Indeed," the Student would have further thought, "how deliberate his tracks look. Reminiscent of one hand clapping." He would have thought other things as well. He was definitely a student gifted with an active imagination.

But now the Teacher was standing on the threshold, swaying. It looked as if the threshold he had stepped upon was the only hard strip of land, before and beyond which existed only empty space of an unknown depth. He was trying to remain upright upon it on his own, without assistance, without leaning or grabbing on to anything, only with the movements of his elbows and shoulders, and in those efforts of his there was a certain humility and a certain resigned dignity, the Student thought. His eyes were not red, nor was his gaze clouded like that of drunkards, it was merely turned aside, in a direction different from that of his actions. In the end he managed to keep his balance, took off his one remaining sandal and hurled it at the group of students. The others ducked with stifled cries, only the Student stayed still and the sandal hit him on the forehead. The wooden sole was not only heavy, it also had sharp edges, and it cut his eyebrow. A thin stream of blood started trickling down, filling his eye with red, but the Student did not wipe it away. He felt like he'd been chosen.

During its flight, the sandal's unfastened strap had hooked a little bowl of ink and overturned it on one of the drawings. It was the Student's own drawing, imperfect in any case. The ink poured down it like a diagonal curtain with long tassels, gradually covering the cone-shaped mountain with its truncated peak: first its snows, then its dark slopes, then the bare trees at its foot, the river and the two human figures—an elderly man and a younger one talking by its banks. Only little islands of the drawing remained, hinting at its content, allowing the viewer to presume that the ink had destroyed a perfect composition, because the human eye tends to find virtues in what is hidden, rather than shortcomings. It was the only possible way his drawing could look beautiful and the Student felt gratitude towards his Teacher.

The Teacher went over to the hearth and grabbed a log. "How beautiful it is that even the lowliest object," the Student thought, "acquires meaning in the human hand. It becomes a tool, an instrument." It was an entirely nondescript log, crooked, gnarled, with one knot, out of which jutted the sharp remnant of a broken-off branch. A loud noise ensued when the Teacher swung it: containers shattered to pieces, paper was torn, the rods of the screens were smashed. The others ran away shrieking. The only ones not making a sound were the Student and the Teacher. It was a dialogue without words. The Teacher was speaking to him. To him alone. Without budging from the spot, the Student almost knew what would follow.

The first blow shattered the wrist of the same hand he used for drawing. A tough lesson, but well-deserved, since he had lost his self-control and raised his arm to shield his face. The second blow tore his ear with that same sharpened remnant of a branch. The Student caught the scent of his own blood in the air and the scent of fermentation from the Teacher's clothes. "Fermentation is a sign of maturation," he thought. He knew there would be only one more blow. He felt so unshakeable that water could not wash him away, nor could the wind erode him, not could the sun desiccate him. It was as if what happened only to the great Teachers was now happening to him. The moment disintegrated into an endless multitude of instants. And in one of them, he managed to grasp his final thought: that most likely the Teacher was not drunk at all, not in the least.

"Tea in the Snow; or, A Brief Delay in the Town of N."

And it's always this and that, and my dearest Misha, and my most obliging Mihail Sergeevich, if only you would drink a little tea, if only you would sit for a bit, my heart aches to watch you pacing the corridor. These things happen, it has happened before, and the newspapers said there were no casualties, just a little patience is all that's needed, while you, Sir, are like a little child, up and down the corridor . . .

And he's always got one eye on the landscape, hoping to catch some movement. But come on now, what movement? Everything's frozen, everything's stiff, as stiff as a dead man, what movement could there be?

While he's like: If only you would sit down a bit, Mihail Serge'ich, we could chat a bit, get to know each other, that's how people meet each other, it's always by accident, due to the circumstances, a bit of patience is all that's needed. While you are like a little child, immediately bored with everything, despairing over everything, you say you're stiff as a dead man, what are these exaggerations? Exaggeration is a bad thing, Mihail Serge'ich, mark my words, it is the root of all evil—not foolishness, not treachery, but exaggeration and nothing else.

And he's always shoving tea into my hands, the sixth cup in the last two hours. I piss in the snow and don't leave a trace, the droplets merely sink into it, leaving no trace, damn this life to hell, you can't leave anything behind, not even a tiny yellow trace, nothing.

And he keeps going on and on and his bald forehead shines, as if reflecting the light from some unknown source, who knows, maybe it's gleaming with its own light: If only you would say something, Mihail Serge'ich, don't leave everything to me, I might slip up while speaking and offend you, but even if I were to say everything perfectly correctly, you'd still get offended, that's just how you are, a bit proud. I can read your face as if I was looking at myself in the mirror, of course, you'll pardon me for saying so, because who am I, yet I know you, it's as if I was looking at myself, how your very soul is bored to tears and your fingers are constantly moving, as if pressing down keys in the air and every note is out of tune, I know them, those sour notes, oh yes, I know them very well, that despair . . .

That's just how it is, I sit here and listen to him, what else can I do. If only the lady from Compartment 6 was here, but the Tatars made off with her. Who knows, it must've been the Tatars, they came out of the snow all covered in snow, nobody saw from where, tossed her on her back over their horses, only her white boots were left kicking in the air. But it's not my job to go saving damsels in distress. Not that he lifted a finger, either, he just watched with tears in his eyes, he loves nothing more than to watch and sigh: Oh, if only Lydia Petrovna (the lady from Compartment 6) were here to sing for us a bit, what a voice, it doesn't caress your ears, but grabs you by the throat, it goes straight for the throat, like a lynx . . .

Well, that's what the lady's life was meant to be, short. Because everyone only lives as long as they're in front of my eyes, afterwards, when they're gone, it's as if the earth has swallowed them up, as if they've turned to dust. Isn't that right?

And he kept harping on his same tune: Oh, Mihail Serge'ich, that's not honorable, it's base, it's downright base to the other person, for the one to talk while the other merely passes judgment and counts up errors without saying a word.

Whereas I could tell you everything. About your childhood, for example, your childhood was—how shall I put it—heroic, your clenched little fists, your loneliness, your pride, you needn't hide such things, you needn't be ashamed, they are beautiful, even majestic.

And later, your military overcoat, that overcoat fit you to a T, you can still see it in the set of your shoulders, you even miss it, as much as you hate to admit it, you miss the discipline, because when it's like this, we have to do things precisely like this, and when it's like that, precisely the opposite, yes indeed, now you have to decide everything for yourself. And you miss the sword, even the sword, it kept your hand busy, now what to do with that hand, the fingers are in the air and everything's out of tune, alas, Mihail Serge'ich . . . Cigarette?

So do I have anywhere else to go? I do not. They're playing cards in the neighboring compartment, but what would I do there, they're already four and I'd be the fifth. Sometimes they even pop in here for a cup of tea, it's rather awkward, but what else can they do, perhaps at the end of the day I am in a privileged position. Besides, after being stuck for so long they've forgotten how to speak like men, all they talk about is cards, "ten of diamonds" they say and smile at you to pour them a cup or at best muster up some "queen of spades" if they want to say something about art.

Of course, all hell's broken loose, the other wagons are full of the lower classes, the broad masses, if you will, are having a gay old time, they've paired off and gotten married, had children, they aren't fazed in the least, they're going about their lives, they're hardy folks, but what good does their hardiness do me?

And him: You oughtn't to talk like that, my turtledove, you really oughtn't. It's bad. Your head is full of nothing but fantasies. But the world is rich enough as it is without our fantasies. Now, take Lydia Petrovna, say, what imagination could have thought her up, those eyes, that bust, and her poor little lips all bluish, bitten, but on the inside, from the outside nothing shows, she says nothing, a proud woman.

Ah, my poor Mihail Serge'ich, you even wrote poems when the time was right for it, poems are a good thing, comforting, they soothe a man's soul and he looks more kindly upon the world, as much as he might complain and curse, he still speaks to it amicably, as if to an equal.

I get up again to go outside, the curtains in Compartment 6 have been drawn, she must be asleep, most people wake up when the motion stops, while she's the opposite, she always wants everything her own way, she must be asleep, all covered up by her coat, and her coat is a fluffy thing, a dead thing, only her white boots are sticking out.

There is no trace, of course. On the way back the fellows in the neighboring compartment are shouting over one another. Don't people constantly talk like that, with their cards ready? You lead, I match you, I play trump, you double trump me. And he says I'm imagining things!

And immediately he starts in again: You love cards, Mihail Serge'ich, oh, how you love them. You're only listening to me now with half an ear, you're following the game. Who plays what, who bids what, you even imagine that you can guess who's holding what and, when someone makes a mistake, your nostrils shrink up, as if you've caught a whiff of some bad smell, oh no, you don't forgive other people's mistakes. Now, if you only had a little something, anything, you'd join in right away, you'd bet it right away, but you've been left with nothing, nor can you ask anything from me, as we well know, and well, whatever Lydia Petrova had she already gave, it's over and done with, what more can you ask of her. But you, sir, always imagine everything like that, coldly, as if you were outside of it, as if it didn't affect you at all, oh Misha, my turtledove, you are a tortured soul, you are . . .

I hold the cup of tea in my hands and every time I bend down to take a sip, my face nods in agreement. This is no way to drink, having to dunk your face in with every sip. It's enough to put you off it completely.

You always twist things like that, my dearest, always imagine them distorted, misconstrued, and now here we are, the train is stuck in the snow, big deal, you just need a little patience, but you immediately turn it into a metaphor, you've brought the broad masses into it. The broad masses are a dangerous thing, seductive, don't get started with them, not even like that, for effect, believe, I know about such things . . .

He's really started waxing sentimental, one of his eyes has started watering like mad when he looks at me and I don't like it, I don't like it one bit.

What were we talking about, oh yes, you somehow twist everything about, Mihail Serge'ich, and now here's the other thing: so the Tatars carried her off, you lost sight of her, or so you say, as if the earth just swallowed her up, her coat was dead, you say, (dead, eh?), you must finally learn to call things by their real names, to hear them at long last, and for me to hear them, too, it's been torturous for me, too, my turtledove, all these hours I've been drowning you in tea. And afterwards your soul was desolate, you were in pain, it's not enough for you to be desolate in the city, now you've set out for the steppe, you need landscape, you say, your emotions are ambitious, my dear, nothing's ever enough for you, you always want more, while your little heart is so weak, it can't hold out, in your place . . .

Here I should've jumped up and once, twice, right in the kisser, but I sit there motionless and somehow everything goes dark before my eyes, and wouldn't you know it, the dirty bastard was right on about that, too, that "my little heart is so weak," and I scream, even though no sound comes out, but he hears everything: There's no such place, scum! There is no such place any longer and there never will be again!

TRANSLATED FROM THE BULGARIAN BY ANGELA RODEL

# SVEN POPOVIC

## FROM *Last Night*

"First Steps"
You said, when all is possible,
nothing is real.
—S. Mraović

SHE TOOK HER FIRST steps in the snow. They melted away. As if she left no trace on the ground. She's twenty-one now and isn't really there. I don't mean to say she's distant, but she simply has this feeling that everything that happens to her isn't real. Like it's happening to someone else. And she's just an observer. Because she felt like nothing was real, she sometimes had to touch certain objects or people to make sure that they were there and wouldn't dissolve like dreams do when you open your eyes.

It's been some twenty years since she took her first steps in the snow. It appears to her sometimes that the days have also dissolved like dreams do when you open your eyes. No sequences, no logical series. Only cracks in Technicolor. It even seemed to her it was all just a dream. In summer, she would lie in her bed and smoke. So heavily that her room would get foggy. At her side always some novel. A Dostoyevsky, a Kafka, a Murakami, a Kamov. She didn't bother reading poetry. Sometimes she would just lie there, brown hair flowing all around and beneath her. She would close her eyes and think of oceans and words that summoned up the eternal. She wouldn't go out until the sun dropped. In winter, she would go to cafés. She would sit by herself. Smoke an entire pack. That amounted to some hundred and fifty pages and two or three cups of coffee.

She met him mid-fall at her university. He was tall, with a bit of a slouch, much too smug. Loud. Always at the center of attention. Nonetheless he disagreed with most people and had difficulty fitting in, despite his charm. In his own way, he sometimes wasn't there either. He insisted he was constantly surrounded with wondrous occurrences, but still it sometimes seemed that he clung to romantic illusions about the past. She would see him hanging out with his friends. Always laughing. Charming punks. The word was they listened to nothing but vinyl LPs together and only watched movies in old theaters. They were constantly starring in their own movies with witty dialogues and the perfect background music. He wanted to be a rebel. She found him completely insufferable. They hooked up at a house party thrown by a mutual friend. He caught her by surprise, using the most idiotic line she had ever heard.

Have you ever kissed to a Smiths song?

That night she did. It was "Bigmouth Strikes Again." He later confessed that he was fed up with them. He wanted to pour gasoline all over Morrissey and set him on fire.

I think you're overreacting, she told him.
    Come on, the guy left the stage at some show because he spotted a grill somewhere in the distance. He's like this sworn vegetarian, "Meat is Murder."
    You're still overreacting.
    Fine, I wouldn't exactly set him on fire, but I would definitely throw meatballs at him.
    How old are you?
    I'm twenty. I think. Why?
    Sometimes you sound like you're six.
    And how does that make you look? Your boyfriend is a six-year-old.
    You're not my boyfriend.
    I'm not?
    No.
    We kissed to a Smiths song.

What does that have to do with anything?
A lot. It's, what-do-they-call-it . . . romance.
What do you do?
Don't try to change the subject.
What do you do, Elias?
I write.
What do you write?
Stories.
What about?
Love.
She frowned. Romances?
No. Short stories about love.
I see.

Do you fall in love a lot?
I don't think I've ever met a woman I didn't fall in love with.
Ugh, that's such an obnoxious cliché.
Fine, a beautiful woman then. One that listens to good music.
And watches good movies. And she has to read.
What do you read?
Cortázar.
What else?
Poetry.
What kind of poetry?
Love poetry. He laughed. His laugh was loud.
And what about you, what do you read, Andrea?
Don't use my name.
What should I call you then?
I don't know. I don't like my name.
Why?
It's plain.
What is a plain name?
She shrugged her shoulders.
Fine, what do you read?
Large books.
And right now?
*2666.*

Bolaño?

Si.

He nodded. I'm gonna change the song. The Velvet Underground. "Venus in Furs."

What's wrong with the Velvet Underground? She asked.

Nothing, but they're not exactly party music.

Her friend was the one who put it on. She wasn't very happy with him playing the Strokes instead. He was switching from New Yorkers to younger New Yorkers.

So what? he said. The Strokes are just as arty as the Velvet Underground, but they're much more suited to parties. You designers and architects always put pose above music.

What a hideous stereotype, she told him.

Sometimes you have to apply them.

But you told me you can't stand stereotypes.

Stereotypes are fun as long as they're not about me.

That's a bit hypocritical.

It's extremely hypocritical.

You're a strange guy, full of contradictions.

That's Zen.

It has nothing to do with Zen.

I like to believe it does.

Are you lying to yourself?

I am naive enough to believe things that are clearly not true.

I'm not sure if that's good or bad.

Me neither.

I think the world might be a better place if we were all a bit stupid. But I'm not sure that I could pull that off.

Me neither.

You know what?

I don't.

These times weren't made for you.

He laughed.

Let's get out of here, she said.

Where to?

My place. I have a bottle of wine at home. You can play the Strokes.

Deal.

~

They got out of there. The moon was a tiny notch against the night sky. He told her that.

How do people forget about the moon? About all of its forms?

I don't know, she said. I like it when I can see its face. You know, like it's howling or at least shocked at all it sees. Like it's saying: "Why the hell are you making everything so complicated?"

It seems indifferent to me.

Oh, so you don't think the moon would mind if I kissed you right now?

That's right.

You know, I'm like the moon sometimes. I observe and I'm indifferent.

I know that feeling. I know this might sound ridiculous, but I'm trying to make my life more like a novel or a movie.

Well now, these topics go better with some wine and music.

Where do you live?

Not far away. We can walk.

Deal.

~

The first time they made love, they were measuring each other's strength. It wasn't as much about sex as it was about proving skill. It was still dark when he woke. The street light was crashing against the window and dispersing all around her tiny bedroom. There was a Modesty Blaise poster above her bed. On her night stand, Murakami's *Norwegian Wood* and Bolaño's *2666*.

He got up, put on his pants and his shirt. Tied his shoes. Took his coat and got ready to leave. Standard practice. He stopped. She was still asleep, her arms embraced around the vacant space where his body lay a moment ago. He picked up her mobile phone and put his number in it. He left the room silently and sent her a text.

Oh . . . sweetness, sweetness, I was only joking
    When I said by rights you should be
    Bludgeoned in your bed.

~

So, you made love? he lit a cigarette with a match. They were standing in front of a diner and it was pouring rain.

Made love? Buddy, I might be a romantic, but I don't think I've ever made love to anyone. He lit a cigarette using his.

Fine, did you penetrate?

Elias blew the smoke away.

Well?

A gentleman never tells.

We're no gentlemen. You're an idiot and I'm a bum. But I'm also your best friend.

My best friend? He raised his eyebrow.

Yes.

What are we, in kindergarten?

Fine, you don't need to tell me, I don't give a fuck. But you're not coming to my birthday.

He laughed. Fine, yes, we did.

Cool.

Cool.

Let's get inside, he tossed away his cigarette.

Let's.

They went back to their table and sat down. Their coffee had gone cold. Elias took a sip.

Yuck.

Yeah, and it's not much better hot.

They sat quietly. Elias was nervously tapping his fingers on the table. Little finger, ring finger, middle finger, index finger. It sounded like a gallop.

I'm gonna get going. I haven't gotten much sleep the past few days and this phone call of yours in the middle of the night was of no help.

Sorry.

Don't sweat it. I'll see you around.

See you around, Maroje.

Don't use my name. That's what she told him. He remembered the poster in her bedroom. Modesty Blaise. Yes, that's what he could call her. Modesty.

They were like two lines that took an eternity to touch, a moment to live out the eternity, and a moment to disappear, uncertain of the possibility of another intersection. Two accidents waiting to occur.

And so he sat in the diner under the arrhythmic flickering of the neon lights. The only thing tying him to her was the pattering of rain on the window. He was nervously tapping his fingers on the table. Little finger, ring finger, middle finger, index finger. It sounded like a gallop. And she was sleeping. Dreaming of walking barefoot in the snow. On a field of snow where the sky is white and as frozen as the ground. The sun frail and distant. Almost as if . . .

## "The Volvox Doesn't Glow in the Dark"

She insisted that I wasn't listening to her or something like that. There was nothing wrong with it, she wasn't upset, but she came to the conclusion that I have trouble focusing. The sun was emerging, the water for coffee was just starting to boil, the waves were murmuring as they caressed the sand. The sound was making me want to take a piss. The sun was emerging and she insisted I wasn't listening to her. I went to take a piss.

I could hear the spoon clanging against the cup. Have you

decided? On what? Whether you're going home or not. Should I stay or should I go? She's talking again, I can't hear her over the stream. I yell, What? I said I knew you would find me.

I can feel her warm breath on my ear. We're at a nightclub, electro blasting and I can't hear her well. I answer by taking a sip of my beer. Ever since we met in that record store, I can't get her out of my head. A miniature hurricane that claimed to go by Megi.

Who did you come with? I ask. My brother. The one who collects LPs? What? she can't hear me. The one who collects LPs? I yell into her ear. She's wearing a subtle perfume. I like that. Wanna get outta here?

Sure, I say. I need to take a piss, wait for me outside. She nods. I go to the can. No line in the men's room. I'm done fast. I close my zipper and get out. She's sipping coffee. She's handing me my cup. The sun is advancing fast. It's no longer a crimson newborn.

I said you didn't have to go.

I answer by taking a sip of my coffee. I ask her if she wants to come with me to the beach. She says she does not. She'll be drinking coffee on the terrace, doing crosswords and Sudoku. I grab a towel and a book, Hemingway's short stories, and take a seat at the table.

You like to go to the beach when there's practically no one around. I don't like the noise, the children screaming. I like the sound of children playing.

I shrug and finish my coffee. I kiss her on the cheek. I won't be too long, I say. I get out and walk toward the beach about a hundred feet away from her house. I spread my towel and lay the Hemingway on it. I go into the water. It's cold and sending chills down my spine, my body instinctively wants to get out. I dive in and decide to swim toward the buoys. There I turn over to my back and let the waves cradle me. No point in writhing, just close your eyes. Peacefully.

I wasn't sure how long the kiss went on. Perhaps only for a second, but perhaps it's been a couple of hours, and the sun is now dawning.

I like you, you're a good kisser. I like Marica from the second grade better. Her socks don't fall down to her ankles like yours do.

Is she as good a kisser as I am? I haven't heard that verb in quite a while, "to kiss." People normally use these gross phrases. Like what? To make out, it sounds so mechanical. So is Marica as good a kisser as I am? Who's Marica?

She lets out a laugh, turns on her heel, and walks toward the club. I follow her and go in. Megi is still doing her crosswords. I leave my book on the table. I'm going to take a shower, I say.

The hot water's out, she yells. Doesn't matter. I get into the shower and let the water run, lukewarm water, like summer rain. That sounds like a cliché. Summer rain! Anyway, it feels good. Salt dissolved in the shower water is running down my body in snake-like curves.

Rain is pouring all over us and we run to the nearest doorway. I press her against the wall. I can taste the rain on her lips, the filthy rain. I tell her that. In return, she slams me against the opposite wall. She says it's a good thing her brother can't see us. He can't stand anyone touching his little sister.

I'm a rebel, I do whatever I want. Prove it to me.

I think about it, and eye the surnames on the intercom. I slide my finger pressing each buzzer. I wink at her and run to the next doorway. I repeat the action. We are running down the street. The lights in the apartments are coming on; people are looking out their windows. The streets are empty. All they hear is laughter.

We're taking a walk in a small Mediterranean town. We summoned the courage to hold hands. It's a bit strange since she's much shorter than me. We are quiet. The silence is comfortable. In fact, that too is a kind of communication. Everything's fine, you don't have to tell me, I know it. We're walking, we soon arrive back at her house, and I tell her I'm going to the beach for a short while. She'll be waiting.

I promised to drop by her place and now I'm climbing toward the Upper Town. I see the city spreading below me, the windows are shimmering like the volvox or whatever-they're-called do on the sea surface. The moon is already so close I could grab it by its horn. I reached out my hand and closed my eyes.

Are you going to spend the night here? Megi takes a seat next to me, hugging her legs, shaking. No. The sand isn't as warm as you are. Then get inside. I'm going to stay for a few more days, I tell her, I get up and I kiss her. The sea lies behind me, almost pitch black. On its surface you can see the shimmering volvox or whatever-they're-called. The moon is so close I could grab it by its horn.

## "The Happy and Dead"

That morning Andrej Kalovski determined he was dead. He was still breathing, his pulse throbbing, his entire body going like clockwork, but fuck it, he was a dead man. He was drinking coffee and using his free hand to tie his tie, a skill he had acquired over the years, working in a gray firm with gray hallways, where everyone wore gray suits, drank tasteless coffee, and ate free lunches that tasted sort of gray. In addition to the skill of one-handed tie tying, he had also developed a sense of apathy toward each and every aspect of his life. The understanding that he was dead came to him with no shock whatsoever, and he continued to sip his coffee, having already managed to tie his tie. On his way out of the apartment, his wife reminded him to take out the garbage.

The outside greeted him with early-morning cold and quiet, there was hardly anyone on the streets. He headed for the bus stop, which is where each day at 7:22 AM he catches the bus to work. Every morning he meets the same set of people at the stop, dressed in the same set of clothes, standing in the same spots. Today, however, he spotted a new person at the stop. A short girl with ruffled black hair reaching chin length. He could distinctly make out the traces of smudged make-up around her big black eyes and the somewhat paler eye circles. She was wearing an oversized black shirt and tight jeans, looking right at him and smiling as if they knew each other. He saw her lips move, but he couldn't hear what she was saying.

I'm sorry, I can't hear you.
I wasn't saying anything.

Oh, I thought . . .

. . . I was just moving my lips.

I can't read lips.

I'll teach you. Try again.

Andrej observed as she moved her lips, carefully shaping each muffled syllable. Do-you-ha-ve-a-smo-ke?

I don't.

There you go! It wasn't that hard. Besides, I don't smoke.

Why would a lady who doesn't smoke need a cigarette?

Lose the lady.

Excuse me?

Why would *you* need a cigarette, she says, stressing the "you."

Oh, right. Why would *you* need a cigarette? He asks, also stressing the "you."

To start up a conversation.

The bus arrives, Andrej gets on, and the girl stays at the stop.

Hey, aren't you getting on?

No, it's too crowded, I'll take the next one.

But . . .

The doors close. The girl is further and further away. Andrej kept thinking about her for the rest of the day. While they were waiting for the bus in the evening, he looked up at his colleague. Do-you-ha-ve-a-smo-ke?

What?

I wasn't talking, I was only moving my lips.

The colleague gave him a puzzled look. Andrej, you're working too hard.

Yes, perhaps.

He got home. Had supper. Didn't fuck the wife. Before falling asleep, he thought about the strange girl from the bus stop. Maybe he'll see her in the morning.

Morning. He was drinking coffee and using his free hand to tie his tie, a skill he had acquired over the years, working in a gray firm with gray hallways, where everyone wore gray suits, drank tasteless coffee, and ate free lunches that tasted sort of gray. On his way out of the apartment, his wife reminded him to take out the garbage.

There she was! She was tying the shoelace on her sneaker while hopping on one leg. The people at the stop paid no attention to her.

Hello! he approached her.

She took one look at him and went back to tying her shoelace.

My colleagues can't read lips either.

She finishes tying her shoelace. She crosses her arms and starts reading the timetable.

What is it, don't you remember? I'm the one you asked for a cigarette yesterday, even though you don't smoke.

She still says nothing. The bus arrives. He looks at her, gets in, and sits down resignedly. Yesterday must have been just a bit of fun for her. The doors close, she hops on at the last moment. She walks up to him.

I dreamed that I was taking a bungee jump from outer space toward the earth.

What?

Yes. It felt amazing.

Why wouldn't you talk to me at the stop?

I did yesterday.

So?

But I didn't get on the bus with you.

I still don't get it.

This way I'm creating a sense of coherence. I didn't talk to you out there, but now I will in here. There you go.

And tomorrow?

What?

What are you going to do tomorrow?

What's tomorrow?

The day after today.

I find that concept a bit vague. I'm not able to look so far ahead.

Oh. So bungee jumping, you were saying?

Yes! The earth was getting closer and closer, and the second before I hit the ground, the rope pulled me back up again.

I never dream about anything interesting.

I don't believe you.

No, really. I only dream about my exams, the hardest ones, from back when I was in college.

So change something.

I don't know how to change things in my dreams.

You don't need to. Change something in your life.

What should I do?

Quit your job.

Yeah sure, should I also leave my wife while I'm at it?

Why not? Do you love her?

I do, too!

So much that it rhymes, I see. This is where I get off. Bye.

She jumps off the bus. For the next couple of minutes, Andrej is confused. So confused that he almost forgets to get off at his stop. Change something. Sounds really nice. Magical, yet simple. But it also takes courage. While he was coming home from work, he looked for the girl. At the stop. On the bus. In other people. The next morning he asked what her name was.

Megi.

Is that your real name?

What is a real name?

What does your ID say?

Why would a piece of plastic know my real name?

Well, what did your parent name you?

And why would they know my real name?

Fine then, I will call you Megi. Hi, I'm Andrej.

He extends his hand, and they share a hearty handshake.

Did you quit your job?

No.

I assume you're still married.

Yes.

What have you changed then?

Nothing.

You're a coward.

I know, but . . .

. . . but but but but! She covers her ears with her hands. Start with little things then. Squeeze your toothpaste from the middle.

How did you know I squeeze it from the end?

I know everything. Angels and prophets whisper to me.

In your dreams?

No. On the streets.

How come I never see them?

You don't have to see them. You only need to listen. This is where I get off. Bye! She jumps off the bus.

You got out on a different stop yesterday, he yells after her.

She shrugs her shoulders. But today this one's my stop. The doors close. She waves at him. He spends his whole day at work thinking about this miniature hurricane. In the evening, he squeezes his toothpaste from the middle of the tube. That night, he dreams about an exam. But he isn't scared.

Misty morning. He was drinking coffee and using his free hand to tie his tie, a skill he had acquired over the years, working in a gray firm with gray hallways, where everyone wore gray suits, drank tasteless coffee, and ate free lunches that tasted sort of gray. On his way out of the apartment, his wife reminded him to take out the garbage.

Do you read? Megi asks him at the stop.

I read the newspapers.

I find newspapers too difficult to read.

What do you mean?

All those articles about accidents, embezzlements, murders, spectacles. It makes me sick.

What do you read?

Poetry.

What kind?

She shrugged her shoulders. All kinds.

I haven't read poetry in a long time.

Come with me to a poetry reading tonight.

Where? And who's reading?

My friends are reading, in their apartment.

Does that qualify as a poetry reading?

Why wouldn't it?

Well, it's not official.

What is official? she chuckled.

OK, I get it. When?

Whenever you get off from work.

Around seven, eight.

Would you like me to wait for you here at the stop at half past eight?

Agreed.

The bus arrived. They got in and continued their conversation. About the fall and the chestnuts. About the morning fog. About the expanding universe. At least that's what she says. Andrej believes it will shrink in the end. The reverse Big Bang. At half past eight they meet at the stop. To his question of whether the apartment is far away, she answers that it isn't. After five minutes of walking, they arrive.

Fourteenth floor. It's not a big place. A room and a bathroom. There were books and candles all over the place, and Andrej had to be very careful not to topple any of the piles of books or vinyl records. There was music coming from the record player (from the speaker, actually, but they only explained this to him later on). He didn't know the band because he never listened to music. Megi told him it was Gang of Four, and that she thought they were a little overrated. Megi's friends were drinking wine.

Who's the fellow, sis? one of them asks. Tall, skinny, with black hair. He looks like he smiles a lot.

Andrej, he says and extends his hand. His name is Pavel. The other boy's name is Ješu. He's a bit shorter, with brown hair and green eyes.

Hana is late, as usual, Pavel declares. But I think we can begin.

Ješu reaches for a book with yellowed pages. I saw the best minds of my generation . . . he begins.

Wait, you can't always do Ginsberg, Pavel protests. You read "Sunflower Sutra" last time.

I read "America" last time.

Irrelevant, you never let go of the Americans, Megi interferes. The discussion continues, a lot of names are coming up, and Andrej is listening, feeling lost amid all the names. Someone rings the doorbell.

That's Hana, Ješu says. Hana is a tall girl with black hair. She makes the announcement that she has a new poem.

Let's hear it, Pavel says, pouring more wine for himself.

Sometimes
    halfway through my automated actions
    I stop
    I look back
    as if I'm telling myself
    it's okay
    as if I'm telling myself
    everything is going to be fine
    you're still here
    you're still in the game something inside me can still alter my
direction
    one day when you're no longer here
    you won't even know about it
    even ask about it
    even look back

That's true, Andrej says, speaking out for the first time. Nothing ever alters my direction. I never look back. I never ask. I fit perfectly into the machine. I don't even need maintenance. And the more I talk to Megi, the more it's becoming clear to me that there are choices, but they can frighten a man, that's why taking the well-traveled road of routine is the easiest way out.

Silence took over. The record reached its end and the amplifier was letting out a humming sound. Pavel took another sip of his wine. You know, he began, your situation is not as bad as you may think.

There are people who go through their entire lives without coming to that realization. And then there are people who live their entire lives thinking they're free, when they're really slaves to unimportant things. In the end, all that you need is already in you. That's hard to grasp. I've known that sentence for years, and still I can't wrap my head around it. My friend had a dream once about the greedy god of all things mediocre and unremarkable, who devoured humans. And some of them had ideas, some of them wanted to change the world, but they sold out their present for a safe future. They entered a bitter race with time. And all of those people, they were happy. Happy and dead.

A moth circles frantically around the candlelight until it finally flies through the flame. It doesn't die, doesn't fall to the ground, and doesn't quiver its tiny legs. It circles on with its wings on fire. Burning. Glowing. Megi opens the window and it disappears into the darkness of the night, turning into an orange spot. For a brief moment, it looks like it might set the dark on fire.

TRANSLATED BY PETRA ŠLOSEL

# JIŘÍ HÁJÍČEK
## *Lion Cubs*

COACH VAŘECA HAD WANTED to hand the five-hundred-crown note in. But when he returned from Budějovice on the midday bus it was still burning a hole in the pocket of his sport coat. He'd spent that whole Friday morning running from one authority to the next. Each time that he took out the white envelope and explained what was in it he came up against creased brows and shifty eyes. All that time he hadn't even had the actual note in his hands, because of the fingerprints. At his last port of call, the police station, he'd been laughed at and sent home.

The bus passed the hostel, a long building that was one of the first in the village. Since midweek this had been fully occupied by some sort of high school excursion, as Vařeca had heard someone say that morning at the store. The bus stop was on the square, next to the tavern. The coach was looking forward to getting out of his coat and shirt and back into a T-shirt. There were beads of sweat on his tanned bald patch. The August sun had retreated behind clouds; it had been muggy since early morning. What bothered Vařeca most about the affair with the five-hundred-crown note—handed, in the envelope, by an unknown man to the juniors goalkeeper the previous evening—was the fact that it had caused him to miss a whole morning of training on the eve of a game. At the store he bought three bread rolls and a two-hundred-gram slice of meatloaf, which he ate from its paper wrapping as he walked. He reached the sports field in the lunch break. Some of the boys were lying under the tree next to the locker room; they greeted the coach from a distance, with respect. Vařeca's assistant Martin Moravec, who was twenty-eight and formerly a midfielder for a club in the second division, was waiting for him in the office.

"How did it go, Franta?" asked the younger man, whose black

curly hair was collar-length. He swung his feet off the desk and walked toward the coach. The two were on very good terms: sixty-year-old Vařeca had been Martin's coach and mentor, making of him the greatest star Semotice and its surroundings had ever produced, and after Martin's precipitous fall, the coach had brought him back as a colleague.

"I don't know what to do about it, Martin," said Vařeca, putting the white envelope on the desk. "At the Sports Association they told me they needed more evidence. At the Soccer Association they said it was crazy to think of dealing with corruption among juniors at district-league level—we'd blacken the name of local soccer, and for no good reason."

"So just forget about it."

"Then what do I do with the money?"

"You're too honest, that's your trouble."

"I don't want to hang on to a bribe."

"It'll go toward running the club."

"And will I enter that in the accounts? They don't have a column for bribes."

"Funny that. Czech accounting could do with one."

Rather than laugh at this, Vařeca continued to look worried as he scratched his gray mustache. "How did it go with the boys this morning? Did they all turn up?"

"Sure did. Pepík Sháněl was complaining about his right calf, but he managed to run it off. And Šustr came up to me again to ask who'd be first-pick goalkeeper. That kid's a dimwit. I told him he'd have to wait for you."

"That boy really bugs me. He's got the height for it, but what about those four fouls in Nová Ves? And remember what happened when Marek got injured against Ouběnice? Twenty minutes to go and we ended up losing a match we'd basically already won. How can he expect me to put him in the team after that?"

"You need to relax, Franta. Finish your meal at the desk and I'll see you outside at half-past. In the meantime I'll get the boys moving. Oh yeah, one more thing. There was a woman here. Wanted to know who's in charge of training."

"What did she want?"

"She saw me with the boys and didn't want to believe I was coaching them. Then I told her you were the senior coach. She asked how old you were and said she'd rather come back when you were here."

"Someone from the village? Do you know her?"

"No. Apparently she's the teacher of those girls up at the hostel."

"There are only girls in that place?"

Training sessions of district-level juniors didn't usually attract spectators; it wasn't like they were Juventus. So Vařeca noticed the woman standing just beyond the white-lime marking of the touch-line the moment she arrived. Although the afternoon session was still in progress, she stood on doggedly by the locker room. As he took his charges through their paces on the field, at first Vařeca paid no attention to the woman. But he began to find something suspicious about her. She was below average height, with short hair of a rich brown, apparently dyed. From time to time he looked over at her: lightly built, she was a little over fifty, he guessed; she was wearing brightly colored knee-length shorts, a loose top, and canvas shoes. The session was almost over before he realized what was bothering him about her. It wasn't just that she'd been at the stadium for almost an hour; she'd been watching the young players with close, systematic attention. Vařeca didn't know what to make of this.

Training over, Martin sidled up to him. "That's her, Franta."

Vařeca instructed the boys to leave the field, then bent forward as he got his breath back, palms on thighs.

"Damn it, Martin. She's sizing up our game and our kids, that's what it looks like."

"Before Sunday's match? Borovnice's coach is a guy, you know."

"There's something fishy about this."

"Anyway, if Borovnice had sent a woman to spy on our training sessions," Martin went on, "it wouldn't make sense for her to be asking for you."

"Maybe she's a scout."

Martin snorted.

"Did she speak Czech?"

Now Martin laughed out loud.

It was five-thirty in the afternoon. Having rushed his lunch, Vařeca was hungry. For the past twenty minutes he'd been sitting in the office in his sweaty T-shirt, trying to understand what the woman sitting opposite wanted from him. There were droplets of sweat on her narrow face. As she spoke, she fixed him with her hazel eyes and often clasped her hands together, as if in petition or prayer. A high-school teacher of chemistry. Slightly agitated, he had forgotten her name the moment she introduced herself. All he had managed to grasp so far was the urgency of the situation. There was desperation in her eyes and an appeal in her voice.

"An orientation course, you say?" he was repeating after her. "From the school of nursing. But what does it have to do with our training?"

"The first thing I need to know is where your boys live."

"Where they live?" He looked at her blankly. "They're either from this village or another in the neighborhood. They come here on bicycles or motorbikes. Some of them are driven in by their parents."

Vařeca was fidgeting with the envelope, which he'd left on the desk. When he realized what he was doing, he stuffed it into a drawer. The woman's gaze darted about the office. In the corner was a net bag filled with balls; under the window were the first-aid kit and stretcher of the club's medic. The office as a whole was in need of a tidy-up.

"One of our students didn't spend the night at the hostel, Mr. Vařeca." This came out in a rush.

Now that the story was out, the lady teacher appeared relieved, although the worry didn't leave her face, Vařeca noticed.

"At lights-out at ten she was still with the others. This morning she didn't appear at breakfast. Some of the girls tried to cover up for her, but, as they sleep eight to a room, it didn't take long for the truth to come out."

"She went out in the evening, then?"

"Right after lights-out. By arrangement."

Vařeca shrugged. The teacher wiped her brow with a folded cloth handkerchief.

"She was with one of your boys. Till morning."

"How do you know that?"

"She told us."

"Is it really such a big deal, Mrs. . . . ?"

"Dvořáková."

"Mrs. Dvořáková. The main thing is, she's back now."

"It was after eight when she got back. We'd been waiting for an hour and a half. We were about to call the police."

"Whatever for?"

"Mr. Vařeca, when a sixteen-year-old girl goes missing, who knows what might have happened to her? Besides, my colleague and I are responsible for her."

"But as you see, everything's fine now, nothing happened to her . . ."

"Ah, but something did, Mr. Vařeca."

Obviously the matter was pressing. The coach sat back in his chair, the sweaty T-shirt cold against his back. The dramatic pause spread out in front of them. Vařeca didn't care to ask any more questions; Mrs. Dvořáková was looking at him as if he'd done something wrong. When the silence became unbearable, he swallowed dryly and asked: "So what happened, then?"

Instead of answering, she looked from the desk to his eyes and back again.

"Mrs. Dvořáková, you came to me because you want something from me. Please don't speak in riddles. Just tell what this is all about."

"I need help, Mr. Vařeca. It's a delicate matter."

"So how can I help you?"

"He was blond. Medium build."

Vařeca detected hope in her voice.

"We've got at least two blond kids of medium build in the team," the coach pondered aloud. "You might even say three. Then there are two blond kids I'd call tall."

"Tell me about them."

"One's a midfielder, the other's a right back. One of the taller blond kids is a forward—a right winger—and the other's a goalkeeper."

"Hang on . . ."

"So which of those are you interested in?" he asked with impatience.

"All of them."

"The whole squad? Here it is." Vařeca pushed a sheet of paper in a transparent sleeve—a provisional teamsheet for Sunday's game—toward her across the desk.

"I need to see them," she said, with a patient smile.

"I've got the players' registrations with photos, but I can't give you those."

Her eyes flashed.

"I'd only need to borrow them for a little while," she pleaded.

"No can do, I'm afraid."

"I'd be so grateful."

It was almost eight-thirty in the evening. Coach Vařeca, in sneakers and a tracksuit, was locking his cottage before returning to the stadium. He set off slowly, his weariness apparent in his gait. In his mind he was replaying the difficulties of his trip that morning to Budějovice, at the offices of the Soccer Association for the Region of South Bohemia, the district offices of the Sports Association, the Department of Physical Education and Sport at City Hall, and the county police. No one had any idea about what to do with the five-hundred-crown note. So he turned his thoughts to team selection for Sunday's game.

She was waiting by the door of the clubhouse. She handed him a plastic bag, and he made a quick check of the cardboard folders it contained: all the players' registrations were there.

"Did she recognize him?"

"She wasn't sure. Those pictures are tiny."

"Are you kidding me? I get it that she's stupid, but surely she's not blind as well."

"Please don't be cynical," she said softly.

"I'm sorry," he said. "But the whole thing seems topsy-turvy to me."

"Truly, Mr. Vařeca, I'm sorry to be taking up your time with this. I understand why you're angry . . ."

"I'm not angry. So he didn't even give her his name, for God's sake?"

"But he did." Her smile was a sad one.

"So what is it?"

"Robert."

Vařeca's smile was triumphant. He fished in his pocket for the keys to the clubhouse and turned back to the teacher before going in.

"What can I say, Mrs. Dvořáková? You know as well as I," he said lifting the hand with the bag, "that there's no Robert here."

He was about to enter the office and close the door behind him. But when he looked up she was still there, her expression serious, patient, and determined. She just stood by the entrance to the clubhouse, looking at him, saying nothing.

"There's no Robert in the team, really there isn't."

"He invented the name, but he's one of yours all right."

"What makes you so sure?"

"Something she told us."

"You interrogated her?"

"We have our methods."

"You're worse than the FBI, you are."

"Pedagogical techniques, Mr. Vařeca."

"The poor girl."

"She confessed to the main thing. Then we left her alone with her best friend. They've known each other since elementary school."

"Why did you do that?"

"To get her to open up."

Still Coach Vařeca stood in front of the clubhouse of Semotice FC with a plastic bag in his hand. Helpless, he was scratching the wreath of short gray hair around his pate.

"Is all this really necessary?" he asked, annoyed now.

"Believe me, it is."

"It seems a bit much to me."

"They had unprotected intercourse."

Silence but for the muted, sorrowful peal of the church bell on the square.

"How do you know that, for God's sake?"

"Repeatedly."

Vařeca was about to say something untoward, it was on the tip of his tongue, but the steely determination in her expression held him back. And there was a surprising intransigence in her body language.

"We train from nine till five, with an hour and half for lunch, Mrs. Dvořáková. I'm responsible for the boys within those hours. If what you say happened did indeed happen, then it was in their free time."

He was suddenly aware of the lightness of her build. She was wearing jeans and a cream-colored sweater. Now he wasn't so sure about her age. The short hair was youthful and *sportif.* This time, it seemed to him, there was something different about her.

"Of course you're right, Mr. Vařeca."

"Then I don't see how I can help you."

"Do you think I could have a look at your gym?"

"The gym's at the school. All we have here is a small weights room."

"That's what I meant."

He unlocked the door of the locker room. They passed through a narrow windowless space, past wooden lockers and long benches. A smell of sweat and dust hung in the unventilated air beneath the low ceiling. Beyond the next door was the little room with weight-training equipment; in the corner were a washbasin and two showers. Mrs. Dvořáková looked around. Her eyes came to rest on the facing wall, where, under a narrow oblong window, there lay a mat with a checkered blanket wrapped around it; there were several empty cola cans on the floor. She looked at the coach.

"Who can get in here?"

"There's one key in the club office, which is always locked. And there are three more that do the rounds among the boys, so that they can exercise on their own."

"Do you keep a record of who uses it and when?"

"We used to, but the boys never used to write their names down. There's no need—it's been years since anything went missing. Who'd make off with any of this stuff? Dumbbells, barbells, and benches."

Still her eyes darted about—desperately searching for any kind of evidence, Vařeca thought.

He laughed. "You were thinking the boy might have recorded in a book that he was in here with a girl?"

She flashed stern eyes at him. "It's plain to me what went on in here."

"So what did go on?"

"So you're going to downplay it, are you? Like all men."

Vařeca had the feeling he needed to put something right, though he wasn't sure what. First and foremost, he couldn't understand why she'd come to him with this. What did she hope to achieve? What she'd do if she tracked the boy down, he couldn't imagine. The woman seemed desperate and lonely, but he was starting to take an interest in her, which was probably why he walked her to the hostel. This time he was the one who broke the uneasy silence, by telling her about the forthcoming game, and about his trek in the regional capital with the bribe. When they stopped in front of the long whitewashed building, at last she was smiling.

"You're a just and reasonable man, Mr. Vařeca. I saw that right away."

He mumbled something in reply.

"Their class teacher and I won't get much sleep tonight, I can assure you."

"I imagine not."

"We're leaving first thing in the morning the day after tomorrow. Could I please ask you for one last thing?"

The next morning at nine Coach Vařeca had the juniors stand together in a line. Eighteen youths in soccer boots and training shirts.

"It's the whole squad, including the subs," explained Vařeca, as he left the locker room in the company of Assistant Coach Moravec,

Mrs. Dvořáková, and a young girl with an alarmed expression. The group stopped where the line began.

"We couldn't get the student in question to come with us," said the teacher, turning to Vařeca. "She won't leave her room."

The coach nodded his understanding. Out on the field like this, it looked as though the referee was about to toss a coin to decide who would take which end and who would kick off. There was a slight nervousness in the air, just as there was right before a game. The players were shuffling from foot to foot, exchanging nervous glances as their boots hit the ground heavily.

The teacher whispered something in the girl's ear. The girl gathered her wits, stepped up to the first player and looked him in the face. The coaches stayed where they were as the other two went from one boy to the next. The boys were restless and fidgety; one snickered, others studied the grass or rolled their eyes in incomprehension. The gangly girl, with her ponytail and summer dress, approached the end of the line in the company of the teacher. Vařeca and Moravec exchanged glances; after they looked away, an expression of slight strain remained in their faces. Having lingered over none of the boys, the girl remained silent; her duty discharged, straight away she lowered her gaze, with obvious relief. Mrs. Dvořáková took her arm and led her away from the young soccer players.

"Well, Lenka?" said Mrs. Dvořáková.

"I don't know."

"Isn't he one of the blond ones?"

"His hair was more reddish than pure blond, Marie said."

The teacher sighed with disappointment and put her hands on the girl's shoulders.

"Let's go one more time. And concentrate. Focus on the eyes. She said they're brown, didn't she?"

The student nodded. This time they started from the other end. In the middle of the line the girl stopped, helpless. She looked at the teacher.

"I really don't know."

"Come on, let's get to the end," said Mrs. Dvořáková. "Concentrate on the eyes, remember."

The scent of grass hung in the air and the sun was getting hot. Now the girl was standing in front of the last player, but she was looking beyond him, toward the white, netless goal frame.

Again Mrs. Dvořáková took her aside and conducted a hushed conversation whose contents Vařeca didn't catch. Martin Moravec nudged him gently and nodded toward the teacher and her charge. Vařeca walked up to them and lowered his head to Mrs. Dvořáková's.

"My assistant and I were wondering . . . Maybe she'd know whether he's a defender or a forward."

The teacher looked at him doubtfully.

"It would narrow it down a bit," he insisted.

The girl was looking at the ground with a pained expression.

The teacher turned to the student and said in a patient tone: "Lenka, what do you think, from what Marie told you?"

"A forward, probably," the girl mumbled.

It was around seven in the evening and Coach Vařeca was still hunched over his desk in the clubhouse, drawing up the final team-sheet for Sunday's game. He was roused from his thoughts by a faint knock at the door.

"I was just passing and saw you through the window," said Mrs. Dvořáková.

He asked her in and pushed up a chair so that it was facing his own and they were sitting just like the first time, the day before. She was wearing a black top and a tweed jacket—a rather masculine style, Vařeca thought—and tiny gold earrings he hadn't seen before. She cleared her throat, breaking the silence.

"How did the matter of the bribe end up?"

"It hasn't yet. We haven't had time for it. How about your situation?"

"To tell you the truth, my colleague and I are of different opinions. It's her first year as a class teacher, so it's her first orientation course, and she's not keen to come across like an investigating officer. She wants to let the matter lie."

"Well, wouldn't that be the most reasonable thing?"

"She's only twenty-five, you know. I've been teaching for nearly thirty years. I wanted to give her all the help I could, but . . . well, it's her class."

"A teacher for thirty years . . ." He nodded his appreciation.

She was gathering her thoughts. When she spoke, Vařeca heard the urgency in her voice, as though she were delivering a message.

"When a group of girls finds itself in the same place as a group of boys, something always happens. Maybe you don't understand exactly what I mean. When something is a possibility, even if the conditions for its occurrence are minimal, occur it usually does. Say there's a top-floor window with eaves outside, you can bet your life someone's going to climb out."

"I can see that your profession's a tough one."

"At this particular age," she went on, as if struggling to complete her important statement, "a thing needs to be only slightly—hypothetically—possible for it to come to pass."

As she leaned forward in her chair, toward the desk and him beyond it, he felt her agitation and saw the fire in her eyes.

"These days there are no working parties for strawberry-harvesting, or apple-picking, or potato-gathering in September. Can you imagine how many working parties and dormitories and hostels I went through with my students?"

He stood up and opened the closet, where cups from various leagues and tournaments were arranged. Although he always had something alcoholic in here, this time he found only an empty fizz bottle and the dregs of some homemade brandy.

"Young teachers today know nothing but these orientation weeks and ski courses in the mountains."

"I was about to offer you something to drink. I'll run over to the store, it's not far. What do you say?"

With apparent reluctance, she agreed. Vařeca checked his watch, then his pocket, then, inconspicuously, all the pockets of his tracksuit. In the end he opened the right-hand drawer of the desk and took out the white envelope. It was barely a hundred yards to the general store, but it was closed. Two cottages farther down, toward the square, Vařeca rang the doorbell. A woman leaned out of the window; she was stout, with blond highlights in her hair and a cigarette in her mouth.

"Would you open up for me, Blanka?"

The woman disappeared behind the curtain, to reappear a few moments later on the doorstep, rattling a bunch of keys. She and Vařeca walked to the store together.

"I've got a few bottles of really good Moravian wine, Franta. It's pretty expensive, but I've been telling myself that if I can't sell it, I'll take it home."

She unlocked the store, walked around the counter, and handed Vařeca a bottle. He read the label.

"Late harvest. Two hundred and fifty crowns a bottle," she said.

"Grüner Veltliner," Vařeca said, nodding. It occurred to him that he hadn't asked Mrs. Dvořáková which she preferred, white or red. Troubled, he scratched his gray mustache.

"I've got a Blauer Portugieser too, from the same wine grower," said Blanka, who might have been reading his thoughts.

"I tell you what, Blanka, give me both of them."

He took the five-hundred note out of the envelope and handed it to Blanka across the counter.

On his return to the club's office, he rinsed out two glasses. Mrs. Dvořáková chose red.

"What are you going to do now?" he asked.

"I don't know. Nothing. We leave tomorrow, right after breakfast. My colleague wanted me to leave her alone with the students for a while."

"She's closer to them in age. Maybe they'll confide in her."

"When I was twenty-eight I had a really torrid week with my girl students."

"A working party?"

Mrs. Dvořáková sipped from her glass. "That's right. Imagine the situation. The hostel of the Fruta enterprise full of girls, and barracks right across the road. The girls and the soldiers looking at each other through the windows. Shouting and waving to each other . . . There was no problem during the day—the girls were harvesting strawberries—but how were we supposed to watch them in the evening?"

"So what happened?"

"One of them got pregnant. At sixteen."

"And then what?"

Mrs. Dvořáková stared thoughtfully at the diplomas in dusty frames on the wall.

"She had the baby," she said after a while, a faint smile on her face.

As he sat there under the club pennants and photos of senior Semotice elevens, Coach Vařeca began to feel embarrassed: slowly their conversation was heading off into the world of women.

"That girl was top of her class. Straight As, exemplary behavior. Parents very well placed."

"A big mess, then."

"I got fired. It was in eighty-eight."

Beyond the window it was getting dark. Vařeca heard her teacherly voice lower and soften.

"I found a job at a high school. I was there for seven years. My qualification is for chemistry and biology. For the last ten years I've been teaching future nurses."

He filled up their glasses. A silence fell.

"It's easy to forget that we were seventeen once," said Vařeca.

"There was a time I had it at home as well as at work," Mrs. Dvořáková resumed. "But my daughter's twenty-five now. Left home long ago."

"Do you have a house in town?"

"No, after my divorce I moved to an apartment. It's little more than a studio, really, but it's enough for me. I bet you have a cottage here. On the square."

"I do, but I live alone. I've been a widower nearly ten years. My daughters live in town. I'm a toolmaker by trade, you know. But I'm looking forward to my retirement. Then I'll have more time for the boys and their soccer."

"You're in charge of twenty boys. I guess you understood my situation because you know all about the world of boys."

Coach Vařeca felt that he was about to venture into philosophizing. He was less shy with Mrs. Dvořáková now.

"I keep trying to remember what it was like for me when I was the same age as those boys are now. Even as a nipper I noticed how grown-up men talked about soccer players who were just boys, and how they watched them. At home, at elementary school, at trade school. When I was eighteen and started work, the older guys would look down on us, thinking we didn't know anything about anything, so they—who were wiser and more experienced—would teach us. But when these older guys stood the other side of the touchline or sat in the grandstand, they talked about the same boys, or boys of the same age, in a different way. How could that be? If they were good, they showered them with praise, cheered them on; sometimes they even looked up to them. I experienced this as a young player myself. I don't know if you see what I mean . . ."

Taciturn Vařeca had surprised himself by the length of his speech. It was a relief to him when she took over, telling him about the first dance she attended, when she was seventeen, in spite of the fact that her parents had forbidden her from going.

"My folks were strict, Dad more so than Mom. We lived in a small town, and he came to the Sokol building, where the dance was taking place, slapped me in front of everyone, and dragged me all the way home."

"How had you gotten out of the house?"

"Through the bathroom window and down the lightning rod," she said, laughing.

His workman's hands—hands like shovels—lay open on the desk. Boy's world, girl's world, that's what he was thinking.

"So, do you think the girl really didn't recognize him from the photo on the registration?" he asked.

"What do you think?" Was her smile conspiratorial?

"I'm pretty sure she knows very well which boy it was. But she's keeping her secret."

The bottle was empty. Vařeca picked up the second, the Grüner Veltliner. He looked about. "Not very cozy in here, is it?" he said. "How about we drink this one at my place?"

The next morning the young class teacher sat at the breakfast table alone. Her colleague Mrs. Dvořáková hadn't spent the night at the hostel. She turned up around ten, just before the bus was due to leave; it was already filled with students. Hurriedly she collected her travel bag and wheeled it out. Her colleague thought how tired she looked, with no make-up and circles under her eyes; yet she looked relaxed and even-tempered, too.

The Semotice juniors won Sunday's district league game against Borovnice FC by three goals to one. All goals were scored by a nimble center forward called Karel Potočný, known to his teammates as Roberto Carlos, after the famous Brazilian player. In its September issue the *Semotice Bulletin* wrote enthusiastically of this young blond talent, calling him the team's "most prolific attacker."

TRANSLATED BY ANDREW OAKLAND

# IDA JESSEN

## *Postcard to Annie*

FOR A YEAR, between the ages of eighteen and nineteen, Mie lived in an attic room on Otto Rudsgade. She had just begun Nordic Studies at the university and only by a stroke of luck had she managed to find a room with such a central location, sharing with two other girls, Bodil, who was a Christian and in her final year at the diaconal college out in Højbjerg, and Annie, who was training to be a bilingual secretary. Mie knew there were many who had to make do with living on their own in dingy basements in Viby or even as far away as Tilst, and she was very fond of her room, from where, when she opened the dormer window, leaned over the sill, and poked her head out, she could see the red rooftops of Trøjborg, the woods, and the bay of Aarhus Bugt. She had painted the sloping walls white, and painted the desk and the bookcase and the chair white, too. On the floor was a mattress, and that was all. She had her own little landing with a large cupboard and a mirror, and the landing opened out onto the hallway where there was a bathroom and a little kitchenette that were shared with the two others. She was happy about living together and had even used the word "communal" in conversation with one of the young men from her study group. "How come you've got three fridges, then?" he asked when she showed him the loft where they dried their clothes and stored their various oddments, and she told him she had bought hers from the previous tenant and had only paid two hundred kroner for it. Afterwards, she had a nagging feeling it had been the wrong thing to say, and not only that, but she felt that it might have been an important moment, too. Something had slipped through her hands.

Painting her desk and the bookcase at home in her parents' garden that summer, she had felt like she was on the verge of stepping

64

inside a new person. In high school she had realized that academic work came easily to her, and when after three years she graduated, she was in no doubt she would go directly on to university. Her parents made tentative noises about the benefits of a gap year and seeing the world first.

"What world?" she asked. "Isn't Aarhus a part of it? Isn't the university? I don't want to waste a year doing something I don't want to."

"Of course, darling, you must follow your will," they agreed, and she could almost feel their relief at her sense of purpose. "You seem to know what you're doing." She pictured herself, the way she would stand in front of the mirror on the little landing as she brushed her hair, how then she would grab her bag and dash down the stairs and out onto the street, immersed in important things to come. But as yet she was only halfway in and halfway out, and most of it seemed halfway familiar. The foolishness and the embarrassment. The joy that remained hidden. The light against the wall in the mornings when she awoke. Sound had been softer this night, and she could tell without moving from the mattress that snow had fallen. It was February 21. She had to get up, her study group was meeting.

Then came three short knocks on her door. It was Annie on her way out. Every day she said good-bye in the same way. But Bodil was still there. Mie could hear her padding about in the hallway. She wore sandals all year with bare feet and slept only four hours a night. She rode a men's racing bike and her eyes were so blue that anyone who saw her could only imagine her being a good, intelligent, an altogether perfect person.

Mie stayed under the covers until she could put it off no longer. She got up and took out some clean underwear from the cupboard before going to the bathroom, which was so small she had to shower with one leg on the toilet seat. When she was finished she scurried back to her room with a towel around her and got dressed. She put her books and the folder containing her notes in her bag, and meticulously brushed her wet hair. After that, she went to the kitchen to make some tea.

Bodil was there, cutting cheese with a slicer. Her movements were vigorous, and she placed the slices in three stacks on a piece of tin foil. Mie recognized her own block of cheese. She had only bought it the day before and now Bodil's efforts had left it miserably concave with two upturned ends of rind. It wasn't the first time things had gone missing from her fridge, but Mie wasn't the sort to kick up a fuss.

"Good morning," she said instead.

Bodil glanced up at her and carried on slicing the cheese. "What are YOU doing up?" she asked, without returning the greeting.

"I've got study group," said Mie. "At ten o'clock."

"And I'm supposed to CARE, am I?" said Bodil with a grin and looked her impudently in the eye in such a way that Mie felt obliged to lower her gaze. Bodil stuffed some cheese into her mouth before folding up the parcel of tin foil and putting it in her bag. "Move yourself," she said and barged her way past. "I'm in a bit of a hurry. I've got study group as well. And this afternoon I've got to go to the dental school and get my jaw sorted out so it doesn't keep dislocating all the time. They think I'm quite interesting for the time being. Ha ha." She turned and gnashed her big white horsy teeth in Mie's face, then swiveled around and went off down the hallway. Mie stayed out of her way in the kitchen until the front door slammed shut. As soon as she heard Bodil's footsteps going down the stairs she filled the kettle and put it on the burner. "Idiot," she muttered, meaning either Bodil or herself.

She made her tea and drank it standing up, leaning against the counter. Through the little skylight she could see straight up into white sky. Soon it would begin to snow again. She thought about having some breakfast, but had lost her appetite. "How does a person get the better of another?" she wondered, but the thought was so complicated as to completely escape her endeavors to capture it. It leapt from her grasp in a display of sparks.

It was nearly twenty to ten by the time she shut the front door behind her, and as she emerged onto the street she immediately abandoned any thought of going by bike. Down on Trøjborggade the traffic crawled along between banks of snow. But the snow made her happy. The city, now wrapped in white, seemed less daunting, less alien to her than before. She almost forgot the incident with

Bodil and was consumed by the feeling that somewhere, one day, there would be a place for her.

She got on a crammed bus, alighting at the city hall, from where she would continue her journey out to Viby. The sky was leaden and grey, the snow fell gently. The traffic, however, was in turmoil, and she realized she had been lucky to even get this far. The bus shelter was packed with waiting passengers staring down the street in anticipation. Now and then a heavy bus came flying past without stopping, and people exchanged stories of woeful journeys to work. One woman had been on her way for three quarters of an hour, another for more than an hour. Not many men went by bus, only a single young man stood out, a student by the looks of him, reading a newspaper.

As she stood there, an elderly woman came along the pavement with quick, sprightly steps, white hair gathered stiffly at the nape of her neck. She walked with such purpose, and seemed almost to pierce her way through the waves of oncoming pedestrians. Her gaze was fixed firmly ahead and she did not seem to be at all bothered by the cold or the slippery pavement. Her coat was unbuttoned and flapped in her wake. From a distance it looked like the kind of garment more suited to summer. And what was she wearing on her feet? Mie couldn't take her eyes off her. Flimsy, open shoes. They looked like the slippers of dark blue leather she remembered wearing as a child. Surely they'd be soaking wet with sludge? And her coat was not a coat at all, but a dressing gown of padded satin with a large floral pattern. Pink peonies and green leaves on a creamy white background.

Mie's heart skipped a beat. She looked at the others who were waiting in the bus shelter, but no one seemed to be bothered. Some were chatting, others were silent, and the young man was reading his newspaper. Perhaps the woman had merely popped out for a minute on an errand. Mie told herself to calm down. There was no point making a drama. Things got so embarrassing when she did. She could work herself up until her voice became quite shrill, and she'd been making such an effort lately to keep herself in control and behave like an adult.

The woman was wearing a nightgown that wasn't properly

buttoned at the chest. Then, at long last, a bus appeared and looked like it was going to stop. It slowed down and people moved forward to the curb. Sure enough, it indicated to pull in. Mie was swept along by the surge of eager passengers and found herself at the doors. But just as she lifted her foot to step inside, she changed her mind and went back to those who had remained on the sidewalk.

Now the elderly woman had reached the bus shelter and Mie saw that her legs and feet were bare, and her slippers were indeed soaked. As she walked by, Mie stepped out towards her.

"Do you need any help with anything?" she asked.

"No, no, thank you," said the woman without shifting her gaze.

"It's a nasty day," said Mie.

The woman didn't reply.

"Aren't you cold?"

Still no reply.

"I can follow you home, if you like. Where do you live?"

The woman said something Mie didn't catch. She had to scamper just to keep up with her.

"Sorry, what was that?"

Another incomprehensible reply.

"Are you going somewhere in particular?" asked Mie.

The woman stared stiffly ahead. It was plain she wanted to be left alone and had no intention of conversing.

"Where are you going?"

People passed by them on the sidewalk and Mie felt increasingly silly, increasingly suburban and conventional. If the woman wanted to go for a walk in her nightie that was her own business, surely? And yet she heard herself repeat her question: "Where are you going?"

"Over there," the woman replied. At least, that's what Mie thought.

"Well, I'll let you get on, then," she said with an awkward chirp of laughter and halted as the woman carried on, looking neither left nor right. But Mie remained standing until she saw the woman vanish around the corner at the next crossing. Only then did she return to the bus stop. The time was by now twenty minutes past ten.

It was no longer worth trying to get to her study group, but nevertheless she stayed put. Her thoughts kept coming back to the woman. She felt relieved. What would she have done with her if she had wanted to be helped? What if she had followed her home, what then? Her head was empty at the prospect. She stared out into the busy street and caught sight of another bus slowing down and indicating to pull in. A number five to Viby. Another surge of passengers, but this time Mie got on.

She stood at the back as the bus pulled away, pressed against the window by people with shopping bags and prams. Next to her stood the young man from the bus stop. Mie carefully avoided looking at him. She wiped a peephole in the pane with her mitten, only for it to steam up again. The air was thick with the smell of damp clothes and stale tobacco. Shortly after they passed Banegårdsgade the bus and everyone in it suddenly lurched to one side. There was a thud that ran through the aisle from the front to the rear. People clutched at each other and let out small cries. Some laughed. The bus drew to a sudden halt and for a second everything was quiet. Then the front door opened and the driver darted out. Mie wiped the pane again. The passengers began to murmur and crane their necks.

"What's going on?" Mie asked a woman whose elbow had been perilously close to jabbing her in the face more than once already.

"I'm not sure," the woman answered. "It felt like we hit something." Then after a moment she said: "They're saying someone's been run over."

"Has someone been run over?"

"That's what they're saying."

"Is it bad?"

The woman gave a shrug. "No idea," she said.

In the ten minutes that followed, talk increased. No one knew where the driver was. Someone pressed the emergency button for the rear doors and a number of people got off, some by the front doors, too. Cold air filled the bus and after a while there was room in the aisle and some empty seats. Mie went further up the bus and sat down, pressing her face to the window. A couple of people hurried back and forth outside. It was coming down heavily now, hard pellets of snow blowing across the road. The traffic was almost at a standstill. A single car edged its way forward halfway up the pavement on the wrong side of the road, wipers going full speed, and in the distance ambulance sirens were heard. One by one, the passengers were leaving the bus. Mie stood up again and went right to the front, and now she could see a huddle of onlookers at the radiator grille, all eyes staring towards the same point. It was true. There had been an accident.

She did not consider herself to be an inquisitive person. She was a nineteen-year-old girl who behaved properly and politely, and refrained from indulgence. Often she would be approached by people who for some unknown reason had picked her out, wanting then to cling to her, to suck her dry, as though it were a kindness she would never have the temerity to decline. And decline she did not. But nor did she assent, or not really. She would steal away through the first available door with a lame excuse, to everyone's bemusement and an intrusion of questions. They didn't notice anything was wrong until suddenly she, the meek, apple-cheeked girl, had torn herself free. She had a feeling, or rather she knew, that ever since high school her fellow students had said of her that she was far too gullible, too easy to take for a ride, sweet and innocent, basically, and it upset her that they should judge her at face value, not least because she felt herself to be permeated by a bone-hard cynicism that came from inside her own heart and made her look straight through whoever she was with, and straight through herself as well. It was why she was so harsh on herself. She never engaged in gossip or tagged along on the heels of others, and did little for the sake of her own slender pleasures and comfort, and that was just about the only medal with which she could adorn herself at this point in her life. This January morning on M.P. Bruuns Gade, Aarhus, in 1983.

But she got off the bus.

The moment she stepped onto the sidewalk an elderly woman turned towards her and told her in an agitated voice: "She jumped out in front. Just jumped out in front."

"Who did?"

"That poor lady," said the woman. "She hadn't a chance." She took Mie's arm for support. "Horrific, it was," she said. The snow was as hard as hail and the fingers of the stranger dug into Mie's coat sleeve like she'd never again let go. Mie felt a sudden jab of pain in her right temple, just above her eyebrow, and she pulled free and stepped aside. The sirens were very close, rising swiftly in intensity, until finally they stopped, leaving behind them a silence in which a door could be heard opening, and then others still, and a stretcher was rolled out, people were forced back onto the pavement, but Mie pressed herself against the front of the bus and remained standing there. She saw a figure being lifted up, swathed in blankets and coats, not even the head was visible. She had never seen anything like it before. Her heart was pounding dreadfully. It was as if it wanted to pound all the fright out of her and assure her that if only it beat with sufficient alarm then everything would be all right, nothing bad would have happened and it would all be over. An ambulance man inadvertently turned up the corner of a blanket, revealing a glimpse of floral print against a creamy white background of satin, and Mie spun round in the same instant to be sick. But nothing came up. She staggered to the sidewalk, gripped a lamppost and felt her stomach plunge as the stretcher was rolled back into the ambulance, and while she stood there she noticed out of the corner of her eye a pair of legs in black jeans step towards her.

"Are you all right?" a voice asked.

"I'm fine," Mie gulped.

"You need to sit down for a minute. Come with me."

She nodded, but did not move.

"You need something to drink."

She lifted her head and saw the young man from the bus stop. He studied her with an impassive, critical gaze, with eyes that did not see her at all, only the state she was in. Had it been the elderly woman of just before, with the distressed voice and the unpleasant, owlish grip, she would have said yes. But she could not go with the young man who now stood before her.

"I'm all right."

"You look like a corpse."

"I'm fine, really."

"You don't look it."

It was starting to get embarrassing. She let go of the lamppost.

"Okay," she said. "All right."

He took her to a café a bit further along the street. It was bright inside, as if all the snow outside had accumulated in the mirrors and the white tablecloths, and Mie's headache grew worse. Her nausea returned with a sudden jolt and she desperately wanted to go somewhere she could lie down. The young man had gone up to the counter and was gathering things on a tray. She closed her eyes and straight away it was as though everything that had happened vanished. A tremendous sense of fatigue came over her.

"How are you feeling now?" said the voice.

She didn't react.

"Are you okay?"

She grimaced, to say: Wait a second.

"Hello-o-o. Anyone there?"

She didn't care much for his tone and opened her eyes. There he was, holding the tray steady in both hands, that same critical look in his eye.

"Yes," she said, offended.

"There's coffee here, and some juice and bread."

He placed a glass, a cup and saucer, and a plate with a bread roll on it in front of her.

"Eat," he said. "It'll do you good." She was still embarrassed and rather in a huff, and the more she chewed, the more the bread seemed to swell in her mouth and she realized to her dismay that tears were welling in her eyes.

"Have some juice," he said kindly, handing her the glass.

"Thanks," she muttered, not daring to look up for fear of crying.

Some time passed in silence as she ate and drank. He sat and sipped a cup of coffee. "Feeling better?"

She didn't want to say anything, but he didn't need an answer.

"You've got some color back in your cheeks now," he said with satisfaction. She did feel a lot better and her natural urge to be friendly was coming back to her, too.

"Aren't you on your way somewhere?" she asked. "You mustn't let me keep you."

"It's all right, I was only going home. I live just along the road here."

"Then I am keeping you."

"I'm not in a hurry. It doesn't matter."

"I don't want to be a nuisance."

He smiled, nothing more. She stole glances at him over the rim of her coffee cup. Her experience with men was limited, but some things she knew. For instance, she was aware that if he had taken her home with him instead of to the café where they were now seated, she would eventually have come to a point at which she felt obliged to repay his kindness by going to bed with him, and she was thankful for the fact that this was not going to happen. In all, she had been with two men, the most recent being Søren, who had noted the three fridges. They had stayed behind in his room after the others had gone home from study group, and when the time passed eleven and they had drunk a bottle of wine, it had seemed to Mie to be the only way of getting home again with her honor intact. He had peeled off her loose-fitting, undemanding clothes, and his eyes grew wide at what he discovered underneath: "Hey, you actually look GOOD!" he exclaimed, with such astonishment that the words, and the sudden gentleness with which they were uttered, remained within her, as immovable as if they had been equipped with barbs. Until then, she had been wholly unaware that a compliment could be so humiliating.

"Where were YOU going?" the young man asked.

She told him about her study group.

"Don't you have to get going, then, or call someone?" he said.

"No, it's not worth it now."

"I see."

"She died, that woman," she went on. "They said it was a woman who jumped out in front of the bus. Or ran, I mean."

"So I heard."

Of course. Slightly at a distance, slightly familiar. Not too much, but not too little, either. And inside, Mie was burning.

She fell silent. She wanted to talk about it some more and searched for the proper, objective words to use that would be quite at odds with the chaos she felt inside. But he spoke first.

"You'll be in shock," he said. "I'll get you another coffee."

While he was away she found a tissue in her bag and blew her nose without making a sound, her upper body twisted over the arm of her chair. She straightened up with a feeling of resolve.

"I saw her just before it happened," she said when he came back, then adding quickly to explain: "I mean, not just before she ran out in front of the bus. It was while we were waiting for it to come. She came along the pavement in her dressing gown and slippers. Didn't you see her?"

"No," he said. "I didn't."

"I even spoke to her. I went after her. But she wouldn't talk to me." As calmly as she could, Mie told him all about it. About what had been said. She told him about the woman's odd determination. "It was like she just popped out to get something," she said. "And I felt so stupid for interfering." The only thing she didn't mention was her relief on realizing that perhaps she wasn't needed.

"She must have been senile," he said.

"Do you think?"

"It doesn't matter how much of a hurry you're in, no one goes into town in their slippers in this kind of weather."

"I suppose not."

There was a pause.

"I didn't think of that," Mie said after a bit. "Or rather, I did, of course, when I first saw her. But then because she answered me and seemed so . . . Where did she come from? What about the people who were supposed to be looking after her?"

"She probably sneaked out," he said, and smiled reassuringly. Mie smiled back. The dark hand that had clutched her inner being released its grip.

"So you don't think it was a suicide?"

"No." He pondered for a moment. "No," he said again. "I think she was a poor, confused old lady who had run away from home. I don't think she was going anywhere in particular, just wandering about aimlessly. She probably didn't even realize she was crossing a busy road. Not from what you've just told me."

"But what was she thinking?" Mie went on, now sufficiently at ease in his company to say what she had been wanting to say all along, and what she in actual fact had been wanting to say to Søren from her study group, indeed to anyone if only they did not appear to her to be so outlandishly obsessive and false. But this young man seemed genuine: "Do you think there was something I could have done?"

"Yes, I do, certainly," he said.

"There was?" she replied, aghast.

"Yes, of course. It's called citizen's duty. Perhaps you might think about it next time." He looked at her, coldly, she thought, and her cheeks bloomed red.

"You can talk, you just stood there reading your paper," she retaliated. "You didn't even try. You didn't lift a finger."

"We're not talking about me."

She reacted instinctively. Without thanking him for his help or even replying to what he had just said, she pushed back her chair, stood up and left the café, burning with rage and without looking back.

She marched along the pavement, not looking where she was going, colliding with other pedestrians, who spun round in astonishment and stared at her as she went. She sensed none of it, but felt herself consumed by bleakness, seething and spuming. How unfair! He had refused to discuss the matter, and had passed judgment on her. But what about him? What about him? She spat out the words as she marched on: "What about yourself, now that we're talking about it? What about yourself? You make me want to puke. Puke!" She came to a crossing and stopped. Anger boiled inside her, and only impulse propelled her along. But when the light changed to green she did not cross the road. She was buffeted by those whose way she was blocking, and stepped aside. All of a sudden she could hardly move her legs. There she remained, rooted to this spot in her life, and so immersed in herself as not to realize it. No one had ever made her feel so shameful and so enraged as this stranger, this young samaritan whose name she didn't even know. She thought about the glass of juice he had handed her, and how to begin with he had studied her as though she were an object in some experiment, transforming before his eyes. She thought about his smile that had prompted her to confide in him. She thought about him having said he was in no hurry, that he was on his way home. It struck her now that he had lied. If he lived in the vicinity of Bruuns Gade and had been waiting for a bus at the city hall he must have been going somewhere else.

But why had he told her differently?

To reassure her.

To be kind.

Because he wanted to be with her.

These were the only answers.

*

Twenty years later she is driving through Aarhus in her car one evening in autumn. She has come from another part of the country and has been on the road for some time. She is going to give a talk at the library in Risskov, and she must find something to eat before eight o'clock. She is rather late. She had reckoned on getting here before now, but there was an accident on the freeway, and a detour. It's now quarter to seven. There's still time to find somewhere.

It's been many years since she was here last. Nothing more than slumbering recollections connect her to the city. Now they begin to stir, gradually. It's October and already dark. Leaving the freeway she took a wrong turn and finds herself now in Højbjerg. She drives through the woods and along the sea, which is inky and restless. The moon is waning, though as yet still almost round. For a brief moment she feels as if she could drive her car across the bridge of moonlight that illuminates the water. "I've never seen it like this before," she says to herself, for she has retained her former habit of speaking out loud whenever something makes an impression on her. With the march of time these utterances she hears pass over her lips are no longer mere exclamations and single-syllable mutterings of despair or rage, but well-composed, sociable sentences, as though some warm-hearted companion were always at her side. She drives along Dalgas Boulevard, then carries on down M.P. Bruuns Gade, past the railway station that has been sandblasted clean and now looks so much brighter than last time she saw it. She turns the corner and passes by the concert hall. The car is driving her. She must find a place to eat, had almost forgotten, so absorbed as she is in seeing her former city again. But then halfway up Frederiks Allé she recalls the café and decides on the spot that she will eat there. Most likely she'll have to make do with a sandwich or a salad, but that doesn't matter, for by now she has little time for dinner. She turns onto Banegårdsgade and slows down as she rejoins Bruuns Gade. She can drive as slowly as she likes, there's hardly any traffic at all. She thinks she remembers where it was, but crawling past she sees only a greengrocer's and a minimart. She pulls in to the curb, gets out, locks the car door, and looks up. The sky above Aarhus is overwhelming. Some gulls screech from the rooftops and she is gripped by a sense of familiarity that feels like a yearning, a shudder that passes right through her. "I'll have a little walk," she tells herself.

She goes along the street to the next crossing. The pedestrian light is red, but there are no cars in sight. She walks over and continues on, peering in at each window along the way. Some she remembers, others not. But the café is nowhere to be found. Eventually, she abandons the idea. She goes back to the car and gets in. She's no longer hungry, more important matters occupy her now: she has not finished visiting herself yet. She is struck by an odd feeling of tenderness at the thought of a timid young girl who was so easy to correct. What a long time ago it was. She indicates and pulls out, turning down Johannes Bjergs Gade, and there it is, the café. Bright and inviting. The very same place.

Inside is empty. For a moment she thinks it might be closed, but the door opens as she turns the handle. She remembers the table at which they sat, and there she puts down her coat and her bag before going up to the counter and ordering a club sandwich with mineral water and a cup of tea. She sits down. The floor is worn. The furnishings are all different now. She remembers the young man had on black jeans, a green shirt, and a navy blue sweater by Zacho, the label was at the cuff. He was still at the table when she went back. He hadn't moved. His newspaper was on the floor and he sat turning his cup slowly on its saucer. But when she came through the room towards him he looked up, his entire face lit up at once, he got to his feet and they swept into an embrace that lasted for many, many years. An embrace.

What would she have done if she had known what was to come? After the first years of eagerness and devotion she wearied and would look for excuses to be on her own. She could be childish when things got too much for her, mustering the strength to pull herself together only after being taken to task. And then one day it was over. She was through with feeling ashamed and left him, the young man who in the years in between had become a very grown-up man indeed, with a displeased and reproachful countenance.

Would she rather have carried on over the crosswalk instead of turning back? It was a silly question. Of course not. Young women lust for life and love and life again, and she felt she almost could have burst as she ran back towards the café. Please let him be there. Please don't say he's gone. Let him be there.

Everything that was to come lay concealed within that embrace. Their almost grown-up children were there.

The waiter comes with her sandwich and drinks. But she has lost her appetite now and can only sip her tea. She's not worried about the evening ahead, knowing herself to be fully prepared.

Yet time passes, it's already twenty past seven. She pays and goes back to the car, and is driving north through the city center when a sudden impulse prompts her to turn past the cemetery. She does not stop until reaching Otto Rudsgade, number ninety-two. The door is locked, of course, everyone has security systems now. But then two women happen to be on their way out. They ask if she wants to go in.

"I used to live here," she explains. "I'd like to look inside and see the staircase again, if it's all right."

It is. "Have a nice time," they say kindly and laugh. Their footsteps disappear along the pavement in the direction of the woods. She remains standing just inside the front door. The wall is yellow at the bottom and white above, and the banister is a mousy grey. She stares blankly at it all.

A moment later she is back behind the wheel of her car on her way to her speaking engagement. She empties her mind of everything other than what now lies before her. She is so used to it that this slow and gradual evacuation of thoughts proceeds entirely on its own. Her empty stare registers the road, the cyclists, and the car behind her, but she pays them no heed. It could all be an uninteresting film she was watching while half asleep. She isn't really present, is neither here nor there, nor anywhere else. But turning into the parking lot in front of the library she emits a snort of laughter that tears her from her soporific state, stumbling suddenly over a recollection that's been hidden away, forgotten all these years.

By the time she got home that evening after the road accident and her first encounter with Ove, she was ravenously hungry. She went straight to her fridge and found a hunk of rye bread and what was left of her cheese. No more had been taken since that morning. The door of Bodil's room was wide open and she could see Bodil herself sitting huddled at her desk, the light from the lamp shining in her waxy, yellow curls. She was making a funny noise. And Mie, who was still being wafted along by the day's sustained and resplendent effusion of caresses and tender lovemaking in Ove's tiny flat on Bruuns Gade, as though she had not yet stopped making love with him at all as she stood there with the cheese in her hand, went in to say hello. She found her drinking oatmeal soup through a striped straw, her back hunched as she sucked.

"What are you doing?" Mie asked. Without sitting up or putting down her straw, Bodil looked at her and bared her teeth, revealing a crisscross of wire and little screws.

"God, I'd forgotten. You've been to the dentist's," said Mie. Bodil replied by emitting a series of sipping and sucking noises.

"What?" said Mie.

"It's her jaw," Annie called out from the kitchen, appearing then in the doorway. "Her jaw!" she repeated solemnly. "Her jaw's been wired together. She's on spoon food for the next three weeks."

"How awful," said Mie.

"Awful!" Annie repeated.

Now, twenty years later, on this contented evening, with the past appearing to her in such forgiving light, Mie thinks this: "I wasn't as alone as I thought." And she decides that when she gets home she will write to Annie. It can't be that hard to find her on the Internet. She won't send a long and detailed letter, just a postcard with a few short words.

TRANSLATED FROM THE DANISH BY MARTIN AITKEN

# MIKKO-PEKKA HEIKKINEN

FROM *The Destruction of the Liquor Store in Nuorgam*

### "The Dogs Down South"

THE WORST ARE THE ASS-EYES on the short-haired dogs. They stare back bare at the stranger walking along behind, stare arrogantly, as that curly little tail twists the sphincter oval-shaped.

That ass-eye says: Watch me, human. I can shit any time I want, plop in the path of your fixed-gear bike. I can shit smack where your vintage Nike's gonna land. I can speckle the sidewalk. And there ain't nothing you can do about it. My owner cares more about me, his dog's butthole, than he does about the vital functions of say that drunk passed out over there on the pavement. I'm untouchable. You don't believe me? Give it a whirl. Touch me. The dog's owner'll clock you in the jaw. What, you don't want to test it? Okay, then, watch how I squeeze out a squiggly brown spiral on the Boulevard. Who's gonna stop me? Sometimes I locomote it out like lava. I got all the time in the world. God, look how crowded the trams are today. My, my, how the trees over there in the old church park have grown. Now it's done. The dog steps daintily to one side. The owner has a plastic bag on his hand like a glove. He bends down and scoops up my shit. The owner, who lives in fucking Punavuori, picks up my shit with his fingers. You see, human?

These ass-eyes wink at you in the tens of thousands in Helsinki. No one knows the exact number, because no one keeps track of mongrels. Tens of thousands of scraggly, sugary animal assholes, in apartment buildings, row houses, detached houses, high on Royal Canin farts.

There's no way this many anuses operating on animal instincts won't leave their calling cards. Brown skidmarks on designer sofas, silk sheets, paper rugs, *haute couture* dresses, mink furs, motorized leather seats. Doggie anuses answering the call of nature meet random doggie noses at street corners in every season. Wet snouts then eskimo-kiss infants that non-family members are not allowed to touch without disinfecting their hands first. Having given the baby the treatment, the dog and its asshole take possession of the living room from the easy chair. All through business hours the beast barks at the barren apartment. Forget how hard the breeders have worked to turn a herd animal into a stuffed animal. The endless yapping in cheap prefab apartment buildings exasperates the neighbors, but even if they complain to the authorities, the owner cares as much about that as if the beast is visibly suffering, you know, because its fur's been shaved off, its snout's been amputated, its nostrils've been tied in a knot, its eyeballs've been sucked up out of their sockets. The only sad thing is that the critters weren't built to take their own lives.

The dogs up north are different.

They live outside in the yard year-round. For one thing, a proper dog is big. It wasn't bred to fit in your pocket. The most popular dog breed in Finland, the German shepherd, is of a magnitude that if it decides to jump up in an easy chair the damn thing collapses at the very thought of it. A dog kept out of doors stays alert and barks only when there's something to bark at. Such as: my nose says Aikio is on his way over here to collect his debt, and he's drunk off his ass, so get your damn shotgun out, owner, and step out here onto the porch to greet him.

A dog is a predator. It is genetically guided to grasp the big picture in hunting-related matters. Outside of Helsinki, a dog's primary task is to help humans fill their freezers with meat that used to run free through the forest. No dog, no meat. A well-trained dog will point at a bear. That's why they call a KBD a bear dog. But what is a Griffon Bruxellois? Something semi-dry, fruity, sparkling? Wikipedia says they "bark easily"; the Kennel Club defines it as "self-important" and "nearly square." What the fuck is that? A snarky bathroom tile?

Many a breed kept down south, with their sparrow frames and

thick pelts, would be perfectly suited for use as a bottle brush. You can't spot the shine on their anuses from a block away, but at least after they've squirted our their evening pee they walk home with a bag of string candy hanging off the backs of their thick furry leggings.

Every last dog denominator has been distilled out of these dogs down south. You don't believe me? Just look at a wolf, which is from the same family of animal as these pets that were domesticated from it. That'll do it. Stand your wolf there, and line up a Griffon Bruxellois and say an ordinary Spitz next to it. Which is closer to the original? And which one looks like a cross between a rat and a sheep? If people were bred like dogs, they'd be selling us in pink miniature versions for use as cake decorations. The dogs down south are dogs in the same degree as Finnish presidents after Kekkonen are statesmen. The travesty is tarted up with trinkets modeled on accoutrements from the wife's accessory drawer: a cute little Burberry jacket, a peepee hoodie, a five-hundred-euro hair dryer, a furry choker collar, and a latex toy for those lonely moments. The end product? A doll, for the doll house.

In the north a dog's anus gets fracked in the frost without forced walks to the park. The ass-eye is cleansed naturally in outdoor activities, in amongst the heather, on the crust of the snow. Most northern dogs run free. They shit in the wild around the house, like the moose, reindeer, hares, and every other damn animal. In the northerly reaches of Lapland you've got about as much chance of stepping in dog shit as you do getting served in Sami at Stockmann's. And dog shit serves a purpose. It's fertilizer. When a KBD drops its load on the melting snow, the sapling that springs up there will be a mighty pine by the time your grandkids are old folks rocking in their rocking chairs.

Humanity. There's two kinds.

There's the kind where you let animals revel in their genes and defecate up and down all the rustling ridges.

Then there's the kind where you squat on Finland's busiest thoroughfares scrabbling up the crap your Griffon Bruxellois has just squirted out of its quivering haunches. And not just scrabbling: you stand there next to the poor little cute thing, coaxing the shit out.

Out there in view of anybody who walks by, so it won't spritz out in the easy chair. The strawberry in the stool: while you scoop up the squirt, you're also atoning for the shame the public pooping has caused the dog. But of course this is all you projecting your own feelings onto a senseless critter, turning it into a kind of honorary human. The dog isn't ashamed. It's a dog. You're ashamed. You imagine the dog feels the same thing you feel so you can go on living your life as a human who humbly, day after day, picks up poop off the streets of the capital city of Finland.

## "Rower"

There went Satan's supper. He sat by his campfire on the Saimaa lakeshore trying to fry himself up a seal steak. No grease in the pan. Fact was, he plumb didn't have any, and you couldn't fucking eat a ringed seal without it. And that damn bear snuck up and stole the seal carcass before Satan could cut himself off some blubber.

He had to go to work hungry. Royally browned off.

It was Midsummer's Eve, the busiest time of the year. Satan's camp was on a tiny island. He'd felled a giant pine and made his fire out of the root system. But now Satan set his frying pan to one side and extinguished his campfire with a thick yellow stream. He filled his nostrils with the cloud of sizzling smoke.

His boat sat perched on the rocks along the shore. Satan banged the boat out onto the water and jumped on the bow thwart. Hooves on the ribs, hands on the oars, goddammit, go! A three-pronged fireplace poker lay ready in the bilge.

His first job was close by. Gathered at a summer cottage was a group of thirty-something buddies who'd been drinking round the clock. Satan rowed up near the shore, enjoying the scene. These geniuses. One young gentleman ran about naked, a spruce branch up his asshole. You couldn't tell whether he was laughing or crying. Another had climbed a birch, sat up there bellowing out some drunken song. The limb broke and the singer toppled down on branch-boy's head. The singer broke his neck and died. Oh dear, the screaming then, the commotion. The women cried, the men howled. They scrabbled about for a phone, dropped it, called directory assistance instead of the emergency center. Satan slid the boat up on shore, grabbed his poker, hooked his hooves up over the gunwales onto dry land, walked over to the base of the birch, to the body. Well, well. Fat disgusting pig. The dead man's head twisted to one side. Satan smiled. So, yeah, let's do this.

Satan poked the poker up through the corpse, heaved it up onto his shoulder, and headed back down to the water. Heavy son of a bitch. Satan dumped the body in the boat and sprang nimbly onto a thwart. The poker poked out of the carcass like a spear out of a deer.

A loon laughed, the sun shone, Satan rowed. His next address was a farmhouse. The extended family had gathered for their usual midsummer celebration. The old man was dying, and the sons disagreed on how the place should be divvied up. Both wanted the main house. A bonfire was burning on the shore, the argument in full swing around it. The big brother looked to be the drunker one. Satan watched the devilment from his boat. Well, get on with it. Belly's rumbling. Big brother blew his top, pushed little brother into the fire. He fell on his back, hard, the burning branches giving way beneath him. For a few seconds he tried to climb up out of there, but sank back down, engulfed in flames. Satan's eyes lit up. At last, something new! It was always knifings, knifings, more knifings. Stabbings with sharp instruments are so boring. Don't people have more imagination than that? And now again the pandemonium, the wailing and the gnashing of teeth! He's dead, save your fucking breath. Satan rowed ashore and walked up to the burning body, sucking up deep drafts of the meaty fumes. The scent of home sweet home! Yeah, so okay, let's get going. Satan jammed the poker into the meat and slung the load up onto his shoulder, oops-a-daisy. The dearly departed plopped into the boat next to the dead tub of lard. The oarlocks creaked as Satan cranked hard on the oars.

Around midnight Satan glided up to a dock where a splash had just splished. A drunken woman was just sinking into the mud at the bottom of the lake. She'd gone for a swim from the sauna, fap as a five-fingered frog. Satan waited a moment before diving down for the lifeless lush. The great thing about drowning victims is that the chilled body feels pleasant against the skin. Satan came up with the blue woman in his arms and flung his fodder on top of the pile, squelch!

Over the next few hours Satan collected six more bodies from Midsummer celebrations on the eastern Saimaa shore; three knifed, two beaten, one shot to death. The corpses lay long-wise at the bottom, cross-wise at the top, to secure the load. The untouched seal steak back on the island nagged at him. Satan rowed the boat toward his camp. All in all a pretty ordinary Midsummer, busy busy. At least the guy with the branch up his ass and the bonfire guy had added a little spice. The sun climbed up over the horizon. Next to Satan on the thwart lay a dead loon. The rower had snatched it out of the lake and strangled it to take home to the little demons. Get the taste of game on their tongues. Satan reached the island. The bow bumped up over the stones at water level. Satan bounced out onto the stones and was about to head for the campfire site when he heard a muffled moaning from the boat. Huh.

*Yyynh.*

Not possible. Not out here.

More moans. *Yyynh, yy-yyynhh . . .*

It had to be coming from the pile of meat. Satan started grabbing limbs right and left, tossing bodies in the water. There went the shot guy, splish! There went the beaten guy, splish! There went one knifed guy, ker-splish! There went the other, ker-splash!

Finally he dug down to the moaner. The drowned woman.

She was still alive. Hacking up water from her lungs, her face blue. You're over the hill, old man. Last time that happened it was what, the fourth Crusade? It was the workload. He had so much to do he didn't have time to pore over every side of beef he tossed in the boat. The woman opened her eyes and raised herself into a sitting position on top of the bottom layer of bodies. His client seemed to be coming to her senses.

"What the devil, hack-hack . . ."

"At your service."

"Some fucking fiend musta drug me . . ."

"Well, yes."

The woman goggled around, noticed the strange scenery and stranger company.

"The hell am I doing here?"

"Close enough."

The women held her head and trembled. Satan sighed: Soo-o. His hooves hove in the shallows. Fresh water softened them, made them ache. He'd had about enough of tonight's work.

"Who are you?" the woman asked, her voice quavery.

Satan reviewed the rules. Should he cart the client back to the death site and see that the whole loss-of-life thing was handled properly this time? Or could he just snuff her here and now? Professionalism above all else. Doesn't matter how low the job is, there's a right way and a wrong way for everything. Back to the basics. Using the poker isn't just a ritual, right. Dammit, get the book. Satan stomped over to the campfire site and rummaged around in his things till he found the red book with the title: *Collecting*. The many-layered fingernails paged through the thick sheets. The paper smelled of smoke. Eye the headings.

*1.3 Choice of work methods.* No.

*2.0 Tarring the boat.* Huh.

*2.9 Spearing the body.* All over that one!

*3.5 Hoof and mouth disease.* Ick.

*4.0 Modern vehicles.* Have to think about that one.

*5.6 Rudiments of seal-hunting.* Famished!

Don't they have anything in here about the living dead? Oh, uh huh, yup, in the section titled "Fatal Disposition" it said this:

If the spearing fails or for whatever reason is left undone, it is possible, though highly unlikely, that the client's vital functions will be restored. If that happens, it is essential to determine the body's spiritual destination or fatal disposition immediately. This measure is crucial, because there is reason to suspect that the revitalization event might have been caused by some virtuous act performed by the decedent during his or her lifetime that the stupidity, malice, evil, or other desirable trait prevailing at the time of death was not puissant enough to push aside.

God, say it so a person can make heads or tails of it! His scalp steamed.

The easiest way to verify the client's fatal disposition is the tunnel question.

Right, right, that was it. Satan slammed the book shut and walked back down to the shore, where he found the woman had climbed out of the boat and was standing ankle deep in the water. She leaned against the boat, swaying.

"Listen, hag, when you were in the lake, did you see any kind of tunnel? After it got warm, I mean."

"Hell no."

"Try."

The woman grimaced and shook her head.

"Uhhhhh . . . maybe there was a tube-like thing flashing or something."

"Was there light at the end of it, maybe?"

"Um, sure."

"What could you see in the light?"

"What? Oh, uh . . . dicks."

Hmm. It was possible she was headed for heaven after all. Whose bailiwick is this in the end? Things are getting complicated. We need solutions. The woman cleared her throat.

"You got any booze?"

That did it. Satan popped her prettily on the chin. She toppled into the water, out cold.

Satan got his root fire started again and rummaged around for his frying pan. The seal steak had dried onto the cast iron. He grabbed the pan and went down to the fat cadaver, the one that fell out of the tree. It was stretched out on its side at the edge of the water. With a grunt Satan fished around inside the holes his poker had made, in the folds of the fat man's belly, and damn if he didn't manage to squeeze out some fat for his pan. Yum-mm!

Satan ate his breakfast with a happy smirk, spitting into the campfire. Every time some gob of fat splatted into the flames, they flared up fetchingly. Satan let out a mighty belch and then pissed off back down to hell. He assigned each of the newcomers the appropriate locations and job descriptions. The one who'd been singing in the tree got the lowest spot. It became his job to translate Finnish municipal law into German.

Only one left on the beach: the naked blue woman.

She woke up toward evening on Midsummer's Day. She had no clue where she was, and of course had no memory of her tribulations. Different spots on her head hurt like a son of a bitch. She yelled for help for a while, but then decided that no one ever went by the deserted island she was on. It so happened, however, that she was the granddaughter of a fisherman, and had actually listened to her granddad's stories. Her diet that summer consisted mostly of raw fish and water. It turned out to be a sunny summer, too, and after the blue woman turned white, she began to tan. In the first week of September she spotted a tugboat chugging along with a log raft in tow. She jumped up and down, screamed, waved her arms, and pretty soon along came a rowboat. She felt a bit embarrassed to climb up out of the rowboat onto the tug with all eyes on her naked body, fried to a honey-brown crisp and red with horsefly bites.

TRANSLATED FROM FINNISH BY DOUGLAS ROBINSON

# GAUZ

## FROM *Stand-by-the-Hour*

NEW RECRUITS. The long line of black men climbing the narrow stairway looks like an unprecedented roped party taking on K2, the daunting summit in the Himalayas. The rhythm of the ascent is measured out by the lone sound of footsteps. Knees angle sharply up the steep stairs: nine, followed by a platform, then another nine, for every floor. The sound of the men's steps is muffled by a thick red carpet that runs right down the middle of a cage that's too cramped to accommodate two people shoulder to shoulder. With the mounting fatigue and flights of stairs, the group thins out. Every so often, there's the sound of someone gasping for breath. After six flights, the first one up presses the large button of a Cyclopean interphone that looks out through the black lens of a surveillance camera. Sweaty, they all wind up in a large, open-space office. There are no dividers to obscure the glass cage that has two letters marking the territory of the dominant male here—DG—and there's a picture window offering a generous view over the rooftops of Paris. Forms are distributed by the dozen. Security guard recruitment. Protect-75 just landed some major contracts for various businesses in the Parisian area and its workforce needs are as urgent as they are immense. Word spread very quickly throughout the African "community"—Congolese, Ivorians, Malians, Guineans, Beninese, Senegalese, etc. The trained eye can easily identify nationalities by clothing style alone: the Ivorians uniformed in Polos and 501s; the Malians with their oversized black leather jackets; the Beninese and Togolese wearing striped shirts jammed in tight at the stomach; the Cameroonians in magnificent, invariably shined moccasins; the improbable colors of the Congolese from Brazza and the outrageous styles of the Congolese from Stanley . . . When the visual cues don't do the trick, all you have to do is listen: the accents that come out of Africans' mouths when they speak French are markers of origin, just as reliable as an extra 21 chromosome is for identifying Down syndrome, or a malignant tumor is for diagnosing cancer. The humming of the Congolese, the chanting of the Senegalese, the staccato of the Ivorians, the back-and-forth of the Beninese and the Togolese, the pidgin of the Malians . . .

Everyone takes out the documents requested for the job interview: ID cards along with the classic CV and the CQP, a kind of administrative authorization to work in security. Here, it assumes the pompous title of a diploma. There's also the infamous cover letter: "be a member of a dynamic team," "participate in an ambitious career plan," "find the right fit for my training and skills," plus the conventions for a formal French letter, the "veuillez agréer monsieur," "sentiments distingués," "l'expression de ma plus haute considération," etc. The medieval circumlocutions and the ass-licking language of cover letters are ridiculous in such a place, under such circumstances. Everyone's got a strong motivation here, even though it differs depending on what side of the office you're on. For the dominant male in the cage at the back, it's to have the highest sales figures possible. By any means. Hiring the most people possible is one of these means. For the group of black climbers emerging from the stairwell, it's to find a stable job. By any means. Working as a security guard is one of these means. Relatively accessible. The training is minimal and no experience in particular is required. There's a ready understanding of administrative situations, the physical profile ostensibly being enough. Physical profile . . . black men are sturdy, black men are tall, black men are strong, black men are obedient, black men are scary. It's impossible not to consider this laundry list of noble-savage clichés lurking simultaneously in the limbic systems of all the whites in charge of recruitment and all the blacks who have come to exploit these stereotypes to their own advantage. But this morning that's not the case. Nobody cares. Plus, the recruitment teams have black members. The atmosphere is relaxed. Somebody even ventures a few bawdy comments about the perky tits of one of the two secretaries distributing forms. Everybody fills out their job applications with varying degrees of concentration. Last name, first name, gender, place and date of birth, marital status, social security number, etc. This will be the most demanding intellectual exercise of the day. Nonetheless, some look over their neighbors' shoulders. Prolonged unemployment results in a lack of confidence. The papers circulate in all possible manners between the black men and the secretary with the big rack. After the initialing and the signing of some pieces of white paper inked with esoteric phrases designed to regulate the working relationship between an employee-to-be and a big-boss-to-be, each member of the group receives a bag containing black pants, a black jacket, a black tie, a black or white shirt, and a monthly schedule indicating the time and place of work. The contracts are for an indefinite period. Having entered unemployed, they all walk out as security guards. Those who already have experience in the profession know what to expect from the days ahead: standing all day in a store, repeating this dreary feat of tedium, every day, and getting paid at the end of the month. Stand-by-the-hour. And it's not as easy as it looks. In order to cope with this job, to maintain perspective, to not succumb to lazy compliancy or, conversely, to block-headed zealotry and embittered aggression, it's necessary to know either how to empty the mind of all considerations that transcend instinct and the spinal reflex or how to have a particularly intense internal life. The incorrigible moron option also works. To each his own method, his own objectives. Everyone goes back down the six flights of stairs in their own way.

AT "LA CHAPELLE." A bar run by a Kabyle guy, a clothing store of a Chinese from Nanjing, the Tunisian lady's bakery, a Pakistani's hardware store, an Indian jeweler, another bar of another Kabyle with a Senegalese clientele, the Tamil's call shop, another Pakistani's hardware store, an Algerian butcher, another Chinese's clothing store (but this one from Wenzhou), the Moroccan's second-hand shop, the Wenzhou-Chinese *bar-tabac*, a Turkish restaurant that you'd better not confuse with the Kurdish *sandwicherie* next door, an Algerian Djurdjura butcher, a Balkan boutique, Moroccan grocers specializing in African and Antillean cuisine, Kabyle bar number three, a mini-corridor of a second-hand shop run by a surly Yugoslavian, a Korean electronics mart, the Malian's

TOPY shoe repair, the Tamil's hardware store, another Moroccan grocer, Kabyle bar number four specializing in alcoholics at the pre-terminal phase, the Korean's African grocery, the backroom Croatian casino, Tamil hairdresser, Algerian hairdresser, African hairdresser from the Ivory Coast, Cameroonian grocer, Antillean boutique selling esoteric objects and *bois bandé*, Jewish doctor's office . . . Going down Rue du Faubourg-du-Temple is like walking on a Tower of Babel that's been toppled by pyrotechnicians and set down between Belleville and Place de la République. What if the hidden treasure of the Templars was this incredible diversity of origins and cultures in the city's old faubourgs? Around the Goncourt metro station, Avenue Parmentier meets Faubourg-du-Temple at a perpendicular. The ambiance here is more Parisian, more French, more Occidentally homogenous, more "normal": bobo bars, Caisse d'Épargne, an old-style bakery with real quality floured baguettes, Le Crédit Lyonnais, Italian pizzeria, Le Crédit Agricole, Apple retailer, bookstore-stationer, BNP Paribas, restaurant mentioned in the Michelin and Hachette guides, Le Crédit Mutuel, sound engineer, Société Générale, a secondary school named after a dead person, Swiss HSBC bank, shoe store specializing in large sizes, another Crédit Lyonnais, two primary schools with lists of children deported during the war, municipal pool . . . Farther east is the 11th arrondissement's town hall, where the gold and the tricolor on its roof of black slate leave no question as to whether it's a building of the Republic of France. For Ossiri, making the trip from there to the Camaïeu store on Rue du Faubourg-Saint-Antoine was like traveling through time.

During the "La Chapelle" era, he and Kassoum would take in all the neighborhood's streets like surveyors: systematically. Up to the shadows cast by the little gilded buttocks of the angel on top of the totem pole at the Place de la Bastille, this part of the 11th arrondissement was, along with the Champs-Elysées, one of the great amusodromes of Paris. Funky bars, concept bars, exotic restaurants for every latitude on Earth, lounges, secret clubs, night clubs, dance bars, little concert halls, etc., attracted crowds every night, especially on the weekend. Less entertaining was the fact that this district had the highest concentration of clothing stores run exclusively by Chinese owners. Legions of their compatriots, mostly undocumented, worked to pay off their border-crossing debts in poorly ventilated areas, windowless rooms, dark courtyards, modified atriums, and rearranged hallways, or out on converted patios. They never took any breaks or vacation except for their New Year, a day that resounded with the popping of firecrackers. Chinese bosses would make a lot from such model—top model, even—employees. The production costs for the latest fashions were very low in a country with high standards of living and consumption levels. Having numerous qualified workers that were underpaid, non-unionized, and all-you-can-exploit was outsourcing at the local level. That's some serious capitalist prowess for the children of China! This meant that those who partied in Bastille were among the privileged few in France who could barf up their surfeit of alcohol before the gate entrances used by the very workers that made the clothes, now reeking of smoke, in which they'd fidgeted, danced, and sweated the night away.

Sightings of bedraggled revelers first thing in the morning, especially Sundays, were among the shared moments that Kassoum and Ossiri cherished the most. At dawn they had to leave their little studio apartment, which they called "La Chapelle" because it was right above the Chapelle des Lombards nightclub, to free up the apartment for Zandro, who worked as a bouncer downstairs. Since they didn't work every day and didn't always know where to go so early in the morning, they'd party it up with the last of them. Ossir and Kassoum would be fresh and lucid. The straggling partiers were tired, drunk, and/or drugged up. With his old reflexes from growing up in the Treichville* ghetto, Kassoum couldn't help thinking that it would be easy enough to relieve these dawdling dandies of some of their jewelry or the money they'd brought with them for the night; he'd had plenty of experience of this sort in Abidjan. But it seemed like Ossiri could read his thoughts, and just one look would get him back in line. "Leave vultures' work to the vultures," he'd often say. So Kassoum had to content himself with having front-row tickets to laugh at the closing-time circus starring

* Treichville: a working-class neighborhood in Abidjan.

the Parisians and those who'd come in from the *banlieue*s. And Ossiri was unyielding, even the day when that completely drunk girl jumped on him, shouting in English "Take me! Take me!" Her handbag was half-open, showing a wad of blue 20-euro bills that seemed to implore Kassoum for a more peaceful sanctuary in his own pockets. He hadn't seen a single euro coin for a week, and even Fologo, the clumsiest pickpocket in all the Colosse ghetto in Treichville, could have pulled it off.

—Kass, leave vultures' work to vultures. *(Ossiri)*
    —Take me! Take me! *(The girl)*
    —But it's really too much, she's just giving it up. There's no off-side when the ball's delivered by the other team, Ossiri. *(Kass)*
    —Take me! Take me!
    —What's she saying?
    —She's saying to take her.
    —I swear, she's taunting me.
    —You touch her, we don't know each other anymore.
    —Take me! Take me!
    —Fucking rich kid!

"Fucking rich kid!" was Kassoum's phrase of surrender every time they disagreed about how to get by during tough times. When the girl started to throw up first on his shirt, then on his shoes, Kassoum decided to "wake up the ghetto inside" to deal this drunkard a "python"—a sharp headbutt, well-aimed and well-timed, that vigorous cephalic strike that his reputation was built on and that made all of Colosse dread facing off against him. "Ossiri, I slept in the ghetto for years and years. Now, the ghetto sleeps within me."

But something in this girl's eyes kept him from striking. Kassoum couldn't do it, but he didn't really know why. Distress, maybe. Distress that he'd read so often in the eyes of his neighbors in the Colosse who didn't know how to face a new day just as miserable as the one before. Or maybe it was the light green of her eyes. In the stories of his childhood, some monsters were described as having green eyes, the color of the deep forest. Kassoum had never seen eyes that color from so close. His reaction must have been noticeable.

Behind him, Ossiri was pushing his luck, telling him to take her to La Chapelle so she could lie down, and to watch over her until she came back to her senses. Zandro wouldn't say anything—he certainly didn't even have to know. He was always too exhausted from his night of handling people who were violent, people who were hysterical, pickpockets, drunks, line-jumpers, the indignant, the paranoid, the depressed, the dealers, the junkies, and all the hotheads who believed they were stronger than everyone else in the world after a line of cocaine or a couple ecstasy pills. By himself, Kassoum carried the girl into the narrow stairwell. Her long blond hair fell onto her sturdy judoka shoulders, and even though she'd withered from the booze, she was a good head taller than him. She must have been descended from white tribes of the great cold and glacial north who had regularly invaded the more southerly shores of Europe to sow terror, chaos, and sperm. Ossiri didn't give him any help, under the pretext that the sight of two black men transporting a semi-conscious white woman down a dark and deserted street would arouse suspicion. He wasn't wrong but, as was often the case, he pushed his logic too far. "Here, betrayal is a sport that became a national institution during World War Two. When the Germans controlled the country, people would turn in Jews and members of the Résistance. After the Allied victory, people turned in the traitors and collaborators. Here, there are always informants and people to be denounced," Ossiri had concluded peremptorily. But Kassoum had already tuned him out. Like a panther straining to pull a heavy doe into a tree so as to protect her from the scavenging greed of a pack of hyenas, he trundled the strapping girl up to "La Chapelle." This is how Kassoum first met Amélie, who was from Normandy and taught English at a high school in the *banlieue* west of Paris . . .

The parvise of the 11th arrondissement's town hall opens onto a roundabout, where traffic is distributed between Avenue Parmentier, Boulevard Voltaire, Rue de la Roquette, and Avenue Ledru-Rollin.

Ossiri's bike goes through the red light and weaves in and out to reach Ledru-Rollin. There's a Monoprix at the intersection with Rue du Faubourg-Saint-Antoine. His aunt Odette has been the department manager there for twenty-eight years. Thirty years ago, when her husband brought her from her village in the sylvan confines in the western part of the Ivory Coast, she barely knew how to read and write and had never seen people apart from those that had been roaming for millennia beneath the vines and tall trees of Issia. She's seen a lot and learned a lot there at her Monoprix. But still, twenty-eight years to get up from her seat at the cash register . . . A melanine rate of promotion? She no longer asks these kinds of questions. She's two years away from retirement. For the two weeks that Ossiri's been assigned to the Camaïeau at Bastille, this stop at Monoprix has been something of a ritual. Tantie Odette offers him a coffee. He accepts, and they go into the break room. He asks her about Ferdinand, and she answers matter-of-factly. She asks after Angela, and he makes up stories using lyrical phrases mixed with general news about their homeland. She laughs. She laughs a lot when he speaks. Then he says he has to go, otherwise he'll be late. She accompanies him through the aisles and presents him as her son when they pass an old colleague from the eighties. A kiss on the cheek and Ossiri detaches his bike from the "No parking" sign. Camaïeau isn't far. He walks.

TRANSLATED BY TEGAN RALEIGH

# ANN COTTEN

## *Chafer*

SHE CANNOT BE SLEEPING. One doesn't do such things when one is asleep. I must acknowledge that there is a conscious mind inside the head that leans against mine, one that considers it a good idea to stroke me in a repetitive manner. We are on our way through arid plains, the lights are dimmed, the whole bus is asleep or dreaming. Dreaming with the bus driver as he hits the tapestry-lined dashboard in time to the music with a many-colored little leather whip, making the tassels wobble. Something—an electric guitar, a flute, or a woman's voice—wanders in serpentines through the upper regions of the human hearing range. In the lower parts, close by us, a karkabèn, crude iron double-clapper, expresses its calm and regular excitement. The young man in the yellow caftan, who has been sitting at the front of the bus in the seat behind the young women passengers for the whole trip, whispering various things to them, his cheek pressed to the back of their headrest—even he is sleeping now. At the first rest stop, as I, smoking, shifted my weight from one leg to the other, feeling odd to be a woman for no reason, like a donkey on hooves, he crossed the road to pick a yellow asphodel. Now his head leans softly against the seat in front of him, where the beauty he was harassing, who ignored him with habitual grace, is sleeping too, or at least holding herself completely still. The two boys who got in without baggage to work for a few months in a place where the bus will let them out by the roadside, are awake and whispering. Behind them their mother, before them seven hundred goats, and in between, dominant in the moment, their beauty, the elegance of their manner, their wise feet. Outside, dusk is flying through the cities through which the bus passes, along the dusty roads under a rosy sky that seems to utter jokes and scatter unmistakable signs. Dusk falls on all inhabitants, those in a hurry and those who linger in the square, thinking of someone or some problem that is scuffed like an old canister and covered with dust every day afresh. And people in business and people visiting relatives, whose inner life I cannot imagine.

Our two sweaty heads have fallen toward one another, rolling in the swell of the road, hidden by the window curtain, flashed by the street lighting. Krassa has laid her thin scarf over our laps, a trick to allow freedom of movement, unwatched. Her small, hot hands take advantage of the little realm she has created to stroke mine. Rolled between Krassa's thumb and fingers, I wonder when it will stop, this going and coming, back and forth. She strokes and strokes. In clouds, in swarms, in schools, waxing and waning in scope.

Please remember this scene. It is to return again and again, disturbing and annoying me. I would like to use an explanation with ghosts. This supplement to the visible world might offer an exit from the circular arguments I have been wasting my time with, using only rational reasoning to address the old problem that it is impossible to understand what is going on and to act at the same time. Not that I was looking for epiphany, but . . . why not? After all, is it not something of the sort that one seeks in literature, in sex, in *amour fou*? The idea that one might be forever just taking turns allowing the other to experience some irreal intoxication one is incapable of feeling oneself. One keeps quiet and behaves as cooperatively as possible so as not to disturb the other's illusion until it's over. And then, in the worst moments, when pressed until survival seems to demand a fast getaway involving the use of a verbal machine gun, one will stumble word for word into hurtful honesty, breathing deeply in surprise at the uncomfortable fact that one does truly forever preclude the other: one never felt anything of the sort.

It is a moral question I am revolving around, but also a physical one: How can it be possible that one person loves and the one he loves dislikes him? Is love not the kind of thing that can only come into being from two sides at once, in a kind of feedback loop? From the party of unrequited love we have enough reports. Regarding it, and regarding supermarkets and tourism and imperialism and other irrational swellings of one-sidedness, it appears to me quite clear that it is a simple case of self-delusion, swelling in time, multiplied by imperious notions of righteousness. And again it's not mere chance that the depiction of delusion is a specialty of literature.

I have always known that to love means to get lost. But I thought it meant losing oneself to the truth, a daring escape from the labyrinth of false ideas that is society. What worries me is whether I am not now, by rejecting a woman in love, betraying the truth, and then putting myself in the hands of society for protection against her revenge. For this reason I have always refused to admit that anyone I don't love might ever fall in love with me, and even now I keep glancing toward the easy way out, to claim that what is driving these people out of their minds is merely a hairball of clichés, not love—otherwise I would be in total agreement.

Now, however, I am able to report from the other side, and willing to do it with the best of hearts. Recently in love affairs I have found myself sprawled on other people's windshields, all six legs scattered around me, the last organs gurgling their elegiac upheavals as I drown in my own blood. It would make sense to draw some conclusion from this, some philosophical insight that could guide me in fixing up some principles, like one fixes a paper collar with chalk. Of course I have for some time been suspicious of my indulged idiosyncrasies, and of the way my own timidity makes a monster of me, as it does with others; but first of all I am worried that I generate brutality precisely through my conviction that I must find some way of dealing with myself before I dare to hand myself in to others. Why is that?

I would like to express directly my disgust with the whole situation: life, with all its dirty lies, and my own distaste for any participation in this idiotic panorama. This may be even more pressing than my longing to be convinced of the opposite. But if nausea is as dictatorial as love, it must be equally easy to dissect. Therefore I retreat, a bit shaken, and continue to watch, fascinated, from a certain distance.

If we take love as the belief, reasonable or not, in a somehow *important* confrontation—just like a thought is the sketch of a relation between facts—it really would be the same situation, and then also the same amount of work, as an interesting conversation. And in quite the same way, I am seized by a terrible impatience as soon as I feel that the other person is heading in a fruitless direction. From then on I can only watch—granted he fascinates me aesthetically. Krassa was brutal: relentlessly she used her competence, her decisive, sensible opinions on me, and I had great difficulty defending my silliness against her. At the same time I sat quite calmly and was full of wonder: What might be going on inside of her? And how spectacularly ugly she was! The question I must ask myself is if I—if I ever had an actual thought about her.

The long time that I spent staring at her blankly, while she, on the other side of the gap, was following some scent or other, seems to me now like the endlessly drawn-out moment of a choice. Max Klinger's *Judgment of Paris* comes to my mind, a huge painting in which, on a high terrace, one goddess after another presents herself naked to the man who is posed, he too naked, on a seat in the shade. The three women stand tall and firm, well dressed in the sporting whim of a morning, and yet they tremble before the painful results of nuances. How cruel the joke is, but also how vast and free! The figures are life-size, the air bright daylight, one seems to feel the wind on the expanses of bare skin, to be able to estimate the temperature. I remember well how the picture impressed me, especially when I saw it for the second time, in Munich. It was October, and I was in the city to take a test to prove I had reached a certain level of proficiency in Japanese. The evening before, however, I had met up with my Munich friend Godiv. He appeared with two other students, both blonde, one girl looking slightly pinched, the other creamy and sprinkled with moles. The way Godiv acted with them, I no longer desired him, which threw me into a raging depression and I ordered round after round of vodka. Godiv was no longer as I remembered him. The two times I had met him before, he had been somehow extended by his own surprise into a longer reach than usual, a shining person he himself hardly knew. But tonight he entangled himself in boring, academic-moralist discussions with the girls, with whom he seemed to be trying to compete. And while I tried to either lose him completely to the girls, so he could unfurl his arts, or find a topic that would re-erect him, they refused to drink more vodka and gave me theirs. In the end it worked, so to speak: Godiv disappeared into the subway car with the girls, and as the doors closed I finally saw that wide-eyed, scared, questioning, screaming, altogether present glance I had wanted to see again.

But it had taken too much to get there. More like a flower than a person I drifted to my hotel, fondled the iron handrails on the way up the stairs and slept the three hours that remained before my test.

Saturated with coffee that held open my eyes like the awning of a long-term campsite resident in heavy rain, I sat at the university in a neon-white classroom, stared for a while at the test paper and began to laugh. Ten multiple-choice questions stared back at me with small, expectant eyes, with delicate fake lashes. Each character was more beautiful than the next. But what did they mean?

I found it absolutely idiotic to waste my knowledge on tracing the line between right and wrong, particularly since the people giving the test already knew the facts they were trying to get me to spit out. I was to cross out two of three characters, which consisted of completely blameless possible parts, in order to participate in this game. Was it not much more important to know and love them each in their own right? To protect them—the right ones, the wrong ones, and particularly the nonexistent ones—by refusing to choose?

Of the three characters in the first question, two together formed a familiar combination. Was it word, literature, book, university, or warning? The third character was the same as the first, only on the left the one had the radical "man," the other "water." And I had always just left that part out when I wrote it, I discovered with horror! I had been learning on my own, no one had ever corrected me. The characters were so interesting. I copied them, in vertical calligraphies that shrunk, tornadolike, toward the corner of the page. Loved them on to the paper again and again and again. Characters, no matter what they may be like, are supposed to fit in a rectangle of a certain size, but you would never guess how difficult that is. After I had spent some time on the refinement of my stroke, I felt farther away from the answers than ever. Something like a hunch crept over me, then a slight dislike for the left side of the page. But the dislike, I reasoned, would probably point to the right character rather than a wrong one, seeing that I am always *against* the right things. Didn't the wrong characters fill the air with the more interesting perfumes of the nonexistent? Finally I handed in two pages of calligraphy, it having morphed on the second page into a series of pinup figures, and went to the museum. I felt three. Free. Free of linguistic competence, free of calligraphy.

At the museum I thought I was able to feel the troughs in the floor where people would stop in front of the pictures and shift from one foot to the other before moving on. When I came to *The Judgment of Paris* I rested my limbs using a bench that was there, trying to imitate Paris's pose. I looked at a Kokoschka, then an oil painting by Schiele. How on earth did the painters remain the masters of their colors? At one time, I too had been able to hit all possible nuances of the skin by swiftly switching the order of the colored pencils in my hand; often blurring the page with squinted eyes as I scribbled. But nowadays, though I had withdrawn to the reduced palette of black ink, not even there could I command my line: it led me on, in figures I had not wanted to breach, it and I in the spell of some obstinate fidelity to something I had hardly the slightest idea of. Thus everything I did was necessary and imposed by its own character; I stepped back when a choice appeared, as if I were in trance or an animal that can be immobilized by simple tricks such as eye contact. Like a child that one can actually prevent from doing anything by giving it confusing choices; like a band of robbers that can be draped in arabesques of heavy-handedness by dropping tidbits of conversation from out of a treetop above their camp. In this manner I would land on the back of any idea, any whim, any strict internal logic that would carry me away from the moment of a choice. Usually something like prodigality or excitedly racing around. But while I languished in the passing time, in the light of my latest lamp, the world forgotten, something else lay beside it all, unnoticed. Had I really avoided the choice? I fear I had merely avoided my judgment.

Outside the window, a desert is passing, briefly illuminated by our headlights. One city after the next. On the back of my hand I feel the delicate pressure of Krassa's hot fingertips. They are going to rub me to insanity. I cannot sleep, but slowly I drift away into the pleasant black cosm. Then a new wave of consciousness arrives, dragged by Krassa's fingers onto the tray of my mind, in candlelight, as it were: w- w- wo- wo- woman, someone wishes a word with you.

I am generous, I am generous, I don't mind, I breathe deeply, change my position in the seat, procure a bit of air for the posterior by giving up some around the shoulders, scatter my hands differently and—great side effect!—they land far away from Krassa's puffy fingers. Air! Freedom! Existence and respiration! Now back to the naked cosm, to sleep.

The idea of being enclosed in the logic of jouissance as by a high palisade remains with me even in my sleep. At the same time, I am in the uniform of an officer of the Czarist army. I stand facing a line of glasses filled with vodka. I don't remember how I got here, but I know I must defend a woman I have kidnapped, whom no one must treat badly. She is a foreigner, a heathen, a tribeswoman. I don't know the significance of the glasses in front of me. I think I have asked for a duel, and someone is trying to change it into a drinking contest. I protest! I want high cliffs, the first light of morning, numbered bullets! They say I should marry her. The idea is closing in on me like a tapestry closes in on a frothy-mouthed dog! They insinuate that otherwise they might not have sufficient respect for her. Swine! Well then, I will marry her if you like, we will marry three times, by the church, by the state, and by the Devil! Except that already now it fills me with disgust that she depends on me. You must educate her, says my friend, a warm moist breath in my ear, good advice, but I shake it off. Make her your equal in society, an equal opponent. That is too difficult. *Too* difficult! Drink! I cry. I empty two of the glasses and leave. With that, I have lost a dozen friends at once: To rise above their games is unforgivable. Now I have only the woman I kidnapped. I stand outside the casino and stare at the starry sky. Its insolence.

Something small begins, an impulse, a miniature movement— yes, a rubbing on my thigh. The Devil, have Krassa's hands now fallen upon my thigh! There, like a patch of oak processionaries, they decide—darling creatures that hands are, in all their plotting—to slowly make their way across my thigh. At this speed it will take half an hour. We have more than thirteen to go, during which we will remain in precisely the same position . . .

What should I think? Should I go searching for reasons to stop the hands' procedures, which do me no harm? I brush them off, that should do it. I pretend to be sleeping, it's not my fault if my honest insides act on their own needs during my sleep. Let brute force take the place of confused delicacy. Why not do away with Krassa altogether? Into the cosmos with me! I am entering slumber, I feel the breeze of nothing on my cheeks, see my officer friends in the distance, greeting me with ironic salutes: they have stumbled out the door to look for me. I call from out of the constellations, I cannot hear myself. I am the kidnapped Circassian woman, soothed by the stars in a song that I am playing on the flute while my officer is at the casino. The officer stares into the stars, which seem to have some pull, the consequential flow of a melody that he cannot quite grasp. It is I, standing on the ground, no, my feet are actually floating, carried by a bus through the desert, above the vibrations of the motor. Some of the reading lamps are on, while most people are sleeping, among them the three Kabyle engineers, one of whom had grown suddenly excited and told us he had spent ten years working here—he pointed into the dark, where on the horizon a faint glow could be seen from the great refinery several miles off the road. Krassa heaves a deep breath and snores a little.

The odd thing is that I am only here because she has a false vision, is fuddled by love. If her mind were doing what it should, she should have no reason to take a trip to the desert with me. "Many a pair of friends," she said, as we leafed through guidebooks, "never spoke with each other again after travelling in the desert." If I succeeded in changing her notions to fit mine and she ceased to imagine love, my presence here would become problematic. If, on the other hand, I went along with her, I would merely be someplace else, which I like so well, right? Yes, but I cannot be there, because she is already there, and so solidly present. I can't? I mean that physically there is no space for me in her thinking. But it is thinking, it cannot be a question of physical space. But one also cannot think two versions of the same thing at the same time. She may desire me, but I think she doesn't particularly like me. That is the bag that caught the cat, the brutality, the misunderstanding. Certainly, I do not like her particularly. Why not? She is amazing. No, she is terrible: she doesn't notice that I don't want to echo her desire, or she doesn't care. She has a dream, and I am supposed to play a role in it. I am supposed to want her dream, I am supposed to enjoy it. I am supposed to want her. Want to enjoy her. I cannot, it is impossible, I gasp for air and she begins to stroke me again. Slowly. She gathers confidence, becomes methodical, regular. Diligent softness, self-confident gestures. I stop her again. A few of her muscles become tense and she turns to me slowly like a superdimensional mechanical puppet. Her eyes, popping out of their sockets, are far too close to my face, her strutting, confident upper lip, crowned with its silky mustache, spits out her full, warm voice: "You don't like?" A voice squeaks out of my esophagus: "No. I don't like. It prevents me from sleeping."

I feel the hard sentence sending waves of disappointed realization through her body, then she is shaken by a few sighs. She turns away from me, rearranges herself, like one shakes up a pillow.

The Circassian, the Circassian, the Devil take me, I had forgotten her for a moment. And yet she is locked in my room all day long. I don't want to teach her to be a lady, I wanted and still want the way she storms through the room, or flies over to me, hair streaming behind, or wraps me with hot silence, wrathful, not punishing. She is the creature in me, I am her carpet, the receptacle for her words; she doesn't understand what I mean by sensible reasoning, by freedom as a mood, easily broken, dependent on the faculty of judgment. Her words, that consider so much of me not worth considering, consider the rules of society no arguments, consider all my moral duties silly, imbecile rituals. She has her own morals, and they demand of me my own, wild kind of fidelity. My comrades, adieu.

We arrive in the morning, not long before dawn. The music drives away with the bus and its place is taken by birds welcoming the morning with their peculiar and drastic song. A native of the town brings us to a café, where he begs a friend of his to sit with us. The air becomes lighter and lighter. My heart pulls toward the music, yearns for the day, wants to walk and walk and walk, as the air bangs my pants about my legs. *Laissez-moi voir venir le jour.* I have to remain seated. I get up and pace up and down. "What's the matter?" asks Krassa, not wanting to displease the guardian, who is there to protect us from dragons, robbers, demons, and our own ignorance. Protection is courtesy in a region famed for its wildness. "No," I say, "I can't sit anymore." I appear weak, unable to discipline my body to meet the standards of good behavior. I roll a cigarette and light it. Krassa and the guardian glare at me. She who does as she pleases, while others force themselves not to, earns eternal jealousy and bitter revenge in time. This cigarette has placed a seal on our antagonism, but as will be shown, Krassa is willing to forgive me several times, at least for the duration of this trip.

We wait, no one knows for whom or what. Someone has called someone else, and therefore someone having something to do with our lodgings will emerge out of the morning, out of this wide world of sand and the city, protected from which we sit under the awning of a café that is as active as sleep-encrusted eyes. The glass cooler is full of fresh mint leaves and bread. Outside lies the world, incredibly beautiful, while the parting dusk retreats like a clear wave on a beach. The way it plays high up into the sky in this particular place makes me admire without restraint the extent of physical objects. It begins here, this world I desire so much. But if I went out into it, leaving behind my little human duties, I would no longer know who I am. Since we are in a desert, the end would resemble all other ends: I would die of thirst, like millions of people have died before me. Or be ashamed if I were to be saved. I acquiesce to my confinement. With sardonically small steps in my heroic garb of billowy striped brown pants and cobalt blue shirt, I go and sit back down on one of the plastic chairs.

The sight of an awning from below reminds me of an image that impressed itself on my mind as a child. It was a rainy day at an arts and crafts fair, and I was sitting beside my mother, who was spinning at a wheel. The drops would slide to the lowest point of the material, which was gathered up in loops, and fall from there.

Only in one place they fell from a loop that was not the lowest, as if giving in to the temptation to fall. They could not know there was a lower loop not far on. With my eager little soul I wanted to tell them, but found no words to talk to drops.

Finally, the proprietor of the guesthouse comes across the square, an elderly Frenchman in khaki pants, fresh convert to Islam, obstinate, stern, friendly, a young grandfather. To walk! To walk! The three of us walk through the town as it grows lighter and lighter, trousers and hair fluttering as if moved by the wind of time itself. In the kitchen of the guesthouse, we set down our things and drink the old coffee out of our thermos bottle. Then Pierre takes us through the town. We pass through a labyrinth of mud walls that rise high above our heads, into close tunnels under ceilings of woven palm leaves, the anterooms of the houses. There is no such thing as public and private space, it seems, only various degrees of familiarity. Not even the families are really private, not even the emptiest part of the desert is really public, as one is so dependent on networks of human culture to survive. Some kilometers on, following invisible paths with a guide in a 4x4, we arrive at a castle on a cliff. The wind whistles through the open windows. It is the only obstacle between the horizons. Three saints lie here in their graves, above which there is a small room with a tin teapot half buried in the sand. The wind has been blowing through the window for centuries. Three coins lie in the sand. Koran verses lie in the mouths of the dead. For help, there are social networks. Help, social networks. One has to behave well, wherever one is, I realize uncomfortably.

Into the walls of the city children or adults have scratched drawings and letters, logos like Coca-Cola and Toyota, portraits of people and cars and cartoon figures. I cannot hide that all this is quite new to me. We pass out of the labyrinth into a wider street leading to the "fortress," which is used as a hotel. Beyond the steep, palm-covered descent, the salt lake begins, *Le grand Erg*. On the edge of the rise lies the source, from which the old irrigation system branches out to supply the whole oasis. Pierre leads us to its mouth, tells us to remove our shoes and to walk into the tunnel of the canal. It was dug by slaves, he says. We wade through the clear water until we reach a bend, lighted from above by a hole in the tunnel's roof. The stark light is a mere placeholder for the heat outside, strengthens the feeling of dark cool. Krassa and I balance in the half-light on sandy outcrops of stone. Then we come back out. The heat seems friendly as it smothers us, like a mother's love. I drop my scarf in the water and wind myself a dark, dripping turban. Under the wet hat I wander on, an odd, theatrical mushroom, breathless at the beauty, shy, step by step, as if on the moon. Krassa too. Her formality is afloat, her Arab pantaloons, her sandals, her feet pattering over the ground, sure and rough in those ugly health sandals. We are dizzy and blinded. I feel excitedly good, like on a tipping scale where balance forces one to be unafraid.

In the guesthouse we prepare ourselves for sleep, it is early evening. A yellow room with no windows encloses us. Woolen blankets with black-and-white patterns hang on the walls and off the ends of the beds, reminding me of outside, serving as vents for claustrophobia. Krassa wafts around in a white, square nightgown, brushing her teeth. At the end of her sleeves, her small hands emerge, not without grace, olive brown like her feet which pad about under the big, white legs. She moves around the hostel, preparing this and that. I have thrown myself onto my bed in my clothes. Then I get up again, roll up the blanket at my feet, remove my bra, remove my trousers, cover myself with the sheet and close my eyes firmly. Krassa shoves herself onto her bed and lies in fetus position, facing me.

"You do not vont to come to me?"

"No."

"Then you do not live the same thing as I."

"No, I don't."

"Hm," she says. "I thought you do."

"Sad, no?"

"Yes. Very sad." A reproach, awaiting something, some kind of hope lies yet in this sentence.

Should I, even now, come over to her? Surprise her with the opposite—fabricated, without conviction? Surprise her with brutality, my only answer to her fondling? Over her, around her—I swear, I would have to stop short after two or three seconds, nothing would guide me. I would build roads of asphalt arbitrarily over her body, and later nothing would keep me there, so close to her, except a feeling of guilt. Every one of her limbs would be too much for me, their heat an ugly hell. Her proximity means my own removal. I praise myself for staying put and keeping my eyes shut hard. I am cool, I am cool, and fall asleep, sending rakish thoughts toward the ceiling.

"So you really do not live the same thing as I?"

I am startled awake, lift my head slightly and answer again: "No."

We have no goal, we race over the rock desert and the dunes with our curves, we clamber over the dunes, climb them like the Himalayas, dust in our lungs, hearts, hands, camp in the flank of one. Stars rise over the dunes, it is quiet, but the silence seems prickly, it is empty, but the emptiness is like a slinky, restless, dangerous animal. It chases my thoughts into eddies as I climb the flank of the dune, shins twisting in the sand, to see the lights of three cities from the top, to the north, to the west, and to the south. Twice we have changed the tires when they were pierced by thorns. Ahmed, the guide we obey, searches and finds secret trails where they lie open on the surface of the desert. We walk a few paces to stare at immense wadis, our clothes fluttering, turn and still Manu Chao is pouring out of the 4x4. We drink water from the Chinese 1.5-liter-bottles whose caps tear around the mouth of the bottleneck if you screw them closed too hard. The senselessness of our driving around is terrible. Should we write poems about the wadi, the distance, the fact that a third thorn would have us stranded? Would it be better if we had a mission: repressing people, for example, revenge, or trade? Rapt, but moody, I continually rewrap my turban and painstakingly botch sketches, rumpled by the careen of the car, into my notebook.

In the evening, on the roof of the fortress, Krassa sits in her bedsheet of a nightgown with the insides of her thighs on my hands laid onto our bench before me, astraddle and almost nose to nose. I continue to extrapolate. I believe I am telling a story about some ex-lover. Is it revenge, is it just a sadistic kind of seduction? I seem to take pleasure, drawn by some strangely irresistible pull, in pushing my cool, solipsistic game further and further while I sit across from her. I free my left hand to gesticulate. She removes herself from the other, of her own accord, so to speak, and sits back, a heavy specter filled with human interest.

Dusk draws in with its army of intensity, we watch it from the parapets of our fortress, a huge phenomenon crossing the great salt lake. On the lake, an inconstant light swerves around, a 4x4 containing a soul full of enjoyment and longing. For the whole hour that we sit there, the light blinks in various places and finally finds its way back into the palm grove, into the labyrinth of small lights and neighborly errands through the dark, the hot excitement of a body that lays itself to rest and celebrates its rituals now that it is cooler.

We go back to our room. My gaze follows Krassa as she moves, in her square nightgown, under the yellow storm lamp, through the room. She emerges from the shower with a hairbrush, she stands on her bed, sits down, brushes her hair, rolls around. Now she is lying on the bed, the nightgown flipped up high on her back, reading an essay on aesthetics. Blanchot, brought from Paris. I look up from *A Hero Of Our Times*, which I am reading for the second time, and find my eye resting on the back side of her legs. How unbelievably hideous they are! White, irregular flesh, pierced by phalanges of black stubble which gather to give off denser comments wherever the mass of the flesh demands a fold, comments that seem to determine the world as grumpily as letters. I understand how necessary it is, and must be to her, to have this loved, loved and forgotten—what is love but forgetfulness?—and in it, through it, to touch her soul . . . I avert my eyes, half in fear that she might catch my glance and misinterpret it, half out of cowardly, lame love for the so regular, disciplined letters that spell out, line for line, the story of Pechorin, and between the lines allow my taste to behave like someone lithe in a uniform, fetching his foil. With a horsewhip I pass through the rows of letters and caress round backs, the soft underbellies of *u*'s, tickle the *k*'s. Ah, if I had the Russian text here, *y* would propel me down into sweet hells; I would come; I would readily come along.

Time passes. In Berlin, outside the window, the sun gazes on the merry and yet somehow wistful-looking foliage of the ailanthus tree as it moves in the air above the parking lot. Sun and trees seem to know that I am using my time badly. Children scream in the pre-school next to the graveyard. A circular saw goes from time to time. Where is the curly audacity with which Prätz just a moment ago approached me, took me around the middle and seemed to entice me to come back into the undefined area that lingered around him on my bed? I turned off the flame under the potatoes I was making for us and followed Prätz, in the distance of his head start that made him invisible, prowling through the jungle of my own apartment, breathless. The scent led me through the hallway past the bicycles to where my bed lies, in the last corner, where I found Prätz's back. Prätz was lying fully dressed on my bed with bent legs, unmoving.

His back looked like an instruction, perhaps a music program, I thought, that on the one hand attracts the newcomer and tempts her to try it out, on the other hand puts her off by giving no information on how to activate it. I took so long to learn to use these programs, to try more and more often, and to try blindly even if I was hoping for beauty—not only in black, angry nocturnal moods where nothing could go wrong because I hoped for nothing. I learned to attempt thoughtless forays, like how Prätz speaks. When he speaks, it's as if joy spewed a satin ribbon out of his mouth and it hung in the air, blown upward by amused zephyrs. Then again he will spit and mumble, address the ground, and sometimes he is, understandably, quiet. Prätz's curse is to be so beautiful that one hardly cares how he behaves and whether or not he works.

Prätz lay there waiting. In front of me was the white alley of his pelvis, a sweet firewall running into the top of his jeans. The covered part of his hip seemed as far away as a place high up on the side of a building across the lot, shone on in pink apathy by the morning light. No hint of a psyche to hold on to. A fold of his T-shirt gave off an idle comment, explaining nothing but itself, the fold. Prätz's nape, confusedly focused in form, stopped any play and seemed to channel my attention like a regulated brook full of long streaming algae, or like the thought of death—as rivers are regulated to avoid floods. Like clouds in a dramatic sunrise, the nape hung between his head and the upper end of his torso. In front hung the belly, softer than usual, inclining a little into my hand. Farther up it was more stony, like the narrow flying buttresses of a cathedral. All centimeter-close, touchable, all completely unattainable because of the silence of the program. I spoke. It murmured: mhe. I asked,

"You aren't sleeping, are you?"

It answered:

"m."

I threw myself grimly onto the other side of this grey entity and saw dark eyes under pink eyelids.

Something like a reproach in the question I had sent with my eyes, which were searching for too much, made me start back, I apologized and gave the backside of the entity a push, catapulted myself onto my legs and went off to do something useful.

This strange program called Prätz lies in me like a heavy, not very nourishing dish. It is good that dodos exist, good that platypuses exist, one shouldn't slaughter them and shouldn't ask them what kind of animals they are. One should make them breakfast and ask them, once, then later once more, one should be more serious and ask differently, I told myself. The sun shone on, it was late morning, early afternoon, late summer, early fall, I had a lot to do, I had done a lot, I shuffled, playacting, through my apartment like a Japanese secretary, I sprang with heavy trumps through my apartment like a slap-happy jaguar in a tree, *pounce, pounce, pounce*. Grabbed some headphones, put on some music, Gruppa Leningrad, oh no, T. Rex, oh no, Can, checked my emails, wiggled my legs, went to get eggs, still awfully confused.

You should have seen Prätz's face when he appeared in the doorway among the flycatching streamers, as if in pouring rain. Face of lead, above it hair like kelp, tired, friendly, and more in tune with the air above him than with himself. If one has traitors above one's head, one must always sally straight upward, that is how I understand Prätz, and that is enough information, one shouldn't overtake others in understanding themselves.

Later, in the night bus, I forget to count the strokes that Prätz's fingers lay down on my arm. With surprise I acknowledge that it is far from being unpleasant to me, although it is exactly the same thing that Krassa was doing. I think, and draw Prätz's long white arm in front of my eyes. His face goads me on, throws me up in the air, rather than pushing me along in front of it like Krassa's. I had become a wheelbarrow and in my imagination I placed her feet in rubber boots. That was mean of me, in her own view her feet were princess-like. I look up at Prätz, he looks up at me, we receive joy, somewhat more than one can get by looking up at the sky on a random day. As if his traits were a kind of code that I would be able to understand one day, I try to learn to read them, today his face looks like

(ima, now).

TRANSLATED FROM THE GERMAN BY THE AUTHOR

# ELENA PENGA

## *The Untrodden*

SHE RETURNED WITH HIM to their hotel bungalow and sat in the shade of the private yard while he turned on his laptop inside. All morning she had been at sea on a boat for tourists, the kind that take you to see the monasteries of Mount Athos. She saw the monasteries, but they were so far away they flitted by like pictures. Pictures of a world clinging to those rocks since ancient times. Odd feeling not to be able to get close, to walk there, to visit. Untrodden. Unscalable. A sacred place forbidding you to set foot there, forbidding you to visit from fear of desecration. What is its opposite? Trodden?

Aboard the boat she was amazed by all the amateur photographers, mostly middle-aged hobbyists, but also old people with professional equipment, expensive cameras with large zoom lenses and other accessories. Almost everyone around her was equipped and taking photos incessantly, the rocks, the seagulls, the sea, the monasteries up there in the distance. Couldn't they just sit still for a minute? Untrodden. A sacred place forbidding you to visit from fear of desecration with all the clicking cameras, the eyes, the brains. A mania, almost nightmarish, to capture everything. To what end? To make it one's own?

From the bungalow now she can see part of a wonderful garden with many red flowers and white circular benches. She can see a group of reporters. They are sunning themselves. They are sitting in the middle of the garden on the white benches. No one is talking.

"Come, Loneliness! Sit down here, Loneliness," someone shouts. Who is he talking to? The voice again, even more demanding: "Come, Loneliness! Sit down, I say, sit down!" Someone has named their dog Loneliness? Who would do that?

The woman is sitting completely still. She doesn't hear anything else. The man comes out of their room, draws near, sits next to her. "I dreamed," the woman tells him, "that we were sleeping with the bungalow doors open, completely open, we had fallen asleep like that, and I dreamed that while we were sleeping a man came into the room wearing a long dress, he walked softly, the garment dragged on the ground and made a weird *scritch-scratch* sound."

"You didn't dream it. It happened. When you were sleeping I opened my eyes and saw him. I saw him from behind leaving through the bushes."

"Weren't you afraid? Who was it? What was it? A thief?"

"No, it wasn't a thief. Something else."

"Something else? What?"

"He wasn't coming for us. It was a mistake. I think he made a mistake."

The man touches her softly on the cheek and goes back in, returns to his computer screen. The woman remains outside suspended in midair. She looks at the book she has abandoned on the lawn chair. She picks it up, brings it close, opens it, tries to read it. She can't, she closes it, she shuts her eyes. Love stories flicker through her head.

There exist love stories that are full of light, she thinks. From start to finish. She knows that because she has lived it. Everything happens slowly, no rush. Sure, there's pain and disagreement, but they aren't the main things. Like in the sixties, she thinks. Not that she lived through the sixties, but she knows they were full of life, hope, people were moved, they had dreams, they gave birth to whole movements. That's the feeling she has from the light-filled stories—like a party, very alive. Maybe their light has to do with the chemistry between people, maybe with mysterious causes that the common mind can't grasp.

There are also dark love stories. And they're like that for dark reasons. Both kinds always involve a hotel. If not more than one, at least one. And that one is a hotel in summer. Near the sea or a lake. And it's a beautiful hotel, she thinks. She has repressed the ugly hotels and remembers only the beautiful ones. She remembers a room with a sea view where she lived a chapter of a light-filled story. She remembers a room with a lake view, a room with sun pouring in, where she lived a chapter of a dark story.

Now she thinks about the untrodden in her relationships. The limits. To desire? To action? And then she remembers some stories where the untrodden suddenly evaporated. She remembers doors that opened wide and she went inside.

She has suffered a loss. And came here to get away from where she was before, from her life. She thinks about what happened, but her thoughts are scattered, her feelings are too raw, she can't interpret the facts. She attempts to put the inside in order, but the order is undone. Best to concentrate on the pictures, plants, flowers, the view of the sea, the sparrows that fly across the sky-blue background. She looks at it all. She is calm as long as she is looking. She stands motionless until she herself becomes a part of the picture, the landscape. The landscape doesn't change. The light doesn't change. No movement, no variation. There's a bar at the hotel entrance and a sentry house with guards who take turns day and night, but from the beach whoever wants can enter. And not just from the beach, but from other points. At night. When the light disappears and the landscape disappears from sight.

The woman turns her back to the light. Now she goes into the room. She sees the radio by the side of the bed and turns it on. She listens.

"Six women demonstrators chained themselves to the entrance of the factory for over twenty-four hours. They were joined by locals in demanding a repeal of Article 36, which legalizes the mining company's arbitrary actions. The demonstrators remained all night at the factory gate, while the locals gathered in the morning from all the neighboring villages. The demonstrators maintain that the expansion of the mines will turn the whole region into a mining belt of heavy industrial exploitation, which will cause irreversible damage to the water, the forest, the air, the people, and the local economy."

She turns off the radio. She leaves the room. She looks out. She sees the cactuses. Many of them. Impervious. There are people with thorns that poke out so no one will touch them. There are people who pull themselves in so no one will touch them. People who turn their backs on you and distance themselves suddenly and forever so you can't get to them. The untrodden. And then there are the others. The invaders. Those who come and come back and break in and get inside.

The reporters in the garden have turned to stone. Or maybe they're asleep. But aren't they going to the factory? Isn't that why they came here? For the demonstrations? Did they come for something else? What else could it be?

Last night the woman and the man went to the hotel restaurant where they eat every night and were told they couldn't eat there. They were told someone had booked the whole place because he wanted to eat by himself, because he didn't want to eat with others. Who was it? Maybe that's why the reporters were there? Was he the reason the reporters came?

Someone is trying to enter their room. Or is it another room he is trying to get into?

She has also tried to enter, to break into the untrodden of the other. Sometimes successfully. At other times a painful failure. Best not to have any aspirations. Untrodden and avatar.

And her untrodden? Her limit? Isn't it madness? In love isn't the untrodden the point where madness begins, the dependence on the other, that point where you lose yourself inside the other?

"I think of relationships like spaces. How exactly is the space that two people create?"

"Maybe it's a country they create, a new country with its own language, its own customs and rituals, its own laws and prohibitions. An untrodden."

"There is violence in relationships. In those that aren't good. The untrodden is nothing when it meets the lie, the lack of integrity, self-interest, small-mindedness, total inability to take responsibility."

"We live in a time when it's easy to support our wrongdoings."

"Don't think about that now. Think about the good relationships. Those you love. Those who love you and forgive you and want you near them."

On Mount Athos there is the untrodden of gender, the-prohibition-against-women-entering-or-staying, the-pro-hibition-against-eunuchs-and-children-entering-or-staying, the-prohibition-against-female-animals-of-any-kind.

Elsewhere there are other prohibitions. And there are still borders with barbed wire, with bars that block entrances, outposts with armed sentinels, police on boats patrolling the sea. And there are all those people who have to emigrate, who are expelled, who arrive on unknown soil exhausted from the waves, the salt, the sun, the thirst, the hunger.

At night some people try to get into the hotel. They wear robes as disguise. Or as protection from the plants, the cactuses, the thorns. *Scritch-scratch-scratch-scratch*, the material brushes past the plants. The glass door of the bungalow is wide open. The invader goes inside. Is a woman waiting for him? Is a man waiting for him? A couple? The invader stops being an invader. He becomes the fulfillment of desire.

"You didn't dream it. It happened. When you were sleeping I opened my eyes and saw him, I saw him from behind leaving through the bushes."

"Weren't you afraid? Who was it? What was it? A thief?"

"No, it wasn't a thief. Something else."

"Something else? What?"

"He wasn't coming for us. It was a mistake. I think he made a mistake."

The untrodden presupposes the notion of the foreign, of the unfamiliar, of the undesirable. But it also presupposes the notion of the invader.

"I have wished for an unexpected moment when you'd invade me. I have wished for a moment when I'd invade you. I don't know the way. I would like to. I don't know the way."

"Find it. Take the boat. Let the waves hit you, let the sun burn you, get thirsty, get hungry, take risks. Find yourself on an unknown shore. And you will find the door open."

TRANSLATED BY KAREN VAN DYCK

# ZSUZSA SELYEM

## *Confectionery 1952*

I ONLY WANT TO EAT like everyone else. That's all. My location is completely subordinate to this life program: after all, *life is too short to be anything but happy.* There are two concrete bunks in the cell and one concrete table with four holes along the edge through which an iron chain is threaded so that the nutriments can be tied down, although at this date there are far more nutriments in the cell than chains. Even now they are bringing in another one.

The moment they hurl it in, before the cell door has time to close, the cellmates start bombarding it with questions: what's going on outside, has the Devil or, failing that, the Western powers taken that foul gangster Gheorghiu-Dej? The new nutriment apologizes, it has no inkling about politics, it was not brought in from the city but from a *malenkiy robot* labor camp in Dobrogea. It is clad appropriately in shabby, torn shoes, shorts, and a short-sleeved summer shirt. I quickly size up my chances: I can get at it at any point. Better still, there's no fat on it anywhere, finding the veins will be a piece of cake.

All this I observe from my house. I have set up my hideout in a crevice in the wall and because I had a jab yesterday I can afford to relax for the next four days. I daydream about how delicious this new butt is going to be. I've gotten tired of the previous lot, the taste of crazies is slowly getting on my nerves; worse, the blood of the nutriments kept here long-term thickens from stress, no matter what quantities of anticoagulants I pump into them. One of them freaked out so badly the other day it started screeching "more light, more light." They came for it, knocked it down, and schlepped it off by the feet.

Everybody has their own drama. I, for instance, couldn't care a continental about light, as I have little regard for vision, but the nutriments are forever whining about the neon light burning non-stop, without which, if they didn't get the black squirt in the morning and if they weren't chased out one by one to the bogs double quick, they wouldn't be able to tell day from night. Nor can they bear the lack of air: there's no window in the cell, and it's only through the thirty-by-fifteen-centimeter grated opening under the door that they get a bit of oxygen. I of course am hardly incommoded by this—on the contrary, it is by warmth and carbon dioxide that I recognize my feed.

For a while this new one doesn't know what to do in the cell where normally two nutriments would fit but at present there are ten. They squeeze themselves together on one of the concrete bunks to make room for the eleventh and tell it everything nutriments need to know in the cell. When they bring in the black squirt it means it's morning. If you drink it you'll feel an irresistible urge to urinate but you are allowed to the bogs only once a day. If you insist on being taken out and bang on the door, the guard yells at you to keep your gob shut, that if he takes you out now it'll be blood you're pissing.

I admit the atmosphere in the cell is a shade less than convivial, but then again, if you really try and don't think too much and just let yourself go with the flow, always finding time to detach yourself, and if you can accept the low points along with the high, and if it just so happens that the only colors you have at your disposal are blue and yellow, and despite it all if you still manage to keep your pecker up, then with a bit of creativity you can mix them to obtain fifty shades of green, for life is but a journey and it is solely up to you how far you get, I for instance ended up living a splendid life because I never let hardship get the upper hand and always kept smiling and so whenever I want I can find the best possible nutriment with my rostrum, almost without moving, and I have time for meditation, for giving advice to others, for showing them the light at the end of the tunnel, for instance, aka the ray of hope.

What if your other need comes over you? If you don't eat you don't need to shit either, one of the old nutriments answers. Indeed the nutriment would rather eat, several times a day even, it has the makings for that, somehow it tends to panic when it's hungry. They would waste what little energy they have keeping track of every single crumb, organizing and selecting from among the bread lumps pushed in for lunch. They even get bean soup, sometimes as many as seven or eight beans floating in one tin cup or another, but that's not enough either, they're always counting and measuring each other up and down, one of the old nutriments used to systematically torment another by fishing out the same bean repeatedly and pretending to swallow it, but lo, one bean was still left in the can, while the other could only stare, close to tears.

In the meantime I found out that the new nutriment's name was Beczásy, formerly a landowner from Háromszék but with the nationalization they took away everything it had: land, house, agricultural machinery, horses. They came for them the night after Shrove Tuesday, the guests had barely left and the housefolk gone to sleep when the maid woke them with the news that five armed strangers were perching on the woodpile and wouldn't climb down for fear of the dogs. Beczásy whistled back the dogs and was instantly told that they were allowed twenty kilograms of luggage, and that they'd better not keep the van waiting. The smaller larva had been promised a visit to the Sepsiszentgyörgy confectionery the day before, so when the van laden with the landowners was rattling into town the little larva asked aloud, Are we going to the confectionery?

I have no name. I am a female of the genus *cimex lectularius*. Our males often fail to distinguish between us, they simply perforate our thorax with their saber-like reproductive organ and through this wound inject their sperm directly into our paragenital cavity, provided it's a female they've mounted and not a male, who under the circumstances is forced to emit an odorous signal to the other to find a more appropriate vessel for his great copulatory drive. Our nutriments have termed the thorax-perforating position *traumatic insemination*, which I must say is awfully nice of them but there is zero trauma, we have no nociceptors of any kind. I've always stuck to the maxim, don't try to be the only female in his life but the one who counts. The one he thinks about, the one he loves, the one for whom he is ready to fight the entire world. Try to be the one for whom he would sacrifice everything, the one he treasures. The one he protects and supports. The one by whose side he walks, whose hand he holds, never leaving her alone unless she asks him to. Be the female who lets him go if he wants to go. For however much it hurts, you must learn to accept that there are things you have to let go. Anyway, what is destined to be yours will be yours in the end; though others may enter the scene, they will be like specks of dust, too insignificant to change the course of fate. For indeed whatever is destined to happen will happen.

The Beczásys were moved into forced residence in Sepsiszentgyörgy and stayed there for one year, then were deported to Dobrogea; the female is still there, the larvae are scattered about.

I get hungry. The nutriments are fast asleep. I climb down the wall to the floor, direct my steps towards Beczásy, pierce the soft skin on the inside of one elbow with my rostrum. As I expected, the blood is tranquil and scrumptious. I fill my abdomen and slowly retire into my house. Another five days of relaxation.

My favorite nutriment has cut down on all life functions to a bare minimum, keeps lying on the floor almost all day long and only turns over if one side starts hurting. It doesn't mope, doesn't think about anything, just lets things be, like someone who's been sent on a cultural detox trip. Three weeks pass by, it only stirs when the bread or soup rations are distributed, and for the morning sprint to the bogs. In this time those unfortunate nutriments that keep brooding about why they were locked up, what offence they might possibly have committed, what they would be asked during interrogation, whatever they should answer, and, not least, what their people might be doing outside and so on and so forth, keep boiling in their own juice until they soften and welcome any kind of change. They give a sigh of relief when they are finally taken to interrogation and, pleased as they are, oblige by chattering about anything they're asked.

But my Beczásy rises from the cement floor when summoned to interrogation like a newly eclosed pupa. They bind his eyes and drag him out of the cell. He is led hither and thither at length, pushed in the end into an office where a nutriment in uniform is waiting for him behind a desk and asks him to take a seat, to write down his whole life on that sheet of paper, the names of his acquaintances, and what, where, when he talked with them. What he knows, what he does, what he hopes for.

He fills the sheet and asks for another. The nutriment in the uniform hands him one, leans back with a smile of satisfaction and starts reading the first chapter. All you can see from outside is that his head begins to grow more and more red. When he reaches the part about the Italians eating the cat, for the cat will always be the Italians' most prized meat, and small wonder since it's the cleanest animal on earth, he starts screaming and smashes the paper into Beczásy's face. What the hell is this? How dare he mock him? Is he trying to sabotage Socialist society, which is built on absolute equality? Has it not dawned on him yet that he is nothing, a nobody, a speck of dust? That it only takes him one move to blow his guts out, to crush him like a cockroach?

I couldn't say the fate of cockroaches is close to my heart, and I have no heart to begin with, but still, this is not a nice thing to say. And Beczásy looks at him with candid eyes and when the one in uniform stops to take a breath he remarks unperturbed that he has written exactly what the comrade major asked him to, that he hadn't the remotest intention of mocking anybody, it is the very truth that the Italian war prisoners working in their orchard in Bolgár after the First World War when he was a small child had indeed caught their cats and . . . The major starts bellowing again. Do you really imagine that you can outwit me, you pest? With your cats and Italians and Bulgarians? What's this got to do with us? When, where, with whom did you plot to overthrow the regime, who are your friends, may God bugger you together with your whole rotting class, why do I have to waste time with such degenerate morons, I'm telling you you'll regret this, you'll regret this bitterly.

In the end the one in uniform shrugs and continues in a lower voice but stressing each syllable: I'll give you another chance. Here's a clean sheet of paper. I want an accurate biography. Write about conspiracy. About politics. Not animals.

Beczásy starts again. The interrogating officer leaves the room; he returns in an hour and says that's enough for today. He puts the densely written page aside for now to spare himself, lights a cigarette, and rings for the guard to remove the delinquent.

The others of course pester him with questions. What happened? Beczásy sighs and tells them what a dirty scoundrel the interrogating officer is, but that everything is going to be fine as long as we keep our calm and sanity. With this he lies down on the concrete floor and closes his eyes. Again, he only gets up for the morning bogs and for eating at lunchtime. Sometimes he stirs a bit and turns over to his other side. I choose a pleasant point on him every five days and indeed, everything is fine, but for the fact that I am not the only one to frequent him now, some of my kin have discovered that his blood is fresher and tastier.

Between two jabs he's usually taken off for interrogation, the one in uniform is raving, for what he gets is either a detailed report on wheat crops, or on the specificities of various horse breeds, and my Beczásy keeps looking him in the eye with preternatural candidness, so that the officer is unable to decide whether this pest is indeed a perfect idiot or a first-class mime, but he'll make sure to beat all those first-class skills out of him, for this is what he in his turn has first-class skills for.

He wants to find out why László Luka, former finance minister, current convict, used to go hunting at his place together with his wife, Betty Birnbaum; he wants to know what they talked about in the minutest details: 1) how they plotted to play Transylvania into the hands of the Hungarians, and 2) what role Lucrețiu Pătrășcanu, former justice minister, current convict, played in this act of high treason. To this, my Beczásy answers with the utmost sincerity: I have never invited that gentleman to hunt, he simply sent word that he knew mine was the region's best hunting ground and that he would let me know the time of their arrival, some time in the autumn of 1947, I couldn't tell you the exact date because after the nationalization my diary was left in Dálnok. I mean, if Gheorghiu-Dej announced he was coming to visit you, would you refuse him?

During the interrogations that followed, Beczásy was not allowed to sit down. As instructed, the officer first exhausts the possibilities of psychic torture by employing a sort of chiasmus: reducing the number of words while increasing the volume of the voice. Repeating the combination of the words *God, bugger, fuck, mother,* until the delinquent stops protesting, stops resisting, and consents to repeat, accept, sign everything. The only problem is that no matter how long he keeps churning out such combinations, even though he goes as far as to describe at length the methods of terminating the lives of relatives, this particular one doesn't protest and doesn't resist, just keeps looking back at him candidly as though he weren't there, so that at the end of some of the sessions the officer is more worn out than my pet.

Beczásy's method of pupation is unbeatable until the officer passes on to the chapter of Relentless Physical Torture. This I regret, for it means I'll be forced to pass on to another nutriment, but then again, ultimately every defeat is a part of our becoming and we have to comprehend that no one is cheating at the card game: today we lose, tomorrow we win, that's just how it goes. Don't expect to get anything back, don't expect your efforts to be appreciated, your talent to be discovered, your love to be recognized. You need to bring every cycle to an end. Not out of self-respect, not because you can't keep up the fight, not even out of pride, but simply because it's no longer part of your life. Shut the door behind you, change the record, clear out the junk, shake the dust from the rag. Forget who you were and be who you are.

First the officer hits him in the face with his bare hand while hollering about treason, a confectionery, nationalism, and Lord Lieutenant Gábor Szentiványi, then hands him a sheet of paper and barks at him to read out loud: "I, István Beczási, together with Dr. Gábor Szentiványi, discussed in the Ária confectionery in Sepsiszentgyörgy on September 27, 1949, between 11:00 a.m. and 1:00 p.m., the methods by which ailing Communism could be eradicated in the county of Háromszék." This is a patent lie from start to finish, Beczásy says and hands back the sheet. The officer doesn't take it but hisses through his teeth: Sign it. Not even if you strike me dead, Beczásy answers, because if I . . . At this the officer gestures with his eye to the two screws at the door, who grab him and schlep him off to the torture chamber.

They lay him facedown on the cement table and beat the soles of his feet with their truncheons. This kind of caning causes such agony in the brain that synapses are sometimes ruptured. Then they lift him off the table and take him back to the officer who holds out the paper to him: Sign it. Beczásy: I cannot, because if I . . . They drag him off again. They drive pins under his nails. Again, he won't. The officer now accompanies them to the torture chamber, carrying a cat under his arm. The two screws tie Beczásy to a chair, the officer jams the cat under his shirt and starts punching it viciously, the wretched animal tries to escape but the two screws won't let it, so it digs its claws into Beczásy. While this is going on, the officer introduces the words *cat, Italian,* and *Bulgarian* into the sequence *God, bugger, fuck, mother.* Then holds out the paper. Beczásy doesn't sign it. Then they tie him to the chair, forcing his legs apart, and beat his testicles with their truncheons. Beczásy faints, the officer is on the verge of a stroke, tries to calm himself down by repeating his maxim to himself over and over again, *Get the losers out of your life,* and with all his strength brings down the mallet on Beczásy's skull. He lets his tired arms sink, spits, and orders the two screws to drag the thing back into the cell for now, it can wait until the morning to be dumped into a hole in the backyard. Then he goes back to his room, takes a draft from the cognac bottle, leans back, lights a cigarette, smooths out the sheet of paper Beczásy refused to sign and in his own, somewhat unsteady hand writes below: Becási.

When they haul him in by the feet, there is a long silence in the cell. In the end one of the nutriments goes up to him and tries to take his pulse at the wrist, then after a while goes back to its place. Then goes back again and palpates the neck. The others watch in silence. Then this nutriment tears off a strip from his soutane, pees on it, and starts wiping the blood off the face, the eyes.

At dawn the two guards come in and see Beczásy sitting. He is sitting on the concrete floor with his knees drawn up. God bugger this, we have dug him a hole in vain. They kick him in exasperation or just out of habit and go off.

I had one more jab from Beczásy but it wasn't so good. The officer managed to persuade his superiors that he had wrung a confession from the convict, that he had even signed a contract of cooperation, so he was let off. I have always believed that if you don't succeed at one thing, you shouldn't give up but instead look for something else that can propel your thinking and your whole life forward, something you can put your heart into. Luxury, glamor, and money are not everything, because they are ephemeral, they come and go. True feelings and timeless human values are much more important, for they are everlasting.

TRANSLATED FROM THE HUNGARIAN BY ERIKA MIHÁLYCSA

# DAITHÍ Ó MUIRÍ

## *Duran*

A FEW MILES OUT OF TOWN, a quiet road, I'd picked a house out on its own, but the door was hidden by a porch thing so I couldn't see if it was closed—a fairly sure sign (in that kind of place) that no one was in. I checked out the two windows—the curtains were wide open—by walking over and back past the gate a few times. Nothing stirring. I'd just go in. And if the door was closed I'd knock, just in case, and then find a way in. But what if someone came to the door, what would I do then? Well, the same thing I'd do if the door was open and they spotted me, I suppose. I'd say I was lost or ask for a glass of milk, when the time came I'd think of something or just run away. I opened the gate and walked in.

The door was closed with one of those yellow notelets stuck to it. Written on it: Johnny. On the other side: key under mat, bottle in cupboard, back at 4. In I went, or we went—I whistled to Nina who was waiting at the gate. We found some money, a few euros on the table. We didn't have too much trouble finding the bottle. Brandy—we'd never drunk that before. We didn't bother with glasses (plenty in the kitchen) but passed the bottle from one to the other and just knocked it back in big gulps—it was important not to spend too much time in the house (as I explained to Nina). Next thing we knew we'd emptied it. As you'd expect—Nina was only nine (birthday April 7th: I was a year and five months and seven days older than her, eight days I mean, or is it nine?)—it nearly killed us.

Without going into everything I'll just say that we went completely wild and wrecked the place, especially the kitchen with the dishes and the food (eggs, milk, potatoes etc., we started throwing the stuff at each other) and the front room too—I pissed in the fireplace, streamed up to the mantelpiece and even managed to reach

the picture hanging over it—a big framed photo of two guys and
two women on the beach in some hot country. Nina squatted down
on the table and did a big shit and then peed on top of that. I was
sore laughing. By then it was nearly four so time to get going—we
fell out on the road, still badly fucked, and then headed on out the
road looking for some other house.

We came across this small bar where somebody had just been
shot dead with a gun. It was the first time either of us had seen
anything like that and it sobered us up—a bit. Right in front of the
place, lying on his back, a man with his arms stretched out and a
few holes in his chest—with all the blood it was hard to make out
how many bullets went into him but five or six or seven, that's what
it looked like. Maybe he was still alive—his eyes were half open,
only the white in one of them—but he wasn't moving.

Gathered all round was a crowd of drunks—some of them more
fucked than us—with drinks and fags in their hands, chatting and
nodding to each other. Something that sobered us up even more:
a young guy with no drink and no fag, long leather coat, coloured
tie and bright shirt—no sign of a gun—standing over the body,
he took his hands out of his pockets, zipped himself down and
took out his willy. With everyone watching (a lot of them stopped
talking) he pissed down on the guy—I was surprised they let us see
that, that we weren't told to clear off. That's drink, I suppose.

Off went the leather coat back down the road towards town,
hands in his pockets again, walking with an easy little sway, not
looking at anyone, not saying anything. No sooner was he gone
than the crowd kicked up a racket—everyone talking at the same
time is what I mean. From what I could hear—Nina was feeling
sick and sitting against the wall while I went around listening—it
was an argument about land, or about some woman, I think, or
money or the three things, probably. I ran into Maria (birthday
September 15th: I was a year and four months and three or four
days older than her—how many days are in September?) in the
crowd—she wasn't at school either. And she'd seen the whole thing.
But before she'd tell all I had to explain about the brandy—she'd
smelled it anyway even if she couldn't tell from the way I was walking—and about the mess we left in the house back down the road

and all, and I showed her the money too. Her eyes were bulging wide for a second and then she just roared laughing—she informed me that the house belonged to the leather coat.

Back I went to Nina like a shot with the bad news, with Maria behind me laughing her head off. We'd have to just clear off right now, quick—we couldn't even chance walking back past the house. Just beside us there was a long narrow road going down to the sea so we could walk home along the shore—if the tide was out. I pulled Nina up, told her to breathe in and out, in her nose, out her mouth, try and walk around a bit. But then Maria told me it wasn't the leather coat had done the shooting and she just laughed even more. Nina didn't catch any of this so I just told her I was willing enough to hang around, what the fuck and all that kind of thing. By this time there was a bit of colour in her cheeks, she started smiling and some of the old cheeky brat came back. She was feeling better now, she said, she'd hang around too, what the fuck. The little rascal, she'd do well in life with guts like that. This was Nina's dream: high points in the Leaving Cert, baby the year after, a girl, marriage the year after that, a bollox, a few years after that off to India with her daughter for five years, travelling from province to province before coming back—she's still in Ireland, her daughter too, Ciara, sixteen (birthday, I don't know: I'm more than twenty years older than her).

Maria passed a fag to Nina, not to me—she knew I didn't smoke (I still don't). Chewing gum was what I needed, something to hide the smell of my breath—my dad had no idea I was drinking though he was sure I smoked (i.e., fags). Maria wanted to go with us to spend the money in the shop, it was just a bit further down the road, but Nina said she'd just wait there for us. I didn't really want to leave her on her own—there were some funny looking characters around, not to mention the leather coat. However many sweets I was going to buy her, ice cream, orange juice, bananas, it didn't matter, she wanted to stay where she was. I knew of course that she could take care of herself but what if two of them grabbed her, three or more or something even worse? I told her then that it wasn't the leather coat who'd done the shooting at all, that I was just showing off before with all that talk about hanging around, but she still didn't care—something else might happen and she sure wasn't going to miss it. By now Maria was pulling at me, annoying me, she wanted sweets, ice cream, orange juice, bananas—what about a race, five minutes there, one or two minutes inside buying stuff, five minutes back, that was just $5 + 5 + 1$ or $2 = 11$ or $12$ minutes and nothing was likely to happen Nina. I knew she was right but even so, I just couldn't make up my mind. Maria began trying to get Nina to race with us, daring her, saying that she probably wouldn't be able to keep up with us anyway, even if we gave her a head start. But Nina was no fool, she knew what Maria was up to, she was staying and that's that, go yourselves, don't bother about me but just then we heard the ambulance siren and there was no more talk about going anywhere at all.

The ambulance arrived and with it the cops, five big uniforms in a white squad and two detectives who got out of a BMW. One of them—tall, fat, bald, small moustache, sunglasses, tie half open, white overcoat a bit dirty—stood with his hands in his pockets over the body looking down, while the other one (chewing gum, big bent nose and white socks) crouched down in front of him to open a black case. The crowd was really quiet, quieter even than when the leather coat was pissing on the dead guy. I thought the detective was going to do it again, just take his hands out of his pockets and zip down his fly when suddenly Nina shouted out: piss on him! Well, she didn't leave me much choice: piss on him, I shouted, Maria got the idea and shouted too: yeah, piss on him— people in the crowd started sniggering. We just ignored the looks the detective gave us (he took his sunglasses off) and went on shouting louder and louder, jumping up and down, clapping hands in rhythm: piss on him, piss on him, piss on him!

The detective walked back to the BMW, I didn't expect it at all, he said something and the ambulance guys and the uniforms got back into their vehicles and they all cleared off—they just turned round and drove back in towards town. This made the whole crowd laugh. But I was really disappointed—I wanted to see more detectives, some guy with a piece of chalk drawing a line round the body, another taking photos, the body being carried to the ambulance in a plastic bag, a pool of blood left behind (who'd clean it up, the cops, the barman, the relatives, or would it just be left to the rain?) and all the other stuff that happens with murders. It was all my fault, trying to look out for Nina—she was far from sick now.

It was Duran did the shooting, said Maria as a start to her story. As for the leather coat (that's what everyone called him), he was just a bigmouth or whatever we called stupid cunts in those days, posing around, big talk, a guy who'd pull his willy out in front of kids, yeah, we'd heard all about his kind. But dangerous even though he was a bigmouth or whatever. Duran, he made use of the leather coat from time to time, when a bully was needed, someone to deliver messages, some stupid cunt to do the dirty work. But Duran himself, he was another story altogether—a real gentleman, even though he'd kill you without mercy if he thought you had it coming or if he had no choice, man or woman, girl or boy, a baby even, and that's not mentioning the hundreds of kittens and pups he'd drowned in lakes and the sea.

Back came the leather coat at this stage, he was twitching with rage, arms going all over the place, ranting and raving about how whoever messed up his house was going to get it. With him was Johnny (I guessed), another bigmouth. He told the leather coat about the black case that was still lying open beside the body—it was forensics stuff, they could take it and do some fingerprinting back at the house. But where were the cops gone, anyway? Twenty fingers went in our direction and some minor bigmouth told on us.

The leather coat's eyes narrowed, he studied each of us and then said: beat it, kiddies.

That's the way he always talks, said Maria as we walked down the road to the sea, like he's in some crappy American movie. She said nothing more about him, nothing about the killing either, we weren't interested anymore. Do you want to hear my dream, she asked us, about what I want to happen me in the future? We were more interested in that. And she had a special place picked out to tell us all.

There was a stream that flowed down between the fields to a place on the seashore where, after the old bridge fell apart, the Council built a new one—all they did was heap concrete over two fat pipes that let the water flow out over the round stones of the shore into the sea. The pipes had already got a good hammering from floods in the stream and storms in the sea: cracks, chunks missing, one of the pipes all blocked up with sand and stones—you could walk (crouched down) inside the other one and look up through holes at the sky, that's what we did before sitting on top of the pipes to listen to Maria's dream.

A car sped down the road and stopped with a screech of brakes at the bottom, twenty metres away from us, around about that, twenty-five, thirty. Inside were four people and they were looking at us: the leather coat and Johnny in the back, Duran in the front with his driver, a young guy, his nephew. The engine stopped running. After about a whole minute—we could see them talking to each other—Duran got out (a big man, agile enough though you could see how old he was by the wrinkles) and walked with an easy sway over towards us, like he was taking a Sunday stroll, one hand in his pocket, his cap pushed back a bit on his head, looking from the rough ground at his feet up to the sea on his left. I turned to face towards the sea, I listened to the measured sound of the shoes till they stopped right behind us.

Then silence.

The sea was really quiet, an unusual thing, no breeze was blowing, no gulls, no shore birds, there was nothing at all to be heard: silence. Silence that Duran finally ended with his soft voice. He talked about the sea, about tides, about fish, about rowing in boats, about storms, words I'd never heard before, words from the old life, as he explained, things the youth of today knew nothing about, weren't interested in, didn't even respect, they were so spoiled by TV and movies, fooled by money, stupid music, ridiculous clothes, drugs, false dreams. He talked about seaweeds, about islands, about fishing, about everything you could say about the sea, probably.

Can any of you give me an answer, he asked raising his voice a bit, to the question I'm going to ask?

There was complete silence. I pricked up my ears, trying to hear something. Nothing. My back was to him, I could see Nina in front of me sitting with her back to the sea, Maria was beside me, a bit behind—I'd have to turn my head round to see her.

Suddenly I realised there was a sound—the stream flowing from the pipe under me out across the big round stones down to the level of the sea, to the rocks and boulders that were covered with mussels still too small to eat, as Duran had already explained, and further away was the water of the bay, so calm, then the far coast, the mountains, the lighthouse, and to the left of that, tiny white spots that were the houses of some village, probably.

Duran: where does the water go when the tide goes out?

Maria said something, an answer maybe, but she was suddenly hoarse. I wanted to turn my head to look at her, and so let Duran see the side of my face: like it was just some casual movement, and then, after a while, I'd look again, I'd turn my head a bit more round, like I was relaxed, a bit curious, then I'd just glance up at Duran's face.

I listened to the water flowing.

No one has the answer to that question, said Duran. And then he went on talking about the sea, about the seals and the jellyfish, the curlews and the redshanks, lots of other things.

Tell me now, children, have any of you ever heard this one: key under mat, bottle in cupboard, back at four? He began laughing, a quiet breathy laugh, and when he finished he sighed—he was sad because he had to drown us, Nina first, because she was the youngest.

I was already afraid, of course, but now I was shaking, in my belly especially, my heart, my whole insides. In front of me Nina was white in the face, her eyes like they'd been since Duran came, still looking down to where her fingers were fidgeting at her knees—she looked like she'd just shit her nicks. Maria, she said nothing. And I kept looking down at the rocks with the mussels that were too small to eat, at the water of the bay, the far coast, the mountains, the lighthouse.

Long, long ago, children, I heard this story about two men who burgled a house. They came across a camera, there was film in it but only a few pictures already taken. So one of them went to the bathroom, pulled his pants down and with each one of the toothbrushes gave his arsehole a good scrubbing before putting them back in the glass on a shelf over the sink—with his mate taking pictures of the whole lot. They put the camera back where they found it, the film wasn't used up yet, and off they went. What do you think of that now?

Nina was shaking, her head held even lower, but I realised she was sniggering quietly. Then I heard Duran sniggering, it gave me a fright, Nina looked up, looked up and past me at Duran, Maria was sniggering too, I could hear her, I turned my head round and she was looking at Duran too. When Duran stopped laughing he sighed again, but now I knew it was because it hurt him to laugh, hurt his chest, his lungs must have been weak.

The leather coat, children, he said in a whisper, I'll tell you this much—he's only a bigmouth.

And he burst out laughing, Nina laughed too, a bigmouth and an asshole, she screeched, and that made Duran laugh even more, a bigmouth and a dickhead, screeched Maria, and I looked round at her before saying what I thought of the leather coat straight into Duran's face (I'd never seen such kind eyes before, nor since either), a bigmouth and a stupid cunt or whatever we used to call people at that time.

The sigh at the end of his laugh, it was still there: longer, louder, a sign of relief because he hadn't laughed so heartily in a long time, since he was a child himself, maybe.

And Johnny, he said with his chest heaving as he tried to hold in his laugh long enough to finish the sentence—another bigmouth! We just roared and roared.

When the laughing stopped Duran started coughing deeply for a while and then he took a gun out of his pocket. It was a pistol, one with a barrel for not five, not seven, but six bullets. He crouched down and looked at each one of us after the other. Here you are, he said and put the gun into Maria's hands. Keep that, a little present for you, he said (of course, it wasn't loaded), but don't tell anyone about it, you know what I mean?

He got up, looked at the sea a while before walking back to the car, just like when he first came, with an easy sway, strolling with one hand in his pocket, looking from the rough ground at his feet up to the sea, now on his right. He got into the car, waited a long time before moving his mouth and then his nephew started up the engine.

I said that was Maria's dream but now that I've put it all down I remember it really happened—Maria still has the gun to prove it.

And my own dream? I didn't get to work for Duran, that was all I wanted from that day on. I was with him a few times, in the same room as him is what I mean, some bar or other, but I couldn't make myself go up and talk to him, remind him of that day, how much it affected me. And then, one day, he was gone. They said it was the biggest funeral in the place in a long time. A great man, they were all agreed on that. There were things he'd done they didn't like but even so, everyone said he was a great man and the leather coat or Johnny were blamed for any badness he was involved with. People always made excuses for Duran, and anyone who didn't you just stayed clear of that person (if you could). I was sixteen and my dream didn't come true, seventeen, eighteen, nineteen, twenty, twenty-one and then he was dead and my chance was gone. For my dream I had to make do with watching the car with its engine running, being driven at speed up the road—Duran's nephew was a really fast (but very good) driver. He reversed the whole way up, a narrow road with a bad surface. He could have turned round, there was space enough at the bottom of the road for a two point turn, but Duran preferred it that way, being driven backwards, because he liked looking at the sea, spring tides and neap tides, tides coming in, tides going out.

TRANSLATED FROM IRISH BY THE AUTHOR

# MAROSIA CASTALDI

FROM *The Hunger of Women*

*Pause with me—Reader—in the suspended time of the eternal present,
and look at the things that have no end, because the book of life, every
book, is an infinite work, and the cut of the frame is arbitrary as a
Pollock painting*

A WOMAN IN A LONE HOUSE vacuumed every morning I saw my life
reflected in her lot Like her I spent my time cleaning and cooking
for my family I had a grown-up daughter who still lived at home
It was just us two but still we were a family I was a widow I passed
my recipes on to her My husband died in a car accident He was in
the hospital a long time I spent sleepless nights beside him as he
suffered He slipped into a coma and I made the terrible decision to
pull the plug Since then the wisdom of the centuries has nestled in
my memory I kept pictures from the happy times when we would
go to the country house we sold later I tell my neighbor about him
I give her recipes like the eggplant one You slice some eggplant
fry it with garlic put it in the oven with mozzarella parmesan and
tomato sauce

Sometimes she would try to cook my recipes like me We have
little dinners we three lone women She looks into our eyes She
doesn't say much Like me she had cut herself off from society When
I went to the neighbor's to eat I would bring pasta and bread from
my house to her table and we would light candles for us three lone
women My daughter didn't always come She said we seemed like a
pair of war widows Our malady was living on anxiety or abandonment Solitude eats the soul—Reader—

The three lone women saw each other at dinner and the neighbor would tell us about the appliance and housewares store she

used to have She would spend hours arranging coffee pots and salad bowls in the window She'd invested all her savings in that business after her husband died The neighbors praised her for her hard work and strong will In the little town where we all lived everyone remembered her shop She had a boundless love for the objects in which she took refuge like an inviting beach after a storm That's where she got the vacuum she now used at home

The sound of the vacuum she used maniacally was a savage drone that ruined sleep and peace Maniacally she cleaned the whole house every day Nothing was ever clean enough She looked around The dust of time was her enemy Ravenous time nipped at her ankles

The sound of the vacuum was a deafening drone that wafted like a storm wind into the houses of the little town where we lived on a hill that held the wisdom of the centuries in the ancient earth Every window had bars and inside a clock and an old pot and a threadbare doily Everything seemed ancient Everyone seemed to know everything about everybody People talked about those three lone women who had the impudence to do business and commerce on their own They cursed the din the vacuum made growling night and day like a bound animal The deafening ticking of clocks marking the time of death and life drove them crazy The neighbor's husband was a butcher who spent his days till ten p.m. preparing stuffed chickens and liver wraps and veal with bay leaf thyme sage rosemary whose roasted scent emanated from the shop They made dinners to order for fifty in the little rich town in the lower Po Valley full of fog and crime in winter when they closed themselves in for the cold and wet skies and sad nights Incest theft violence multiplied In the drawer they kept a gun

The neighbor devoted herself to dusting her terracotta and porcelain knickknacks left over from the shop she ran for years She'd had the inside painted in blue and white stripes It was the envy of all the neighbor ladies who gossiped about her enviously She was still young They said she'd gotten the money for her shop using her graces like a slut on a rich businessman in the area who had a candy factory Every day they saw him taking packages to the blonde widow with her beautiful arms She'd put on weight since her husband's death A good meal was all she wanted after a day's work She ate the businessman's candy lazily and ravenously while the neighbors whispered

The store was white blue and bright When it was quiet the neighbor ducked out to look at the street and the oaks and the alders on the boulevard Everyone in town went to her for wedding and baptism favors The coffee makers the cups the glasses showed the sun their skin from which the dust of time had been lifted by the hands of the shopkeeper who dusted them daily The dust of time, time was her sworn enemy At home and in the store she silenced every annoying tick-tock every screeching alarm She would die from the madness of clocks

She looked around and found refuge in a sandwich or dessert that filled her yearning for love and affection I gave her my dead mother's recipes I'd seen her in a white shroud Before she died I brought her pasta with fresh tomato sauce You take a bunch of tomatoes sprinkle them with salt sugar and oil and basil no garlic and after a quick sauté pour them steaming hot over pasta al dente

I gave her my mother's pastry recipe You combine flour with equal parts butter and sugar Mix everything by hand and knead until it's a dense coarse ball that you leave to set under a cloth after carving the sign of the cross You place it on the counter and roll it out then place it in tins with fruit cream and glaze You bake it at medium heat for half an hour

The shopkeeper tried to cook but she wasn't very good Her true talent was cleaning

After the housewares store she got bored and got rid of the knickknacks and replaced them with shoe selling The empty shoes watched the road like sentinels of time They were empty of themselves as if waiting to be filled by the warmth of a foot They held the enigma that shoes have like in the Edita Broglio painting where they're waiting like vestals with a lamp and oil for when the time comes for all to leave the earth She even dusted the shoes maniacally and was eager to try them on her chubby feet She gave me a pair of red shoes like a pair I had as a little girl a gift from my mother In exchange I gave her my recipe for puff pastry You mix flour water oil and salt into a silky mixture by rolling it out and kneading it for a while until it's a stretchy dough that you roll out over a large surface until you have a big layer of dough that you cut and put onto sheets to make rustic pizzas filled with meat and vegetables You cover the sheet with dough and bake on medium until the pizza turns golden These dishes are filled with centuries of Mediterranean wisdom My mother passed them on to me and when we were little the smells from the kitchen wafted through the old house like the indelible trace of what has been *Be quiet be quiet* my soul's voice repeats when my mind turns to the chapped white hands of my noble mother worn by the strain of extreme domesticity that ate away her life Only by passing on the taste for the preparation of food that her mother had passed to her did she earn a crumb of eternity on earth

I taught the neighbor simple things like bread with butter and tuna or sugar and bread with oil tomato and salt or caponata campana which you make by soaking a piece of frisella and covering it with diced tomato mozzarella oregano salt and oil Those heavenly slices of bread taste like childhood I also gave her the recipe for stuffed peppers You roast the peppers until the skins come off then stuff them with pasta and olives and sauce or with oil soaked bread and capers parmesan parsley and olives You lay them out in a pan and cover them with bread crumbs

One night when I invited her to dinner she ate four peppers ravenously It was a joyful hunger My daughter looked on astonished It was a joy to watch her as warmed by wine we drank our coffee She told us about her shoes enumerating them like daughters The shoe store shone throughout the neighborhood

My daughter had no interest in housekeeping or cooking After working my whole life I lived off interest from my savings I didn't look back I didn't want nostalgia or remorse

As we were having dinner I started thinking about a trip to the sea we could take together and as we ate I could see in my dead mother's eyes centuries of Mediterranean wisdom My mother died thirty years ago eaten away by the disease of the century that confined her to bed for nine months the time to give birth to her death and her life and to go to the land from which there is no return where she would be reunited with my dead brother The lands of the *nevermore* are invisible to the eyes of the living but apparent in the wisdom of madness and delirium We dined on dishes made from her recipes which my daughter had as little interest in as house-keeping We ate fried anchovies You coat rinsed anchovies with flour and fry them in boiling salted oil You can also marinate them cold with salt parsley lemon and oil As she ravenously devoured the fish I told her about my mother's endive pizza and other pizza recipes In the kitchen that was the prison and salvation of her life my mother made the dough by mixing flour yeast water and a little salt and oil She kneaded the mixture until it became a dense and stretchy ball that she left to rise under a cloth in a warm place for an hour after carving into the raw loaf the sign of the cross that was on the missal and the prayer book that she kept in the cabinet that's now in my house full of papers her bills her recipes and her jewels as if the recipes were worth the same as gold She passed on to me the wisdom of the recipes that earned her a scrap of eternity on what we call earth Then she would take the mound of risen dough roll it out with her hands dip the round shapes in boiling oil then cover them with tomato parmesan basil and oil or would roll out a circle of dough on a sheet and put on top basil tomato oil and mozzarella and bake it in the hot oven for twenty minutes

In the evening we sat at the kitchen table overlooking the sea finite lashed furrowed by ships carrying centuries millennia gold wines spices oils crafts freemen slaves This sea struck by waves by lights from which a vessel a lighthouse a house never disappears This sea of buried dead And back come the millennia and centuries past the buried and reanimated dead and dark women huddled chafed They weave cloth by the sea They wait rip sew gather rip scrape cut crumple They give substance to the sea A sea written drawn corporeal They make it the closed open body of the ancient sea barred with columns with vessels with lighthouses Sea of war sea of earth paper sea of flesh paper Egyptian Sicilian African sea Italian sea sea of Spain France Greece Albania Rome sea inked handcrafted articulated sea worn out never tired of setting forth Mediterranean

We would eat pizza and salad with broccoli tomatoes and potatoes and green beans dressed with garlic basil vinegar and oil and oregano drizzled over the fresh steamed vegetables We ate in silence I would grab my brother's ears to distract myself from my father's gnashing teeth and smashing jaws as he ate silently as if just sitting with us were a favor to my mother At Christmas he didn't accept her gifts He would open the packages and put everything aside until the following year when he finally decided to use the socks or housecoat she had given him the year before At Christmas our mother became sad and cried over his semi-rejection and scorn for her consideration and care but my father was tired too eaten away by his job selling fabrics that took him all over Campania and Lazio One day he brought home a Jewish textile merchant named Ettore Diveroli who had sold out his stock of fabrics Our mother wasn't comfortable with my father's colleagues but even for them she would draw on her age-old culinary wisdom Knowledge of food is the knowledge of the Mediterranean centuries that were alive in my mother's eyes She prepared a dinner for Diveroli and our father that was like the one we ate on New Year's She made tagliatelle with clams and sole in butter and poached salmon That morning she called me over and showed me how She combined flour eggs water salt and a drizzle of oil to get a dense stretchy dough Then she rolled it out over the counter She let the thin rings of dough rest on the flour and then rolled them and cut them into small strips That evening she boiled the pasta and dressed it with the oil and fish The Jewish merchant praised her and gluttonously devoured those wise foods My mother looked on barely eating at all When she cooked a lot and was tired she rejected her own wisdom Her ancient sadness spread to me That was the origin of the seed of sin and waste that later I saw in food Before it had been something divine simple and natural and then something controlled organized and terrible But food preserves the nature of the centuries and the wisdom of God That was when I abandoned my childhood habitudes which I perhaps had already buried when my grandmother died and became what I was: a creature destined like my mother to carry on the wisdom of the centuries in food In our food there is the wisdom that lives inside this sea finite lashed furrowed by ships carrying centuries millennia gold wines spices oils crafts freemen slaves This sea struck by waves by lights from which a vessel a lighthouse a house never disappears This sea of buried dead And back come the millennia and centuries past the buried and reanimated dead and dark women huddled chafed They weave cloth by the sea They wait rip sew gather rip scrape cut crumple They give substance to the sea A sea written drawn corporeal They make it the closed open body of the ancient sea barred with columns with vessels with lighthouses Sea of war sea of earth paper sea of flesh paper Egyptian Sicilian African sea Italian sea sea of Spain France Greece Albania Rome sea inked handcrafted articulated sea worn out never tired of setting forth Mediterranean

TRANSLATED FROM IRISH BY THE AUTHOR

# MĀRIS BĒRZIŅŠ

## FROM *A Taste of Lead*

I FEEL QUITE SPRIGHTLY coming down the stairs on the morning of November 18. I make my own breakfast, brew coffee, carry in some firewood, and light the wood stove. The frog in my throat begins to scratch and act up, but I don't panic. I've learned my lesson—a pill under my tongue and a mouthful of water to wash it down. After fifteen minutes the cough is gone. My mood is easy and upbeat. I want to sit idly and enjoy the lovely winter scene outside the window, but then I remember Wagner and, with him, my tuxedo. So be it, what must be done must be done—having pulled out the suit from the wardrobe, I brush off the dust collected over the summer. I just have to remove some stains still there from That Time. Dried-in soil doesn't yield easily, but if it's soaked long enough, out it comes. Then I heat up an iron and press my suit pants under a dampened cheesecloth. I also iron a shirt. I clean off my patent leather shoes with half an onion, then rub in some Vaseline and polish them until their surface becomes a mirror. It looks like I haven't forgotten anything, everything is top-notch, and I'm totally ready for battle. I take another codeine tablet so that Tamara won't have the slightest doubt about the state of my health and, sitting down once more by the window, I continue to celebrate the day. A monument should be erected to those who discovered this wonderful medication. If it were only possible, I would embrace and kiss them. I mustn't forget the tablets at home, just in case I have a relapse during the performance.

"You look quite dashing, Matīss." Tamara studies me as she starts to get dressed for the performance. "Do you feel alright?"

"Uh-huh!"

Each in our own corner of the room, we put on our finest

clothes. Every now and then we exchange looks and smile at each other, but when we've finished, we jostle at the mirror.

"How debonair you look!"

"Hey . . ." I poke her chest. "You're pretty classy yourself!"

"Like it? I'm going downstairs, there's a bigger mirror there."

When she's gone, I put the bottle of codeine tablets in my pants pocket. It's not too good, the bottle bulges. Should I take just a few? Yes! I slide a couple of the tablets in my breast pocket along with a white handkerchief and put the rest in my overcoat pocket. If I need them, I'll go to the cloakroom and take some.

"Hilda, I have to be at the hospital right after the performance," Tamara says as she fastens a belt around her waist. "May I keep the dress until tomorrow?"

"Since I'm not giving it to you for free, for all I care you can wear it for a week."

"Oh, really?" Tamara freezes for a moment. "How much do I have to pay then?"

"Not much. Boris will soon have finished that good medicine. If you could again . . ."

"Already? Well, fine then . . . I'll bring the dress together with the medicine."

"Yes . . . but the sooner the better."

"But you just said—for all I care after a week." Tamara smiles.

"I meant the dress, not the medicine."

"I understand, I do understand, I'll try tomorrow . . . Well, how do we look?" Tamara hooks her arm in my elbow.

"Well, almost *zu schön*. You will be the most beautiful there for sure!" Hilda clasps her hands with delight.

"And with that tuxedo the gentleman has nothing to be ashamed of, but will be admired and respected by all. By the way, after the performance don't wander off to some *soiree* because I'll be waiting for you outside and will be freezing all alone in my coach."

"You'll also drive us back? How nice of you!"

"Such refined upper-crust folk can't be crammed into a tram. It's too bad you have to go to work. After the performance I had intended to celebrate a bit our now obsolete Independence Day."[1]

"Oh yes? Well . . . in my thoughts I'll be with you."

I gaze at my beloved and conclude—an observant person should notice in her Latvian-flag-red dress a hidden message. It's not overtly daring but it might warm the heart of some countryman of ours.

We're about to leave when Boris, unshaven and disheveled, enters the room.

"I need water."

"But I already put some by your bed." Hilda tries to take her husband's hand, but he breaks away.

"You're laughing? I need much more water. And we must tell all the residents to keep barrels-full at hand. But don't you worry; I've found a way to announce this to the whole country via my radio." Boris smiles cunningly. "The Americans have altered their plans—their soldiers will now be sent by mail. Each Latvian citizen will shortly receive a package. The idea is simple, but brilliant—the United States Secret Service has infiltrated the German postal system. The post will appear to be sent from Germany, but the packages will contain American soldiers. And I totally agree with Roosevelt, this is much safer."

We all gasp almost in unison.

"What are you talking about, dear?" Hilda tries to push Boris away, but he stands firm like a cliff.

"You know that man is three-quarters water. The Americans will dehydrate their army, place them in small boxes and send them here, but we'll put them in water until they swell up again, are revived, and once again ready for battle. If the plan succeeds, then there will soon be a hundred thousand here and that will be the end of Hitler."

"How did you find this out?" Rūdis asks.

"From an announcement in code."

"On the radio? From newspapers?"

"No, these things don't happen so openly any more!" Boris wants to laugh at Rūdis's naïveté. "I have Gershwin's records. One recording is called *An American in Paris*. And as we all know," Boris says

---

1 Latvia's Independence, declared November 18, 1918, was understandably not openly celebrated during the German Occupation in 1941.

with a victorious look on his face, "Riga is 'Little Paris.' Correctly read it should be: *An American in Little Paris*. See how this has all been planned? I'd already received this important news before the Russian and the subsequent German invasions."

"Of course . . ."

"Yes, and the messenger also confirmed it."

"What messenger?" Rūdis steps forward quickly and unintentionally frightens Boris.

"I can't tell you that." Boris suddenly deflates and turns to leave. "Oh, I left there . . . left some pressing work . . ." Boris hastily rushes into his room.

In my opinion the comment about the messenger is the same sort of nightmare as the rest, but Rūdis for whatever reason ascribes some significance to it. He gazes fixedly at Hilda.

"Do you know by any chance why he mentioned the messenger?"

"Why does he mention Americans? Oh, my God, how am I to know . . ." Nervously shrugging her shoulders, Hilda looks aside. Her evasive look is cause for more suspicion to Rūdis.

"He hasn't gone outside, has he?"

"No . . ."

"Really? Hilda, I have to know if something like that has happened. For our own safety's sake."

"Oh, now you're really pressuring me! Just because of such a trivial thing, it's nonsense and not worth talking about. I had fallen asleep, Rebecca also, and he sneaked out for a moment. But I caught him quickly. Right here on the porch. He didn't manage to get away and no one saw him, and he also didn't see anyone. The messenger is just a fantasy, the same as the rest of it . . ." Hilda falls back into a chair and begins to cry. "Oy, how worn out I am! I can't take it anymore . . ."

Tamara hurries to her and, leaning down, hugs her.

"Now, Hilda, please don't cry." Hilda's tears drastically change Rūdis's interrogative tone. "You do understand—I had to clear this up."

"Yes," she sobs. "But nothing has happened after all."

"Well, that's good then, Hilda! Let's move on." Rūdis glances at his watch. "Hey, my dears, we really must hurry now."

"Hang in there, friend! It'll all be fine!" In saying good-bye Tamara embraces Hilda again warmly.

Rūdis lets us off on Vaļņu Street. It wouldn't do to have us roll out from a beat-up truck in front of the Opera House. Not only the car, but also my coat is worn-out from extended use, so I quickly take it off as soon as we enter the lobby. The first thing that catches the eye are the gesticulating arms of officers and the women's luxurious fur coats.

Our seats are excellent—in the second opera box, first row. Of course, no one would give a seat in a remote corner behind a post as a birthday gift to Tamara, the lady doctor. Maybe the threat implied by military uniforms creates a deceptive impression, but, it seems that the majority of men in the audience are soldiers. At least that's the case in the parterre section and the bel étage. I assume that there are normal people seated higher up, in the balconies.

On entering the White House, as Latvians tend to call the opera building, I thought I'd be nervous, surrounded by so unfamiliar a public, but that's not the case, I'm calm and in an amicable mood. I glance at Tamara and she too is behaving like a true aristocrat. Her head held high, something akin to Mona Lisa's smile on her lips. Several Latvian culture workers and artists are also seated in the parterre section. I recognize their faces from the newspapers. The Fritzes cast bored looks around, maybe lingering a bit longer on Tamara, but a few Latvians examine us thoroughly. I guess at what they must be thinking—those two are not from the usual opera crowd, they've never been seen here before, and they're dressed up as if for a festive concert celebrating Latvia's Independence Day. In particular the young woman—a dark red dress with a sparkling silver belt and, pinned above her breast, an ornamental national broach of real silver decorated with rubies. And it wouldn't enter anyone's mind that beside this sublime creature sits a common housepainter from Torņakalns. Or even more ghastly—a gravedigger from Ziepniekkalns.

An elderly officer and his wife take the seats beside us. The wife is young, she could be his daughter, but could just as easily be from a brothel—she's difficult to categorize. Slightly inclining his head he greets us. We're just as polite. The Opera House slowly grows dark.

The beginning of the overture almost jettisons me into a tumultuous sea. It slowly calms down, after a moment to surrender again to thundering power. I close my eyes and imagine myself standing on a heaving ship's deck. Involuntarily my fingers clench the edges of my seat, but the stormy gale subsides, and, when I open my eyes the curtain also goes up. A mariner chorus, Daland, the Steersman, and the Dutchman sing so magnificently that the first act slips by almost unnoticed.

Tamara doesn't want to stroll back and forth in the corridor during intermission, she'd rather stay seated, asking about my health and describing her impressions of the performance. At the second bell, I'm overtaken by the feeling that someone is watching me. Glancing around the concert hall, I look up and see Hermine sitting in the balcony. Well I'll be damned! I'd never have guessed that she'd be interested in anything more than pop music. She stares fixedly at me, as if in reproach—how dare you sit in such good seats, moreover with such a lovely and elegantly dressed woman. But maybe her eyes are not throwing daggers, it just seems so to me. At such a distance one can be mistaken and imagine God knows what. Noticing that I've spotted her, Hermine quickly turns toward her escort. In such an emphatically loving manner, it's laughable. The somewhat slight officer—I can't tell his rank—seems like he hasn't yet tired of Hermine's chatter and the periodic graze of her ample bosom. He too studies me. Would Hermine be telling him of our past exploits? Well . . . she's capable of anything. It's quite disconcerting to have an old flame leer at you from above. I'm able to pay attention to the second act only when Tamara has nudged me lightly. I sneak a look at the balcony—now Hermine's eyes are boring a hole in Tamara. She can't give it a rest, she'd have done better to sit back and enjoy the performance. I sense that the long accustomed-to yet constant taste of lead in my mouth has become more pronounced. What now? I assume that Hermine is capable of ruining anyone's mood from whatever distance, but for the life of me I couldn't have imagined that her presence would have such a negative effect. But maybe the soldiers in the concert hall are to blame? Regardless, having shoved three fingers in my breast pocket, inconspicuously I grab two tablets and put them under my tongue.

At the next intermission, we decide to walk about a bit. To the men's room and the lady's room. It's good that I'm not on the same floor as Hermine. Tamara doesn't have the slightest inkling about her existence.

During the third act the drama takes place only on the stage, because I've calmed down. I immerse myself in the waves created by the *Flying Dutchman*, and Hermine can stare to her heart's content, her presence no longer disturbs me.

After the performance, on leaving, Tamara kisses my cheek and thanks me. I don't understand why I've earned this. Thanks to you too.

Rūdis's truck is parked in our agreed-to location at the corner of Kalēju and Audēju Streets.

"Get in on the double, my feet are frozen to the pedals."

As soon as we take our places in the cab of the truck, the windows immediately steam up.

"What hot breaths. Did you have drinks, or what?" Rūdis wipes the windshield with one hand, his other hand steering the wheel.

"If you were to take off your boots and raise your frozen feet, we could blow on them and warm them up."

"Yes . . . now I understand why you like Matīss."

"Why?"

"Because he has no comeback for your sharp tongue."

"You're wrong. My tongue is as smooth as silk and as tender as down."

"More likely as smooth as a scalpel."

In such a way they banter back and forth until we reach the hospital. Having got out with Tamara, I indicate to Rūdis not to wait, but to take off. I'll walk the short distance home. I want to accompany Tamara for a few steps.

"As you wish. But don't kiss too long or you'll get a sore throat," Rūdis warns. I slam the truck door shut but he rolls down a window. "Matīss, don't forget, the cognac is waiting."

"Oh yeah."

"Oh! Why did you let him go? Like this your cold will get worse. Give me a quick kiss and run after him. Tomorrow morning I'll come to see you."

"Yes?"

"Yes, for sure. I have to tell you some things."

"Really!? Once you start, you have to finish."

"Oh, God . . . who loosened my tongue," Tamara is annoyed with herself. "I'll just explain all tomorrow, so, please, be patient. How stupid of me, now you'll imagine God knows what."

"Hey . . . At least you could give me a hint of what this is about."

"Don't get uptight! It's nothing bad, just the opposite. You've got a bit of patience, don't you?"

"Uh-huh . . ."

"Well, good then."

She gets up on her toes and we kiss much longer than Rūdis could stand. It's biting cold, but I don't want to let Tamara go.

"I laughed at Rūdis, but my feet are freezing too," Tamara taps her heels one against the other, and our embrace is undone.

I always feel that this last moment of farewell is the hardest—who'll be the first to look away and turn to go? Tamara has the upper hand, but she hesitates. Backing away step by step, I raise my hand and wiggle my finger tips—bye, bye, bye. Smiling, she waves in response, then turns and briskly walks away.

Life isn't so bad after all—a wonderful opera just now, Tamara so lovely, there are no words to describe her. My mind is filled only with bright thoughts, and my steps skip along with them. My toes are freezing from the cold, but that's just trivial, in a minute Rūdis and I will sit with a glass of cognac in a room warmed by a fired-up woodstove. What more can one small dust particle seeded in the infinite vastness of the cosmos wish for?

At the turn-off to our street a big, horn-honking truck with a tarpaulin-covered bed forces me off the road. Curious, I stop—where is the truck rushing at night, what is it after? Out of the corner of my eye I notice sitting in the cab beside the driver my neighbor Pēteris, who is showing the driver where to turn by poking his finger at the windshield. Seemingly he hasn't even seen me, or he would have said hello or maybe even stopped. Probably he and his company are going to a party. Well, all right then, why shouldn't they, just as we did, to celebrate the eighteenth of November. They're Latvians after all.

I wait for a bit, for the truck to roll on to its destination. Let my neighbor's crowd disappear into his yard, then I'll continue on. God forbid that Pēteris should see me and decide to invite me to join them.

What now though? The truck stops at my house. The tarp is thrown back from the truck bed and three, four . . . five policemen . . . no, it looks like even more jump out. It's dark, if it weren't for the snow, nothing would be visible. From the cab more men clamber out—altogether there are some eight or even ten of them. If I'm seeing correctly, all with weapons in hand. Two or three, I can't quite discern, remain shifting from foot to foot by the fence, while the rest hurry into the yard. I want to go and ask what they're doing there, but my legs have a mind of their own—they slide backward, until my back is hugging the gate of house number one on the street. Where will you run, you madman, hide, while they still haven't seen you! Get away somewhere, it's dangerous here! My head is in a muddle, but my steps are certain and quick—in just a few seconds I'm already beyond the street corner. They'll be arrested, that's for sure now. God forbid that the police should start to shoot! That can't be allowed but how to stop it? What can I do? I'll tackle one policeman but meanwhile another will arrive with a rifle, and *alles*. Some reinforcements would help . . . hell, what reinforcements? Kolya as an old partisan maybe could think of something, but it would take some time to reach him. . . I can't do anything, just throw snowballs. Helplessness strangles my breath. My neighbor Krūmiņš's dog Džeris is barking non-stop. He, of course, would be ready to leap into the fray with bared teeth and claws. Crawl into your doghouse, little idiot, you might get pilloried for running off at the mouth like that.

For sure that piece of shit nosed out something. But how? We lived so quietly, protected ourselves like nuns from sin, and now look. Maybe Hilda didn't tell us everything about Boris's breakout. My fingers grope for a cigarette pack in my pocket. Must have a smoke and a think. My hands tremble like those of an old drunk, the matches break. My back is wet and my whole body is trembling. That's from anxiety, old man, not from the freezing cold. I must pop some more pills, for relief. I throw a couple in my mouth, topped with a handful of snow. What to do, where to go? To Tamara's? Yes!

I speed up, but my patent leather shoes slip and slide until my legs give way, and I collapse to the ground. I get up and start to wade through the snow at the edge of the sidewalk, where it hasn't been ironed into ice. My progress isn't as quick as I'd like, but I make headway.

When I approach Robežu Street, I slow down. Events unfold almost as they did a half a year ago in June—once again I'm in a tuxedo and once again I'm fleeing, just that now I'm on my own. That time Rūdis had reached the other side of the railway tracks, and would shortly have been herded into a cattle wagon to be deported. Stop! Where am I going? What will I tell Tamara? That I looked on from around a corner and skulked by house foundations like a lost and frightened dog, but now I've run to her to cry on her shoulder? I'll just upset her needlessly and what good would it do? When everything is explained, then yes . . . Maybe it won't be so bad, but let Tamara live in peace, take care of the little ones, as long as . . . as long as she still can do it. I turn around and hurry back.

I start to feel ashamed that in my animal-like fear I had lost clarity of mind and strength of heart. Just as the captain of a sinking ship shouldn't abandon the deck before his crew and passengers, I too, as the owner of the house, had to clutch onto the door jamb until the very last. Please God, give me the strength to be firm, to not flee and to weather the storm together with Rūdis and the rest. If I can only manage to get there in time now. I stretch out my fingers—they're not trembling as crazily anymore. However, my whole body suddenly shakes—as I hear the thunder of a machine gun round. My legs once more function on their own accord—from fear they stop and freeze. What's happened now, forward, move,

move! Stumbling, falling, I run, my shoe soles slip like hell, until they drag my butt up in the air. I fall on my back and remain lying there. My tailbone aches so badly that even with a mighty push I can't stand up. While I'm reeling sideways, from around the corner the same big truck pulls out and speeds away in the direction of the city center. It seems to me that I hear Hilda's screams and policemen's curses from the tarp-covered truck bed. Up on my elbows, I wave for them to stop, but the driver flashes a bored glance through the window at me and barrels on, as if saying, he's not going to prop up some drunken bum.

My head hung low, I crawl forward. I've managed to save myself but I feel like a traitor. I can, of course, console myself that this is the finger of fate or a lucky happenstance, that I was delayed with Tamara. Maybe the Lord had planned to save me, it could be, but it doesn't become easier because of it. Joyful little Rebecca . . . what's going to happen to Boris's and Hilda's child? If it hasn't happened already? There were gunshots, after all . . . but maybe they aimed in the air only, for a scare . . . for a short while I can still hope that's the case.

My thoughts are pulled in all directions—to flee, save my life, or with head held high return home, and what will be, will be? It's true, who's to say if there's anyone really inside. If I flee, it would be good to be dressed more warmly, to change from shoes to boots. I must look inside—there's a gap between the heavy curtains. Wading half-bent to the window, my heart pounds as my mind once more feels shame. I'm in my own yard, after all, but I'm sneaking around like a thief. I stand up straight and examine the room. I don't see anyone. What now? Stepping back from the windowsill, suddenly I'm overcome with indifference and apathetic calm! Enough screwing around and jerking about. Slowly I'll collect my belongings and I'll head to Kolya's. Should I jump into the wolf's jaw just because the others have suffered a misfortune? Would any good come of that?

Walking along the path to the door I notice footprints in the snow, and further on, by the arbor, someone lies face down in a snow drift. Shot and killed . . . Rūdis!? He was trying to escape for

sure, but can one escape a bullet! Just imagining it my legs turn
to stone. I'm afraid to look at my friend's numb cheek, I want to
remember him alive, but I can't leave him there. Placing my feet
in the trampled footprints in the snow, I approach the corpse.
It's Boris! His coat shredded to bits, the snow soaked with blood.
It's obvious he was fleeing . . . for God's sake, why did you run?
Had the Americans showed up again? Jesus, in front of your wife
and daughter . . . oh, how the little girl must have . . . to envisage
Rebecca's feelings is beyond me.

I take Boris by his arms to try and drag him to the woodshed. I
won't get far this way, I must try something else. I enter the house
and take the blanket off his bed. I spread it beside his corpse and
roll Boris over on his back. His eyes stare glass-like at heaven. I try
to press them shut without success. It can't be that they've already
frozen! Should I put coins on the eyelids? Fine, but I'll do that
later. I grab the corners of the blanket and drag it further. It slides
much more easily. Having pulled Boris into the woodshed, I lay
him down between the stacks of firewood and cover him from both
sides with the edges of the blanket. Tomorrow I'll put you on a sled
and pull you to the graveyard.

You're lucky, Boris, no more terror and grief. Maybe I should
hang myself right here beside you—so my eyes don't see and my
ears don't hear . . . No, I don't have the strength to look for a rope
and I dreadfully want to sleep. It seems that it doesn't matter in the
slightest—if I live or die. And if it doesn't matter, why do anything
needless. I'll live, come what may. But you, Boris, sleep. Not knowing if according to Hebrew law it's a desecration, I still make the
sign of the cross. There's nothing you can do now, Boris, so you'll
have to endure this Christian tradition.

It's good that you sleep like this, you're not cold, but I still have
to heat up the rooms in the house. I load birch firewood on my left
arm and turn toward the yard. A piece of firewood falls on Boris's
stomach. Forgive me, that wasn't intentional. It seems to me that
he lets out a moan, but it's only the wind, which breaks in through
gaps in the woodshed walls. When you're exhausted you see all sorts
of phantoms.

Having thrown down my coat, I shed my suit jacket. I gaze at the bowtie as if it were a foreign body, for it seems that I was at the opera not this evening but a year ago.

TRANSLATED BY MARGITA GAILITIS
EDITED BY VIJA KOSTOFF

# JONATHAN HUSTON

## *Moondust*

THE ASTRONAUT WHEELS DOWN the sterile white hall under the blur of florescent lights. He inhales through his nostrils. The smell of antiseptic would make most men gag. But not him. He's calm, his heartbeat and breathing are regular, his blood pressure is normal. A woman stands with her back to the wall. She flashes him a thumbs-up. He likes how her back is straight and she has big white teeth. He feels the pressure building between his legs. She's too old for him, otherwise he might go to bed with her when he returns. He winks and salutes her the way he does all pretty civilians, and then he forgets her.

The astronaut is hooked up to something: a tube protrudes from his thin, naked forearm and ends in a transparent bag slung around the top of a pole. A clear liquid pumps into his vein, glucose or saline solution, probably to keep him hydrated on the flight. He's had enough of the prodding and pumping. He's ready to go. He's worked hard for this, he's healthy and strong, and his mind is sharp. He's rolling down the hall in a chair like a wheelchair to relax his muscles before the flight. He can barely feel his legs. They must be strapped in very tight. He whistles wild blue yonder and wonders why he's not wearing his spacesuit.

The nurse wheels him into the common room.

"Claire's here," the nurse says. A young woman is hunching on the sofa by the coffee table. Her hair is too black to be natural, she has too many earrings crawling up her lobe and helix, and she's too thin and too young for him, the astronaut thinks. She's probably still in high school, maybe a freshman in college. Sometimes they're too old, sometimes they're too young.

The astronaut isn't flying to the moon today. He tries to get up from his wheelchair but his legs haven't moved in years. Okay, he says to himself, you know where you are now. Focus. But who is this girl. He tries to keep an open mind without letting it wander. He can do this.

The nurse parks him and his drip next to the girl and says she'll leave the two of them alone now. The nurse has gray hair tied up in a bun. She's got a tough look about her. She's probably Russian. He smiles anyway as she leaves the common room and the memory of her already dissipates like vapor.

The astronaut stretches out his hand to shake the girl's. "How do you do," he says. She must be a young admirer.

The girl doesn't shake his hand. "Mom says hi," she says.

The astronaut doesn't respond.

"Your daughter," Claire says. "I'm your granddaughter, okay?"

The astronaut doesn't know what to do with this information. He doesn't remember the girl. Maybe she comes to visit him regularly, or maybe this is the first time he's ever seen her and this is an emotional moment in their lives. He doesn't want to make her feel uncomfortable but he does want to know what she wants. He has a routine for dealing with situations like this.

"Would you like a cookie?" the astronaut asks, gesturing to the floral-patterned saucer perched on the coffee table. Claire shakes her head.

He reaches for a cookie himself. Peanut butter. Not his favorite. He takes a bite and the crumbs fall into his lap. He leaves them there.

Claire takes a cookie after all, but she just holds it in her hand for a moment before putting it on the table, uneaten, next to the saucer. She shifts to the end of the sofa and stretches her legs, letting her feet touch the floor. She's wearing black shorts and her legs are skinny. It's summer in L.A., but she's wearing bulky brown boots. He doesn't like her boots. Her hair falls over her bare shoulder as she reaches into her red canvas backpack. The astronaut likes her muscular shoulders. They remind him of his own. She should wash her hair.

She pulls out an iPad. He has one of those too. He watches Star Trek episodes in bed and plays a game called Doodle Jump. He loves Star Trek, but he loves Doodle Jump even more: a cartoon creature with a trumpet nose and four tiny legs jumps up an endless series of platforms, higher and higher into the sky, all the way into outer space, using spring shoes and propeller hats and rocket packs to gain altitude. If you're not careful, the creature falls between the platforms and dies, or it gets eaten by a space monster and dies. The astronaut is pretty good at Doodle Jump and it keeps his reflexes sharp. He's better than anyone else at the nursing home, except maybe the nurse who wheeled him into the common room today. He's asked her out, several times, always in vain. She'd be just the right age for him, and he likes her, even though she's Russian. The device this girl holds in her hands has more computing power than the entire Apollo program. He wonders if she'll ever fly to the moon. He remembers sharing rainbow ice cream at the pier with a black-haired girl once, but she was a lot younger, or he might have seen it in a movie. He remembers the smell of the sea and the flavor of artificial fruit.

"Can we start now?" Claire asks.

"Sure," the astronaut says. He's adjusting to the new situation. He reaches over and picks up Claire's chocolate chip cookie and eats it. It's too crunchy, and the chips are too hard. He likes them just out of the oven, fresh and chewy, like his wife used to make them.

"Well, will you look at that," the astronaut says and wipes the crumbs off his lap.

The astronaut imagines Claire's a reporter, interviewing him after his moon flight. But he knows it's been a while since his moon flight. He has a habit of imagining things now, and he doesn't like it. Sometimes, even when he's not playing, he imagines he's that little creature with the trumpet nose, jumping up up up into space and never falling, or he's on a mission to explore . . . but now he's going to concentrate on the task at hand and try to remember, not imagine.

Claire adjusts the iPad cover so she can type comfortably.

"What did it feel like to walk on the moon?" she asks.

"I don't care what it felt like," the astronaut says. His words come out much too harsh.

Claire stops typing. She looks patient, as if she's been expecting this. "I'd still like to know," she says. "It's important to me."

The astronaut softens his tone of voice.

"I don't remember what it felt like," he says. "But I remember what I did. I had a job to do."

Claire stops typing again and picks at a chipped, purple fingernail. She has pale hands with long, thin fingers. He's seen fingers like this before.

"Mom said you'd say that," Claire says. "I know this is hard, but I want to get at the inside, even if you're not used to talking about it."

The astronaut wants to end this conversation with his unknown granddaughter, call the nurse, and get back to his room to play Doodle Jump. But he doesn't want to disappoint her. He doesn't want to disappoint anyone who comes to visit him. He closes his eyes and rummages through the ruins that make up his three days on the moon. He's told the stories so many times, he can't sort out his fading memories from all the verbal wallpaper he's plastered over them. If he remembers anything, he remembers the stories he's told. He clenches his fist. He feels the arthritis in his fingers and he remembers how hard it was to pick up rocks through his gloves, to wrench them free of the boulders that embedded them. There were a lot of rocks.

He says, "When Carl and I left the command module and entered the LEM, for a moment I—"

"The LEM?" Claire asks. She rubs her fingers against the screen of her iPad.

"The lander," he says. "One astronaut stayed in lunar orbit while two of us landed on the moon in the lunar module. We called it the LEM. Carl and I collected rocks and set up experiments to figure out what the moon is made of. You should know this."

"I know what a LEM is," Claire says. "It just sounded funny when you said it."

The astronaut doesn't believe her. He isn't sure he likes this granddaughter of his. He doesn't like her attitude, and she isn't prepared for the interview. This generation will never make it back to the moon, even with all their powerful gadgets.

"Why are you here anyway?" he asks. He's surprised by his anger and he tries to suppress it. She's just a girl. He wishes he had a glass of milk to offer her. "Are you sure you don't want a cookie?" he asks. "The last one's peanut butter."

Claire pulls back into the cushions of the sofa. "I want to know what it's like to be the last person who remembers the moon."

The astronaut had forgotten that. He's the last man alive who walked on the moon. He must be really old. When he dies, the last memories of the moon will die with him. But his memories are dying already before he has the chance to. He curses himself sometimes. He tries not to let himself get distracted, not by the television blaring in the corner of the common room or the chatter of his fellow residents, the smell of stale food and disinfectant, the growing pressure in his bladder, his questions about who this girl is across from him, or why he can only remember snippets of anything. He struggles to piece his memories of the moon together now like a broken mosaic. Some of the stones are already lost or crumbling, or cracking and loosening as he speaks, or pilfered from other mosaics stuck in the crevices of his mind. He tries to reassemble the memories that must be half a century old by now. He remembers steel sunshine rippling off fields of blinding dust. He remembers indigo beads of molten lead and orange clumps of clay buried in mounds of powdery graphite. Can that be? He remembers specks of olive-green crystal strewn over charcoal plains, house-high boulders of basalt and rubble, breccia blasted from craters created by meteorites raining like bombs from the deep black sky, blood-red lava pouring from mouths of ancient volcanoes before they died. Or maybe he read that somewhere, when he was preparing for his mission.

"There were a lot of rocks," the astronaut says. That's something he's sure of.

"Rocks," Claire says and types something in her iPad that's longer than "rocks." She must think he's an idiot. "Sounds like a buzzkill," she says.

But in the end it really was all just rocks. He was an Air Force pilot pretending to be an astronaut pretending to be a geologist. If he'd been chipping away at all those rocks, clammed up in a Teflon and Mylar spacesuit in the California desert instead of a lunar highland, breathing artificial air that stank of sweat and stale farts, his fingers and arms hurting so bad from gripping hammers and pounding probes with gloves that barely flexed, he would have called it all a sick joke and gone back to bombing Communists for a living. He still can't think of anything more boring than geology. This is one thing he has in common with his granddaughter, whose eyes are surveying the craggy, lopsided faces of the other old people in the common room. He doesn't want to be like them. He hated those rocks. But that was all there was. No water, no air, no fire other than the sun radiating down on them when they weren't shivering in the shade. He and Carl were a space-age Adam and Eve collecting rocks in a barren garden where even God and Satan never set foot. No new life and new civilizations to seek out. Just rocks and dust as far as the eye could see. And in empty space the eye could see so far: nothing was muted, nothing soft. The desolation of gray hummocks and tan craters and white mountains stretched out before him until his gaze hit the black envelope of the universe, punctured only by the sun and the crescent of a planet so far away. But the planet looked magnificent, like a piece of blue bubblegum hovering right in front of him, wrapped in white cotton candy, as if he could just reach up and pluck it from the sky and put it in his mouth, and he wonders what it would have tasted like if he'd—

"Did you ever feel guilty?" Claire asks.

"Why would I feel guilty?"

"Because of when you came back." Claire shrugs. "And because it took a lot of money to send you to the moon," Claire says. "Cold War propaganda while children on Earth were starving, college students were being shot, families being lynched. Vietnam, Cambodia, Nixon. That never bothered you?"

The astronaut never felt guilty about that. He really has to go to the bathroom. "You can't just always fix things," he says. "Sometimes you have to build things."

It's easier for him to reconstruct the moon than the state of the nation fifty years ago or his family. There was no time on the moon to think of family and friends and barbecues and church and football, let alone politics and the meaning of life. No room to think of his wife, waiting for him to return alive, cheering him on in front of the TV screen, cookie dough ready to go. Twenty hours of moonwalks over three days on an airtight schedule left no space to be homesick or to philosophize or wax poetic. There was no time to think of anything other than engineering and geology, trying to remember which rocks were interesting, cleaning off the moon-dust that gummed up their instruments, trying not to screw up and die. His whole lifetime had been compressed into the only three days of his life that mattered to anyone or that anyone would ever remember. He remembers the stress and his heart racing and pain-ful breaths. And when he got back to Earth he was depleted and confused. Like coming back from a war. He screwed a topless wait-ress at the Boom Boom Room in Nassau Bay. Now *that* felt like life for a while, slipping back into living breathing flesh, his body wiry and tough with the heroism only an astronaut can bring back from the moon.

"Coming back was like landing on an alien planet," the astro-naut says.

"Do you feel lonely?" Claire asks.

"What?"

"Nobody else alive has experienced what you've experienced. That must make you lonely."

"I have my friends here, they like to hear my stories," the astro-naut says, gesturing at the decomposing humans around him. He's afraid he'll wet his pants but he doesn't want to leave just yet.

"Were you lonely on the moon?"

"I wasn't lonely," he says, "I was just tired. Really tired." He's remembering more now, and he spurts it out before it melts away: "I was tired the morning I set foot on the moon. I hadn't been able to sleep in the LEM. We were protected only by its thin skin, sur-rounded by pumps and valves that clicked and hissed. The adrena-line kept me going that day, but I could barely think. I just wanted to sleep. The lander stood there perched on the rim of a small cra-ter, ready to topple with the slightest gust of wind. But there was no wind. I put on my spacesuit and climbed down. The dust was springy under my boots, like walking on a sponge, and I felt queasy. I didn't want to throw up in my suit, especially not on television. I wobbled away from the LEM like a drunken man. I got my tools from the LEM's equipment bay: hammers and rakes and scoops and tongs to scratch the surface of the moon."

"This is good," Claire says. She's scooted up to the edge of the sofa again and is typing words rapidly into her iPad. She takes a bite of the last peanut butter cookie.

"There was a huge boulder at the far edge of the crater near where we landed," the astronaut continues, "and I rounded the crater to probe it. I heard only the sound of water pumping through my suit as it tried to cool my limbs, the oxygen flowing around my body, and the buzz of Mission Control and Carl's voice in my ear. I'd never sweated that much before. I glanced up at the Earth. But it was distracting me, so I forced myself to forget it, and I reached the boulder. Everything was gray. But then a crystal lodged in the rock caught my eye. Its color was alien, like a rainbow trapped in amber, graceful and fragile and bound to give the geologists on Earth wet dreams."

The astronaut hesitates. "Sorry about that," he says. "I was getting carried away."

"I can handle wet dreams," Claire says. "Go on."

The astronauts looks away from his granddaughter and stares into space, as if through the walls of his nursing home. "There were billions of years of history right there, in that single rainbow crystal. I'd never seen anything like it and I never would again. I scraped and hammered, tugged and pried and tried not to lose the dust and pebbles as I scooped them into my pouch, struggling to free the crystal. I almost had it when I dropped my hammer. I swore and hoped the mic didn't pick up what I said. The hammer just flew away and bounced off a rock and twirled across the moonscape as light as a pinwheel. I hopped and spun after it and when I finally grabbed it with my glove again, I didn't know where I was. I looked back and I saw my overlapping footprints spiraling up a crater around a boulder and all I heard was static. I couldn't see Carl or the LEM. The hills in the distance blurred together. I couldn't tell what was near and what was far. The moon was like a hologram, every tiny fragment a blurry likeness of the whole. Every black and white rock and crater and mound of dust was a reflection of every other. I saw myself wandering the moon forever, drifting from dune to dune, stumbling over shattered meteorites, falling into pillows of ash. Vomit rose into my esophagus and I was afraid I'd choke to death. And then—"

The astronaut struggles to find the right words.

"You had an epiphany?" Claire asks.

The astronaut looks at Claire's face. She's very young. She must be hoping that his trip to the moon and her visit to the nursing home might turn out to have been worthwhile. She doesn't know much about life yet, or about him.

"No," the astronaut says. "Then Carl's voice crackled in my ear and guided me back to the LEM. I left the moon with rocks and what I came with."

It's all becoming vague in his mind again, like a dream swirling away at daybreak. He clings to the memories of memories, but they slip from his grasp. The rest is quickly told: tired cheers, routine debriefings, half-hearted hugs, and a life and a nation that gave up on shared projects and moved on to—what? He scans the deliberate, cheerful wallpaper of his old folks' home, masking chips and cracks in plaster. He remembers the waitress from the Boom Boom Room now, her long, pale fingers, her black, black hair. He remembers her yelling at him that he never left the moon, and he remembers the way their daughter shrugged away from him years later, the last time he saw her, as if she were related to someone else.

His granddaughter waits for him to say more, but he doesn't. "Is that it?" Claire asks.

"I'm afraid so. It was a lot of work, but I did the job."

She gets up and packs away her iPad.

"Thanks, Grampa," Claire says. She steps toward his wheelchair and almost hugs him but doesn't. He's glad she doesn't: his pants are wet. He doesn't think she notices the smell, but he doesn't want her to get too close. "Mom hopes you're comfortable here. If you remember anything else, let me know, okay?" Claire says and then she's gone.

By the time the Russian nurse comes to pick him up from the common room, the memory of Claire is gone, too. The nurse wheels him back through an empty hall to his room. She helps him clean up his accident, he slurps his dinner like an astronaut in space, he watches Star Trek in bed and dreams of becoming a starship captain. He breaks his record in Doodle Jump and falls asleep.

He wakes up a few minutes later and remembers the smell of moondust, and he remembers the girl he met today. He wants to tell her how it smelled when he returned to the LEM from his moonwalk. He stripped off his spacesuit and he was caked in moondust. It was the first time he smelled and tasted and touched the moon without a helmet or gloves or boots. It was the only time the moon didn't feel like a simulator. The alien dust invaded his pores and dirtied his fingernails and filled his nostrils and lungs and made him sneeze. It made him feel alive but alien, as if he belonged to the moon now. Back on Earth, the dust no longer smelled like anything at all. But here in the lander on the surface of the moon, it breathed oxygen for the first time, and it smelled like spent gunpowder, or like the remains of a barbecue on a rainy Fourth of July. It smelled like the ashes of an old body scattered into the sea. He wants to hold onto that memory until his granddaughter's next visit. He's the only man alive who remembers the smell of moondust. He can do this. He focuses on it and nothing else. He banishes every other thought. He rehearses the memory of moondust over and over again. His mind is sharp and powerful again, remembering what moondust smelled like, what it felt like in his hands, clinging to the unshaven skin of his face, the sandpaper pain of it in his lungs, and again that fleeting smell of exhaustion. But finally he falls asleep and he dreams of the Russian nurse, and by the next morning when he wakes up, no one remembers the smell of moondust.

TRANSLATED FROM GERMAN BY AUTHOR

# UNDINĖ RADZEVIČIŪTĖ

## *Opium*

"Opium," said the Scot, opening the box. "You lose yourself completely but at the same time you also lose fear."

But the Scot did not need opium for fear.

He had been stabbed with a knife a month ago but that didn't stop him from going about his business at night.

The Scot in the city was as illegal as the opium.

An invasive species.

Only no decision had yet been taken to shoot him like some kind of raccoon destroying the nests of nightingales.

Even though, as has been mentioned, he had already been stabbed with a sharp object.

Most probably he used opium not to dampen down fear but as a form of spiritual therapy to heal his wounds.

"Where's it from?" asked Winston.

"What?"

"The opium."

Winston could not tell if it was really opium or just some new kind of "grass," and he was left with two possibilities: to believe what the Scot was saying or—not. Opium was rather rare in twenty-first-century Europe.

But if you couldn't believe the Scot, who could you believe?

The Scot was his oldest and best friend, and now his best friend was preparing an opium pipe in accordance with Chinese ritual.

You could also choose to believe that or not.

The Scot had bought the nineteenth-century opium pipe a year ago in the Netherlands.

He had bought the special table to hold the opium tools in West Berlin from some dealers in Chinese antiques.

It was dirty with bits peeling off when he bought it, but then he had it restored.

The Scot didn't seem very pleased with the restoration, but the cherry blossoms depicted with shell inlays warmed his heart so much that he finally managed to suppress his displeasure and calm down.

The opium was kept in a dark-blue cloisonné metal box decorated with pink lotuses, which the Scot had also bought in the Netherlands.

The special knives and the five-centimeter-high copper ashtray, funnel-shaped and tapering down towards the bottom, in a London flea market.

The instrument for measuring out the opium looked like a miniature barrel, with crudely engraved flowers and birds.

The Scot had bought it in Berlin as well.

The tools for cleaning the pipe he had ordered from local artisans.

And the artisans had made them from brass to the Scot's drawings and grainy black-and-white photocopies.

The Scot had everything.

For the opium.

Only there had been a shortage of opium for a long time.

"Where's the opium from?" Winston asked again.

"From the same sources," said the Scot

"From the same Scottish sources" was how he also got an endless supply of legal products.

Chinese tea directly from a plantation. Less than twenty days after it had been picked.

Dark-blue Uzbek raisins untreated with any chemicals.

Green almonds, braided dried melons, chocolate that a week earlier had been judged to be the best in the world.

The Scot's world seemed somewhat bigger than that of the people around him, and if the town were to find out about the Scot's Scottish life, they would stab him with knives more often and with even greater enthusiasm.

The Scot lived his life without paying the least attention to how things were supposed to be in the town.

For that reason, people no longer greeted him.

He hid in the shadows but Winston had never noticed that there was not enough light in the shadows for the Scot.

Or that is was too cold for him.

As it was, the Scot as a Scot would disappoint anyone.

His hair was not red, nor was it curly.

And he never went out into the street without his underpants on.

He looked like a rabid fox crossed with a French musketeer from a twentieth-century film based on an Alexandre Dumas novel.

He wasn't even able to produce any documents to prove that he was a Scot.

Only ones that showed he was like anyone else.

He was a Scot only according to the stories told by his family.

And those stories, about the doilies and mirrors from his grandmother's younger days but also reaching as far back as the seventeenth century, were different to other people's stories.

The Scot always insisted that his family were not some kind of economic refugees.

They had been invited. To a new town being created in the center of Europe.

And its ruler had invited them to that town.

Invited them because of their faith.

They were, after all, Protestant, the new town was Protestant, and they were wealthy.

Somewhat.

Out of all the Scot's Scottish stories there were two that Winston liked best.

One of the stories was about how one of his ancestors was going to build a Scottish house in that Protestant town.

And build it next to the town hall.

And the town hall, as it happens, was also being built at the same time.

By the municipality.

In keeping with the traditions of house building in that town at that time, many of the buildings stood joined to one another and shared a common wall.

The town elders tried to negotiate with the Scot's Scottish ancestor regarding the common wall and wanted to divide the cost in half, but the Scot's ancestor completely stopped the construction of his house.

And disappeared.

And reappeared only after several years.

When all six walls of the town hall had already been built.

The Scot's ancestor surveyed the town hall and, quietly, without any hindrance, adjoined his house to it.

"You see, Churchill, that's the Scottish way of doing things," said the Scot, explaining the situation.

"You call deceiving people the Scottish way of doing things?" Winston then asked.

"No," said the Scot. "It's just that the Scots are a very patient race."

"Wait for what," asked Winston.

"The moment," replied the Scot. "The right moment."

That's probably accurate, yes.

Especially taking into account how long the Scots waited for the right moment to exit the United Kingdom.

The other story about the Scot's family was about how one of his ancestors, probably the same one, opened a tobacco shop in his new house and taught all the locals to smoke.

In a civilized manner.

A pipe.

He ordered some long white Dutch porcelain pipes from the Netherlands.

Half a meter in length.

But after five wars—two of them world wars—all that was left were shards.

But were shards not proof enough?

The Scot's opium pipe bought in the Netherlands looked like a real work of art, even though it was an ordinary bamboo one, with a modest Yixing clay—and not ivory—bowl.

But.

With silver rings, jade tips, a tiger eye cabochon, and a beaten silver plaquette, decorated with a Foo dog, its teeth bared threateningly like a lion.

Most often these Foo dogs can be found in pairs outside Chinese restaurants.

Guarding the doors.

"That's enough," said the Scot's black beard.

The Scot had the shortest beard of all the members of the rugby veterans' club.

A French beard.

He came to this town because of the rugby.

It was through rugby that they had become friends.

Winston had to shave.

Not because Churchill needed to, but because the town's inhabitants did not trust people and in particular mayors hiding half of their face under hair.

"How's your side?" asked Winston.

"Healing. And how's your blood pressure?"

The whole town already knew about the Mayor's blood pressure.

"It's jumping up and down."

"That thing may quieten it down," said the Scot.

Although opium both heals and kills. And one had to be careful in using it.

When you have been friends with someone for more than twenty years you only need to say one word.

Or two.

Winston did not want to ask what the stabbing with the knife meant to the Scot.

An end to his career?

But he asked anyway.

"Are you coming back when you're fully recovered?"

The Scot did not reply.

But the opium covered up for him.

Would an international-class rugby referee return to the playing field after his side has healed?

The answer was obvious.

No.

And the reason was not just his wounded side but age as well.

What one could be jealous of the Scot for was his wife.

Not so much his wife but the fact that she had run away to America.

The fact that she had left the Scot forever and had moved beyond the horizon line from where no one would ever be able to bring her back.

Excepting the Russians.

Not unless the Russians were to turn the world on its axis and all of America found itself underwater.

As a result of the opium?

A thought came into Winston's head: it would be good if his wife were also to disappear.

Disappear in such a way that he would not even know to where and there would be no point in looking for her.

The Scot stood up holding his side in an unusual way.

He had no fat around his waist.

As far as one could see.

Crimes did occur in the town, but it was usually women that were attacked.

It wasn't clear if the perpetrators were locals or the visitors who came in from elsewhere for the remedies.

Perhaps they were locals since they had more energy and less to lose.

Besides that, only the visitors found things of interest in the town, while the locals were bored.

Besides that, the male visitors on arrival found companions amongst the women who were also there for the remedies.

They drank the mineral water together and took turns rolling around in the mud.

Whereas running around the town streets with a knife in their hands was really not their thing.

The Scot was still in pain.

That was clear.

But as a real rugby veteran he had enough self-esteem not to show it.

After all, they were like gladiators.

At least that was what their trainer used to say when there were no other arguments left to motivate them.

"The Geographer," said the Scot, yawning and shaking off the effects of the opium, his head enveloped by the pleasant smoke. "He's flown in."

The Scot hardly smoked any but still had to free himself from the effects.

"I heard," said the Mayor. "Tell him to buy an airplane because that helicopter of his is doing everyone's head in. And not to fly around at night high on opium. One disaster is more than enough for us."

"What disaster?" asked the Scot.

"What disaster? The ecological one."

The Geographer was one of those people whose presence was always felt even when they weren't around.

Everyone still talked and thought about him.

It would be better if the Geographer drove a car instead of flying.

But there was nothing anyone could do to change that.

What happened to him also happens to many people who suddenly, unexpectedly find success in life.

A sudden, irrational fear took hold of him.

The Geographer gradually began to be scared of intersections and traffic lights.

And then he became really afraid.

Several years ago the Scot had even asked him if anyone had ever driven into him or if he had been involved in any kind of accident. But the Geographer could not remember any accident.

"He flies around at night? I hadn't heard," said the Scot.

"You sleep well."

"And you sleep badly?"

Wherever it went, the conversation always seemed to veer off in the wrong direction.

Perhaps the opium was not of the best quality, perhaps it was not the opium at all, or perhaps because they were not smoking too much of it but only sampling it, Winston was still just about aware of his own feelings but no longer of any threat coming from the world.

"He doesn't have enough for an airplane now," said the Scot. "His chemical plant is up against the wall."

"From the Greens?"

"No, it's more serious than that. That's why he's flying around. That's why he's flying and looking."

"For what?"

"A direction."

"What??"

"A new direction. He's running like an elephant fleeing from a jungle fire."

"Did he find the Mercator?" asked the Mayor.

"Yes."

"Where?"

"In Belgium."

"How much?"

"Too much."

"A mill?"

The Scot nodded.

"Euros?"

People who become more successful than others suddenly, with that success, acquire all kinds of fears, both explainable and unexplainable.

One of them was that it was easy to lose everything.

But together with those fears he also acquired faith.

That somewhere there was a talisman able to protect him from all of that.

If Winston's hope was placed in a dried-out orange and his fear was limited to shortness of breath at night in bed, then it was the Geographer's belief that he could only be protected by two Mercators.

Even though the Scot said: one should not look at everything like that.

They were only toys.

Those Mercators.

Two toys for more than a million euros each.

Each.

To be more precise, three Mercators for almost four million.

Because everything began with a mistake.

The Geographer bought two Mercators but one of them was, it turned out, not a real Mercator.

This was confirmed to him by experts in sixteenth-century cartography.

And now it had to be replaced by a real one.

The one that was not real also appeared to be from the sixteenth century but not by Mercator but by another cartographer.

The experts suspected that the globe could have been made by Hondius even though officially he was not known to have made any globes.

"Registered?" asked Winston.

"What?" asked the Scot.

"That Belgian Mercator."

As the Geographer had told the Scot: only twenty-two pairs of officially registered Mercator globes were left in the world.

Twenty-two terrestrial ones and twenty-two celestial ones.

"Is that Mercator registered?" Winston repeated his question.

"No, it's not registered," said the Scot.

The Scot was interested in rarities.

He himself was a rarity.

And the Scot was interested in rarities that one could buy with the sort of money the Geographer had. The Geographer had bought a real Mercator terrestrial globe and a celestial globe that was not a real Mercator.

The fact that the globe the Geographer had acquired was not a Mercator was not, as it happens, difficult to ascertain.

One had to know only one secret.

That secret in the whole story about the globes was the one the Scot liked best.

In the world there were no two Mercator terrestrial or celestial globes that were the same.

In the world there could not be two globes exactly the same dedicated to the same person or at least not officially.

In the case of the Geographer, his celestial globe could not have been dedicated to George of Austria, Prince-Bishop of Liège, since such a globe was already registered in America.

In the Harvard Map Collection.

So, the Geographer's first foray as a collector of globes was half-way unsuccessful.

From that moment the Geographer's passion grew only greater and the hunt began.

He even managed to sell the fake Mercator globe.

For several thousand euros.

Without deceiving anyone.

But all that was from five years ago.

And the Geographer's hunt for a real Mercator celestial globe reminded Winston of looking for a bride in Arabian lands.

With the help of a portrait.

Those globes gladdened the Scot's heart.

Even more so than his set of opium tools.

Winston almost did not remember the globes.

Even though he had seen them.

In photographs.

All he remembered was that on the terrestrial Mercator globe North America was *separated* from South America.

A large Hippopotamus was depicted on it.

And then some kind of strange land was to be seen on it.

A Land of Pheasants or Penguins.

"What kind of land was that?" asked the Mayor.

"Where?"

"On that terrestrial globe?"

"On the terrestrial globe?"

"Yes. What name did it have on the globe? Land of Dolphins or Penguins?"

"Land of Parrots," said the Scot. "The opium must be working on you."


The Geographer used to recount how in some of those antique maps the European masters would intentionally mark out completely non-existent towns.

On the territory of America and not somewhere in Europe.

So that no one would suspect the deceit.

So that if anyone attempted to make copies of their maps the ones that made those copies could be caught out.

To prove their guilt in court.

"What did the Geographer have to say about those made-up towns?"

"I don't remember anymore," said the Scot.

"About the master cartographers specially making up all kinds of non-existent towns."

"Oh, they did that to protect their maps. It was a kind of copyright."

"Made-up towns," said Winston.

"What are you on about?" asked the Scot

"Those towns."

"Get those towns out of your mind."

The effect of the opium on the head had subsided and the desire to talk came on.

"Did he show you any photographs?"

"Of what?"

"The new globe."

"He did but all I remember is the backside of a centaur. That was probably the constellation of Sagittarius."

"And what did that backside look like?"

"Like that of an Arabian steed," said the Scot.

"Like that of an Arabian steed, meaning what?"

"With its tail raised."

"And what were the defects?"

The question was a professional one.

They talked so often about the Geographer's globes that they had almost become specialists in antique cartography.

The Geographer himself used to say that if you wanted to buy a sixteenth-century globe you had to come to terms with its defects in advance.

It was impossible to find a thing that was four hundred years old without defects.

"There's no shortage of defects," said the Scot. "It's dirty, damaged, stained, the worse for wear, and covered in shit."

"Covered in shit?" asked the Mayor.

The effects of the opium had worn off.

"Fly shit," said the Scot.

"Any mold?"

"No one had said anything about any mold. The lacquer might also have worn away," said the Scot. "And in places the paper joints have come apart."

"Come apart?" asked the Mayor.

"On the papier-mâché of the globe itself," explained the Scot. "In some places as much as several millimeters."

The Scot had a remarkable memory: he could remember everything for everyone.

"And the frame is broken," said the Scot.

"According to what's being said it seems to be real."

"That's quite possible," said the Scot.

Winston walked home, looking like the celestial globe—dirty, covered in the lake's toxic algae, damaged, stained, the worse for wear, and covered in fly shit.

From the inside.

Dawn was breaking.

TRANSLATED BY ROMAS KINKA

# SNEŽANA MLADENOVSKA ANGJELKOV

## *Beba*

FROM THE TALL APARTMENT tower, which I would often go to just so I could ride the elevator to the roof, there were the loveliest views of the surrounding buildings, of the park, and of the winding Vardar river. I would lie on my belly, pressed firmly against the hot tar roof, perched on the edge of a fifty-meter drop toward death, taking in everything around me. Sometimes I would bring some apricot seeds with me to play tricks on the passersby. Here, from up high, things look different. Owing, perhaps, to the sense of awe. The poplars aren't as tall, and the eggs in the crow and magpie nests are within reach. I loved these trips up into the sky. I didn't tell any-one about them, because of the girl from the police station, whose face once appeared on the ten-denar banknote after she survived a fall from the fifth floor, thanks to a hedge. I didn't want to put my luck to the test.

If I hadn't gone up to the roof, I would never have discovered the secret to Auntie Beba's good complexion. She appeared one sum-mer's day with suitcases and a young man with whom she spoke in French, showing up at the same place where two years before she had left behind her daughter, Ana, in tears, trying desperately to break free of her grandmother's grasp. The adults claimed that Auntie Beba ran a brothel in Paris, a gift from a patron, who is probably Ana's father. Perhaps they said it out of malice or envy, because Auntie Beba was a very beautiful woman, and as the old maids said: "She could have any man she wanted." Almost every day that summer, Auntie Beba climbed up to the roof of our build-ing with a hammock chair, a bottle of water, and a book in hand. From my vantage point on top of the apartment tower I could see her clearly in her denim shorts and red bra, finding the sunniest spot. Her colorful kimono was draped over one of the ventilators protruding from the roof, which I thought were chimneys. Then that young Frenchman of hers would come and rub lotion all over her, after which Auntie Beba gleamed like a goldfish. He would take her hand, kiss it, and, bowing deeply, take leave of Auntie Beba, who would be smiling from ear to ear.

It was fascinating to watch. Especially because Auntie Beba had no idea that anyone was watching. At least that's what I thought. One day she straightened up, shaded her eyes from the sun with her hand, and looked over at me on top of the apartment tower. I wanted to melt into the roof tar, or fall into a hole and just disappear together with all my shame. I kept my gaze firmly fixed on the ground. My heart was pounding fast.

Please stop looking at me, I thought to myself, just let me crawl away from here. I promise I won't stare at you anymore.

Slowly, I raised my head. Auntie Beba was standing in the same position. She beckoned me to come over. Dear God, how embarrassing! She'll tell Mom. Everyone'll find out. I shrank into myself. Auntie Beba was still beckoning to me.

I don't see another way out; I'll have to go over to her. I'll apologize, I'll cry for a bit, and then she'll let me go. With my heart racing, I descended fifty meters vertically into hell, then fifty meters horizontally through purgatory, and twenty meters up the stairs to . . . I reached the roof of my building. Lying next to the ventilator were the black kimono with colorful flowers and a pair of bunny slippers with tails, which we just used to call "bunnies."

Auntie Beba turned to face me, and with a smile said:

"You've arrived, chérie. Sit down here beside me."

She was holding a book in her hands—*Intimacy and The Room: Two Stories* by Jean Paul Sartre—with a nude woman on the cover.

"It seems as if we have something in common, chérie."

I stood there silently, awaiting my verdict. Everyone always pays a price for crime.

"What's your name, chérie?"

She addressed me warmly, which just made me feel even more anxious. I was on tenterhooks: when will this burst of friendliness erupt into hell.

"Speak up dear, don't be afraid."

"Maja," I lied.

"Come over here, Maja. Sit down beside me."

I sat down on top of the ventilator, right beside Auntie Beba.

"Do you like to look at things from up high?" she addressed me warmly again.

I nodded in agreement.

"You feel that you are omnipotent, like God!"

I said nothing. I didn't have that feeling. It was just that I could see much further. I could see a lot more than what you can when you're standing with both feet firmly planted on the ground.

"Do you know my daughter, Ana?" continued Auntie Beba with a smile on her face.

"I know her, but we don't hang out together," I replied.

"Why don't you hang out together, chérie?"

I was still trembling, I didn't have an answer to that question. I remained silent.

"Well, I suppose she's older than you, she's got other friends, but I'm sure you have something in common."

"I collect doilies." I figured that was the only thing that Ana and I could have in common.

"I don't know if she collects doilies, but I'll ask her," Auntie Beba said in a calm voice. "I sent her many things from France, but I don't think she's kept any of them. If she has, you can do a swap with her."

After a short pause Auntie Beba broached the main question that had been hanging in the air the whole time.

"Why do you climb up to the top of the apartment tower, chérie—what if you were to fall?"

"I won't fall," I replied quickly, staring at her "bunnies."

"Who are you checking out from up there? A young man, perhaps?"

"No," I answered curtly.

"Have you been doing this for a long time?"

"Well, for about two years, ever since I wanted to get away from Severjan."

"And who's Severjan?" Auntie Beba inquired with a smirk.

"A young Gypsy boy who was in love with me and followed me

around constantly. I felt stifled by him, so I had to get away."

"So you decided to watch how he runs after you from up high," Auntie Beba said, again with a smirk.

She had me firmly in the palm of her hand. I felt powerless.

"Better I should watch him than for him to hassle me," I said gathering up my courage.

"And what happened with Severjan, chérie?"

"Nothing. He fell in love with the girl from Galičnik and started following her around. He'd sit on the bench opposite the apartment block with a newspaper in his hands. He'd cut out eyeholes in the newspaper so that he could see through them."

"Hmm, cute, like a detective." Auntie Beba was attempting to enter into my story.

"There aren't any Gypsy detectives," I replied and turned my head toward the "bunnies."

"My boyfriend's a Rom," Auntie Beba said with pride, and let out a heavy sigh.

"Is he a detective," I asked in amazement.

"No, he's not. He plays the guitar. He's a true artist, chérie."

"But, isn't he French?" I asked in astonishment.

"Yes, but of Romani origin."

"Here at the market there's a boy, Kay. His mom's a Gypsy, but his dad's one of us. They live in Germany but stay here through the summer," I said, revealing my secret love to Auntie Beba. "He's very handsome, like your Frenchman."

"When you grow up, he might become your boyfriend."

"Oh, there's no chance of that! Mom'd kick me out of the house."

Auntie Beba burst into friendly laughter. I tried to memorize the way she tittered and chortled, the way that every muscle on her face moved when she laughed, so that I could practice it afterwards and laugh like that as well.

"When you're all grown up, your mother won't be able to tell you what to do. You'll do as you please." Auntie Beba wanted to steer me along her own path.

"But, if I make a mistake, there's no turning back."

"There's no turning back, but there is looking forward. What do I lack? Each day is better than the last."

"I sometimes sing at lunchtime." I wanted to see if there was any truth to the myth of the connection between singing at lunchtime and marrying a Gypsy.

"I sing, too—now more than ever since I have someone." Auntie Beba leaned forward in her hammock and grasped my hand in a gesture of farewell. "I enjoyed our conversation together, but don't ever let me see you on top of the apartment tower again."

I nodded in agreement, said a brief "bye," and went off.

That afternoon the girl from Galičnik and I climbed onto the garage roof to sunbathe. I'd attempted to make Bermuda shorts out of a pair of old jeans, just like Auntie Beba's. Up top, I had on a short vest with fringes, like a Native American. I had great strength within myself. I felt as if I could fly. I told the girl from Galičnik that one day I'd get married to Kay. She burst out laughing. Insulted, I turned away to face the street in front of our building. What appeared to be a bundle of rags was falling from the roof of our building toward the entrance. It fell at great speed. I heard a scream.

"What was that?" the girl from Galičnik gave a start, grabbing hold of my arm.

"Something fell from the building. I didn't see exactly what it was."

A crowd of people gathered at the entrance. They began calling out for help. Auntie Beba came running out in her colorful kimono as well. A crazed shriek had replaced the laughter on her face. She was no longer gleaming like a goldfish.

TRANSLATED BY PAUL FILEV

# PHILIP HUFF

## *A Comfort of Sorts*

ISABEL EMERGED FROM the house's shadow in her socks, trainers in hand, holding a blue cap over her eyes.

"Good afternoon, signorina," I said.

I was squatting near the little wall next to the swimming pool, and put the trowel back into the black bucket containing the last of the cement, sweat pouring off my back and brow.

"So, sleepyhead," I said, walking over to the deck chair in the shadow of the large holm oak. "Did you sleep well?"

Isabel nodded, still somewhat sleepy.

I put my arm around her waist and pulled her tightly to me, her running shirt taut over her breasts. I pressed my head against her belly. The fine hairs on her thighs had a golden sheen. Isabel put her hand on my neck and turned my head toward the staircase I was in the process of constructing.

"So," she said. "You've been busy."

"Inspiration," I said, pulling her shirt up and kissing her flat stomach.

Isabel freed herself and moved to sit in front of me, on the foot of the deck chair. She put on her shoes. There was dirt under her fingernails. Her lower back was the color of caramel.

"You're already getting a tan," I said.

Isabel nodded, pulled up her socks and then rolled them down just a little bit. She stood up with a sigh. Her legs cast two thin shadows on the terrace.

I put my hand on her calves. "Show-off," I said.

"Well, a little bit, yes," she said, now appearing to also feel the heat. "But at least I still can. For a while. Not long. Soon I'll be round as a frying pan." She pulled up her nose and stuck out her tongue in disgust.

"Be careful," I said.

She put on her cap.

"Of course."

As Isabel disappeared among the quiet blue spruce trees at the end of the road, I turned to the steps. They would lead to the outdoor kitchen that was to be built on this side of the house.

When I had bought the house from a local official seven years earlier, it was a modest three-room dwelling. It had expanded over time: an addition with an extra bedroom; a larger swimming pool; a garage; a second terrace that caught the afternoon sun. The next obvious step was an outdoor kitchen.

I had built that garage myself. I had poured its foundations. I had leached planks, built a frame, and put up a roof. The latter was the most difficult. And I had wanted to do it well. I used more than twenty tubes of adhesive fixing the shingles. I later told this to the contractor who was building the outdoor kitchen, causing him to almost wet himself laughing. "For a roof of this size," he told me, "two tubes should be more than enough."

A twenty-minute cold shower, washing away the heat of the day. A clean pair of linen trousers. A shirt. A bottle of wine, silently uncorked, poured into a solitary glass.

The absence of work, of course, but also of a social life. No friends, no dinners, no birthdays, no acquaintances encountered in the grocery store. This was what drew us to Umbria again and again. Isabel and I could go for miles without coming across anyone we knew.

I packed the small blue box that I would give to her shortly, my book, two glasses, and two bottles: white wine for myself, water for Isabel. I set down two ceramic bowls on the table. These were local products that Isabel had bought. One of them was filled with pistachios.

I opened my book at the folded page and started to read. I only looked up again when I was disturbed by the drone of a helicopter. Once the helicopter passed, I noted how silent and empty it had become.

It was half past six. The sun was approaching the end of its high arc through the sky. I looked at the blue box.

What time did Isabel leave for her run? At three? Half past? How long did she usually stay gone for?

I got up and walked to the edge of the terrace, up to where the graveled path began. Fixed to that spot, I gazed out over the valley. There was no movement, no sound; even the river seemed to be quiet. On the other side of the valley, the dark trees on the hill were utterly still. Behind them the sky was soft, and pale, and bottomless.

A bird appeared, flying up from behind the hill, tracing slow circles in the summer sky.

Then the gravel cracked under the broad tires of the neighbor's car at the curve in the road.

I walked down the path, just as Isabel had done, heading along the spruce trees, through the open gate, and stopped the approaching SUV. The tinted window on the passenger side rolled down. I greeted Mrs. Vierchowod and her husband, Silvio, in the driver's seat. Mrs. Vierchowod's hair was freshly dyed raven-black, her skin turned dark brown by the sun, wrinkled and sagging down into the deep décolletage of her dress.

"What's the matter?" she asked.

I smiled at her carefully. "Have you," I began. "Have you by any chance seen Isabel?"

"Isabel? Just now?"

I nodded.

"No," said Mrs. Vierchowod and turned to her husband.

"She went for a run more than two hours ago," I said. "Usually she doesn't stay out for so long, but now she's, of course . . ." But the words got stuck in my throat.

Near the dilapidated, large wooden billboard for Casa Vattimo, on the way to Todi, we saw a car on the side of the road: an Audi Cabriolet. The road surface was torn up. It showed fresh brake marks.

Mr. Vierchowod put the SUV into reverse, parked it on the

shoulder, and pulled up the handbrake. He switched on the hazard lights. As he opened his door, the car emitted a long piercing tone that cut through the regular tick of the hazards: the headlights were still on, illuminating nothing, a safety measure.

Even with my espadrilles on, the surface of the road warmed my feet. I walked towards the vehicle, sweat on my brow. The Audi was damaged on the front right-hand side. The headlight was cracked. The metal of the engine valve was slightly contorted. The air smelled of rubber.

That was when I saw Isabel's blue cap lying in the grass, spattered with drops of blood, like a darker and more permanent version of raindrops.

I looked at Mrs. Vierchowod. She had lifted her hand to cover her mouth. A car came racing past at high speed.

"Please, don't worry about it too much," Mrs. Vierchowod said on the way to Perugia. "This kind of thing usually turns out fine. In my experience . . ."

I wasn't listening. That's the advantage of a foreign language: if you don't focus on it, you don't have to understand any of it. I looked out the window, at the sycamores lining the road. "Army trees" is what my brother used to call them. He was dead now. I hadn't though of him for some time, although I saw those trees every day.

But then some of Mrs. Vierchowod's words did reach me after all: *ospedale, la tua Isabella, niente.*

I met Isabel for the first time in Rotterdam. It was summer. We were at an office party. She was standing in the hallway, queuing for the men's toilets, wearing a thin summer dress. Her bra was clearly visible.

"Quite the party," I said.

"Yes," she nodded, her drink's straw clamped between her pearly teeth, her long, slender fingers wrapped around it. The skin of her shoulders had the sheen of an orange. I felt the need to touch her.

"Let me introduce myself," I said.

Isabel let the straw fall back into the glass. "Isabel Niemandsverdriet." She stuck out her hand.

"What a beautiful name," I said. "Niemandsverdriet—No man's sorrow. Is it your own, or your husband's?"

She gave an almost invisible smile. "My father's."

"And what else did you inherit from your father? Your passion for the law? A castle? Musical talent?"

"Well, not exactly," she said, this time with a bigger smile.

We both glanced at the toilet door. It was still locked.

"You work here in the data room, right?"

"Yes. And I'm still studying."

"What?"

"International and European law."

"There you go. You inherited the passion after all," I said, taking a pack of cigarettes out of my inside pocket and offering her one.

"My father works for the harbor." And: "Thanks, but I don't think we're allowed to smoke inside."

I lowered the cigarettes. "Not even tonight?"

"Not even tonight."

We shared a moment of silence. I was hoping that whoever was occupying the toilet would take his sweet time.

"You're taller than I expected," Isabel said.

I gave her a questioning look.

"Word on the street is, you're a little despot. But you're actually quite tall."

Later that evening, when I let her walk ahead of me into the hotel room, I touched the skin of her shoulder for the first time. It was even softer than I had imagined.

I entered the room through two sets of automatic doors. It smelled of antiseptics and plastic. A squat woman in a blue uniform and disposable hair cap approached me. Before she could say anything, I saw Isabel.

She was lying in a large bed, between green sheets. Her torso was covered with all kinds of tubes and cords. There was an ECG monitor behind her. Then I heard the mechanical drone of the respirator, echoing the sound of the helicopter, and started to shake all over: my hands, my knees, my arms shivering. As I stepped closer, I felt my heart tighten.

Isabel's face was as still as a high and empty sky. A sky where there was nothing to see.

I visited her grave for the first time ten days after the funeral. It was an anonymous spot in the earth, not yet covered by grass.

"It is a pretty place," I said, "where you're buried. Your mother, in any case, finds it quite beautiful. It looks just like the garden at your old home. So she says." I had to smile. "You know, Bel, I think your mother still doesn't quite like me . . . But what I said about you at the funeral . . . Well, at least she thought that was nice. I think. I decided to rather not tell her . . ."

But I couldn't finish the sentence. The remaining air in my lungs escaped in spurts and gasps.

During the funeral, I had felt emptier than ever, all emotions having been wrung from my body. It was with difficulty that I hoisted myself up from the wooden bench to address the people present. My mouth was so dry that the inside of my lips kept sticking to my front teeth. The microphone hissed every time I pronounced an S.

The world became blurry. "It's unreal," I said, kneeling at Isabel's grave. "And I'm sorry about it. But I have real difficulty picturing your face. Even though I want to. The only thing I can imagine with any degree of sharpness is your hands. And your belly. That too. But I can barely remember your face. Or your voice. So I call your cell phone, to listen to your voicemail. It's wonderful to hear you speak. A comfort of sorts."

"I'm not a smoker anymore," she said the next day, in the hotel room. "Haven't been for four years now."

"But," I said, "when you, when I, when yesterday we . . ."

"Telling you then would not have been a good start," she said. "I wanted to give you some space. To figure out what you wanted."

And upon parting she said, "I would quite like to see you again soon. But that's up to you."

I smiled and thought: I will remember this until the day I die.

I'm kneeling behind Isabel on the bed. It's warm in the room. My hands slide slowly over her back. I can count the fine hairs. I take off my underpants and throw them onto a chair in the corner.

Now she's lying before me on the bed, her legs folded underneath her body, her rump facing me, her arms alongside her body. I slide my fingertips further down, along her spine, down to the shallow basins above her backside. This is the softest place on her body, softer even than her cheeks or shoulders or the hairless streak behind her ear. It's the softest skin I have ever touched.

I kiss the two hollows, the two soft parts. A selection of fine hairs, quite isolated, quite vulnerable, are pulled upright as her skin tightens with the excitement of gooseflesh. My hands slide down the side of her back to her belly. I slip my fingers under her black panties and feel a clump of short, coarse pubic hair. Isabel breathes in long and gently, arching her shoulders backward.

I let my hands slide up her and take hold of her breasts. Then I move my torso slowly up her back, until my chin reaches the vertebrae of her neck, and I press my lower body hard against her rear.

"I want you so badly," I say.

"Yes, I can feel that."

I push my hard cock through the fabric of her underpants, deeper into the cleft of her buttocks.

"What do you want?" she asks.

"I want to fuck you," I say.

"Where?"

"Where I said I wanted to fuck you this morning."

"And where was that?" she asks.

I place my right hand firmly on her ass, between my body and hers, and slide a finger into her panties, pushing it up against a small opening, and further until my fingertip is engulfed.

"Here."

She didn't think when she was out running. That's what she enjoyed about running: the thoughtlessness, the automatism of putting one foot ahead of the other.

As was her habit, she set out to cross the road diagonally. She would continue down a path that curved around the hill, leading to the house.

She didn't look before crossing. Didn't think of it. She was running.

When a young woman stepped in front of the vehicle, it was too late for the driver to slam on the brakes. He swerved to the side.

She needs to concentrate when I enter her, but it's a nice kind of concentration, she says. It lets her feel like she's completely surrendering to me, and that I am occupied with her and her alone. That we are the only people on earth, the only bodies that matter.

I carefully slide myself into her, only the first few centimeters until I notice the resistance waning and the muscles in her thighs beginning to relax. Then I go deeper.

"You belong to me," I say. "To me and to nobody else."

"Yes," she says. "Yes. I belong to you."

Barely visibly, her shoulder blades keep tempo with the mounting rhythm of my hips.

"The point is that you are here," I say. "Here, and nowhere else. In this moment. In this place."

I got down on my knees and touched the grave's dark soil. The ground was wet and cool. I produced a small box containing a ring out of my jacket's inner pocket and opened it. Using my thumb, I pushed the gold deep down into the earth. I sat there for some time, staring at the pores of my skin, the loose hairs. I tried to breathe out the rage I was feeling and to find some of the other emotions I used to have.

I knew that ultimately we are time, and that time is nothing more than a place we continually have to leave behind. But she wore the sunlight so well, I thought, and I would have loved to keep her close.

I covered the holes left by my fingers with earth, stood up and brushed off my hands.

As the cemetery gate shut behind me, a murder of crows took off from the tree near the entrance. Cawing loudly, they flew over the grassy field next to the cemetery. I followed them with my eyes until the last of them disappeared into the shadow of a tree on the other side of the field and once more it became quiet. I got into the car.

TRANSLATED BY JAN STEYN

# MIKKEL BUGGE

## *Surrounded*

"I'm so glad we have a daughter," my wife says after she finally manages to get Marie to sleep. "If there's something I hate, it's these gangs of teenage males." I glance up from the local paper. A couple of pages back I was reading about how the neighborhood is being taken over by immigrant gangs from North Africa. It said that I was the only one who could prevent chaos. I could use all necessary means. I had been given a mandate from the highest order.

Our apartment has two small rooms and a kitchen. At night we lie close together, but we haven't had sex for several months. The electricity fails several times a day and the butter is soft when I take it out of the fridge in the morning. The windows are small. While we eat breakfast I hear the dull sound of iron bars beating on flesh and bone. The youths don't stop. Do the cries come from the old man in the cellar? From the caretaker? I know my turn is coming soon, but I don't say anything to my wife, who is feeding Marie with a little plastic spoon.

Two nights later, on the way back from the corner shop I am surrounded. They have black batons and pocketknives. I throw myself backwards while I fumble for the gun in my ankle holster, but one of them strikes my skull and the pain pounds through me. They stab me in the arms, they hit me in the face. Static noise reverberates in my ears. Somehow I manage to get hold of the gun. I fire the first shot, then the next. I can't feel anything anymore. Two of the boys fall, the third one runs away. I shoot him in the back. He falls, but keeps crawling along. I get up and hop towards him on one leg, then I shoot him in the head as he lies there.

When I wake up, I'm in a hospital. The walls are not white, but a greyish beige. They say I've had an accident. I've lost sight in one eye and the movement in one of my arms, but the most important thing is that I'm alive. A woman enters the room, cries, and hugs me. She smells like linen and jam. Beside her stands a girl who says, "Hi Dad."

I hug the girl. Her body is as compact and solid as an athlete's.

An investigator wants to talk to me. He apologizes for the injuries I have sustained and assures me that the interview is a pure formality. I have done the neighborhood a big favor. The boys I killed were scum.

"We should have more people like you," he says, taking my hand. It's sweaty, and he pulls back his own a little too hastily.

I am moved back into what used to be my home. I do my best to behave as if I understand what is happening. When she who calls herself my wife tells me about her day at work, I listen and nod.

We lie next to each other, curled up like little balls. We constantly invent new movements. We are animals, and animals will not be subdued. We don't beg for help. We are not to be pitied. We fall asleep lying close together. It must be completely acceptable to get up in the middle of the night and go to the toilet or out on the balcony to smoke a cigarette. I should be able to resist. I lie there, looking at her in the light from the hallway, and don't manage to move. I want to stretch out my hand and stroke my fingers gently across her cheek.

*

It is Sunday. A girl leaps from the fifth floor wearing an Alice in Wonderland costume. Her friends pull her up from the concrete and take her to the emergency room. It's late winter. A slushy winter.

The broadband isn't working well. At least twenty percent of your portfolio should be weighted toward emerging economies. Inflammation. Bulging eyes and the hope of a short convalescence. Impatience. Information. Intravenous. Solar eclipse. Suicide. Sanitary napkin. A chaotic tumult.

Marie screams.

She kicks and hits.

She has lost the green duck.

I bend down by the sofa, stick my right hand under it, and press my fingers forward in order to grab hold of the little duck which is lying a little further in. I press myself more closely to the floor while I attempt to squeeze my shoulders underneath so my hand will reach further and my fingers will find their way, but first I have to lift the sofa itself with my left hand, which is not and never will be as strong as the right hand, but which nevertheless succeeds in lifting it high enough so that both my arm and my head slide underneath it just at the moment when my fingers encircle the duck's head.

*

I sign up for duty in a foreign mission. It's not a personal desire, I tell my wife one evening, it's a mission. We fly low over a mountain chain at night, and I see no sign of life beneath us. At the camp I meet a young man whose name is Omer. He has a scar across his left cheek. His eyes are glittering. We are given the task of cleaning the toilets together, and we tell each other stories to pass the time. He tells me that his father grew up in a Yemeni village more than eighty years ago. At the age of sixty he left the village and married Omer's mother. He looks around when he tells the story, speaking in a low voice. There is an intimacy in his tone. We scrub the urinals assiduously.

In the twilight, just before I fall asleep, some people approach me. They encroach on me from all directions, but I can't see what they are holding in their hands. Suddenly, I am surrounded. They stand there for a couple of seconds. Then they start shooting. They can't be bothered to aim, they just lift the barrels of their guns and fire away. The bullets are fired again and again. I shoot back. The first shot hits the closest one in the thigh. He falls immediately, but the rest of them remain, unflustered, and continue to hammer the bullets in our direction. I spot Omer. He is lying in a pool of blood on the floor. I can't help staring at his hands. Afterwards all is silent.

*

One day.

Then another.

Then yet another.

Desert.

One of them extracts the toenail of my big toe. I scream with pain. Another stretches out my cock and makes an incision along the shaft.

I writhe away, but they hold me down.

I pass out.

I am woken by the pain in my crotch. It stabs me all the way up into my stomach. I lie in a small, dark room. I feel around with my fingers. A stone in the floor is loose. When I kick at it with my heel, I catch a glimpse of the light in the floor below. I understand that I am supposed to find my way out of the room. I dig and tear away stones until the hole is large enough. Then I jump down. The room is empty. I approach a door, open it, and start walking down a corridor. Suddenly I see a man leap from behind a box. In his hand he has a machine gun which peppers bullets towards me with a deafening blare. I attempt to fling myself sideways, but it's too late and the bullets riddle my body, again and again. I get up. I throw myself at him and strangle him with my bare hands. His neck is so soft. He looks surprised. I don't let go until I hear the sound of others nearby. I find a pistol and shoot those who are coming towards me. I regain control of my body and storm on. I am in a zone where everything is possible. The bullets whine past my ears. I get hit in the shoulder, am torn to the ground, but refuse to fall, and continue running.

*

My doctor has a mild, warm face, and tells me that she has a daughter who is the same age as mine. I think to myself that it's easier to imagine how her face looked when she was cramming for that first exam in physiognomy than when she gave birth to her daughter. She asks if I am tired, are you tired, she asks, emphasizing the first part of tired, as if she is as tired as I am.

I constantly find new reasons to visit the doctor. On the padded chairs in her hallway, others sit waiting, but they are not like me. I have showered and am freshly shaved. I don't badger her and always remember to pay. She refers me to specialists, but it's her I want to talk to. At night I sneak into the toilet and masturbate while I fantasize about her. She doesn't undress. She remains sitting in her doctors' coat, watching me while smiling. Then she stretches out her hand and touches me. She holds me tightly. When I am having sex with my wife, I close my eyes and think about her. She allows me to come closer to her than anyone else. We grow together. I have to fight to avoid coming straight away and open my eyes. My wife has closed her eyes. She leans her head backwards. I hold out.

One day at work I look up her Facebook profile. I don't understand why I haven't done this before. I hear footsteps behind me and I immediately click back to the order invoice I was typing on. A colleague says:

"We have three outstanding from Kronberg, should I take them, or will you do it?" "I can do it," I reply, and he turns behind me and says "Facebook-babes, huh? Thought you were settled."

*

I'm standing in a park. It's Sunday. My daughter sits in her stroller next to me. We have forgotten to bring water, but my wife has been shopping. She crosses the street, her head at a slight angle, as if she is zooming in on me with her eyes. I think that I have now succeeded. This was all it took. It's morning. There's hardly anyone around. Only the birds.

The car that hits her is a yellow Golf with grimy side windows. Afterwards she lies completely still on the pavement. I turn the stroller so my daughter won't see. The driver is a woman in her fifties wearing a large shawl. She drops down onto her knees next to my wife. This is the moment when I should go towards them, but I just stand there, hearing my daughter cry.

Three days later there is a letter in the mailbox. It's a love letter from my wife. She loves my mouth and how I get European capitals starting with B mixed up. Budapest, Bratislava, Berlin. Bucharest. I can recognize her cough anywhere. The thin body that rattles with every cough.

*

I have stopped waking up.

   I go to bed every night.

   I brush my teeth.

   I take out my contact lenses.

   I read a comic about zombies.

   I fall asleep and dream that it's morning.

   My daughter is already up. She is standing in the kitchen making breakfast. She is wearing a pink bathrobe and preparing crisp bread with brown goat's cheese. She is talking about how drunk she was when she came home last night. Then she continues to read the paper. Her face is hard. It's overcast outside, but the light is still terribly sharp. I understand that my wife is dead. She has lost the battle against lymphatic cancer and was buried a few weeks ago. I am uncomfortable in my new role as sole caregiver. Marie looks at me and asks if I want something to eat. I say I don't feel well and am just going to lie down a little. She looks at me with a worried expression. I assure her that it's not serious and go back into the bedroom. I lie down and fall asleep almost immediately.

   It's dark outside. There is no one else in the house. I lie there listening to the cars driving past. Everything is the same, nothing changes. I know that there are enemies under every roof. I can see that the leaves on the trees are concealing larvae. I am conscious of what is happening. I have a definite will. I am aware of the difficulties.

*

Marie and I travel by ferry from Trondheim to Båtsfjord. I am going to show her Norway. We have been saving up for eight months. Our cabin is airy with a large window facing the horizon and the islands in the open sea. In the evening we have the Fruits of the Sea menu together with a couple from Botswana.

The next morning I get up before her. I walk around the almost empty ship. We are far out at sea, and it's still dark outside. Out on deck I catch sight of a man who is taking photos of something in the water. When I get closer I see that it is the man who tortured me. I go over to him. I stand there studying the fingers holding the camera. The nails are bitten a long way down. I leap up and kick him in the neck. The camera flies over the edge. I tumble to the ground. The man hangs over the railing. Suddenly I feel unsure of whether it is him or not. He turns. Now I'm sure. It's not him. But I've seen his face before. Maybe we were once childhood friends. Maybe we sat next to each other at a bar counter. I want to apologize. I want to make the situation different. But he leaps at me, grabs hold of my head and starts banging it against the deck.

*

I start again.

This time I am in the Arctic wilderness. It's twilight. I creep along an iceberg that's several hundred meters high. In the distance, I can hear the ice crack. I am on a mission to locate a defector from Ukrainian special forces who has stolen three nuclear warheads and has a plan to destroy the world. With my night binoculars I see everything. I have walked for several miles and will continue for several more, but suddenly I can sense my motivation failing me. I don't want to, I think. I sit down. I think of Marie. It gets warmer and warmer.

*

It's morning. Marie comes in with breakfast for me. She says that I am going to get better soon. She's gotten a job in the Research Institute of the Armed Forces. She now has a boyfriend who is a top diplomat who can speak six languages. They do a lot of hiking in the mountains and have already decided never to have any children. I grind my teeth and know that the sound is unendurable. I open my eyes wider and wider. I press my fingers into my thigh.

She disappears. It's light outside, but the blackout curtains make the room dark.

\*

I start again.

I am the token female in a comedy show on TV Norway. I squeeze my thighs tightly together under my short skirt. This does not make sense. I am in an institution. The walls are not white, they are a greyish beige. On the TV close to the ceiling, I see the token female in a comedy show. She squeezes her thighs tightly together under her short skirt. A nurse comes over to me. He asks me to come with him. I struggle to get up from the chair but manage it in the end. He accompanies me to the Director's door and lets me enter alone. The office is opulent and old-fashioned. Heavy teak and books lining all the walls. The Director gets up from the desk and approaches me. He is a man in his late forties. I take his hand and sense how he is attempting to signal his own vulnerability without using any words. I stroke my thumb across his thumb and take in the thoughts that come streaming. He has an oral fixation he does not dare to realize. He tries to find new ways of concealing his hair loss. He sometimes views his patients as cattle moving through a labyrinth which he alone has a full view of. He has never stopped eating his own snot, the consistency of which makes him ever more curious.

We sit down. He says I am making progress. He views me as a bright person who has made some wrong choices. I try to answer him, but he gets up and comes towards me. He lifts the other hand: it is disproportionally large and full of grazes, bites, and cuts. First I try to get away, but then I let him do it. He lays it over my face, presses two fingers into my eyes, and squeezes.

\*

A man sits smoking in the corner of my room. I can't make out his face. He says he knows I've got one more mission in me.

"I have known you for so long and I'm sure you'll manage this," he says.

His voice sounds familiar, but I can't place it. My stomach hurts. It's burning and I make an effort to avoid showing any pain.

"This isn't a simple mission. If it had been we wouldn't have come to you."

The man disappears. I get up and step out of bed. My feet feel stronger than they have in a long time. I have been given a project. I have an aim. I have to manage this.

I take a shower, get dressed, and go out. The house is surrounded by identical houses with gardens, trees, and children cycling around. Neighbors greet me. I don't need any help. My car is a red Mazda from the sixties. It has more horsepower than I need and soft leather seats. The weapons in the trunk, under the seat, in the dashboard, and in the door make me feel safe. I roll down the windows and play the Rolling Stones at full blast while driving.

I screech to a halt in front of the school and jump out of the car. There are almost no people in the streets. I open the trunk. It's now or never.

*

I start again.

Minesweeping using people. IV drips. Tractor tracks. Her face before she falls asleep. Things that begin with S. Sewage system, sun cells, sister of the Shah. Rain over Esfahan. I am torn to pieces. The Khmer Rouge. The Kalahari Desert three years later. I meet my wife. We kiss on the way to work. I like her more and more. I run to catch the bus. I can't get over how lucky we are. We have to sleep now but can't help talking. The words continue even though we are no longer there. A boy who lives in the basement cuts off the tip of his little finger. Hang in there. We're not comparing ourselves with anyone. We meet a fat couple on their way home that night. They look so happy.

I start again.

This time I am the dictatorship of the proletariat I am Pakistan's secret police I am Queen Elizabeth I am South Ossetia I am the genocide in Rwanda I am Acquired Immune Deficiency Syndrome I am the Janjaweed Militia I am the last copper virus I am Guantanamo Bay I am the Niger Delta I am the categorical imperative I am Huntington's Disease I am Anna Politkovskaya I am NATO I am the pancreas I am the Democratic Republic of Congo I am the Prophet Muhammad I am the Victoria Falls I am Pol Pot I am the Waffen-SS I am resistant tuberculosis I am Jerusalem I am the Industrial Revolution I am the American Ambassador to Afghanistan I am gulag I am Leukemia I am Cambodia I am The Great Migrations.

TRANSLATED BY SARAH OSA

# AGNIESZKA TABORSKA

FROM *Not As In Paradise*

### BROTHER-IN-LAW

J. was shopping in the supermarket of a small town in the Auvergne where for years he had spent his holidays. In the frozen food department, a gentlemen ran up to him with a huge smile on his face. Before J. managed to place the pack of bacon he had just taken off the shelf in his cart, the gentleman flung his arms round his neck and kissed him twice on both cheeks. Having extracted himself from the man's embrace, J. put the bacon down in the cart and took half a step backwards to get a better view. He scrutinized the stranger but remained convinced he had never seen him before. Meanwhile the man continued to show signs of joy, patted J. on the shoulder, kept repeating "What a meeting!" and laughed so loudly that other shoppers glanced over at them intrigued. Losing patience, J. struggled to stay civil. "It's very nice of you, but we don't know each other," he said. The man stood still for a second in amazement, after which he roared with even louder laughter. "What on earth do you mean?" he yelled. "I didn't realize I had a joker for a brother-in-law!" "Brother-in-law?" "Surely my brother-in-law! Who else?" he yelled, louder still. J. was not amused by the scene that was dragging on too long. "I am not your brother-in-law!" he repeated several times more, but the other only thumped him on the back with ever greater energy. The incident ended just as suddenly as it began. The exasperated J. finally took his driving license out of his pocket and shoved it under the stranger's nose, thereby interrupting the cascade of laughter and back-slapping. Then he walked away without saying good-bye, pushing the cart with the bacon in front of him and postponing the rest of his shopping until another day. He left the pseudo-brother-in-law with mouth wide open in astonishment, a wounded heart, and the conviction he had fallen victim to a monstrous conspiracy.

## WAITERS

In *The Discreet Charm of the Bourgeoisie*, in one of the scenes where the protagonists experience yet more frustration at being unable to eat a meal, the perpetually surprised Parisiennes learn that the kitchen is even out of water. M. and I once ordered freshly squeezed orange juice in a café. I don't know whether the waiter had seen Buñuel's film, but he returned with an equally courteous explanation: the juicer had fallen apart while processing our order. Another incident happened to us one late afternoon in a pub near Wilanów. I received my potato pancakes very quickly. I finished eating and was admiring the setting sun. M. was still waiting. As usual, he had ordered the most complicated dish. I had been wondering how in such a modest dive they were going to prepare the snails, which featured nevertheless on the menu. I got the impression M.'s choice had been noted with a certain anxiety . . . The sun went down, traces of dried froth glistened on the sides of our beer glasses, it grew chilly. M., not for the first time, held forth to me about the virtues of genuine cuisine, which in contrast to fast food requires preparation. On this occasion, however, his words of truth did not allay my disquiet. The fact that we were the only customers in the garden did not bode well. Abandoning M. to visions of the chef bustling over his meal in the kitchen, I went to have a look around. The restaurant, however, was shut, the lights switched off, the chef and waiters long gone home. I was not surprised, only troubled by the thought of M.'s disappointment. Perhaps we should have been more suspicious earlier on, when a knife and fork appeared on the table instead of a snail skewer. Had the staff run away because professional honor prevented them from admitting they didn't know how to prepare a dish listed on the menu? Before they fled, had they come to blows in the kitchen? Had they done a bunk through the back exit after locking the main door from the inside? Otherwise we surely would have noticed. Or perhaps the chef had been the victim of a crime? Bleak scenarios teem inside my head as the hungry M. and I leave the deserted garden, above which a full moon is just beginning to rise.

## WATER BEDS

I took a liking to H. from the time of our first conversation when, asked what he most missed in Warsaw, he replied: "junk mail." In those days we didn't really understand what he was talking about. H. arrived in Poland in the mid-1980s during the death throes of socialism, by mistake. The University of Warsaw had sent a leading authority on Baroque architecture to Cleveland on a year's exchange, expecting in return a scholar of equivalent status. The university administration was not functioning at its most efficient, however, and so it was H., a sculptor and hippy, who disembarked at Okęcie Airport. He came with his large family, all very laid-back, smiling and amicably disposed toward the world. Unaware of the mistake, H. and his wife took up residence in a regular tower block and sent their kids to a local school, hoping ten months would suffice for them to pick up the hissing language. Then they set about familiarizing themselves with a country stunned by their presence. During that year a fire broke out in their uninsured American house and destroyed everything. On their return, they had to start all over again, like eighteenth-century settlers. The first thing they did was purchase water beds—for the whole family plus guests. This impulse, understandable in their situation, was prompted by an advertising campaign unleashed in the newspapers and on television at precisely that moment. Soon afterwards M. and I flew to the States. On our way from the East to the West Coast we visited them in their new home. We spent a sleepless night lying on a double water bed, taking care lest any movement from one should catapult the other onto the floor. We genuinely enjoyed our reunion with H. but, confronted by the prospect of another night, we cut short our visit. Not long afterwards, like thousands of Americans who had succumbed to the fleeting fashion, H. and his family were faced with the difficult task of disposing of the beds, as several hundred liters of water had to be pumped from every mattress! How they managed it, I have no idea. Ever since then, whenever I cannot get to sleep, instead of counting sheep, I remember my night in Ohio. I then feel a little better. Although I continue to regret that, thanks to the inventor of water beds, we didn't stay longer with H. As a souvenir of that visit, we have a ceramic dragon standing in our Warsaw bathroom. No one remembers water beds anymore, but the dragon—transported across so many states and masterfully packed for plane travel—looks brand new.

## AIRPLANE

For the past quarter century I have been travelling twice a year across the Atlantic and have watched a lot of films in airplanes. For reasons I would rather not go into, a fair proportion of them portray if not air disasters then at any rate panic on board. I have seen *Turbulence*, *The English Patient*, and *Airplane!*, in addition to other films which, despite the melodrama, were bad enough to erase themselves from my memory. Who selects the intercontinental repertoire? The most logical answer would be: representatives of competing airlines. Passengers on a flight from Ohio to Detroit, however, did not have to wait until the start of the screening for their nerves to be severely tested. Here is the description of an event recently supplied by the press. It began with a female passenger, next to whom a nun from the Convent of Our Lady of Mercy in Dayton, Ohio, sat down. Having settled comfortably by the window, the nun pulled out her rosary and began to whisper her prayers in Latin. "I was at once suspicious," the passenger said later. "She was wearing a Muslim headscarf and just before takeoff was mumbling something in Arabic." "As soon as she entered the cabin, I noticed she had an odd grim look about her," another passenger testified. The alarmed stewardess asked Sister Cora-Ann for her documents. Hearing her name sounded like Koran, a third passenger sitting nearby informed the rest of the travellers. "Once we discovered the suspect was called Koran, we couldn't control our emotions any longer," explained someone from the back row. Before the hysteria reached its zenith, someone else pushed a piece of ham in Cora-Ann's direction. If she fails to eat it, then it will prove she is a Muslim. Since the incident took place during Lent, the nun did not eat it. The passengers calmed down only after she had left the plane. "As soon as she got off, we felt as if a huge burden had been lifted from our shoulders," rejoiced the next passenger. Meanwhile the only Muslim on board, Abdullah Abdullah XXIII, kept his mouth well sealed, just in case.

## SPELL

I had the misfortune to visit one of our Polish cities with a foreign friend who had hired for the occasion a local guide. He was a young man exuding an icy professionalism, typical of his generation, that wiped the smiles from our faces. Another reason for our wilting smiles was the masochistic, martyrological tone of the information he imparted. Even I, raised after all in this land, was impressed. In a voice that bore no contradiction, the good-looking fellow informed us about wars, invasions, rapes, and betrayals, perpetrated by our so-called allies, and the indifference of the world at large. The powerful word "genocide" summed up every event described. His gloomy monologue was interrupted only by questions directed at my friend and disapproving frowns at her answers, which proved her ignorance of the history of this country. The poor woman muttered something in reply with an escalating sense of guilt, no doubt mentally cursing her decision not to have chosen a more cheerful destination. The list of nations waiting to do "us" in was so phenomenally long that my own birth started to appear barely possible. The guide's attitude toward the perpetrators was highly personal, and the punch line to most of his tales prophesied well-deserved revenge. I had already begun to tremble for the safety of the tourist who did not belong to our clan, when he revealed a human face, magnanimously announcing that we had forgiven the Swedes their invasion of four hundred years ago. My friend and I eventually emerged from our tour unscathed, though whether she will ever visit me again, I am not at all sure. Shortly after this adventure I listened with joy to another acquaintance's story about her visit to our country. This one did not hire a guide, since her purpose in coming to Warsaw was to uncover the secrets of tea-making ceremonies. For it was here that a Japanese master had chosen to pass on to posterity the arcana of his art. My friend therefore walked the streets I knew well, without looking around unduly, preoccupied with going over in her mind the freshly confided mysteries. Of the local color, she remembered one thing. Like all foreigners, she was amazed at the natives' habit of tormenting fellow passengers in train compartments with mobile phone conversations. She was quickly reassured however by the sight of a girl sitting by the window. When the course on tea ceremonies came to an end and my acquaintance was preparing to depart, she described to me her encounter on the train: "A girl sitting by the window was also irritated by the people with mobile phones. Unfortunately for them, they were too occupied with shouting into the receivers to observe that she was no ordinary person, but a cat-woman! She had a predatory look on her face, sat motionless like a cat with her tail no doubt tucked under her skirt, had catlike ears, and held her hands under her chin like cats hold their paws. She paid no attention to me but stared at the mobile users with glassy green irises as she cast her spell upon them. Both she and I knew it was their last journey. It was fantastic!"—my friend assured me.

## BANANAS

To a potluck party someone brings banana ice cream. Among the many excellent dishes, this is the one that arouses the greatest interest. Far from approving. In the cross fire of questions, the person who brought the ice cream confesses he made it. A murmur passes through the little crowd. Eventually the first brave guest pipes up and says he too does not know what to do with bananas. A second admits the same. And a third. And a fourth. The tension provoked by the appearance of the ice cream slowly dissolves into a sympathy generated among the partygoers, solidarity with others in an equally difficult situation. A fifth guest still hesitates a moment before saying that although she had decided many times to buy no more bananas, she always returns from the shop with the hated bunch. Community spirit now unites the majority of guests. It turns out that almost all feel confronted by a similar dilemma. Although they do not eat the bananas, or only nibble them at best for the sake of a clear conscience before chucking them, they are unable to control themselves on their next shopping trip. Ashamed at their weakness, they return home with shopping bags laden. Is such a love-hate feeling linked to the bananas' phallic shape? To the place they occupy in obscene jokes? Their role in slapstick comedy? The fact that they cannot be kept in a fridge, so the obligation to eat them arises the very next day after unpacking the damn bag? The ensuing hour of lively discussion engages even the most taciturn. It transpires that the strange affliction is not alien to them either! Thirty plus people randomly assembled are all suffering from banana phobia. Did they really meet by chance? Are they victims of a conspiracy? Or—following the model of cat-food producers—is someone injecting the banana flesh with an addictive additive, surely harmful to one's health? Who? Large trading networks? Plantation owners? Terrorists preparing a new biological weapon hidden in banana skins? How to fight it? Create support groups? Appeal to the authorities? Emigrate, if it's possible, to countries still free from threat? Long into the night we discuss plans to cure ourselves of the addiction. We all feel a weight has been lifted from our hearts, since we have at last overcome the psychological barrier, and are talking openly about something that has troubled us for years. We have stopped denying the issue, but this is merely the start of the recovery process. The next day we will devise a plan for group therapy. In the meantime, we have to clear away the mountain of melted yellow dessert that no one has touched. Its creator isn't upset: the most important thing is that he got rid of six pieces of unwanted fruit whose name begins with a B. I return home exhausted. It's not long before dawn and I must try to get some sleep before the day that could bring a solution to the embarrassing problem. I decide however to take a quick shower. On the way to the bathroom I try not to look at the four brown crescent moons ominously rotting on their silver stand.

## PREMONITION

It's obviously not worth wasting time on either printed or internet gossip magazines. D. did so, however, and immediately found my photograph. I appear as the lover of an aging pop star. On one side of the page, there he is with his wife, on the other—separated from them by a colorful jagged line—there I am, the instigator of their divorce. A friend of the couple, cross-examined by a gossip columnist, simply cannot believe my cruelty. I do not know the pop star. My picture was taken by the alleged lover, hence it pops up whenever her name is entered into Google. The editor must have been illiterate, since the caption indicating who the photograph represented did not ring any alarm bells. I tell this story to A., who is not in the least bit surprised. "I knew you would call," she says. "Last night I dreamed about you. We were trudging through the snow on our way to a New Year's Eve ball, and you were wearing high-heeled sandals. Each foot a different shape and color. And what's more, asymmetrical. I asked if you wouldn't catch cold, and you replied: 'Haven't you noticed I always wear fur boots in summer and sandals in winter? Otherwise it would be so banal!'" Visions of a new collection by the reincarnation of Elsa Schiaparelli prevent me from being angry. If A. only dreamed such a dream in order to predict my telephone call, then even crap articles have their *raison d'être*.

## POLONEZ

In the early 1980s I passed my driving test. I should never have received my license because I did not know the highway code, drove too fast, and, just to make sure, did not look to either side. There were fewer cars around then, so I did not immediately cause an accident. But luckily it happened soon enough for me not to be a danger to others for too long. In the middle of the empty Constitution Square, I veered to the left and sideswiped a white Polonez driving straight ahead. The little Fiat 126 survived the collision better than the other vehicle, at that time a symbol of socialist affluence. The attitude in those days to one's own means of transport, acquired after many years of hard slogging and saving, was such that I could expect a lynching from the driver, carried out with the full understanding of the gawping onlookers. Meanwhile, opening the door with difficulty, a kind lady got out, while an elderly gentleman emerged with greater ease from the other side and asked if I had fainted. My maneuver had been so irrational that it did not occur to them that anyone could have performed it who wasn't about to have a heart attack. I did not dare initiate them into the arcana of my driving art. So we took out our documents—they were magnanimous enough not to call the police—and I realized I had smashed up the car of a well-known Warsaw figure, the director of the Museum of Caricature. Many years of working in that place no doubt afforded him such a cheerful reaction. Then we politely said our good-byes and got on with pushing the cars onto the sidewalk. The whole business upset me a great deal, of course. Not only had I damaged the little car belonging to M.'s aunt, who had been unaware of the danger to which it was exposed, I had also wrecked the vehicle of such a nice man. And yet everything ended unexpectedly well. Less than three weeks later I heard a report on the radio connected indirectly with my hapless adventure. The Director of the Museum of Caricature, said the announcement, had won a competition to guess the scores of World Cup football matches. His prize was a silver Polonez. "Well timed," added the commentator. "His old one had to be scrapped following an accident."

## TIME LOOP

After twenty years of living in the States, E. came with her adult children to show them their old house in the Sadyba neighborhood of Warsaw. The house had changed little, except that in these ecological times a glass recycling bin had sprung up beside it, yet was barely visible beneath the mountain of smashed bottles. E. was too deeply moved to let the sight upset her, though she did not at any cost want her children to notice it. She wanted them to have the best possible impressions of the country. Trying to direct their gaze the other way, she began to tell them a rumor she remembered from those dim and distant times. In the house next door, a pretty woman had lived with two husbands—which back then, even in artistic circles, had caused something of a sensation. The children liked the story. There was still hope they wouldn't notice the ecological shambles. And then, as they stood with their backs to the bottles, in the window of the flat where a quarter of a century ago the pretty woman had lived with her husbands, the curtains were drawn aside. Against the backdrop of a brightly lit interior, a girl appeared. A moment later a young man popped up by her right side and kissed her on the cheek. She had no time to respond with a smile before a second young man approached from the left and also kissed her. She took half a step back snuggling up at the same time to both. The man on the left and the man on the right put their arms around her. The whole troika froze in a state of bliss, staring at the autumn—early that year—beyond the window. E. and her children were afraid to move lest they should shatter the spell. Tears trickled down E.'s cheeks. For the first time in her life, she had observed how time goes around in a loop. In order for the miracle to happen, very little was required. It was enough to concentrate one's thoughts on something as banal as a heap of broken glass.

## MYSTIFICATIONS

N. likes to say that she would rather fall victim to a chance murderer than a terrorist attack targeted at her as an American. In her final moments she would rather not be part of a group. I understand her well. Recently, in less dramatic circumstances, I was twice made to feel what it meant to be pinned to a place. As a consequence of one of my books being translated into French, I was invited to a magical spot in the Pyrenees for a festival devoted to literary mystifications. The story of the female saint dreamed up by me had already been described by the catalogs of two major Warsaw libraries. The authors of the first entry understood my heroine to be an historical figure, the second—a figment of Surrealist fantasy. The Warsaw librarians had no faith in my imagination. In the Pyrenean village things took an even worse turn. As I presented Leonora's story among the academic papers about literary mystifications perpetrated by now dead writers, silence descended on the room. Disturbingly few people laughed. It took me a little while to realize that the festival participants, like the Warsaw librarians, had taken my tale seriously. During supper, someone asked me what the Vatican archives had to say about my heroine. Someone else muttered that interest in saints was proof of naivety. The penny then dropped (the festival participants were convinced an arrival from a Catholic country could not make fun of saints), forcing me to climb onto the podium on the final day and confess the truth. What happened next also astounded me. Part of the lecture theater applauded in relief, part sat looking offended. Shaking his head in disbelief, the editor of a cultural radio program handed me his card. I could not believe that he too had believed! In the moment when a well-known writer was persuading me he had seen through the mystification immediately, his wife approached saying, "You see, wasn't I right? Leonora de la Cruz did not exist." Before leaving, I overheard a conversation in which someone accused me of not treating my audience seriously. Having returned home from that beautiful remote corner of the Pyrenees, I watched an animated film based on a fairy tale I had written years before, dubbed with foreign distributors in mind. It was about a magic clock that went fast in bad times and slow in good. The American translator, however, rendered the sentence the other way round, giving the story a masochistic twist. Again I felt I had been pinned to a place. English-speaking viewers were confirmed in their vision of the Slavic soul. The clock born out of it rushed ahead in happy times, to the undoing of the kingdom's subjects, and prolonged—in so far as it could—the unhappy ones.

## BUREAUCRACIES

One could go on about bureaucracy till kingdom come. Here are some random examples. I once wanted to recharge my phone in America. Buy a card with a code, which I would then tap into my mobile, acquiring thereby a given number of minutes of conversation. However, as the nearest kiosk was out of cards, I decided to avail myself of the widely advertised service of charging my phone via the internet. An internal voice told me this was not a good idea, but it was raining, discouraging me from walking to the next kiosk, so I returned home and connected to the T-Mobile website. I was already disturbed by the message explaining that a company representative might wish to obtain additional information from me, but it was Friday evening and who, on a Friday evening, needed additional information? Besides I was charging my own phone and paying with my own credit card. What could be so concerning to the representative? Less than half an hour had elapsed before he rang. He requested the number of my driving license, my mother's maiden name, and the name of the secondary school I attended thirty years earlier. I refused to answer his question about the name of my long-deceased dog. I assured the representative that despite the weather, I would go to a kiosk. The representative was surprised: the questions were meant to establish my identity, so easy to forge in this era of electronic crime. I did not hear him out. Under an umbrella, I went to a kiosk and ten minutes later tapped the coveted code into my phone. Although it's hard to believe, at more or less the same time M. had an even stranger adventure. For no reason at all, his credit card refused to obey him. Alarmed, M. made his way to the bank, where he learned to his relief that the cause of the trouble was a purchase he had made earlier in the day of three books. The books were to be sent to his home address, so the bank's precautions seemed somewhat excessive, but since it was better to be safe than sorry, he said: "Please unblock the account as soon as possible." The clerk threw up his arms in despair. The account was closed irreversibly! It took M. several weeks to open a new one. The associated tensions reached new heights. Such heights, that when the new card eventually landed in his trembling hands, another catastrophe struck. In the old days you used to put a card into the ATM and activate it by entering your PIN. *Not anymore.* Today an official introduces over the phone a long list of offers lying in wait for the customer. Only when the latter, by now on the verge of madness, agrees to one of them or plays really tough and rejects them all, does she reluctantly activate the card. During the course of their conversation M., like many before and after him, had to occupy his hands. Certainly, he could have done something significantly worse, but what he did do had inconvenient consequences. Convinced he was destroying the old card, he pedantically cut up the new one. The procedure began all over again . . . And finally, an optimistic tale. P. did not cut up his Green Card, although he had every reason to do so. In a world marked by terrorist phobias, he functioned for ten years with a document on which, as a result of a clerical error, his "sex" was stated in black and white as: female. And it's not without significance that P. (accustomed to the adoration of women) had reason to be rather proud of his virility. Yet no one ever questioned him at any border. No one cast doubt on the authenticity of the card or its owner. P.'s decision not to rectify the mistake sprang not from anarchist sympathies, but from fear of the bureaucratic maelstrom which would have sucked him in on his first attempt at correction. It would have been easier to change sex, but for that—as I said—he was not prepared.

## POINT OF VIEW

Enthused Internet surfers outdo one another's comments on the subject of good news. It concerns the reaction of an American Airlines pilot who decided to wait five minutes for the final passenger—a grandfather hurrying to the funeral of his grandson, only a few years old, murdered by his daughter's boyfriend. The surfers are unanimous: it's the first good news in a long time!

TRANSLATED BY URSULA PHILLIPS

# DAVID MACHADO

## *The Commander's Endless Night*

WHEN HE OPENED THE DOOR to the building he noticed the dense shadows in the stairwell and began to tremble with fear. Immediately he moved his hand behind his back to the place on his belt where many years before he always carried the combat revolver they had given him in Moscow, and the absence of the firearm left him breathless, because he was sure they would kill him. Groping his way along the wall, he tried the light switch several times until he realized it wasn't working. Then he summoned his old warrior's instinct: he stood still, quieted his breathing, and looked into the darkness without fear. He coughed twice and shouted, so loud that he could be heard throughout the whole building:

"I won't see you kill me, motherfuckers. But you won't see me die either."

He advanced with one arm protecting his face and the other raised in front of him, expecting the enemy to appear, climbing the staircase step by step as if each one would be the last, until he reached the second-floor landing without incident, and with his open hand he pounded on the door in anger. The door was locked, just as he had left it when he went out the day before. The darkness and the silence squeezed his heart, but from deep in his guts he drew the courage to insert the key in the lock and then to turn it. He opened the door, walked in, closed it after himself and then stood, his eyes open to the dark, waiting to feel the first gunshot from the past pierce his flesh. He remained this way for about two minutes, and when nothing happened, he placed his keys on the table, took off his jacket and threw it on a chair, and finally, without bothering to turn on the lights, crossed the hallway to the living room and sat down in an armchair draped with tribal blankets with a dry sigh of contempt.

"I'm going to sit here all night," he said. "Come on and kill me whenever you want."

His name was António Ferraz and he was a nurse in São José Hospital, and because he'd had to do several shifts in a row, he hadn't slept in thirty-seven hours. And the reality was that no one was there to kill him. He was so exhausted that he couldn't tell if it was morning or afternoon, he didn't remember walking home through the hills, or the fierce brightness of the dusk at eight o'clock at night, which was the time he arrived at Bairro Alto, where he lived, and also the time that he awoke from his daze. In fact, he could have gone on alert well before opening the door to his building and encountering the omen of the shadows on the stairs, because as he crossed the narrow streets of the still calm neighborhood, he became aware of the lines of black soldiers who greeted him solemnly from the other side of his remote suffering. At a given moment along the way, an official with an unshaven beard and an opaque glass eye approached him and said: "Commander, let's leave for the bush as soon as the moon rises." He gave no reply and waved his hand so that they would not bother him for the rest of his life.

Back at home, sitting in his armchair and trying to suppress the memories with menthol cigarettes, he heard the troops start to march north, he heard a chorus of voices singing an Angolan *rebita*, and finally he heard the same officer shout out to him from the underbrush of the forest: "Good-bye, Commander. We'll see you at the river bank in two days." And then he heard the impossible silence of the African mountain, its flanks still streaming with the blood of the last battle. Until, in Lisbon, the phone rang.

On the other line he heard his mother's voice and was startled that it was already Sunday, because she always called on that day of the week. She explained that it wasn't Sunday, and also that at eighty-eight years of age she didn't need appointments on special days of the week to speak with the only creature left to her in this world. António didn't say anything more and waited. His mother caught her breath and then told him that she had been feeling upset since the early hours of the morning, without knowing why, and she was at loose ends with a restless need to talk with him. Because she had a tendency to have premonitions, she paced back and forth, wandering about in a sea of recurring palpitations, certain that something terrible was about to happen. Finally she ended up realizing that whatever was going to happen had already happened, and that all the upheaval in her chest wasn't anything more than the distant echo from another time.

"Tomorrow morning it will be twenty-three years since you called me in tears," his mother said. "You were in Angola, lost in the middle of the war, and I was here in Coimbra, in the same place I've always been, without being able to help you. At first I thought you'd been shot, but right away I remembered I hadn't heard you cry since you were two years old, and then I realized it was something more serious than a bullet."

She paused, waiting for her son to say something, but António remained silent and she continued.

"It's just a memory, I know. In any case, take care of yourself."

He said good-bye to his mother with a few words, and hung up. The next instant he saw Captain Elias Vieira step out of the shadows of his living room with his face covered in sweat, his arm in a sling strapped to his chest due to the explosion of a mine that missed killing him by a thread, and chewing the same wad of tobacco from three decades earlier. He crossed the parquet floor limping on his left leg, just the way António Ferraz had always known him, and he tripped over everything, looking astonished at finding himself in a fully furnished living room on the Angolan plateau. Even in the dark, there was no chance of not knowing who it was.

They had known each other from the time when Elias was still a slave on António's father's farm, and they had become friends on an afternoon when the black man had been sentenced by the foreman to fifteen lashes for distributing revolutionary propaganda among the other slaves. Back in those times, António Ferraz was too naive to separate acts of rebellion from the skin color of those who committed them, but even so, the punishment seemed excessive for a single man, and he spoke out in defense of the black man, who thanked him, days later, leaving two books at the door of his room that would end up changing the direction of his life.

Marx's *Das Kapital*, and a collection of Lenin's speeches. Some years later, when António Ferraz returned to Luanda after a voluntary period in the Soviet Union, where he learned to fly airplanes, not to mention all the finer points of how to arm a revolution, he met up again with Elias Vieira by chance and the first thing he said to him was: "I'm back, Comrade. Now the whip will change hands." Elias Vieira chose to ignore the pale skin of his old boss and four centuries of tyranny and took him on a campaign through the jungles of the whole country. Everywhere he introduced him to the troops as Commander Ferraz, recently arrived from Moscow, with a doctorate in war maneuvers and versed in original Communist doctrine. Since then, he had become his right hand, his most faithful protector on the battlefield, and sometimes his immovable confidant. Until the day of the stealthy and solitary desertion of the Commander. Because after that, they had never seen each other again, not even in their dreams.

"It's not time to sit down yet, Commander," said Captain Elias from his involuntary memory. "There are only four of us here and we have the first night watch."

António Ferraz lit up another menthol cigarette and looked askance at his friend.

"I've been on duty at the hospital for almost forty hours," he shot back. "And it's been twenty years since I've set foot in Africa. I just want peace."

"And so what do we do with this war, Commander?"

"What war, Elias? The war is over."

The captain moved in the shadows of the living room and squatted down next to António Ferraz with a wide smile.

"Commander, you know very well that this war goes on forever," he said. And then, without hurry, he added: "I'll be waiting for you behind the boulders. Don't forget your weapon."

Then he stood and disappeared through the mists of the hallway. It was almost ten o'clock at night and António Ferraz turned in his chair to fall into his delayed sleep, although he knew ahead of time that he wouldn't be able to, because even though it had rained all day on the plateau, the night air was becoming warm and thick like a wool blanket and the mosquitos were starting to bite relentlessly. From a distance, out near the kitchen, he heard the hoarse voices of two soldiers who were having dinner. The strong smell of grain stew and also the sweet vapors of cane liquor gave him encouragement. He felt the urgency to get up from his chair to join them at the hearth, but he waved the urge away with his hand. He knew the two of them well. They were called Inácio Montenegro and Zeca Baião, they were from Benguela and they had joined the group of guerrillas three months earlier. A year later, during the last battle he was in before fleeing through the jungle to the Congo, he would see them die, not far from each other, by two accurate shots from the enemy.

And, nevertheless, he heard them very clearly as they talked in the kitchen while they had dinner, and then he heard them tune their guitars and play loose chords, and finally he let go of the weight of that insane longing and yelled:

"Zeca!"

"Yes, Commander," they replied.

"Play a Sofia Rosa song."

And they played. And finally Commander António Ferraz dozed off, if only for a few brief moments, and he dreamed of the patients in the hospital that entered alive through one door and left dead out of the other. Until, around midnight, he felt the light touch of Captain Elias's hand shaking him, and he awoke to the lulling music of the interminable song.

"Three soldiers have arrived with a prisoner, Commander," said the Captain.

António Ferraz looked at the other man through time and answered from the depths of his troubled soul.

"The prisoner here is me," he said. "Leave me alone."

Captain Elias Vieira explained there was nothing in life that he'd like more than to leave him alone, but that he couldn't, since the order came directly from the President and it was urgent to follow it. The missive that accompanied the prisoner was short and so clear that António Ferraz would remember it the rest of his life: without any other reason than the fearful signature of the President, the prisoner would be shot at dawn. The Captain was going to tell him the name of the man they had brought to die, but the Commander interrupted him in time.

"I forbid you to say the name of that man again," he shouted. "I've known it for twenty years."

"Very well, Commander, but there's one more thing."

Then António Ferraz stretched out his arm and lit the lantern that was on the table next to the armchair, a sad light spread through the room, illuminating the horizon of the Angolan night. He got up, bringing with him one of the blankets covering the chair to protect himself from the inevitable winds of the plateau. He took one step ahead and his eyes came within a palm's width from Captain Elias Vieira's face.

"No, there is nothing more," he said to him with a deep sigh. "I know what you are going to say now, and I'll tell you right now, that when it's six forty-two in the morning, I will not put another bullet in the head of that poor wretch who already died once."

Captain Elias Vieira put a hand on the Commander's shoulder and squeezed it affectionately. He said:

"I know it's hard, Commander, but there's nobody else."

António Ferraz knew as well as the Captain that there wasn't anyone else. The three men who had brought the prisoner were going to eat what was left of the grain stew and then they were going to return to the town on the other side of the valley. Inácio Montenegro and Zeca Baião were still too green to give them that nefarious order; and the wounded hand of Captain Elias prevented him from shooting a weapon with the funereal precision that the task demanded. It had not been the first time that he had killed a man, since he had participated in enough armed conflicts to know that at least one of the bullets he'd shot had ended up hitting someone. However, this was the first time that he had done it against a defenseless man. He remembered the litany of slogans about the revolution, learned in Moscow so many years ago, and he anticipated his heart starting to palpitate at the orders regarding execution of traitors, archenemies, and other obstructions to the implanting of the doctrine. Above all, he didn't understand why they were forcing him to kill the same man again, twenty-three years later, instead of leaving him in peace with what remained of his life.

He sat down again in his armchair, wrapped in the blanket, and turned off the diaphanous light of the lantern. In the darkness of the room, he searched for his lost peace, but found only the turbulent tremor of his memories. Then he repeated the same lament as before.

"Elias, leave me alone," he said. "I'm adrift in this sea of big waves and the only thing I want is to arrive on dry land. Let me sleep tonight without the memories of other nights."

The face of Elias Vieira appeared in the middle of the gloom like a miserable angel.

"I would like to leave you, António," he said. "But the two of us know very well that to be left in peace you have to die."

Then he disappeared again into the shadows of the room, but António Ferraz still heard him add a useless bit of advice: "Rest there until daybreak, Commander. I'll take watch on my own."

The commander lit one more cigarette, even though he knew from the depths of his being that not even the sweet pull of menthol would be sufficient to drive away the ghosts of the past, much less the certainty of what would happen in the first few minutes of the morning. He passed the next hours trying in vain to invite sleep, but at every moment he was disturbed by the invisible noises of the jungle, by the distant thunder of the sky, by the guffaws and chatter of Inácio Montenegro and Zeca Baião. At three in the morning, he saw a wild dog in the shadows between the disconnected television and the wall, and a little while afterwards he heard very clearly the voice of the prisoner declaiming the salty stanzas of Arlindo Barbeitos to the clouds of the plateau. He was at the point of accompanying him in reciting those final lines, but he considered that doing so would be as if acknowledging defeat to the traumatic memory of that remote day. He got up and shouted:

"All of you stay there in the middle of the war. This time I'm deserting earlier."

He walked through the apartment as if he didn't know where he was, trying to find an exit from that old Angola, but quickly he realized that the doors were closed forever until the next morning. So he advanced to the door of the privy, where the prisoner was locked in and taking courage in the words of the poet. He had decided to knock down the door to let the man who had already died long ago run away, so he wouldn't have to kill him again. It was in this agitated state that Captain Elias Vieira found him and wrapped him in his arms, urging him to calm himself and to get some sleep, while he answered from the depths of his exasperation that that's what he most wanted, but that the bullet he had to shoot in a few hours didn't let him. And the captain led him cautiously in the dark, between the boulders of the plateau and the English furniture he had inherited from his uncle, until he was back in the armchair, and he passed the bottle of cane liquor that kept him company on the nights he was on watch, so he could recover from his torment. The commander drank without protest and felt the same slow burn down his esophagus as in the old times. Then he said again:

"Leave me alone, Comrade. Please."

The captain nodded an acknowledgement, got up, and limped away into the dark.

"I'll come wake you when it's time," he said before disappearing into smoke.

António Ferraz remained immobile in the armchair in the African night of his apartment, struggling against that dizzying disturbance.

He was still in the same position without having rested when around six in the morning Captain Elias Vieira appeared in front of him with a mug of coffee and a piece of dry bread. He took a tiny bite of the bread and two sips of coffee and afterwards, inconsolable, threw the rest to the earthen floor. When he passed the empty mug to the captain, the officer handed him the revolver, the same one they had given him in the Soviet capital, holding it with two open hands as if it were a military relic. He saw the weapon and became frightened. But even so, he took it and placed it on his lap.

"It's time, Commander," declared the captain.

He looked at his old friend, lacking the strength to continue resisting that relentless duplication of destiny, and he rose with the revolver hanging in his hand.

"Let's go," he said. And he advanced in the dark, followed by the Captain.

Zeca Baião was waiting for them at the privy door, still dazed by the early hour, his posture expressing a certain solemnity. As soon as he saw him, the commander divested him of his illusions.

"Don't bother trying to look like a minister of state," he said. "What will happen here is for the hyenas. Open the door, comrade."

The soldier said nothing, lowered his gaze and took the rusty key out of his pocket that he then used to open the lock. Inside, the darkness was even denser and the presence of the prisoner was barely distinguishable from the voice whispering the Barbeitos verses to the tiles. Zeca Baião came in. A few seconds later he came out with a six-foot-tall black man, his hands tied and his forehead bloody. Nobody said anything and Captain Elias Vieira made a signal for them to follow him, at the very moment that the first rays of the sun started to fill the plateau. They walked about thirty meters and stopped. The captain ordered the prisoner to kneel on the ground. And from this side of time, mocked from all sides by the onslaughts of his memories, Commander António Ferraz pointed his revolver at the right temple of the man and for the second time in his life killed him with a bullet of his own shame.

Afterwards, trembling, he went back to the armchair covered in blankets in his living room in Lisbon, picked up the phone and dialed his mother's number in Coimbra. Tears began to run down his face.

TRANSLATED FROM THE PORTUGUESE BY ELIZABETH LOWE

# RUXANDRA CESEREANU

## *Haritina*

I HAD ALWAYS BEEN FASCINATED by women, whom I saw as lionesses with great, piercing eyes. I was never indifferent to men, but since what I liked about men was chiefly their wisdom and sharp-edged, effulgent quality, I left it to women to carry the weight of the strange, invisible, ambiguous, and slippery side of this world. I cannot say I was friendlier with women than with men, but only that, given I was the same as them, it was easier for me to perceive the undercurrents, innermost parts, and subtle tissues of women's so special world. Women smell of oven-baked apple. Men smell of quince. Women have sharp, rending nails. Men have tidily trimmed nails. As for myself, I hoped that one day I might become a pedicurist to the angels.

Naturally, the most important woman in my life was my mother. To be more precise, it was my mother's peerless skin, from which I brought to the surface all kinds of psychically charged stories about what it meant to be a woman. But the second magisterial woman in my life was Haritina, before even my grandmothers, aunts and cousins, they too special one and all. Because Haritina was the one who foretold that I would become a storyteller, at a time when it had never entered my head to be anything other than a poet through and through. She did not tell me this in plain words, but convolutedly and in the cant of rustic witches. For Haritina was a kind of witch and dwelled somewhere in the North, in a village close to the monasteries whose exterior walls are painted with all kinds of devils, celestial ladders, and other scenes of torment or redemption.

I met her when I was eighteen, in the summer after my first year at university, while attending a folklore studies camp. The dice had been cast and they fell in such a way that during that long, dry summer I had to dig around and find out about the art and wisdom of witches. And so, inquisitive and awkward, I began my search. It was not hard to discover Haritina, since the whole village knew of her and pointed the way. But before anything else, I was surprised by her unusual name: neither Maria nor Ana, but rather that monastically tinged name of hers. Without a doubt, Haritina came from *har* (divine grace), although her grace was not divine, but mischievously magical, if I may put it like that. I presented myself to Haritina one Monday, at ten o'clock in the morning. Neither the day nor the hour was suitable, for I found Haritina's gate shut. She was very curt and did not wish to speak to me. And rightly so, for who and what was I, after all? An uppity student with a ballpoint pen and a notebook, in jeans and a t-shirt emblazoned with "Pink Floyd," hair plaited in some twenty pigtails, wearing hippy-style sunglasses and with an unlikeable, bookish face. I stood by her gate, in the hope that Haritina might relent, but the witch looked at me with such mistrust that I gave up. I came back at dusk, but I still wouldn't have had any more success then, if my skin-tight jeans had not ridden up my hips, exposing my left ankle, on which I wore a strange piece of homemade jewelry, which I had fashioned at a rock festival not long before: an anklet made from an aluminum fork. Well, that fork bracelet around my ankle was what mollified Haritina, who, with an air of complicity, let me cross the threshold of her house. My jeans, scrawled with the words to Pink Floyd songs, were likewise a kind of crossroads, ever yearning to guide those who saw them to the understanding that there is always a right path and a left path. The words to "Shine on You Crazy Diamond," written in ballpoint on the legs of my jeans, seemed to Haritina to be strange signs, precisely because she did not, as may be suspected, speak English. And besides, I used to mumble the words to the song almost continuously, even when I ate or slept. That was how I saw things back then; it was a kind of personal magic spell, an acoustic amulet: *Remember when you were young / You shone like the sun / Shine on, you crazy diamond / Now there's a look in your eyes / Like black holes in the sky / Shine on, you crazy diamond . . .* And so it was that Haritina permitted me to cross her threshold that evening, and on that occasion, even if we did not speak about the things I wished to know, I tasted one of her special pies, filled with gooseberries and rhubarb, which is said to clarify the magical eyeglass through which the world can be viewed back to front. We spoke of nothing special that evening. Haritina merely told me that she would put me to the test. When I left, I only pretended to leave, for I went back and stood in wait by the kitchen window, which had remained half open: Haritina had undressed and was washing her body, and her body was covered with floral and geometric designs, the likes of which I had never seen before. I do not know what her body was painted with; I supposed that it could only be a dye derived from plants, and which in time would vanish. As for Haritina's hair, although the witch was around forty years of age, it reached down to her hips and was bluish, for it had the tint of a frozen lake. Haritina did not live alone: she was married to the village woodsman and had a son my age, who worked in the town. But for as long as I had dealings with her, I never glimpsed either of those two men.

That night, in the hostel where we folklorist-philologists were staying, I dreamed like a madwoman; I dreamed I was wandering through the floral and geometric designs on Haritina's body. As you might say, I dreamed a myriad of labyrinths in which I lost myself, delighting in the bare, narrow paths that loomed from my nocturnal illusions. The next day I went to her not early in the morning, but at dusk, as she had demanded. By day, Haritina worked in the village barbershop. She was a hairdresser and it wasn't for nothing that she dealt with the hair of so many people, for she stole the life force from the shorn hair, which, along with other ingredients, she put to use in spells and cures. The second time I entered her house at dusk I saw a jar in which were stuffed a number of glossy crow's feathers, I saw a string of bear's teeth, ground-up pieces of quartz, dried cloves of garlic, and a music box, within which were some intricately woven bronze chains, like handcuffs, for making and unmaking the world, as Haritina whispered to me ironically. The music box surprised me most of all, since it was something that belonged in a well-off house in town, rather than in the abode of this spell-casting peasant healer woman who was known to be a witch. In any event, in that second dusk, Haritina recited a number of spells to me, which I painstakingly transcribed in my little note-book, highly satisfied with my booty. But it was all a trick.

The third dusk was to be the most trying, however, since Haritina was to check to see whether or not I was cut out to be a witch. When I arrived at her house, Haritina was busy boiling a potion of fresh walnut leaves, into which she had mixed pepper and cinnamon. She made me undress, and after the potion had cooled she anointed the whole of my body with it, including my hair. She then made me lie down on the long table in the kitchen, covering me with a sheet. I felt a bit cold and was shivering slightly. It was then that I started singing "Shine on You Crazy Diamond." I divined that I would have to do something unusual under the influence of the walnut-leaf potion with which I had been anointed. But to my misfortune or fortune—who knows which?—I did not have any vision or hallucination or illumination. I saw nothing at all, by all that is holy. Nor did I fly or journey through other spaces or leave my body. Something else entirely happened to me: my tongue loosened immoderately and I started telling stories by the dozen: stories I never knew had been lying inside me, dwelling in my pores and inner reaches, stories that belonged to none and to all, which gushed out in an unexampled torrent. That whole night I told stories, until dawn came and I fell silent. My jaw ached, my tongue was swollen, and I was hoarse. Haritina laughed softly and made me a thick tea of linden flowers and honey. You are not cut out to be a witch, she told me; that is not what you are made for. But you are a weaver of tales. That is what you are and what you will always be. It is a good thing, she added, because that means that you will be able to comfort others. A weaver of tales! I exclaimed in amazement. I thought that I was a poet and nothing but a poet. Yes, a weaver of tales, Haritina concluded.

A year later, when I met the man of my life, he asked me, in the oddest possible way, what I was: I told him all in one breath that I was a weaver of stories. Then that means there are now two of us on the same path, he replied, chuckling to himself, and gave my hair a gentle flick, as a kind of covenant known only to weavers of stories.

During all the other dusks I spent at Haritina's house, I zealously wrote down spells for all kinds of things—illnesses, misfortunes, and joys—but never did I witness any witchcraft. As it was not in my blood to be an apprentice, Haritina walled up her witch's skills to keep them away from me. Later, I understood that the jar of crow's feathers, the bear's teeth, the quartz, the garlic, and the music box had been put there just to beguile and test me. If she really was a witch, Haritina kept the secret to herself. As for the spells she dictated to me, they were real, but they were just words. Without the magic adjuncts and the witch's special gestures, they had no effect.

For the ten days I remained in that region, I was always Haritina's guest at dusk. And when I left, I left forever, for I never went back and never sought her out again. But it's not seldom that I dream that I'm wandering through the labyrinths traced on her body.

In the life of every woman, as I now know, there are three "diamantine" women, as I call them. The first diamantine woman was my mother: from her I learned what the skin and touching are. The second diamantine woman in my life was Haritina, the peasant hairdresser and witch from that sun-scorched village in the North. From her I learned that I am and will be a weaver of stories. The third diamantine woman has not yet appeared, and who knows when she will cross my path, if I be lucky enough. As for me, perhaps I too will have played the role of a diamantine woman for other women like me. Perhaps my other name, Mesmaea, besides my rightful name, Ruxandra, plays this role. Might Esther, Dardina, and Sharashka (known to you, reader, from my story "Three Witches and an Apprentice") bear witness to this? I do not know.

As I said at the beginning, I like both the world of women and the world of men. But the world of women seems to me more redolent, more viscous, more caught up in mysteries than that of men. It is a world whose innermost parts are like delicate tracery and above all a world of stories with colorful illuminations. A world of long fingers with cabbalistic rings, bodies and minds that smell of oven-baked apple. Such an aroma is indecipherable and for this reason dwells far away over the seas and lands, encircling our world in a ruby-colored halo. As for Haritina, when I recall the second diamantine woman in my life, my parole will always be "Shine on You Crazy Diamond." In her honor, I sometimes braid my hair in

dozens of pigtails and wear on my left ankle the strange bracelet
made from an aluminum fork.

TRANSLATED BY ALISTAIR IAN BLYTH

# LIZA ALEXANDROVA-ZORINA

## *Bad Town*

THE TOWN WAS NO BIGGER than a thumbnail, and the deserted villages huddled up to it like little children to their mother. Across the river the church domes glittered, and there were cattle grazing. A metal container stood in the middle of the field, which was bare apart from a single birch tree, sticking out like a splinter. From the riverbank one could see the Tajik woman mixing flour and water, cooking flatbread on the fire while the man smoked, using his other hand to try and drive away a swarm of midges. He was as thin as a stick, and his clothes hung off him, so that from a distance he could have been mistaken for a scarecrow. Tanned black by the sun and dressed in brightly colored clothes, the Tajik family seemed out of place in the dreary scene. They looked more like cuttings from a color magazine that some joker had stuck onto a picture of a typical Russian summer.

They herded the farmer's cattle from early morning until late at night. Their boy's voice could be heard ringing out across the field, bright like a bell. He had nicknames for all the cows, taken from overheard conversations and TV shows. As he cracked the whip against their backs he called out the names of American celebrities and the milkmaids from the farm.

"How can you tell them apart?" his mother laughed.

The houses looked like they were rooted to the ground. They were little bigger than sheds, but each one had a satellite dish sticking out from it like a cocked ear. A television blared from an open window, and the Tajiks pressed against the fence, listening closely.

"A black-assed man lives a black-assed life," said the bald old man, scowling as he watched them.

In Russia, the Tajiks christened themselves with Russian names, Sveta and Kolya. They laughed when they said their real names—the Russians couldn't pronounce them. The boy wanted to keep his name, Zafar, and he would say it through clenched teeth, staring at the ground. But at the farm they turned it into the more familiar Russian name, Zakhar. The villagers didn't like new words, and they still called the new farm the kolkhoz, Soviet style.

On payday Sveta shifted impatiently from foot to foot at the door of the accounts office, her gold teeth flashing and a feeble smile sliding across her exhausted features like a solitary cat. "Please, just a hun-dred rub-les, we've got no-thing to eat," she said, breaking the words into pieces as if she was tearing flatbread. The accountant dismissed her without raising her head, and the guard pushed her out into the street.

"Bad town," the Mongol hordes had cursed Kozelsk back in the thirteenth century. "The people here are mean," said the Tajiks, shaking their heads.

They threw their scant belongings into a bag and got ready to depart for Moscow. As they passed through the village, an old woman with a face wizened like a baked apple made the sign of the cross over their stooped backs. At the bus station they managed to beg enough money for their tickets. But when they got on the bus the guards from the farm appeared and threw them into the car like sacks of potatoes. They took their passports and brought them back to the container with the door which flapped in the wind like the wing of a wounded bird. "Next time we'll break your ribs," they said.

The rain poured all day long, beating on the metal roof like an uninvited guest. The Tajiks huddled under the quilt, letting light through the door to save candles. They lay in silence, staring at the field, too tired to talk.

Even the name of the village, Deshovka, sounded unpleasant: it meant cheap in Russian.

"Be-cause life isn't worth two ko-peks here!" Sveta said in a fit of anger.

"But what about in Dushanbe?" asked the milkmaid snidely.

"There it's worth no-thing at all," said Sveta.

The locals grumbled when they saw the Tajiks: "If it's not the blacks, then the saints!" The saints were the Muscovites who had settled there after the restoration of the Optina monastery. Barefoot and grubby, their children raced around the neighborhood just like the village children.

When they got back from the field the Tajiks found the things which some of the people of Kozelsk had collected for them. They ripped the parcels open right there and then, trying on the clothes and stuffing their mouths full of bread. Zafar pulled on some colorful girls' tops, and the grown-ups looked on, laughing softly. Sveta handled the pots with a doleful look. She only knew how to cook flatbread, so they weren't much use to her. In the evening Zafar raced around clanging the frying pan against the pot, so that the old folks began to cross themselves, thinking it was the fire bell.

Every day Sveta would bring in the cows, and the chubby milkmaids, flushed from vodka, fed her leftovers. She was usually quiet, but one time she began to open up: "I got used to hav-ing Kolya a-round, shame to have to give him back."

"Who to?" the milkmaids asked.

"His wife," Sveta replied. And she described how they had met while travelling from Tajkistan and had already become a couple during the train journey—in Russia, as in war, it was impossible to survive alone.

The jasmine was in bloom and the air was sticky and cloying like Eastern sweetmeats. Shashlik kebabs were roasting, and guests had come together around the long table, their conversations sparking up and ebbing like the coal flames on the grill.

"I've decided to do some good deeds," announced the fat man loudly, wiping his hands on his trousers.

Laughter broke out around the table.

"One good deed a day—surely that's not too much," he said, offended.

"You've got an alarm clock in place of a heart," tutted the host, "everything right on schedule."

The fat man grew indignant, and the priest sitting next to him, his beard wet with wine, said with a loud cough: "The Lord welcometh the intention."*

* From St. John Chrysostom's (Russian: Ivan Zlatoust) Paschal Sermon: "The Lord accepteth the deed and welcometh the intention."

Children were swarming around like midges.

"Such wide expanses all around," said the hostess, gesturing with arms outstretched. "How on earth could we have lived in Moscow?'

"We envy you!" said the Muscovites, nodding. "When we go back, the advertising boards all say 'Welcome to Hell.'"

"And peoples' eyes say the same thing," said a thin man, taking a notebook from his pocket. "I began to note down the random thoughts which come into my head," he went on. "Here, listen: man lives as if already dead, and comes back to life only after his death, in books, gossip, and remembrance speeches."

He straightened his glasses nervously. Silence fell around the table. Each of the guests thought their own thoughts, staring at their plates, and even the children were quiet, exchanging looks which asked why everyone had stopped talking.

"In the kingdom of heaven we trust," said the fat man, crossing himself in the direction of Optina.

The priest nodded wearily. "What else could we trust in . . ."

Darkness fell quickly, as if someone had switched off the lights, and the hostess brought candles. On the far bank a fire could be seen.

"They don't even have electricity," someone mumbled.

"Just like the middle ages," someone added.

They poured the wine, reminiscing about Samarkand, hikes to Karakul, and Moscow street cleaners as black-skinned as earth, and they cursed the slave-driving farmer. And when the bottles were empty, they decided it was time to make a stand for the Tajiks.

Their jeeps roared through Kozelsk, waking the dogs, which barked fit to choke. The night was dark and there wasn't a single star in the sky. Navigating the muddy tracks with difficulty, they came to the meadow. They hooted the car horn again and again, and the fat man knocked on the metal container, which shook as if in fear.

The Tajiks came out, holding hands, squinting in the blinding headlights. "You stay home," the fat man told Zafar, patting the boy's cheek.

They took Sveta and Kolya to the farmer's place. Along the way they picked up a couple of men from Kozelsk, and an officer from the army base who hugged his double-barreled hunting rifle close like a lover.

The inhabitants of Kozelsk called this street the "Poor District." The grand town residences towered over the humble village dwellings, which looked like sheds in comparison, and the farmer's house had turrets and battlements, like a medieval castle. High up on the fence, light glinted off a crest of arms depicting an imperial eagle with cockerel heads—the man who had forged it with such skill had worked all his life in a poultry farm, and he still chopped wood as if he were chopping chickens' necks.

But the farmer did not meet them alone, he came out through the gate with his guards. The Muscovites sobered up in an instant. The farmer smirked, the guards looked on menacingly, and the dogs pulled at their chains, snarling. The visitors had already begun to regret that they had come. No one wanted to speak first and it seemed as if they stood there, in silence, all night. They could hear a drunk woman swearing somewhere in the village, the Tajik woman sniffling, and the heavy breathing of the bulky farmer.

"It's not right, you know," said the officer at last. "You should pay them, they're not serfs after all."

One of the guards, the back of his head tough like an old turnip, fixed a heavy gaze on the proceedings, looking as if some distant memories were coming back to him.

"Come on, we Russians know how to do a deal," said the farmer, blowing his nose with a snort in the direction of his feet.

The Tajiks huddled close to each other.

"A deal!?" yelled the fat man. "What makes you think you can treat people like cattle?"

The farmer gave a sign and disappeared behind the cast iron gates. The guards tugged the Tajiks out from the group by their hair, as if pulling carrots from the ground, and dragged them towards the car. The officer made a grab for his rifle, but was floored by a blow from a knuckleduster. Sveta saw blood, and began to wail. The car took some time to start, and she could be heard inside, beating against the window.

Left alone, the Muscovites looked around confused, and the

officer spat blood. Curtains stirred in the neighboring houses, but no one came out.

"That's a nice state of affairs," said the thin man, grabbing for the notebook in his breast pocket as if clutching at his heart.

Suddenly the gates opened and the dogs shot out. The farmer looked on from his balcony as the visitors dispersed in panic, the dogs ripping their clothes to shreds, while the officer tried to fend them off with the butt of his rifle. Some of the visitors managed to get to the safety of the car, from where they hooted the horn to scare the dogs off.

Seeing the farmer, the officer quickly raised his rifle and fired a shot without taking aim.

There was a sound of breaking glass.

"The kids just smashed a kitchen window," said the hostess, returning.

The candle flames petered out and a moth flapped futilely inside a glass jug.

"You've watched too many gangster films," said the thin man in resignation, picking nervously at the pages of his notebook. "What kind of people would set dogs on you? It's a criminal offense."

Their mobile phones lit up like glowworms in the dark, illuminating the road ahead, and the visitors started off for home.

"We'll visit the farmer tomorrow in any case," said the fat man, getting up from behind the table.

"You've put that in your list of good deeds, have you?" said the hostess, chuckling.

The women cleared the plates from the table, throwing the leftovers to the cats rubbing up against their legs.

"You don't know the local people," said the host shaking his head. "We've seen some sights in the last ten years. They'll start a fight over a bag of potatoes, and when they're drunk they'll kill a man for nothing."

Unprompted, they turned together to look at the river. On the far bank the fire had long gone out, and the container had dissolved into the thick darkness.

According to the calendar it was already autumn, but the

summer was like a clingy girlfriend, hanging on into September. The town was growing emptier as the holidaymakers departed, leaving behind their boarded-up cottages and their children's laughter, which had tumbled through the cracks between the floorboards.

The herdsmen were no longer needed, so the farmer dismissed them.

The Muscovites passed a hat around for donations, the fat man struggled for a while to find the right words, but in the end he just shoved a carefully wrapped parcel into Kolya's hand, giving a low bow.

"Bad town," whispered the Tajiks as they left.

But next summer they came back. Construction works were underway in the town, and the locals looked on bemused as the dark-skinned Asians plastered the church walls. Among them were Kolya and Zafar. The boy mixed the plaster and carried the tools, while Sveta swept the pavement. "Back home's even worse," said Kolya, gesturing in resignation.

New herdsmen had moved into the container on the other side of the river. Smoke rose from a fire in the field, and a grubby boy herded the cattle towards the river. The container had begun leaking after heavy rains, and the herdsmen had covered it in a piece of tarpaulin stolen from the building site.

And on the container someone had written "Bad Town."

TRANSLATED FROM RUSSIAN BY MATTHEW HYDE

# IVAN TOKIN

FROM *Molecules*

### "Tender Girls"

TENDER GIRLS ALWAYS have yellow hair and blue eyes. Their eyes are always green. They always have black hair, which is always red, and their eyes are the color of chestnut, and black. They're tall and skinny, beautifully plump with small breasts that are, as a rule, big. They have delicate bones and protruding cheekbones that don't show at all.

Tender girls are always beautiful, except when they, quite often, aren't. They have long, flat nails on their long, slender, shapely fingers which are blunt and crooked and with nails that are bitten. Tender girls without exception have long and short legs, with sturdy ankles and dainty, beautifully shaped feet that are narrow and wide, rough-skinned.

Tender girls are young. They are exactly twenty-nine years old, they are four years old and only like wearing leggings, they're always about fifty-eight years old and they follow fashion. I know a young, tender girl who is sixty-five. I remember one who at the age of seventy-four was the youngest and tenderest of all the young and tender girls that I have met.

Tender girls are always and often and never born, they are most often sometimes and only born of beautiful poems and sometimes all of them often appear at sunset, and especially always and very rarely at sunrise. It virtually never always happens. Because I know one that was born of a waterfall, of water drops in the air through which the sun shone. And another one and all of them that appeared out of a simple gaze at the open sea.

Tender girls have black skin that is white, always yellow and red. They have big round white bellies, flat and tight. They wear high heels with flat air soles and nothing but summer sling dresses and long sleeves. They're as tender as a razor blade melting into the veins. As a summertime dusk, on the sea coast, at about nine-thirty, in June.

You never ask tender girls anything, you ask them everything, and they won't say a thing when you talk to them about everything. They move at the speed of light while being completely still, in someone's arms, while sleeping in their nightgowns carefully tucked in, naked and uncovered, with their bare feet with socks on, wandering around the bed.

Tender girls are tender on purpose. They're silent on purpose when they talk and careful when they randomly choose who to dream with while awake. Tender girls have nothing in their heads but wisdom.

Tender girls are numerous. There are really a lot of tender girls. There are so many tender girls that it can make a man go crazy. Tender girls are only fewer than the ways you can love them.

### "On Stumbling"

A man stumbled on Starine Novaka Street. A tall, serious man, with a beard. It was a man with an agenda, going somewhere, completely aware that he was on the street, that there were others on the street too, and that they might be looking, even studying him. This man was going around, playing his part, with a bag over his shoulder, in a brown jacket and jeans and black shoes. He was passing between parked cars when his left foot slipped down the white slope of the curb of the sidewalk. In that moment, completely stripped of his role, the man's entire being became absorbed in one single objective—restoring the balance that had been lost.

It was just a short moment. A moment in which the man, single-mindedly, directed all his abilities towards a simple goal. In that moment, although I couldn't know what he was thinking, I knew that he had nothing else on his mind, and that his body didn't move for any other purpose. In that one short excerpt of his life. It wasn't just me who noticed it; any of you could have seen it, had you been there. And you would have recognized the situation in which you find yourselves from time to time. Something goes wrong, something completely harmless, something you can't predict, and everything else simply disappears—you're left alone with your problem, and it gets the best out of you. If there's even a slight chance to get out of it, you will, because you'll do your best. It's not something you plan, or something that happens because you practice positive thinking—you just give your best, because you have to.

Somehow you always count on getting where you're headed. The risks are understood, and you manage them unconsciously; you don't cross the street when you see a bus coming, you don't take a shortcut by jumping off a bridge instead of going down the stairs—things like that. But you never think: "I must take care not to stumble."

Being close enough, I had a good view of the man's face. His foot had slipped, the whole body followed, and his face told me everything. It showed surprise first, then the acknowledgement of the situation, and then the beauty of it all—dedication, as well as freedom. All else ceased to exist, his entire life and everyone in it, and all other plans disappeared before a simple task—keeping the frail body away from the potential danger caused by stumbling on the very edge of a busy road.

In order to be able to experience whatever there is left for you in life—to see the woman you love or your children busy with their own lives a certain number of times, to sit at the pub as many times as your liver allows you to, to earn another, say, two hundred and eighty paychecks, one hundred pension checks, or a completely unpredictable number of fees, move to the seacoast to grow olives and watch your own wife walk barefoot along the shore of that sea at least two hundred and fifty days a year—that frail body of yours needs to be kept alive.

I saw the face of the man in the moment when he was giving his best. I saw it clearly, and I was jealous. I was jealous of the unity of his body and spirit, of the fact that, for him, in that moment, everything else was gone. All that he loved most and that drove him crazy and all the other fripperies in between. There was a situation, and he remained alone in it.

To be alone in a situation, with one's entire being perfectly engrossed in it—well, I can't think of anything better. How I wish I could cook one lunch in that state of mind. Not wander off the topic when talking about something. Not start crying.

Let me tell you something—that man pulled through in a second. He found his balance, and he did it safely too. His left knee cracked a little, but his right leg was strong enough to deal with the situation on its own. His body jerked backward, and he found himself on the sidewalk. He was back in his normal state, with everything that he is, distributed evenly on both the left and the right side of his being. His face became calm, satisfied. And he forgot what had happened right away. That's what we all do. It goes away instantly. If I met him again in a while and asked him: "Do you remember that one time when you stumbled on Starine Novaka Street some ten days ago, about five-thirty in the afternoon?" he would remember. But if I didn't ask him, the situation would most surely fade into oblivion—he'd never think of it again. Just like the rest of us wouldn't.

But we should. There aren't many things that I'm sure of—I can honestly say that there is almost nothing that I'm sure of—but I couldn't be surer about this stumbling thing. You stumble on the curb of a road and get a glimpse of an excellent version of yourself. Then, you use that version every time you have to fight to survive, and you'll have nothing to worry about. Just like the bearded man, who, only a moment later, was a regular guy again, on his way to finish some errands. Like anybody else in that street.

## "The Dog"

A gray bird is on the window ledge. A yellow-brown dog is on the floor. His tongue is out, his ear drooping to the side. The bird flies away, the dog stays. Why does the dog stay? I ask the dog: "Why do you stay, day after day?" The dog is quiet, the dog is asleep, the dog can't hear me. The dog is old and almost completely deaf. The dog stays because I feed him. The dog stays because it's warm when it's cold outside. The dog stays because there's a place where he sleeps and his water bowl. I ask the dog: "Why do you stay, day after day, all these years?" No answer from the dog. He's asleep, with one cheek pushed up toward his eye. That's just the way the dog is comfortable.

The dog runs in his sleep, moving his hind legs. That's what he's always done; he also shakes while he sleeps. Sometimes he moans. It often irritates me, because I don't want to worry about the dog. Sometimes I just don't feel like getting into what's wrong with the dog. But the dog doesn't hold it against me, I can see that he doesn't. The dog sometimes sleeps, sometimes eats, there were times when he used to run wild across the fields and maybe laughed sometimes, and now he just looks at me quietly, deaf and with weak hind legs, through the well-developed cataract on his left eye. He looks at me with his whole body, with his soul, the way he always looked at me, but the dog had to go deaf and blind for me to realize that you can look at someone with your soul.

The dog is peaceful. The dog is powerless but he doesn't feel sorry for himself. In this last phase of the dog's life I've been learning valuable lessons from him. I'm frantically attentive, but I'm not much of a pupil. I'm human, therefore I'm weak and selfish, always thinking about how to make use of things. I'm always thinking that it should be *me* achieving something. Thinking. Achieving. They're disgraceful, such schemes and pursuits. But I can't do better, so I think and achieve the best I can.

The dog is asleep and can't hear me yelling: "Why are you with me, is it because of the food?" The dog is as deaf as a post, especially when it comes to stupid questions. He can't hear anything stupid. That must be nice.

Compared to me, the dog goes through life with such good grace that it's really quite sad. For me, of course; for the dog, it's the most normal thing. The dog looks as if he has it all figured out, although he doesn't know anything. It must be a perfect state of mind—everything makes sense, and yet you know nothing.

The dog licks his paws, the dog coughs, the dog barks, the dog wants to go outside. The dog is ready at his place and is watching me expectantly, while I'm writing to myself in vain. In vain do I try to understand certain things. For a brief moment I did, but I forgot what I'd just understood, and then I started to think, and now I'm going to walk the dog, and then I'm going to bed so that, tomorrow, I can achieve something.

Eventually, the dog is just going to die, quietly and meaningfully. And I will be ridiculously heartbroken, I won't see the plain truth right before my eyes. Or I just might get the gist of it, by a stroke of luck, in honor of that dog.

### "It's Easy"

Standing on the edge between worlds, on a thin, slack rope of comprehensible truth, on one's tiptoes, dazed or unconscious, stupidly confident, insecure but persistent, staring at something small, at colors, at the way the stage is set, at the form or the content, hypnotized by beauty, sounds, word meanings, sequences of sentences, questions, eyes that meet, movements, enchanted by the gestures and positions of the body, broken by cruelty, discouraged by one's limits, encouraged by one's limits, healthy and sick at the same time, washed, with trimmed nails and clean ears, staring through a water drop at everything that there is—it's easy for the man to survive.

TRANSLATED BY JOVANKA KALABA

# MAJA GAL ŠTROMAR

## *Think of Me in the Good Times*

*To my father and to you who believe in happy stories.*

No, THIS IS NOT A *story*. It has no structure, no beginning, and no end. It is but a single *wish*. Captured in full flow. In the middle of nothing. Between what are mere hints of a beginning and an end. Like the full moon above a Karst forest clearing, like a *man*, standing amidst the dead grass, keeping silent about the incipient eruption of the sun, unable to cry the word out loud. It is but a word, thrust straight at the ferocious soil, like a stake, hollering with cruelty as it is driven into the sodden earth, until the sun assumes its place. Do not think this is a beginning. It is not; it is but a continuation.

### INTOLERABLE BEGINNINGS

It would have been enough if I had fallen. Fallen into the flow. As you might, one summer, accidentally fall into the river that you have for so long been merely contemplating from its bank. For some cogent reason or another (yes, all reasons are always cogent, especially when their purpose is to distance us from something), you never dared step into it, despite being, according to certain statistics, almost at the halfway point towards the point where it spills into the sea. It would probably have been enough if I had at least caught a *fish* in this river. I call it a fish—it could just as well be described as the *befitting thought* that hounded me ever since I first stepped into this world. I am not sure when the need to chase the *befittingness of the thought* actually arose, so I assume it has been there since the start. From the beginning. It occurred at the source. It would thus be appropriate to begin at the beginning. Should I take the beginning to be the moment my umbilical cord was cut? Or should it be the moment my mother's water broke? A narrow warm slimy stream, trickling down her leg, and Father rushing her off to the maternity ward in our white *Fičo*, the Yugoslav version of the miniscule Fiat 600. To help her deal with the intense labor pains, he lights her a cigarette. She draws and puffs like mad. *Waters, the Fičo, a cigarette*, and the man with his back turned towards me. He is driving a car. A beginning that sets off a tremendous pain as the pelvis widens, intolerable pain. Birth as a moment of simultaneous pain and fleeting joy. A slip. A cry. A cut and a cry. A trigger in the lungs, the amniotic fluid disappears and you take your first breath. On your own. Independently. From pain to joy. A cry, a cry of joy. And the man with his back turned towards me. Leaving, standing, or just leading the way, is it not therefore obvious that he would have his back turned towards me?

. . .

To be honest, it is not the thought which is ripping me apart, nor is it something I want to capture, or particularly wish to put into words; it is merely some sort of tangled substance, maybe an image, something complicated that only rarely offers a glimpse of its comprehensible resolution. Only at certain moments does it appear as a coherent ending and the confusion elucidates. At such times it brings hope, a bright, clear gap of relief. *Release and relief.* Perhaps this is what I would like to capture. But it only appears occasionally and in abrupt intervals, usually when I'm on the move, driving along in my car, no longer the tiny Fiat, but my own car, my red, *sixteen-valve rosso malizioso*. Leaving, standing, or just leading the way, is it not therefore obvious that I would have my back turned towards me? As I drive along then, never at home. *Never at home*, I repeat to myself with surprise. Why never at home? What does being at home mean? To reside? To live? To be? To exist within the four walls of adulthood whilst still roving around the home of your childhood like a stranger, like a secret agent. Snooping about? Snooping on whom?

. . .

It would have been enough if I started with this: What does having a home mean? The river. A *riverhome*. Then I could continue to explore where one home ends and another begins, to find out where the river I want to wade into flows. Because until I step into it, I will not flow, I will not pass. This is probably why I stand on the riverbank, stand like a goddess. A belated goddess. Afraid of *flowing downstream. Flowing conclusively.* Better not start something you don't know how to end. Is being homeless a sign of weakness?

. . .

I don't know *why* I am writing all this, just as I don't know why, for the past months, I have been watering and tending an unidentified plant on my balcony. I keep asking random people passing by whether this overgrown thing could be a potato, strawberry, or tomato plant. Something that might be useful. Something that might feed me. It grows vigorously, greedily spreading new leaves, demanding a good bucketful of water every day. It occurs to me that it could just be a weed. Maybe I'm growing a plain old weed. Something resiliently stubborn and parasitic. Something that *sane* and focused people pull up and discard, suppress as soon as it germinates. *Because it cannot feed us? Kill something living simply because it doesn't feed us? Should the growing of anything be tied in with meaning, self-interest, and premeditation?* And here am I, allowing its uselessness to spread and propagate. Waiting for it to bear fruit. *Bear fruit or disappoint and go to seed?* Do weeds bear fruit?

. . .

It would probably have been enough if I had simply fallen in. Fallen into the flow. And stopped being an outside observer, an *external correspondent on my own life.* Perhaps someone could push me. Push me into the river. Push me towards happiness. Perhaps I could even ask somebody to push me, like the time I asked a friend to attach little training wheels to my bike. I was well over twenty.

Father never taught me how to ride a bike and I was afraid of just rolling down the hill without anything, afraid of losing control. I *needed* the training wheels to hold my balance. I asked the friend to adjust the wheels every day without me noticing. I would know, of course, but could masterfully pretend that I still had the support until I was ready to *confidently* set off on a long cycling marathon. Then again, someone could push me in out of sheer mercy, push me into the river, into happiness, into the flow. I would start trusting despite my trust originating in a white lie. I would start living, for I still get the feeling that I'm not in the flow, that I'm still on the riverbank, occasionally sticking my feet into the gravel washed up against the bank, occasionally washing myself in the ice-cold water, leaping into the water for a brief moment and immediately looking for a rock to grab hold of and climb back out again, only to once more watch the river flow past me, a silent observer. *An external correspondent on my own life.*

. . .

I am forever awaiting something. I try to remember that first push, that urge to breathe on my own, pushing my head towards the exit. I try to sense the force with which the crown of my head stubbornly falls towards the crevice of light and relentlessly widens and tears my mother's bones. I try to remember the moment I raced with a ferocious horde of sperm towards the egg. I try to remember the triumphant moment when I realized I had made it. The only one out of the millions of other marathon runners. I would like to remember how the head of the sperm cell burrowed into the soft surface of the egg, pushed deeper into the yolk of creation, and shed its tail when it was no longer needed. I try to remember the creature inside the parental cell. Inside the cell that splits into transience and eternity. I try to remember with what bravado and self-confidence I did so. It was evident that I wanted to be born. Evident that I wanted to become, evident that I was a bearer of life. I had made it. I, who am incapable of running a mile without doing my back in, without my untrained lungs betraying me. I try to remember the sensation of that initial triumph, the sense of accomplishment, the tranquility of resting inside the egg of conception and the curiosity of growth that awaited me. Was I capable of love then?

. . .

Some people mention happiness as the moment they call *belonging*, within oneself, being present, this curious, evasive rapture that dissolves as soon as it occurs in the brain. That's where it all supposedly happens, inside the brain, through chemistry and hormones. Some people like to repeat this too often, probably only as an excuse, using science to escape anything that might surprise and surpass them. Subvert their command. Perhaps science is just as much of a speculation as other divinations, its difference being that it uses equipment—how *funny*, equipment that was nevertheless created by the limited human mind. I cannot agree to anything definitively because I do not know. I'd like to, though. I'd like to fall into the flow of *relief*. To find my own home. To be, meaning to be both relieved and happy. To live within myself. Always. Without doubts, without control. On the sofa, the pullout sofa that can double as a heart, a pullout heart, a beer or Coke in hand, one that can be a wheat field of caresses with a cup of chestnut ice-cream, can be a children's book, legs on the table, can be the horizon that never offers an identical repeat performance by the setting sun. Was this what the moment of my birth was like? Was I happy then? Was my first cry one of being deeply moved by the fact that I had condensed onto this planet? Who is to say? Mother says I sang. Not cried, but sang a kind of musical scale. A scale with a particular tonality, a particular syncopated rhythm. What was this tune like? A happy one in a major scale or a sad one in a minor?

. . .

Happiness does not exist in verb form. Perhaps this is because it contains no duration, it is only a blast, a friction. A suspicion, simple, never continuous. Like a momentary realization, a fleeting acquaintance that buds inside us and then instantly sinks into oblivion. Only encounters can withstand duration. And even that is limited. (*Another realization.*) With a sell-by-date on the box. From – until. From discharge to discharge. From the initial discharge of semen to the final discharge of the river into the sea. In between come the encounters. The sell-by-date is printed on the packaging. Best before, recommended time. Once past this date, it has to be discarded. So, arrive to encounter, then leave.

. . .

I keep dilly-dallying. This is still not a beginning. I am not yet capable of a beginning. I need to rewind the film a few more times. Is it really that difficult? Difficult to say that I am sitting on a chair, staring into the void? Trying to remember, to recall. People in the room wait respectfully. They are patient. Silent. They know how hard it is to stare at an empty chair. Is the chair I am sitting on really empty?

. . .

So I return to this *befittingness of the thought* that keeps pursuing me, return to its evasiveness. Perhaps, instead of its beginning, I could try to seize its end, then we could pretend that it is easy to catch the *fish* by hand. But it seems we are never well-enough equipped to pursue befittingness . . . I could only grab a loose end, a frayed thread, one of those at the end of the seam of the soft fabric of the nightdress I never took off as I waited to grow up. A nightdress patched up over and over again. Or maybe I wish to consider the whole, look upon it from afar, through a wide-angled lens, the way a tailor sees a gray factory-wound thread on a cardboard spool and knows exactly where to find both ends. The way only sailors know where the sea starts and where it ends. Maybe I'd like to write a story, a novel, a screenplay, in order to understand it, to untangle the ball of wool. I could become entangled myself along the way. Entrapped. Yes, a trap. Is this writing of mine not a trap? This wish for completeness? The wish to slacken the meanders, the unknown knots, in order to find out. Find out what? *Step into the river that I am merely observing, shouting after it to wait for me.* I would draw out the thread into a straight line from here to there. On it I could mark certain points, years perhaps, events in my life. All the embankments I have stopped at along the way. I could thread them as tiny pearls onto a necklace and hang it round my neck. I would know for sure, I should see, should realize, what it is that is ever present, what exists within me as some kind of *eternal accomplishment. (Inside me everything would still agree: "This is a word, only a word, incapable of expressing any substance!")* But in this straightened-out timeline it should be obvious. As I say this, I am already nearing *restlessness*, at the same time cherishing a kind of burning, hollow desire for a final cut. As if I want in a single stroke to both understand the world and end it. *To stop being so restless.* To catch my life by one end of the thread that has all along been flirting with the other end. Wrap everything up and, in doing so, throw over my shoulder all that is redundant. Into the wastepaper basket. Like in basketball. A free throw. One zip. I'm in the lead. I'm winning. Losing in order to win. But I no longer want to compete. No more comparisons. No more trading. *All I am is sad, sad and restless. And I no longer want this.*

. . .

No, I don't really want to simply wrap everything up. For all you know, I'm probably talking about *death*, but it has to do with the appropriateness of the word that poets like to stick on their covers to elicit in their readers an awed, perhaps morbid admiration, thinking that they, the writers, know what dying means. (*As in any good film, here too you need to have a little death, a little sex, a little birth, and a little pain. Any good manual will tell you as much.*) No, basically I wish to start anew. Talk about birth. Start from zero. From the beginning. Tie the thread between two dwellings, two homes, *between the home of my childhood and the home of my adult womanhood,* and then, with light ballerina steps, walk across the abyss. As a child, that's how I imagined the beginning of life. I drew a boy and a girl on a sheet of paper. They were clumsy, little more than circles, one with a skirt and the other with straight lines for pants. I was young and these were the limits of my artistic abilities, simple, clean lines, joining the circles that were their tummies with a thin line. No genitals of course, just a thread linking their bodies, and along it, tiny figures, genderless and unidentifiable, marching from father to mother in an even row. From navel to navel. Father was very angry, waving the sheet of paper above my head as I lay in my bed, ranting and raving about who the hell had filled my mind with stupid rubbish like this. I didn't understand what I had done wrong. What I was guilty of. All he did was shout and wave the sheet of paper around. Probably out of embarrassment. I don't know, we never talked about it. I wanted to understand how I had begun. My brother smirked, I know it was he who told on me. Then it was all forgotten. No more talk about how I was born. How it all began. They bought me a few children's sex education books with titles like *Time for the Stork to Retire*. There was one about a mommy going to the hospital and the diligent daughter cooking sausages and pudding for daddy. How I wished my mother would become ill and have to go to the hospital so I could stay alone with him and show him that I know how to cook dinner. But Mother was always healthy, active, seemingly invincible. She was only consigned to bed once, after a miscarriage, but she stayed at home. Thus I could only dream of evenings with pudding and Father. *According to some quasi-literary sources of supposedly didactical nature, time with the father is only possible in the event of the mother becoming weak, frail, and absent. What a grim, heavy anchor for all generations that were fed such juvenile fiction: out of the way, Mother, remove yourself, surrender part of your domain of kindness and healthiness to the father! Mother, do not repress him with your saintliness!* Yet to start anew, start from zero, is probably the same trap, the same face, just that is appears on the opposite side of the coin. A malady of the impatient and undernourished.

. . .

Perhaps I should start at the end that is not an end. Where it all starts to unravel. In life we think we have an infinite amount of time left ahead of us. In death this time condenses, flattens. Time disappears. We sink into the bosom of lost nights. As we die. (*You can claim that writers, with a touch of perversity, still habitually dabble with thoughts about the end.*) It occurs to me that ultimately it could well have been the umbilical cord that marked me with the thought about the end. I was born with it wrapped around my neck three times. Some said that even then I wanted to leave. Get it all over with. Take a quick peep and slam the door shut again. Process it in a single charge, to experience a summer storm, to feel the wind, and then forgo this worldly mess. In return, cause immeasurable pain to my young creators and deny them the joy of their tiny screaming achievement. So I preferred to drag it out a little, perhaps out of curiosity over what hides behind it all, or just to be obliging to my parents. I still like wearing necklaces. And I am, to this day, obliging. What a strange notion, wearing beads around your neck, not to show off your attractiveness or out of vanity, but to accentuate your transience. People are unaware that the decorative kitsch you wear is a reference to your finality. A string of beads that now restlessly roll towards the sea.

. . .

*To begin. To end. To try to pursue befittingness.* Yet in essence I am still here, waiting for deliverance. Procrastinating. Waiting for someone to corner me and force me to launch. For someone to remove my training wheels. For someone to push me into the water. Waiting for a magical deliverance. How pathetic. Where do I get that from? Deliverance can come in the form of a pot full of cooked spaghetti and a tin of red beans, enough to fill us, settle the intestinal disquiet and, though only for a short time, fill our emptiness. Our pancreas tells the brain that all is fine and tricks it into replacing the ever-growing emptiness that is becoming the shadow of itself. I don't really know. All I know is that what remains is the record, the empty space of deception. Recovery? Like a river running through the Karst Plateau that disappears underground and then reappears. Even though we know all the tricks of how to replace this emptiness with being healthy, with running or other exploits, a sort of echo of it is always present. With determination we pedal our mountain bike up the hill until our back hurts and our knees ache, and even after an operation, after you've been interfered with and tagged, marked with certain words, scalpels, broken illusions, you still pedal away, sweat and curse the hill which you are at the same time grateful to for being so merciless, for not giving in to your wish that, for a moment at least, it would let up; for then, once and for all, you would have to face the fact, you would be forced to see. There, on the flat section, everything is visible, everything is exposed. The pellucid valley spreads before you like the lines on the palm of your hand. Yet seeing things too soon cannot be good. The bright light, the over-powerful rays of truth, might burn us out. Whose truth? Not to leave. Not to die. By knowing, will I die? Is *finding out* really linked to *dying*? With tying the thread between two dwellings, two homes, *between the home of my childhood and the home of my adult womanhood.* Will I dare step above this abyss?

· · ·

That is why you pedal up the hill, because you never see the summit. You never see the end. And just as you believe you have reached the top, another summit appears beyond. Or you insanely create one yourself. Again and again, you step before the Wailing Wall. Again and again, you fear the realization. Realization of what? *That upon the final acceptance of love you would have to die?* And if the difficult track levels out, only for a brief moment, you start thinking, and you always start thinking about it when it's least appropriate to do so.

· · ·

If only I would *come to terms* with it, be like the thin trail of white sugar accidentally sprinkled across the table, I would discover that it is always there, still present, and what's more, that it has never moved from there because I don't want it to move. Always landing on the same wobbly table, the cherrywood table from my childhood. And I would stare up at myself in the presence of my favorite face that is no more. *Father's face.*

TRANSLATED FROM THE SLOVENE BY GREGOR TIMOTHY ČEH

# KARMELE JAIO

## *Two Stories*

### "The Mirror"

THE STEAM FROM THE SHOWER stall has clouded the mirror before you. You can hardly see your naked body in it as you towel yourself dry.

You put cream on your skin, slowly, very slowly: breasts, chest, neck, inner arms, outer arms, elbows, belly, butt, inner thighs, outer thighs . . .

As you smell the cream, the same old thought comes to mind: you can't compare women to flowers, that's a terrible thing to do.

Kepa used to do that. Again and again, he compared women to flowers: if she wasn't a carnation, she was a rose. Women were always like flowers to Kepa. And he always lived among the flowers at the university, surrounded by young students, students who never get old since they are the same age every year. He thought he was the same age every year too.

You also work surrounded by young people at the high school, even though fewer and fewer of them choose your Latin classes, but you know all too well that the only one in your classroom who gets older from year to year is you, and that for the students before you, you are a dead language, like the dead body of a cat on the edge of a highway.

Some clearings have opened in the steam on the mirror. You can see your face in one and in another, lower down, your belly.

You are starting to appear.

You were also a flower for Kepa, at least for a time. It's been two years since he left, left this house, left this bathroom as well, even though you have not yet thrown away that bottle of his aftershave there. And now you are beginning to realize, after fifteen years

255

together, that in the last few years you were still a flower for Kepa, but no longer a rose, a carnation, a poppy in the meadow blowing in the south wind. For Kepa you were a geranium by the end. A geranium in a pot.

And given the choice, he would rather have the freshness, vitality, and freedom of a wild daisy. Because a daisy grows on the mountainside, in a green meadow, in any park. The geranium, on the other hand, grows in a pot; in a pot on an old lady's windowsill or balcony. Daisies laugh at the sun, geraniums cough in the narrow, dark, and windy streets of an old city. And when winter comes, old ladies cover their geraniums with plastic so they won't die. Not daisies, daisies die and come back to life endlessly. They are always young, like university students.

The steam on the mirror hides only your chest, everything else is visible: your face, arms, belly . . .

You shake lavender water into your hands and spread it over your chest and between your legs. You like the freshness of lavender, it banishes the smells of your body.

Your skin has started to smell more and more these last years, especially since Kepa left. You have begun to understand how that unbearable and stifling smell emerges in old folks' homes. The smell of your body has become a specter that haunts you. So, with the idea of banishing all smells, you started turning the shower head directly on your pussy, close up, and you still do it, though not exactly for the same reason. Now you enter the shower stall seeking the caress of the water.

You get into the shower, change the mode of the spray, and when a narrower and stronger spray comes out, aim it at your pussy and set your soul to dancing. From your pussy up to somewhere around your navel the waves rise and you feel them breaking inside your body, *crash* and *crash*, one wave after another. You finish with your forehead against the glass of the stall, gasping, and let the shower head fall to dance like a crazy snake. Your face against the glass, like old ladies who spend their lives looking at geraniums.

You would like to be neutral, like the deodorant you put on. You are afraid a man will smell the wet smell of stagnation on your naked skin. It frightens you that a man could smell the attic smell on your body, and maybe that's why you haven't even tried to have sex with anyone these last two years. Why Kepa's aftershave is still in your bathroom. Maybe that's why.

No, that young girl, that student of Kepa's, she was no daisy, nor were you, and you are not a geranium. Comparing women to flowers is a terrible thing to do. People don't know anything about flowers. People don't know anything about women. Not even most women.

When the steam on the mirror disappears, you stand looking at your naked body, and see that black hairs have grown around your nipples.

They are very black. And yes, they look like the thorns of a thistle.

## "The Scream"

I write at night. When my husband and children go to sleep, I turn on the computer in the corner of the living room where I've set up a sort of desk—my home isn't big enough for *a room of one's own*—and that's where I work, playing with words, or perhaps more accurately, fighting with them. But even before I start writing, I'm writing in my mind, thinking over what I will write at night. In this way, by writing without writing, I've made many strategic decisions for my creative work. Two years ago, for example, I was on my knees at the tub lathering my children's hair when I decided that the protagonist of my latest novel would have a hidden passion: he would be a great painter hidden behind the mask of a lawyer; and I've been known to decide whether to kill off a character in a story or let him live while I make dinner. There are lives at stake while I beat the eggs.

I don't make a living writing. I work in the library at the Fine Arts Museum. It's no coincidence, then, that a passion for painting has appeared in my latest novel—a writer's life sneaks into his or her fiction like a lizard among rocks. I wouldn't say I don't like my job, for it's no bad thing for someone who loves culture to spend the day surrounded by art books, and I do especially like painting, but the eight hours a day I spend there is time I would more happily spend writing. For the moment, however, I have no choice but to write at night, and I manage quite well that way, even though the next day I'm nearly falling asleep while I sort the books.

That's how I've written until now, but things have changed in the last year, because something has happened that makes it difficult for me to be alone in the living room at night. And as a result, the way I write has been completely disrupted.

My husband is a soccer fan. Or rather, not merely a fan; he is a true believer. He is a passionate follower of Athletic Bilbao, but his passion goes beyond that, and it is soccer itself, soccer in its entirety, that is his greatest passion. Soccer is inscribed on his mind in capital letters. Or rather, not merely on his mind, but on his heart. My husband loves everything about soccer the way another person—the protagonist of my latest novel, for example, or I myself—might love everything about painting. You might be an ardent lover of Monet, but that doesn't prevent you from greatly admiring Cezanne, Goya, Renoir, Zuloaga, Gal, Zumeta, or Kahlo.

So it is with my husband. He loves soccer, not just his own team. He'll watch Barcelona or Bayern Munich without even blinking, but he's equally capable of feeding his passion by watching Eibar or Lemoa. He enjoys the goals, passes, and free kicks by the stars of Real Madrid, Manchester United, or Chelsea just as much as a counterattack by Deportivo Alavés or a save made by the goalie of Bermeo, the club from his parents' home town. And what can I even say about when the national teams play? When the players line up and the anthems play, he gets nervous and raises up his head, as if he too were on the field with them, staring off into the distance. I am a World Cup widow.

So soccer has changed my writing routine. Or to be more precise, soccer itself is not at fault; I blame those who decide on the match schedule; those who have decided that soccer matches should be not only on weekends, but also during the week, and starting late besides. Ever since soccer matches started being scheduled at ten o'clock at night, I'm no longer alone in the living room. Now I have my husband at my side. And it's just not the same.

This past year, I've been sharing the living room with my husband, twenty-two players, and three referees. And that's not counting the television announcers and all the fans in the stadium. What used to be my realm at night, that solitary living room, has become a soccer stadium. And it's hard to imagine a writer, desk out on the field, writing in the middle of a stadium. That's how I saw myself at first, and it was impossible to write a single line. At that time, I was even looking forward to going to work in the morning, because at least there I could feed my soul by reading passages from art books or looking at photos of works of art. I started looking for writings by artists about their most famous works, perhaps trying to find a hint that would help me understand what I was looking for in literature. Then I read a sentence by Edvard Munch that stuck in my mind. He said that he found the inspiration for his famous painting "The Scream" when he saw a sunset with clouds as red as blood. *The colors were screaming*, he wrote, remembering that moment. *The colors were screaming.*

This last year, I have had to accept that I have no choice but to write while my husband watches soccer on television. And I still write like that now. Our living room is large, the corner where I write is far from the television, and I write with my back to the television in any case. My husband uses headphones so I won't hear the sound.

"You do your thing, and don't mind me," he tells me.

But he doesn't realize that from time to time I hear

"Ohhhh . . ."

Sometimes it's

"Hmmm . . ."

Or

"No, no! How could that be a foul?"

I'm sure he doesn't realize he's doing it. I know that he's very careful not to make a sound, and he bites his tongue to stop himself from screaming when there's a goal. But it doesn't matter if he screams "Goal!" or not. When a team scores a goal, I hear a sort of muffled hiccup behind me, a silent scream that moves the pictures on the wall a millimeter or two, a sigh, and I look over my shoulder and see my husband leaning forward a centimeter or two. Stretching out his neck and his legs, eyes wide and fingers spread apart like two spiders. His whole body screams *goal*, even if he doesn't open his mouth.

Ever since I've been writing with my husband in the room, I keep thinking that if I could excite a reader with my writing half as much as soccer excites my husband, I would be happy, it would meet all my literary dreams and desires. But I don't think that anything I've written has ever inspired such emotion in anyone. Sometimes I wonder why I write, for whom, and whether my words have what it takes to move someone. And if they can't stir anyone more than a soccer ball, whether it's really worthwhile to keep writing. This is why recently I've been looking for a purpose in the writings of artists—Frida Kahlo, Van Gogh, Picasso . . . —a clue that will make me believe that it's worthwhile to keep believing in art.

My husband doesn't feel the same burning desire for literature that he feels for soccer, nor for what I write, there's no doubt about that, and I've had to accept it since my first book was published. He reads my books, or it might be more accurate to say he starts reading my books, but I know he doesn't finish them. When I publish a new book, he picks it up, makes a comment about the cover, makes another about how thick it is or about my picture on the back cover, and says:

"It looks good."

Or he'll point to my picture on the back and ask the kids:

"Who do you think this is?"

Or he'll read the first few lines and say:

"It starts off well, doesn't it?"

But I know he won't make it past page ten. His bookmark stays there for months, right in the same place. Right on page ten. He doesn't ever make it to page eleven. As if the number eleven were reserved solely for soccer.

Ever since I started writing while my husband watches soccer, ever since I keep hearing *ohhhh*, *hmmm*, and silent screams behind me, one idea has become my obsession. I look at the screen, then I look at my husband with his eyes glued to the screen, and I ask myself over and over what on earth does this sport have that inspires such passion in my husband and in millions of other people? What is it that rouses their most basic instincts? And in my mind this question has become my obsession: is it possible to transfer that passion to literature?

With that question in mind, I started trying. I started writing while looking at my husband, as if I wanted to bring his passion to my writing, as if I wanted to suck his blood like a vampire. I look at the screen first, then at my husband, screen, husband, screen, husband. Like a painter looking at the horizon, I keep looking up at the man sitting on the sofa with his headphones on. When I see his lower lip tremble when they're about to make a risky throw-in, I ask myself how I can achieve the same effect in a reader, using only words. What adjectives should I use? What arguments?

And in the last few months, something surprising has been happening to me. Watching my husband's emotions from so close up—I had never noticed how deep his passion was—the words have started to bubble out of me. Ever since I started watching my husband while I write, I write better, I write with greater passion, it feels like the letters seize the page with their fingernails, the words bite when you read them. And the words come to me one after another endlessly, to the extent that I managed to finish the novel that I haven't been able to finish for the last two years. Watching my husband released a knot I carried inside me.

Watching my husband, I decided that the protagonist of my latest novel had to rebel, leave his job as a lawyer, and start painting, following his true passion. And when he finished his paintings he would cry, he would sob, with happiness, with satisfaction, with pleasure. And he would start a new life, a new and happy life led by his passion.

When my editor read it, he called me at one o'clock in the morning. He couldn't wait until the next day to call. He said my writing had made him cry, it was my greatest novel, it would be incredibly successful, and so on, while I stood there in my nightgown rubbing the sleep from my eyes.

The novel was published a month ago, and my publisher's predictions have come true. It's at the top of the best-seller list and has had good reviews so far. In their comments, the critics use words like *emotion* and *passion*. I receive emails from readers, many of them thanking me for helping them unleash their true passion, some have found the courage to begin writing, others have started singing, a few have revealed the attraction they feel for people of the same sex. That is, they have started doing what their passions dictate, because of my novel.

And surprising as it may be, the book has had an effect not only on my readers, but also on my husband. He left page ten behind long ago and this week I keep seeing him around the house with the book. Apparently, for him, it's not just another one of my books. If I speak to him when he's reading, he doesn't answer, just like when he's watching the World Cup on television.

And I am grateful to soccer in a way I never thought possible. Every day, I keep watching my husband as I sit in the corner where I write. And little by little I'm coming to realize that I'm watching him more and writing less, because it's so moving to see the tears in his eyes when his team fails a penalty kick, or the way he gulps at a direct free kick.

Today I got up from my chair and went to sit beside him. He has my novel right next to him on the sofa. The bookmark shows that he's almost done with it. I sit next to him to feel his body heat and ask him to take off his headphones so we can watch the match together. I read in the newspaper that it's an important qualifying round. (Ever since I've started writing while watching my husband, I've been reading the sports pages.) And I felt a closeness I haven't felt for years, with both of us doing the same thing, side by side, together. That moment watching television together was one of life's bright and shining gifts. One I hadn't experienced since we used to go to the movies when we first started going out.

And there we were, when suddenly my husband looks away from the television, picks up my book from the sofa, and starts reading. I can't believe it. I can't even look at him, I don't want him to see how surprised I am so, as if what's happening is completely normal, I keep looking at the screen.

And there, on the screen, I see the ball rolling down the field, and behind it, four sweating players. The one in the red shirt touches the ball with his right leg and the others run after it, urgently, as if their hearts were trapped in that ball. The announcer says that the white team is putting on the pressure and that that makes the red team's counterattacks risky. The red player has the ball, he shoots, another player breaks away, now he's got it, he's running with it, he's all alone, it's just him and the goalie. The announcer talks faster and louder, the spectators are on their feet, the goalie moves forward with his hands and legs outstretched, and suddenly the forward kicks hard, he shoots, and the ball goes right between the goalie's legs and into the net.

"Goal!"

My husband looks at me, astonished.

"Did you just say goal?"

"Me?"

"Yes, you just screamed goal."

"Don't be silly, it must have been your imagination."

"Would you mind using the headphones? I'm just finishing your book . . ."

I want to tell him I don't need the headphones, but I see him concentrating so hard on my book that I put them on, and now the announcers are inside my head, speaking right into my ears. They speak with passion, I can hear their heartbeats through the headphones and my own heart starts to beat faster.

My husband watches the replay of the goal and then goes back to reading. This is unbelievable. I could turn off the television and start writing, but I don't feel like it. And now I'm afraid that I might not be able to write if I can't see my husband's excitement as he watches a match.

There he is. He's not even blinking. But he's not watching the match; he's reading my book.

On the television, in the meantime, the score is tied at one and there are five minutes to go. The announcer says it could go either way. And my husband is reading. I need the answer to one question. Is my novel really more interesting to him right now than the last five minutes of a qualifying match? That can't be right. I have to test this. I take off the headphones and turn up the volume on the television.

"What are you doing?" he asks.

"The match is almost over," I say.

"Okay, just a second though. Turn it down a little, I'm just about to finish . . ." he says without looking up from the book.

And I put on the headphones again. I look at him out of the corner of my eye, he's on the last three pages, and then I notice that his eyes are bright. *Mmm*, he says, taking a deep breath and letting out a long sigh. Yes, even though I can't quite believe it, my husband is about to cry reading my novel.

I look back at the screen, at the last five minutes of the match, and my hands start to shake, and the blood is moving faster than ever through my veins.

It's a miracle.

The white and red shirts of the players, the colors of the referees, spectators, and advertisements around the field, green, yellow, blue, black, and orange all mixed together make a palette of colors; the players passing to each other make strong white brush strokes, the forward's dribbling is a swirly Van Gogh line, there is a certain plasticity that gives volume to the screen, an impressionistic intensity of light, and above it, suddenly, when the announcers' voices get louder, I see the goalie of the white team stretching out his arm the way Michelangelo's Adam reaches toward God. But his hand does not quite reach God's ray of light.

Goal!

I see red shirts jumping up and down and hugging each other, red banners waving among the spectators, a sparkler ignites the screen. And in the middle of it all, the forward who got the goal, on his knees and looking to the heavens, screaming ecstatically.

The tears in my eyes give the image a *sfumato* effect, blurring the edges and bringing unity.

I can't contain my tears. The colors are screaming on the television screen, and my eyes can't bear so much beauty.

TRANSLATED BY KRISTIN ADDIS

# CARLOS ROBLES LUCENA

## *Don't Ask for Gagarin*

*For Jaume Bonfill, cognate*

### Ten

As he's been fascinated by space travel since he was a boy, the Commissioner is euphoric when—in order to acquire some authentic space gadgetry for an as-yet-undefined exhibition—he convinces the bank managers to fund his trip to visit the Baikonur Cosmodrome.

The Baikonur launch facility was the main center of aeronautical innovation during the Soviet era and, although geographically located in the state of Kazakhstan, it still belongs to Russia according to a special agreement that remains in effect between both republics.

After making some inquiries at the consulate, however, the Commissioner cannot really be sure how much activity still goes on at the Cosmodrome.

### Nine

Spurning the small sheaf of dollars, the Kazakh taxi driver argues that he's got no passport and will go no further. He abandons the Commissioner in the middle of the desert, right in front of the ruinous marker that represents the border. In a surprising rush of obsolete English, the driver encourages him to step lively and make quick work of the three-mile walk to the space station before he finds himself stranded in the freezing nighttime temperatures. During the walk—the sun beats sharply on his temples to the rhythm of his suitcase clicking behind him on the asphalt—he imagines that he's treading upon the remains of an underwater city to which, strangely enough, no water ever arrived. The sides of the highway are littered with the accumulated scraps of antediluvian vehicles covered with lichen and sprouting reeds. A group of camels stand there nibbling on them. The Commissioner cannot stop thinking that those inexpressive oval pupils were the first to ever observe the launch of the R7 spacecraft that carried Sputnik nestled inside its hull.

## Eight

Inconceivably—or so they've led him to believe—the Commissioner has managed to find lodging in the outbuildings of the Cosmodrome for three consecutive nights. The interpreter they've assigned him, with a white—or almost golden—smiling sexagenarian mustache, comments in an English worthy of Marlowe—seemingly the norm around these parts—that he's part of a pilot project to turn the old complex into a kind of resort; that due to the reduced funds arriving from Moscow they need to be capable of generating their own income.

The Commissioner turns out to be the only guest in the enormous room filled with rusty iron cots and flickering florescent lights. The interpreter asks him if he wants dinner. The menu consists entirely of space flight rations.

Before going to sleep, the interpreter shows him the Cyrillic letters carved into the dormitory door. They are the names of all the cosmonauts who went into outer space and returned alive, he says, slowly tracing the outline of the letters with the tip of his ring finger.

## Seven

The Commissioner sleeps badly, stiff with cold between ragged, moth-eaten blankets, at the mercy of the building's rumbling intestines and a strange dream about an exhibit that contained at least one exceptional piece, some of the best-kept experiments of the secret Soviet cities, namely: the granddaughter of the space dog

Laika maneuvering within an armored Red Army combat exo-skeleton; the hypnotizing satellite that would spread communism throughout the West by means of a danceable balalaika rhythm; and the robotic mole needed to burrow under the earth into America in order to put an end to the Cold War.

## Six

That same morning, after the interpreter takes him to visit the abandoned repair shops, the pre-computer age offices, and the rail depot where they loaded the rockets to take them to the launching area, the Commissioner discovers that his mission is not only turning out to be ridiculous, but that it's flat out doomed to disaster. The Space City is in a ruinous state and has almost no remaining equipment, materials, or workers to speak of. The people in charge have sold almost every piece of value—or copies of the valuable pieces—to small-time scrap metal dealers and other two-bit peddlers.

## Five

Over dinner, the Commissioner tries to explain to the interpreter the problems he's going to be facing if he cannot secure an interesting piece for the exhibition. The interpreter nods as he pours boiling water into a pouch of freeze-dried blinis.

After a while, he tells him that he can design an exhibition that tries to explain the true story of Yuri Gagarin.

The Commissioner, meanwhile, putting the vodka gelatin to good use, thinks that the Russian is only trying to earn a tip, or his admiration, but he listens to him as the afternoon fades into night beyond the dining room's large dirty windows.

The interpreter explains to him that when he was a young man he was Yuri Gagarin's personal secretary; he met him in the flight academy when they were both aspiring cosmonauts. The official story says that they selected Gagarin, from among all the hardworking elite candidates, for his courage and his short stature. Vostok 1, the tiny capsule used to send him into outer space, was not powerful enough to carry any man weighing more than seventy kilos.

On the afternoon when they had to say good-bye to one another, Gagarin confessed to him a different theory: he suspected that the real reason he'd been chosen was his amazingly photogenic looks. Later, the cosmonaut's life devolved into a never-ending sideshow, a pantomime of alcohol and honors, and Gagarin, only thirty-four years old, crashed his fighter jet on a routine flight over the steppes, barely five kilometers from Moscow.

Probably due to that suspicion, says the interpreter with a sad look. A look, thinks the Commissioner, that contains the flaming ruins of the MIG 15, the useless helmet with a cracked five-point star, and the anguish of the young pilot condemned to orbit around the ever-present camera eye, like the dead body of Laika tracing infinite ellipses around the solar system.

Four

The Commissioner finds it no easier to get to sleep the second night, but this time for reasons other than the soundtrack of coughing heaters and the punctual tap dance of the rodents. With increasing clarity he imagines the exhibition he is going to mount about Gagarin's secret life, but he first wants to tell the interpreter about it.

In the morning, when he explains it to him, the interpreter nods and tells him that it's not a bad idea, but that making a work of video art only for connoisseurs might be too conformist. The interpreter says that he shouldn't try to hide the story inside such cutting edge contemporary jargon, that he needs another perspective, a pop culture one, for example.

The interpreter adds that it could be something about Gagarin and Soviet science fiction films; he describes how in his favorite one, two cosmonauts flying aboard a strange rocket land on the moon; the young men, without air tanks, slip on some skis and go slaloming down the lunar slopes, the mountains of the moon that all the young people in the fifties grew up dreaming about. Can I find those tapes? Maybe even see them? asks the Commissioner. The interpreter shakes his head and says "Only in here," while delicately tapping his temple. The Commissioner refills the thermos

with hot water from the central samovar, and stows his little pic-
nic—he's sick of freeze-dried space rations, and the interpreter has
managed to get him a few sandwiches—in his backpack for what
looks to be their last outing.

## Three

When they go outside, the interpreter removes his uniform shirt
and drapes it over a cactus in flower. He huffs and snorts while
he busies himself with an old dead golf cart bearing the logo of a
Mediterranean resort on the side. Help me attach these, he tells
him, and shows the Commissioner the parachute cords that he's
trying to hook onto the saddle of a camel sitting there resting, either
distracted or completely resigned to its fate. The Commissioner
laughs until he understands, and then he quiets down and takes off
his shirt, too, and helps the interpreter properly secure the knots to
the anchor points, taking care to not disturb the camel.

Once they set out on the road driving towards the old launching
site, the animal's strength leaves the Commissioner amazed. Then
the interpreter tells him that the interesting story he needs might
not only be Gagarin's; he also knows another. A little while later the
interpreter hauls back firmly on the reins of his retro-futurist stage-
coach. The hot sun glares off the dry cracked earth.

When the Commissioner considers how camels, with their abil-
ity to serenely travel such long distances, were the forerunners to
spacecraft, he thinks it was probably right that the beasts had the
privilege of being the first spectators in the world to witness these
launches into orbit.

## Two

At the launching pad, the launch tower still stands, like a mega-
lithic monument to abandonment. The Commissioner thinks he
spots some pieces of a rocket hull on the surrounding tarmac and
tries to convince the interpreter to let him take them with him.
The interpreter answers that he would sell them for at least a hundred dollars, if they weren't really just scrap metal from old cars. It

doesn't matter, says the Commissioner. Besides, we wouldn't even be able to pick them up, the Russian responds, under this sun the metal alloy can heat up to a hundred degrees centigrade.

While the Commissioner takes some photos of the old launch tower, the interpreter asks him if he can tell him the other story he'd alluded to. As the Commissioner doesn't answer, wrapped up in examining the labyrinth of options on his digital camera, the interpreter begins to explain how during one of the endless publicity tours on which he accompanied Gagarin, he drank too much and made some remarks about a union leader's fading beauty. The comments reached the ears of the Committee three thousand miles away; they forced his transfer and his descent down the party ladder. The interpreter ended up spending several years working as a janitor in the Classics Department at Moscow University. That apparent tragedy—the miserable pay, working like a slave, and public dishonor—eventually opened up for him a new, personal horizon.

The Commissioner interrupts him to tell him that a hundred degrees centigrade isn't really so very hot, that his wife who is seven months pregnant takes the lasagna out of the oven when it's twice that hot using just a pair of teddy bear mittens. The interpreter nods and both of them, with great care, using their shirts to protect their hands, begin stacking pieces of tin and bolts from the presumed fuselage in the golf cart.

After barely five minutes they decide to stop to smoke a cigarette and then, for the first time, the Commissioner hears the interpreter's thin lips pronounce the name Vladislav Illich-Svitych. Svitych's story is difficult to explain, he says. It begins with his linguistic studies and then intersects Gagarin's space flight and the death of both men under strange circumstances.

One

Svitych was born the same year as Gagarin. His Nostratic hypothesis is perhaps mankind's principal secret discovery, says the interpreter, and his lively expression invites the Commissioner to listen closely to his recollection. When Svitych was twelve years old, during some

Cultural Olympics, he first had the intuition that all languages are descended from a common ancient ancestral tongue. Years later, at university—distressed by Gagarin's recent orbital flight, disappointed at not being the first citizen to achieve this feat—he discovered that his linguistic theory had already been formulated, but not developed. That same afternoon, he understood what his own odyssey would be, which border he would have to cross.

The Commissioner keeps loading the tin into the golf cart, but he starts following the interpreter with his eyes. Svitych, says the interpreter, trained a cohort of young philologists who devoted themselves to the comparative study of ancient languages, trying, through their concerted efforts, to see if they could trace the path backwards or, rather, plumb the depths of time: through lexemes and endings, uniting the Altaic family with the Uralic, the Uralic with the Indo-European, long before genetic mapping was able to show us with certainty that humanity truly descended from a single original trunk.

The Commissioner freezes spellbound before a hex nut while pausing to catch his breath. Yes, says the interpreter, Svitych found the rudiments of that prehistoric tongue, the common seed of all the civilizations. Later he killed himself on the steppe, like Gagarin, barely five kilometers from Russia, in a little car belonging to the linguistics department, two years before the cosmonaut's jet crashed. It seems he cranked the wheel ninety degrees while driving on a straight road and the car flipped and rolled. The previous semester the authorities had sent one of his colleagues to the gulag for being Jewish, and they had also terminated all Nostratic studies, declaring them to be both unpatriotic and insufficiently pro-Slavic. As the interpreter finishes the story, the Commissioner places the last scrap of iron atop the pile in the golf cart and the three of them, Commissioner, interpreter, and camel, start to head back with great difficulty, the humans walking on both sides of the cart. Two hundred meters further on, descending the slope of a sand dune, one of the pieces of iron slips loose and plummets downhill, striking the camel and slicing a deep wound into its right side. Suddenly the front hooves come to a halt and the animal collapses head first onto the sand. Noticing the desperate expression on the Commissioner's face, perhaps because the man is imagining yet another death on the steppe, the interpreter explains to him that people will come looking for them in a few hours. GPS? asks the Commissioner. The interpreter doesn't answer.

## Zero

Night falls over the desert. To ward off the cold, the Commissioner and the interpreter huddle up against the side of the wounded camel, which emits an occasional groaning bleat. They've tried to stop the blood but the wound keeps bleeding profusely. The Commissioner misses his tattered moth-eaten blankets and wonders if it wasn't a mistake not to have scratched his own name into the door alongside the cosmonauts who came back alive. The interpreter watches the sky, naming constellations to try to fall asleep. The Commissioner has his eyes closed and thinks about Gagarin and Svitych, and about Svitych and Gagarin.

During that night, for the first time he understands that the two stories actually make up one single story. Beyond the fact that both men were born the same year, and both died in ridiculous accidents on the outskirts of Moscow, the story of the linguist and the cosmonaut seem to him like the very semblance of the downfall of the Soviet Union.

The superhuman challenge of the conquest of space reduced to four-color posters bearing Gagarin's likeness, petrified into hundreds of smiling sculptures, in burned negatives of children's science fiction movies.

The dream of radical equality between peoples exterminated by the rejection of Svitych's common ancestral language, exiled from any scientific vanguard, confined to Siberia, erased from the textbooks, completely ignored like some two-bit Paleolithic Esperanto.

And the effort of both to construct that new society, to expand the boundaries of the Revolution—the Commissioner keeps thinking as he listens to the interpreter's strong, calm breathing, and the camel's plaintive groaning—annihilated and converted into the catastrophe of forty thousand square kilometers of spaceport city filled with rust and weeds: without any other future than becoming a destination for nostalgic tourists or cynics. Communism as an amusement park in ruins.

When the morning finally comes, a vehicle arrives to pick them up. Out steps a space station worker with two blankets and a Kalashnikov. The man hands them the blankets and aims his rifle at the camel. The sound of the weapon jamming reminds them of the long cold night all over again. The worker removes the magazine, checks the weapon, and reinserts it. This time it fires. This is the first time that the Commissioner witnesses the execution of a mammal. The worker feels the camel's neck for a pulse. The Commissioner wonders how they're going to drag that pile of metallic space scrap all the way back to the base.

TRANSLATED BY BRENDAN RILEY

# GIOVANNI ORELLI

## *death by Laughter*

I'M NINETY-NINE POINT NINE years old, a hundred let's say, thus I am, and have been for a while, a *depontanus*. What's a depontanus? Let's look to the Latins for a little illumination. Varro, a prodigious erudite (116–27 before Christ), says that depontanus was the term for the aged who, once they turned sixty, were cast off (*deiciebantur*) a bridge. Hitler used less spectacular methods to get useless old people out of the way, out of circulation.

There are a thousand ways to die. Of illness, from external violence. From hemlock to the electric chair. By being cast off a bridge to a firing squad. Can you die from laughing? You can! I recall three of my schoolmates. Names Zeferino, Sebastiano, and Severino. The three, at the time aged fourteen, with their parents' permission, had decided to take an Easter ski trip to the Blinnenhorn, a glacier Swiss-German tourists loved. Heading towards the summit, the three followed the Germans; but going down on that holy Thursday they veered off the path of their sage confederates. Zeferino, the boldest of the three, had a daring gleam in his eye. Go, he said, where I go. Do what I do. And he shot off. Three hundred meters down he lifted his arms for a big jump. Sebastiano, a few meters behind, imitated him instinctively, without knowing why, and Severino did the same. Zeferino was the only one who realized that they had jumped a crevasse. It could have been a negligible crevasse, just another wrinkle on an old man's brow; it could have been a proper crevasse, the kind from which you don't come out alive and it's a miracle if they can find your body and put you to rest in the cemetery like a normal person. The tragic thing, as Sebastiano would say years later, telling the story for the hundredth time, the tragic thing was that Severino had started laughing like a idiot. At first the other two had also laughed, but like normal people. When they noticed that

Severino's laughter was becoming convulsive, as if a legion of lice were under his jacket tickling him, and his face started turning red, they yelled for the Germans, who were also skiing down the slopes, but like orderly and prudent Swiss people on the less adventurous but more secure trail further away. Luckily, one of those Germans must have been a doctor, because as soon as he saw Severino's face and terrorized eyes, he gave him two good slaps around his mouth, all agape from laughing. Severino stopped, just like that. He was still all purple, but safe.

Less than a year later, two of those three guys from the Blinnenhorn set off, not *magnis itineribus*, but at a moderate pace, stopping to ask people they came across whether they were headed in the right direction for the city villa where they had been invited for a Sunday meal. Yes, this is the way, someone finally replied: here you are, buon appetito, boys! The two were Severino and Sebastiano, one of whom had ended up in high school with the priests, the other in another high school with the non-priests. Another path had been chosen by or for Zefirino. A path that could have been considered foretold by the kids' alphabet book under the letter Z: *Zefirino goes to Zurich*. Zürich vier. Where he would discover crevasses altogether different from the ones in the Blinnenhorn glacier between Ticino and Valais. He would also quickly discover the sheer size of the city: long gone the mumbo jumbo of his two mouth-breathing buddies from the Blinnenhorn. He would soon learn to distinguish the five work days and the two weekend days, easy. His teacher was a clever fox, an astute and enterprising woman, a girl from some Mediterranean puddle of the northern city, where it was as if the crevasses were covered and concealed by damned fresh light snow. You could only discover them by falling in. At any rate, they weren't fatal. The two mumbo-jumbo brothers, having reached their destination for that Sunday's meal, weren't thinking about crevasses. Sebastiano proclaimed: let's hope there's no chicken.

—Why, you don't like chicken?

—It's not that I don't like chicken, I do, but I like to eat it with my hands, not a knife and fork. Like the bourgeois with their deli-crapitudes do.

At Sebastiano's reply, Severino fell silent, into private meditation. Thinking of Severino, even when he grew "up" (he was nearly 1.65 m tall, with five cm extra for having been declared *fit* in the formidable Swiss army), of what one would write on his gravestone to epitomize his life, a conclusive phrase—assuming that a life can be summed up in the half line that goes beneath one's first and last name and dates of birth and death (a line like, for someone who was a teacher, "devoted to school and family")—his phrase could be *keep stirring your coffee, even after you're dead and gone*. OK, that's not an acceptable phrase. But that was him. That was his signature, his calling card. Once he'd taken his cup of coffee, he'd stir it for at least five minutes, never laughing, not even smiling. With sacerdotal seriousness. One daren't say like Christ, because they say in the Gospels (as, for example, St. John Chrysostom in the sixth of his Homilies on the Gospel of Saint Matthew) that Jesus was seldom to laugh. Or smile. They also say, going further back, that for a time laughter was not permitted in the Academy. Some say that no one ever saw Pythagoras laugh or cry.

Severino stirred at length, even if uselessly, as the sugar had long dissolved. He was afraid a few granules had not. Was he risk averse? It could be said of him (if one were so bold, after Leonardo when he mentions all those who come into the world as mere passage for food) that he had come to the globe to stir the sugar into his coffee. Naturally for him, just as much as for the many other passages for food, no one had the right to keep them from dressing up those actions, essential for them, with occasional, casual chatter of various sorts: sports, for example, especially sports, but sex too, and other things.

Occasionally, Severino's laughs were gigantic, with his mouth opening all the way to his ears—as if he were facing a sudden, unforeseen, terrifying crevasse. With his mouth yawning like a sea monster's swallowing hapless little fish.

With the second laugh that may warrant a brief recollection, it is important not to forget the location. Right on time, the two mumbo-jumbo brothers, Sebastiano and Severino, greeted, as one does, not in mumbo-jumbo but in the vernacular, the lady hosting the lunch. Who had invited them to an "engagement" (as the locals call it) because during the ration years during World War II (which is unfortunate to have to mention, especially for the good percentage of female readers who prefer to busy themselves with fashion, good recipes, domestic architecture), she spent her summer vacation months in the hometown of the two mouth-breathers turned high schoolers. Whose parents had provided at convenient prices and even given away delicacies from the local salami shop and cheese shop. Naturally, the lady, delicate by definition, didn't expect from the two the least compliment about the decor per se, or its "ontology" (to use a word often repeated by her firstborn), and not especially in its metrically calculated location, much less for the genealogical tree of plates and saucers, though the lady of the house had naturally made sure to get the best service, even for those two who, as you could tell by their faces, would have eaten out of a shoe as long as they were eating, without stopping to ask if they could wash their hands (Matthew 15). With their publican hands, clumsy and squat, they greeted the dowager and her two not unpleasant—au contraire!—daughters, about ready to move from high school to university, thus to getting lucky, or more likely, seeing as they were girls, to getting married. She led them straight to sup (is that the right word?) to settle the engagement chop chop. In moments like this, the capital question came back to the fore: what is there to eat? Motivated, this question, not by the what but the how. As with refined aesthetes in the field (field?) of poetry. Let's pray (the two: *avertat Deus*, from the two greenhorn-yokels, *utinam* . . .) it's not chicken. Here you can't eat with your hands. Never ever, not yet being aesthetes, would they have dared to do so (not at age fourteen or fifteen, but later on: the fastest thing in the world is perhaps the passing of years), like the Swiss sculptor who came down to this southern canton on the invitation of a troupe of local artists. Served first, as was polite, he didn't wait a half minute. He grabbed his T-bone with both hands and gobbled it up like an animal, moving a young literature teacher to effuse in his tablemate's ear a little parody of a sonnet he'd been teaching at school: "Of the modern arts no concept / that a single bone doth not confine / with its flesh:

and its bone align / the mouth that obeys . . ." The teacher paused. Obeys what? asked the neighbor to whom the poetic variation was addressed. It's a matter, the teacher was quick to reply, of finding a rhyme for the term "concept" that Michelangelo placed at the end of the first line. It's not a difficult rhyme. I can even rhyme with Giacometti, his spines like spaghetti, thin as a machete, all bone and no flesh, in short the complete opposite of our friend's steak. We're back to the baroque! Whereas Sebastiano and Severino were struggling with the classical. Classical chicken, tough like Cicero.

—It's not chicken, it's turkey, the Hostess curtly specified. But more curt than her genteel correction was a sudden backhand of a bone. Because the knife in Sebastiano's grip, due to an excess of vigor (his hands and arms were specialized, to put it sportsmanlike, in pitchforks and shovels, not table forks and knives), caused him to project off his plate a bone from that stupid turkey or subpar chicken, whatever it was. It shot off like a puck in a hockey game with just seconds left on the clock, the home team up four to three, and a defender in the penalty box for interference. And so someone hits the puck across the ice: either it'll make it or it'll be over. The bone landed just to the right of the hostess, who jumped like a referee ready to call a foul. And a whistle, shrill and short (though a malign coincidence of Fate), was heard: perhaps it came from the street, from an officer who had damned to holy penance a reckless biker? Maybe even an Italian.

There at the table, tangible, immense in its heedless vulgarity, cowardly, country, uncivilized, medieval-hottentot, unqualifi-able-zulu, came Severino's cackle for the foul expulsion committed by Sebastiano. Who wanted to say, for his part (finally, about time!): mind that he's not laughing, he's yelling, crying, as if on the edge of a crevasse on the Blinnenhorn. Is he laughing out of despair? And instead, with the same astonishment, he started laughing too, but not with his mouth boorishly agape like Severino's, which would keep on going if he had no ears to stop it . . . what a buffoon.

Naturally the lady shot up, with newfound athletic prowess. She left the two fools without uttering a word, calmly stepping away in her heart from those beastly peasants who kept on breeding indis-criminately based on the great heavenly command to go forth and multiply, assiduously encouraged in this by the priests, those hucksters. Her two daughters, the schoolgirls, to cancel out the vacuum created by the crevasstic cackling, asked, almost stealing the words from her mouth, if people in the mountains often ate turkey.

—What? Sebastiano said awkwardly.

—Turkey, the younger schoolgirl clarified.

—It's nicer than chicken.

—Of course, why yes of course we eat it. My aunt makes it very well.

This was, for Severino, such a colossal lie, that he managed to hold back the urge to laugh. He looked at Sebastiano as if to say, like a father-confessor (with their tone of "How often do you touch yourself?"), how many lies do you tell in a month? But the light in his eyes changing abruptly seemed to silently and abruptly suggest: quiet, we're concentrating on our meal. Schoolgirl Number One, more detached from the conversation than her sister, took the salad *with her hands*, but they were fairy hands, electric fingers. The second observed with a smile that the two ate like Germans—or chickens, who mix all their courses into one big dish, including the salad. We separate, Italian-style. *Distingue frequenter*, says the philosopher. You haven't done philosophy yet? And at the pair's "no," she asked: So what are you studying? Sebastiano said to Severino:

—You talk, you're second in the class, silver medal.

—My compliments, said Schoolgirl One. —And who's first?

—Some guy who the Latin teacher, a priest, always gives high scores on everything he turns in, he even takes his hands . . .

And here instead of more words came a giggle quite like the one from the crevasse.

—He touches him? Schoolgirl Number Two asked, serious.

Severino nodded emphatically, still laughing with his entire mouth, already a little purple in the face. He became so consumed by a coughing fit at the thought of the battles over getting to the head of the class and making all the parents and relatives happy that pragmatic Schoolgirl One took his hand and practically dragged him to the privy, i.e., the can, the bathroom. There he could cough without making a scene. But back at the table, all it took in the silence was the sound of a fork making a banal cling against the plate, all it took was a light kick in the shins from Sebastiano urging him to compose himself, or as they say at school, to behave, to provoke more laughter.

Sebastiano believed that with someone like Severino one laugh *fatally* (he underlined the adverb in his head) prompts another, due to which he had determined that in such circumstances it was opportune (he'd just learned *oportet* in Latin) to move on to the thank-yous, thanks a million, and good-byes, in any case. Unfortunately Schoolgirl Two had another question, which was no longer about philosophy, but again food.

—So what do you eat up in the mountains?

Of course not always turkey, actually never, Sebastiano thought. But he deemed it opportune to censor himself about breakfast. There were a few too many of them at the table, they were in good health, thus with perfect appetites. Often, to quench that early morning appetite, they had a pan with roasted mashed potatoes. The competitors' strategy hinged on the rate that the food disappeared. They ate the first three-quarters of the pan quickly, but still like normal people. After that came the rush, the race. You had to go for the last spoonful not too soon but especially not too late. Just like cyclists or athletes coming in all at the same time at the sound of the bell for the last lap around the track. Like choosing the moment for the final shot, the decisive one, neither too soon nor too late. Or like when the consul (the president) of their little community (the *vicinia*) set a day when the townspeople could go up to the little field behind the houses to make that pile of hay that belonged to everybody and nobody. There was a rule that was unwritten but had been passed down in the memory of all and was respected by all: the first person to land his scythe in the grain that belonged to everybody and nobody shall have the hay. One of them who didn't give a hoot about that clump of hay but woke up at three in the morning at the first glimmer of light anyway would rush to get there before his hated neighbors. To be a peasant, sometimes you have to have a strong stomach and iron arms, but also a hard head. Schoolboy Latin, in comparison, is as soft as fresh bread.

Severino also censored himself, remembering one night a question an out-of-towner asked one of the four peasant women sitting on the church pew after the evening rosary.

—So, how big was your family?

—Nine kids. Plus Ma and Pa. They eat too.

And another, with pride:

—There were twelve of us, eight girls and four boys. Wanna hear the names?

No, please. The one with twelve went on:

—Luckily, five died as babies.

The visitor who had stopped to chat with the local women:

—How on earth did your mother manage: the land, stable, house, twelve children!

The local woman said:

—One time a city girl came asking about the food, and she talked in city dialect. My mother told her: *O per quell la tavola l'è granda*: If you're worried about that, the table's big enough. Had he been the one to ask the question, at that reply Severino would have had another laugh on top of his Blinnenhorn-crevasse–*crevassus maximus* laughs. We could have all cracked up. Instead he had it, his laugh, far back, at the priests' high school, fourth year. The good English teacher, trying to learn the language of Dante, had also asked about peasant dishes, and Severino concluded his appreciated report with the response-turned-maxim previously given by the *depontana*: *o per quell la tavola l'è granda*. At which the English teacher stated: that "o per quell" isn't quite clear to me. How could I translate "o per quell"? he wondered. And then half a minute later he replied in a triumphant voice: *No problem*, the table's big enough. No problem.

But the table in the town from which the English teacher came was even bigger. And if the poor, as a philosopher once said, are the blacks of Europe, the blacks of Africa and the non-blacks of other countries in the world are even blacker then the blacks of Europe. Having said this, the English teacher had a slight, immeasurable smile, such that, irrepressibly, Severino replied with one of his most desperate Blinnenhorn laughs: how many crevasses there were in the glacier of the world!

He, Severino, also wondered (the two high schoolers returning to their respective residences in Sunday silence), who doesn't have even a table? Who who who hoo-hoo hoo-hoo! Or any roosters chickens old hens for the Sunday meal or broth for the week? Does an old hen still make good broth? Even on Friday? Even if Friday is (was) the day of leanness and fasting. Lean, okay, but as for fasting . . . An empty sack can't stand, the peasant declares, and maybe the Latins said so too. On the road back, the two didn't talk anymore, much less about salad or chickens or turkeys or whatever it was. Severino had of course resumed "stirring his coffee," as he had taken very seriously that detail about the five babies who, unlike the other seven, had been fated to a difficult birth and after birth passed from the risk of death to death in fact. Amen. But the intriguing thing for someone like Severino (who promises, growing up, to become *Severo*) is that three of those children, baptized, according to the will and timing of others, went right to heaven, and two of them to limbo.

About limbo, someone like Sebastiano or Severino had an idea that came, in an elementary, reductive form, from the priest's explanations during religion class. A place where there is neither weeping nor gnashing of teeth (of course, newborns don't have teeth yet), a place neither good nor bad: a place without rooms, set apart, in the solitude of the outcasts. Without demons and their hooks, like the ones woodcutters use to bring down larch and fir logs to their hereafter. As for the place itself, Severino and Sebastiano both pictured it like the waiting room at the local train station, the night of their first nighttime New Year's. First they cheered and drank with the others at the birth of the freshly newborn and perhaps not yet baptized year. But a few hours later, once the party was over, they found themselves with other teenagers, rowdy, drunk, waiting for the bus or the train. In a corner of that limbo there was also a woman with two little children. An attentive rail employee had let the woman off the train, explaining to her that to get where she wanted to go she needed to take the train to Zurich, not Basel, which went in a different direction. They could wait for the right train in the waiting room. In limbo, amidst the scraps of paper and empty bottles on the ground, amidst the din, what entered into those babies' delicate memories? Was it like the precipice of a crevasse in the Blinnenhorn for them too? They were all sleepy but couldn't fall asleep. Must real limbo last for eternity too? It's a monstrous punishment. Really something to think through, before saying to some guy, some girl, *go to the devil, go to hell,* or even (from the less violent, heard less often) *go to limbo.* A curse so monstrous—and on the first of the year!—that it triggered, in someone like Severino, a Blinnenhorn-laugh: fatal, or just about.

TRANSLATED BY JAMIE RICHARDS

# WAYNE PRICE

## *Everyone's the Same Inside*

MY FATHER WAS THE FIRST of the family to stay on at school. His older brothers left as soon as they could, at fifteen, and apprenticed themselves to various jobs at the colliery; his sister earned a small wage as an assistant at the village chemist's, then was married and out of the family home by seventeen. My grandfather never quite forgave him, I think, but my grandmother was immensely proud to have a scholar in the family. At exam time she insisted that he be allowed to study at the back of the garden in my grandfather's pigeon cot—up until then the old man's own, jealously guarded refuge—away from the overcrowding and endless squabbles of the little terraced house.

One morning, my father opened the door to the cot as usual and was astonished to see a sparrow hawk roosting alongside the pigeons, eyeing him steadily from behind the chicken-wire doors that fronted the perches. He told me he'd wondered if he was seeing things in the shadows, after the brightness of the morning outside, but no—as his vision adjusted to the gloom, the hawk's features grew definite: the charcoal bars on its pale, out-thrust chest; the gold rims of its eyes; the brutal little bill-hook of its beak. It was almost twice the size of the racing birds beside it.

For a while my father simply stood there quietly and stared. It must have swooped for a pigeon just as the birds were being called in after their last evening exercise, flashed after its prey right into the cot itself and then somehow been hidden by the other birds when the roosts were closed and latched.

He had no idea what to do next. The pigeons seemed calm enough—it was clearly no threat to them inside the roost. If he tried to free it, which was his first thought, he knew it would attack him and cause panic in the cages. Maybe one of the racers would damage itself, break a wing or its neck. Then, Christ, there'd be hell to pay. He examined the hawk's talons on the wooden perch and imagined them at his face and eyes. The scalpel point at the tip of the beak, too: bright black, like the tip of a nib dipped in ink. But if he did nothing, his father would certainly find it after work and kill it through the wire with a garden fork, maybe, or shears.

At a loss, he sat down, turned away from the strange visitor and opened his books to study, and my father's story was interrupted at that point and I never found out what became of it. In my mind's eye it's there still, looming at my father's back like calm King Death himself, and all the other birds perfectly peaceful, roosting alongside it like it was one of them, no stranger to them at all.

My father's great friend in those days was Alf Morano, a boy whose grandparents had come from Italy to the coalfields in the twenties. They'd opened a small café and ice cream franchise that survived all the way into my boyhood, until the long strike finally put paid to it. My father's and Alf's main pleasure in life, in the summer holidays at least, was fire-starting on the mountains above Aberdare and the Cynon. Along with Alf's little brother, Tony, and sometimes a rag-tag band of other no-good boyos from the village, they'd light the grasses, gorse and heather after any long dry spell and try to set half the parish ablaze. The fun of it, my father told me, was racing the flames for dear life if the wind switched round and drove the smoke and fire after them. The beatings he took for it from his own dad (who always smelt the smoke on his clothes and knew) were legendary, and held up as a gold standard of punishment to my brothers and me.

My father and Alf Morano remained friendly all the way into adulthood, though by then Morano had grown into a difficult, quarrelsome man. At some point he'd taken fiercely to religion and preached sometimes at the Gospel Hall where they prayed in tongues and boasted that God could mend anything from cancer to hemorrhoids if you believed enough and let them lay on hands. He never courted or married and as far as I know had no cronies apart from my father. Over time he feuded so bitterly with the elders at the chapel he was finally told to worship elsewhere. He even worked alone—an unusual thing in that close-knit mining community—window-cleaning, odd-jobbing or welding in a small, zinc-roofed hut he'd built for himself one summer. Smothered top to bottom with black pitch, it sat crookedly amongst the brick garages and workshops that over generations had strung themselves out along the village brook. If I ever passed the shed when he was busy there, the rusty door would be wide open, whatever the weather, and a weird, Plutonic music would be drifting out from the record player he'd set up inside, running off a diesel generator. I know now he was listening to Gregorian chants, of all things, though as a boy the sounds were other-worldly and ominous to me.

But even more than music and quarreling, Morano loved to fish for trout and was safe enough company then, so when my father took me fishing, he would offer Alf a ride up to the Brecon Beacons with us.

The water we fished was a small, remote reservoir deep in the Beacon hills. Its high, crenellated dam reared up at the head of a narrow valley like some long-lost Norman battlement, and the single-track access road ended in shadow just below it. I don't recall ever seeing another car or fisherman there, though I suppose sometimes there must have been and my sense of the place's loneliness has cancelled them from memory. It was a bleak spot, even in summer, the banks steep-sided and the water so peat-stained it seemed you were casting your line onto black oil where nothing could possibly live. But we pulled the occasional wild trout from there some days—wiry, half-starved, needle-toothed things.

One day, deep into June it must have been because I remember being in the midst of my last school exams, Morano took me fishing there without my father. God knows why—we'd never fished without him before and I was a morose, generally silent adolescent, at least around anyone older. I must have been bad company at the best of times and no kind of company at all for the most part. But we made the long drive anyway to the tall, overbearing dam hidden in its fold of hills, toiled up the grassy slope beside it in the late afternoon sun and began our fishing as usual, some distance from each other.

It was getting dark when I sensed him standing at my back. I hadn't heard him approach and had no idea how long he'd been standing there in silence, watching me. I turned and nodded. Any luck? I asked.

He shook his head and stared past me at the flat, dark water, then up at the hills beyond, the lonely blue crowns of distant Cribyn and Pen y Fan.

I'd waded in a little way—not far because the bottom shelved so dangerously past the margins—and when I turned to slosh back to where he waited on the bank the sound of the water breaking around my feet seemed unnaturally loud in the stillness. Now that evening was drawing in the sky had grown milky and vague. The air was still warm, though, heavy and clammy, and midges were beginning to lift like vapour out of the heather.

I joined him where he stood, laid my fishing rod flat with its tip in the water, and lit a cigarette.

He watched me, still wordless, and shook his head.

Keeps the midges off, I apologised, and blew the first stream of smoke away from him.

I've been watching you, he said simply.

I took another drag. Oh, I said.

He nodded slowly. I see a lot of unhappiness. Too much of it in a bright young lad like yourself.

I laughed, embarrassed. I'm fine, I said.

No, he said.

We were both silent again for a while and I smoked the cigarette down greedily, desperate to finish it and be able to wade back out into the water.

Is it a girl? he asked, and I laughed again, incredulous. I could feel my throat begin to tighten.

God, mun—I'm fine! What's this all about? I flicked the half-smoked cigarette away onto the stones.

He didn't answer immediately, but something about his manner kept me rooted there in front of him.

When I was your age, he said at last, and troubled like you, I used to cure myself of all that by thinking about what was inside all them pretty girls. You know, all the organs and guts and everything.

Not a pretty sight, if you ever got to see it. He nodded to himself. It stops you thinking any of them are so special they're worth ending yourself over. You see what I'm saying? There was a quiet urgency in his voice suddenly and I was afraid he might reach out and grip my arm, or shoulder. That's how I saved myself from that kind of thing, he said.

For some reason, I remembered a story of my father's about how when they were boys Morano would sometimes press-gang the younger kids of the street into acting out long, elaborate melodramas that he'd written in stolen school exercise books, stage directions and all. He'd direct them in a kind of frenzy, and of course it always ended in disaster when they couldn't learn their speeches or got bored and rebelled. Strangest of all, though, my father reckoned, was the way he'd devote days of fevered writing and tyranny to each project and then, when it fell to pieces, abandon the whole thing in a moment and turn his mind to something else entirely, as if the whole thing had been just some kind of dream he'd woken from and instantly forgotten. I felt myself edging backwards now, but still couldn't seem to turn my face from him to end the conversation.

You see what I'm saying? he repeated.

I don't know, I said. I could feel the gnats settling and biting on my forehead, crawling into the hairs. I could feel them at the rims of my nostrils, and stepping on the lashes of my eyes.

He nodded again, thoughtfully. Everyone's the same inside, see, he said.

Aye, I said, and rubbed my itching face with both hands, breaking the awful stillness between us, maybe looking then like the desperate young lover he'd decided I must be.

Put some of this on, he said, and fished out from a deep pocket in his coat a small glass jar filled with some kind of white ointment.

What's that? I said.

It'll keep them off, he said. Better than those dirty smokes, see. Put some on your face and hands.

It smelled faintly of petrol and almonds and went on thick like greasepaint, and whatever it was, the midges loved it. I remember cursing, furious, then crashing into the cold water and doubling over to scrub away the crawling mask. And all the time I could hear Morano behind me, cackling like a fiend—the first and last time I ever heard him laugh—and when I finally straightened and turned to confront him he was kneeling on the stones, as if sick with hilarity, or praying crazily with it, and all my anger vanished and I was helpless with laughter too.

Six months later, when the snow and ice of the worst December in years must have made the smaller roads into the hills almost impossible, Morano drove alone to the little parking spot below the reservoir and ran a length of hose from the exhaust into the cab. I was at university in England by then and hadn't yet come home for Christmas. One night when I telephoned, shivering, from a call box on the campus, my father told me that a Water Board engineer had found him sitting there, frozen solid like meat inside an icebox, nearly a week after the petrol tank must have finally coughed itself dry.

We only spoke about it once when I got home. It was late on Christmas night, I think, and my father told me about the last time, as kids, they'd set fire to the mountain. The wind had turned and the three of them—dad, Alf Morano and his little brother, Tony, eleven by then—had run yelling and whooping as usual ahead of it. But whether because the wind suddenly got stronger or because some of the grass was too green and the smoke was thicker, Tony got into trouble, maybe panicking or half-blinded, and the flames overtook him. He stumbled screaming down the slope towards the river, the two older boys not realizing in time and only reaching him when he'd already plunged in. He was alive, though the carpet of burning grass had melted away the rubber soles of his shoes and he'd been running on bubbling skin until that had scorched away too. We did save him, my father said. We did save him.

They carried him, all three boys hysterical, back to the house in Windsor Terrace and then, as if miraculously, he became completely calm and Morano's mother was able to comfort him and lay him down on the bed. He died of shock just after the doctor arrived, and my father marvelled, as he told me the story, that other than the burns to his feet there wasn't a mark on him.

I know of course that my father told me the story as some kind of confession. I know he thought, in his guilt, that it must have had something to do with Morano's own death, up there under the dam in the snow. And maybe that's how it was, though I never told my father about the strange conversation about love we'd had, just Morano and me, looking out over the water to the big Beacon hills on that one evening he took me fishing. Maybe it all comes down to the same thing in the end, anyway. Finding out so young—too young—that you could be saved at last, and it could still not be enough.

TRANSLATED BY JAMIE RICHARDS

# AUTHOR BIOGRAPHIES

LIZA ALEXANDROVA-ZORINA, a prize-winning author, popular journalist, and public activist, was born in 1984 on the Kola Peninsula and settled in Moscow after graduation. She was a finalist in two important literary competitions: the Debut Prize and the NOS Literary Prize for her novel *The Little Man*; she also won the Northern Star Prize in 2010. Her books include *The Little Man*, *The Rebel*, *The Broken Doll*, and *Man is a Noun*. *The Little Man* and *The Broken Doll* were published in French. *The Little Man* was also published in English and Arabic. Critics compared *The Little Man* to Dostoyevsky's *Crime and Punishment* and to Zvyagintsev's prize-winning film *Leviathan*.

SNEŽANA MLADENOVSKA ANGJELKOV was born in 1977 in Skopje. She completed her MA in Film and Television at the Faculty of Dramatic Arts in 2012. Her first novel, *Eleven Women* (*Ili-Ili*, 2011), won the Utrinski Vesnik Award for Best Novel of the Year. She has also published *True-to-Life Pictures* (2014), a theory on film editing and its vital role in shaping creative documentary film with an emphasis on the documentaries of Macedonian director Vladimir Blaževski. Angjelkov has extensive experience in television editing and has creatively shaped over five hundred documentaries, reportages, travelogues. She is currently working on her new novel.

MĀRIS BĒRZINS was born in Riga in 1962 and has written nine books—novels, short stories, plays, and children's literature. His plays have been performed in Latvian theaters, while several of his short stories have been produced as films. Bērzins's current historical novel *A Taste of Lead* was adapted by the National Theatre of Latvia within a year of its publication. Due to its extensive popularity with readers, the book has been reissued several times, gained the interest of film producers, and has as well received six awards, including the Latvia Literature Prize for Best Novel of the Year and the prestigious Baltic Assembly Prize.

**IANA BOUKOVA** was born in Sofia in 1968. She has a degree in Classics from Sofia University. She is the author of two books of poetry, as well as the short story collection *A as in Anything* (2006). Her novel *Journey along the Shadow* was published in 2008. Iana Bukova's poems and stories have been published in anthologies and journals in Albania, Argentina, the UK, Greece, Italy, Mexico, the US, Serbia, Hungary, France, Croatia, Sweden, and Chile.

**MIKKEL BUGGE** was born in 1978 in Vesterålen, just north of the Lofoten archipelago in Northern Norway. He made his debut in 2007 with the short story collection Perimeters. His first novel, *Go Under Ground*, was nominated for Norway's two biggest readers' awards and won him the Havmann Prize in 2011. His third book, the short story collection *The Rope*, was published in 2014 and was shortlisted for Norway's national book award, the Brage Prize. Bugge has also written two plays for the stage. He currently lives in Oslo.

**MAROSIA CASTALDI**, born in 1950, is a writer and painter from Naples living in Milan. She has published numerous collections of stories and novels. Her highly lyrical and experimental work gravitates toward abstract and eternal themes like time, death, emotion, and art, as well as place and the Mediterranean. She is critically acclaimed but undoubtedly underread.

**RUXANDRA CESEREANU** was born in 1963 in Cluj, Romania, and is Professor at the Faculty of Letters (Department of Comparative Literature) in Cluj and member of the staff at the Center for Imagination Studies (*Phantasma*). Cesereanu has published eight books of poetry as well as two experimental volumes co-authored with Andrei Codrescu and Marius Conkan. Her poetry has been translated into English, Italian, and Hungarian. She has produced seven books of fiction, including the novel *Tricephalos*, the short story collections *Nebulon* and *Birth of Liquid Desires*, the cyberpunk novel *Angelus*, and her most recent novel *One Sky Above All*. An English translation of Angelus was published in the US in 2015. Cesereanu is also known for her research and critical writing, with seven books of non-fiction published in the first decade of this millennium.

ANN COTTEN was born in Iowa, USA, grew up in Vienna, Austria, and finished her studies with a work on concrete poetry. Her first publication, *Fremdwörterbuchsonette* (2007), consisted of 78 double-sonnets in a hairpin formation, which surprised the German poetry scene. This was followed by *Florida-Räume* and *Der schauernde Fächer* (Suhrkamp), *Hauptwerk. Softsoftporn* (Engstler), and, in English, *I, Coleoptile* (Broken Dimanche Press). Her most recent works are the illustrated epic poem *Verbannt!* and the forthcoming English collection *Lather in Heaven* featuring text and photography (Broken Dimanche Press, 2016).

GAUZ was born in Abidjan, Ivory Coast, as Armand Patrick Gbaka-Brédé. He immigrated to France with a degree in biochemistry and has worked many different jobs, including as a security guard in a store. The protagonist of Gauz's début novel *Débout-payé* (2014), Ossiri, is a "vigile," or security guard, which puts him in a unique position to comment on race, consumerism, and immigration in contemporary Parisian society. The book won the Prix Lire in the "First French Novel" category as well as the first-ever literary prize attributed by Gibert Joseph, awarded in 2014. Gauz has also written the screenplay for a film about young immigrants from the Ivory Coast, *Après l'Océan*.

JIŘÍ HÁJÍČEK was born in 1967 and grew up in rural South Bohemia. He now lives in České Budějovice. Since the late 1990s he has published two novellas and three collections of short stories, including *Vzpomínky na jednu vesnickou tancovačku* (*Memories of a Village Dance*, 2014), from which the story in this volume is taken. Hájíček's first novel, *Dobrodruzi hlavního proudu* (*Mainstream Adventurers*), was published in 2002. His two subsequent novels—*Selský baroko* (*Rustic Baroque*, 2005) and *Rybí krev* (*Fish Blood*,

2012)—won Magnesia Litera Prizes. Gale A. Kirking's English translation of *Rustic Baroque* was published in 2012 by Real World Press. His books have appeared in English, Italian, Hungarian, Croatian, Macedonian, Belarussian, Polish, and Bulgarian, making him one of the most successful writers in the Czech Republic today.

MIKKO-PEKKA HEIKKINEN, born in 1974, is a Finnish journalist who writes serious, humorous prose about oddball residents of the hinterlands facing the pressures of the modern world—and how they pressure the modern world right back. He debuted with a collection of hilarious short stories, *The Destruction of the Liquor Store in Nuorgam* (*Nuorgamin Alkon tuho; Johnny Kniga*, 2010), from which the stories in this volume are taken. His first novel, *Invasion of the Snowmobiles* (*Terveiset Kutturasta*, 2012), was a genuine breakthrough whose incisive humor immediately won over critics and readers alike. The following novel, *Bullheaded* (*Jääräpää*, 2014), also became an admired bestseller. The film rights to his fourth work, *Reindeer Mafia* (*Poromafia*, 2016), were optioned already prior to publication.

PHILIP HUFF was born in 1984 and graduated from the University of Amsterdam. He is the author of the novels *Days of Grass* (2009), *The Empty City* (2012), and *Book of the Dead* (2014); the short story collection *Good to be Here* (2013); and the essay collection *The Sadness of Others*. Huff won the DJP Literary Award and the Hollands Maandblad Prize for Prose. He wrote the screenplays for three films: *Days of Grass* (2011), based on his debut novel, *Greenland* (2015), based on a short story, and the forthcoming *The Empty City* (2017), directed by Michiel van Erp. He lives in New York City.

JONATHAN HUSTON is a writer, translator, and creative writing teacher living in Liechtenstein and Los Angeles, writing in German and English. His collection of German short stories, *Mondstaub – Erzählungen*, was published in March 2016 by the Van Eck Verlag, Liechtenstein, and presented at the Leipzig Book Fair. His short fiction has appeared or is forthcoming in publications in Liechtenstein, Switzerland, the United Kingdom, and the United States, including the *Jahrbuch des Literaturhauses Liechtenstein*, the *Dreck hält warm – Grüsse aus dem Unterholz* catalog of the Kunstverein Schichtwechsel, the Future Reloaded anthology of the Collegium Helveticum, and the literary magazines *Jupiter, Origins, Cicada*, and *Quiddity*. He can be found at jonathanhuston.com.

KARMELE JAIO, born in Vitoria-Gasteiz in 1970, has written three collections of stories: *Hamabost zauri* (*Fifteen Wounds*, 2004), *Zu bezain ahul* (*As Weak As You*, 2007) and *Ez naiz ni* (*Not Me*, 2012); two novels: *Amaren eskuak* (*My Mother's Hands*, 2006) and *Musika airean* (*Music in the Air*, 2010); and a book of poetry, *Orain hilak ditugu* (2015). The novel *Amaren eskuak*, which was very well received by Basque readers and has received a 2016 English PEN Translates award, has also been adapted for the screen and was presented at the San Sebastián International Film Festival. Her stories have also been adapted for the theater and published in many anthologies.

IDA JESSEN is one of Denmark's most acclaimed and popular writers, having authored a score of novels, short story collections, and children's books since publishing her first book in 1989. A recipient of the Lifetime Award of the Danish Arts Foundation, she has twice been nominated for the prestigious Nordic Council Literature Prize, most recently in 2014 for her collection *Postcard to Annie*. Her latest novel, *En ny tid* (A Change of Time), will be published in the USA by Archipelago Books.

STÉPHANE LAMBERT, born in Brussels in 1974, is a poet (*The Penis and the Hand; The Garden, the Earthquake; Chapel of Nothingness*), novelist (*The Man of Marble; The Colors of the Night; Paris: City of the Dead*), and essayist (*Farewell to the Countryside: Claude Monet's Water Lilies; Mark Rothko: Dreaming of Not Being; Nicolas de Staël: Faith and Vertigo*). The major themes running through his works are desire, the body, the family, death, the chaos of the contemporary world, and artistic creation. In 2016, critics warmly embraced his book *Before Godot*, which examines the link between a painting by Caspar David Friedrich and Beckett's celebrated play.

**DAVID MACHADO** was born in Lisbon in 1978. He is the author of three novels, *Deixem Falar as Pedras*, *O Fabuloso Teatro do Gigante* and *Índice Médio de Felicidade* (European Union Prize for Literature, 2015), the last of which will be adapted for film and translated into about a dozen languages. He has authored several prizewinning collections of short stories for children. His books are published in Italy, France, Brazil, and Morocco.

**DAITHÍ Ó MUIRÍ** is the author of five collections of short stories: *Seacht Lá na nDíleann*, *Uaigheanna agus Scéalta Eile*, *Cogaí*, *Ceolta*, and *Litríochtaí*. He was awarded the Cló Iar-Chonnacht Literary Prize in 2001 for *Cogaí*. He is the author of one novel, *Ré*. He lives in Connemara, Ireland.

**GIOVANNI ORELLI**, born in 1928, is a central figure in Swiss-Italian letters. He is the author of more than a dozen novels, as well as several books of poetry, and he has long been active in the cultural sphere of Ticino. In 1997, he was awarded the Gottfried Keller Prize. His novel *Walaschek's Dream* was published in English translation by Dalkey Archive Press in 2012. His most recent work is the short story collection *I mirtilli del Moléson*, published in 2014 by Nino Aragno.

**ELENA PENGA** was born in Thessaloniki. She studied theater and philosophy at Wesleyan University and screen and theater writing at the University of Southern California in Los Angeles. Three collections of her short stories have been published by Agra, one of Greece's best-known literary publishers. *Tight Belts and Other Skin* is the winner of the Ouranis Prize from the Greek Academy of Letters (2012). Her plays were first staged in New York's Off-Off Broadway scene in the 1980s. Since Penga returned to Greece in the 1990s, her plays have been extensively translated and performed in Greece and elsewhere. She also wrote the screenplay for Lakis Papastathis's award-winning film *The Only Journey of his Life*. She teaches playwriting and lives in Athens.

SVEN POPOVIĆ was born in 1989 in Zagreb, now located in Croatia, but back then in Yugoslavia. His short stories were published in the anthology of young Croatian writers *Bez vrata, bez kucanja* (2012), in the short story collection *Record Stories* (2011), and in various magazines and webzines like *Quorum*, *Zarez*, and *Arteist*. He has contributed as a freelance journalist to a number of magazines like *Zarez*, *Aktual*, and the Austrian leftist magazine *Wespennest*, as well as writing literary and album reviews for various webzines. His collection of short stories *The Sky Is in the Gutter* came out in 2014 and received excellent reviews.

TERESA PRÄAUER is an Austrian fiction writer, essayist, and visual artist. She is the author of the novels *Johnny und Jean* (2014) and *Für den Herrscher aus Übersee* (For the Emperor from Overseas), which won the Aspekte Literature Prize for best German-language prose debut of 2012. In 2015, she received Droste and Hölderlin promotional awards, and was shortlisted for the Leipzig Book Fair Prize. In fall 2016, she will release her third novel, *Oh Schimmi*. She regularly publishes on the subjects of poetry, theater, pop culture, and fine arts. She is currently a Samuel Fischer Guest Professor of Literature in Berlin and in spring 2017 will be a writer-in-residence at Grinnell College.

WAYNE PRICE was born in South Wales but has lived and worked in Scotland for many years. He has won or been shortlisted for many international short story awards, including the Bridport, the William Trevor/Elizabeth Bowen, *Glimmer Train*, the Sean Ó Faoláin, and the Raymond Carver Prizes. His first short story collection, *Furnace* (Freight, 2012), was long-listed for the Frank O'Connor Prize and nominated for the Scottish First Book of the Year Award; a novel, *Mercy Seat*, was published by Freight Books in 2015, and his recent pamphlet collection of poetry, Fossil Record (Smith|Doorstop), is a Laureate's Choice. He teaches at the University of Aberdeen.

UNDINĖ RADZEVIČIŪTĖ, born in 1967, is a Lithuanian writer who is known for her intellectual black humor, her use of multi-layered texts, her fusing together of East and West, as well as her mixing of the philosophical with the mundane. She graduated from the Vilnius Academy of Arts where she studied art history, theory and criticism, and after four years she left her doctoral studies for a job in an international advertising agency. She worked as a creative director in a worldwide network of advertising agencies for over a decade. In 2003, 2011, 2013, and 2015 her books were shortlisted for the Most Creative Book of the Year Award (Lithuania). In 2011 and 2013 her books were shortlisted for the Best Book of the Year Award (Lithuania). Her fourth book, *Fishes and Dragons*, won the 2015 EU Prize for Literature.

CARLOS ROBLES LUCENA was born in 1977 in Terrassa, Spain, and holds a degree in Humanities Studies from the Universitat Pompeu Fabra in Barcelona. He works as a teacher of Spanish Language and Literature in the Aula Escola Europea. His short stories have appeared in such magazines as *Quimera*, *The Barcelona Review*, and *Bonsái*. His first book of short stories, *No Pregunten por Gagarin* (Don't Ask for Gagarín), is published by Ténemos Edicions.

ZSUZSA SELYEM is a novelist, critic, translator, and Associate Professor of twentieth-century Hungarian literature and literary theory at Babes-Bolyai University, Cluj, Romania. One of the most important experimental voices of mid-generation Hungarian fiction, she has published two volumes of short stories, a novel, and five volumes of criticism to date. Her 2006 novel *9 Kilos (Story about Psalm 119)* was translated into German and French. Several of her short stories can be read in English translation in *The Missing Slate*. "Confectionery 1952" is part of Selyem's forthcoming volume, *Becási*, consisting of self-standing short stories which together make up a highly unusual family history, mostly narrated from non-human points of view and embedded in the traumatic history of communist Romania.

MAJA GAL ŠTROMAR, writer and actress, was born in 1969 in Slovenia. She studied Italian, French, and acting at the Jacques Lecoq International Theatre School in Paris. Her literary works so far include three collections of short stories: *Goga 66000*, *Na Predpomlad Mi Reci Ti* (Call Me By My First Name Before Springtime), and *Že Češnječas* (It's Cherry Time); five novels: *Amygdala's Heart, Lju.beznica ali Svetloba po dekretu* (Little Love or Light by Decree), *Misli name, ko ti je lepo* (Think of Me in the Good Times), *Potaknjenci* (Cuttings), *7kg do sreče* (7kg to Happiness); a theatrical monodrama, *Alma Ajka*, published in Slovene and Arabic at the Biblioteca Alessandrina in Egypt; a poetry collection, *Boginja z zamudo / Dea in ritardo* (Belated Godess), published in Italy with an audio CD; an educational manual on theater, *Črkolandija* (Letterland); and the charity story "Anina zvezdica" (Anna's Little Star). Maja has also written many plays for children and adults and several radio plays broadcast by Radio Slovenia and the Italian National Broadcaster RAI.

AGNIESZKA TABORSKA has published seventeen books in Poland; some have been translated into English, French, German, Spanish, Japanese, or Korean. Her titles include essay collections: *Conspirators of Imagination: Surrealism, Topor's Alphabet, and American Crumbs*; short story collections: *The Whale, or Objective Chance and Not as in Paradise*; and literary mystifications: *The Dreaming Life of Leonora de la Cruz* (Midmarch Arts Press, 2007) and *The Unfinished Life of Phoebe Hicks*. Her books have won awards in Germany. *The Black Imp and Other Sprites* won the award for Best Polish Children's Book of 2014. Agnieszka Taborska has translated novels by Spalding Gray, Roland Topor, Giselle Prassinos, and Philippe Soupault.

IVAN TOKIN was born in Belgrade in 1971. His first novel, *Najnormalniji čovek na svetu* (The Most Normal Man in the World), published in 2014, had eight reprints in less than a year and was shortlisted for the annual NIN Award for Best Novel of the Year 2015. His collection of short stories *Molekuli* (Molecules) was also published in 2015. He lives in Belgrade. He hopes for the best.

# TRANSLATOR BIOGRAPHIES

KRISTIN ADDIS translates primarily between Spanish or Basque and English, and is one of few who translate directly from Basque into English. She specializes in literary translation (short stories, novels, poetry) and has also translated works about the Basque language and culture. Ms. Addis has spent many years in the Basque Country; she currently resides in Iowa.

MARTIN AITKEN is the translator of a host of works from Danish, including books by Kim Leine, Peter Høeg, Dorthe Nors, and Helle Helle. His translation of Ida Jessen's novel *En ny tid* (A Change of Time) will be published in the US by Archipelago Books.

ALISTAIR IAN BLYTH was born in Sunderland, England, and attended the universities of Cambridge and Durham. He ended up in Romania at the end of the last century and has remained there ever since. His translations from the Romanian include, most recently, the novel *The Bulgarian Truck* by Dumitru Tsepeneag, published by Dalkey Archive Press.

DAVID BURNETT was born in 1973 in the Greater Cleveland area and has lived in Leipzig, Germany, since 1995. His first book-length translation was the East German novel *New Glory* by Günter de Bruyn, published by Northwestern in 2009. He received a 2014 PEN/Heim Translation Fund Grant for his translations of Prague-born Johannes Urzidil, a selection of which is forthcoming from Pushkin Press.

GREGOR TIMOTHEY ČEH was born and brought up in a bilingual family in Slovenia. After studying at UCL in London he taught English in Greece and then completed a Masters at Kent. He now lives in Cyprus and regularly translates contemporary Slovene literature for publishing houses and authors in Slovenia with translations published in both the UK and US.

PAUL CURTIS DAW is a lapsed lawyer whose translation of Evelyne Trouillot's novel *Memory at Bay* was published in 2015 by the University of Virginia Press. His work also appears in *Words Without Borders*, *Best European Fiction 2016*, *Subtropics*, *Cimarron Review*, *K1N*, *carte blanche*, *Indiana Review*, and nowhere. He serves as an officer and director of the American Literary Translators Association.

PAUL FILEV is a freelance translator and editor living in Melbourne, Australia. He is the recipient of a Dalkey Archive Press Fellowship. He translates from Macedonian and Spanish. His translations from Macedonian include *The Last Summer in the Old Bazaar* by Vera Bužarovska and *Alma Mahler* by Sasho Dimoski, forthcoming from Dalkey Archive Press. He is currently working on the translation of a novel from Spanish, *Blue Label* by Eduardo Sánchez Rugeles.

MARGITA GAILITIS was born in Riga, Latvia, immigrating to Canada as a child with her family. Gailitis returned to Riga in 1998 to work as a translator of Latvian laws into English in support of Latvia's application for membership in the European Union, achieved in 2004. Today Gailitis focuses her energy on literary translation and poetry. She has translated some of Latvia's finest poetry, prose, and dramaturgy and is a tireless advocate for Latvian literature worldwide, for which she was awarded in 2011 the prestigious Three Star Order by the President of Latvia. Gailitis's own award-winning poetry has been published in periodicals in Canada, the US, and Europe.

MATTHEW HYDE is a literary translator from Russian and Estonian to English. He has had a number of translated short stories and novels published by Dalkey Archive Press, *Words Without Borders*, Pushkin Press (forthcoming), and Vagabond Voices (forthcoming). Prior to becoming a translator, Matthew worked for ten years for the British Foreign Office as an analyst, policy officer, and diplomat, serving at the British Embassies in Moscow and Tallinn, where he was Deputy Head of Mission. After that last posting

Matthew chose to remain in Tallinn with his partner and baby son, where he translates and plays the double bass.

JOVANKA KALABA is a Belgrade-based literary translator, passionate about finding exceptional pieces of Serbian and Yugoslav fiction and contributing to their worldwide recognition through her translations. Her most important translations include Jovanka Živanović's novel *Fragile Travelers* (2016, Dalkey Archive Press) and "Mila and the Stranger," a story by Ivo Andrić, the Yugoslav winner of the Nobel Prize in Literature.

ROMAS KINKA works as a forensic linguist and literary translator; he believes one discipline complements the other. His translation of Kristina Sabaliauskaitė's *Vilnius Wilno Vilna: Three Short Stories* was published in 2015 and his translation of Undinė Radzevičiūtė's novel *Žuvys ir drakonai* (Fishes and Dragons) is scheduled for publication at the beginning of 2018.

VIJA KOSTOFF is a linguist, language teacher, writer, and editor. She has collaborated with Margita Gailitis in translating the novels, short stories, plays, film scripts, and poetry of many of Latvia's major writers. Born in Latvia, she now resides in Niagara on the Lake, Ontario, Canada.

ELIZABETH LOWE is the founding director of the Center for Translation Studies at the University of Illinois at Urbana-Champaign and currently teaches in the New York University MS in Translation. She has translated both Brazilian and Lusophone writers, including Clarice Lispector, Euclides da Cunha, Machado de Assis, J.P. Cuenca, Antônio Lobo Antunes, and most recently João de Melo. Her translation of J.P. Cuenca's *The Happiest Ending for a Love Story is an Accident* (2013) was a finalist for the IMPAC award. The Brazilian Academy of Letters recognized her for the second translation of the national classic *Os Sertões* by Euclides da Cunha (*Backlands: The Canudos Campaign*, 2010). She resides in Gainesville, Florida.

ERIKA MIHÁLYCSA teaches twentieth-century British and Anglo-Irish fiction at Babes-Bolyai University, Cluj. She is the editor, together with Rainer J. Hanshe, of the arts journal Hyperion: On the Future of Aesthetics (Contra Mundum Press), and is a prolific translator of contemporary British and Irish fiction and poetry into Hungarian. Her translations of contemporary Hungarian writing have appeared in World Literature Today, Two Lines, Trafika Europe, and Numéro Cinq.

ANDREW OAKLAND is a translator of fiction, poetry, and biography from Czech and German. Novels in his translation include Radka Denemarková's *Money from Hitler* (Women's Press, Toronto, 2009) and Michal Ajvaz's *The Golden Age* (Dalkey Archive Press, 2010; a 2011 BTBA Fiction Finalist) and *Empty Streets* (Dalkey Archive Press, 2016).

SARAH OSA studied Japanese and Chinese Studies at Cambridge University, UK, and Arts and Cultural Management at Pratt Institute, New York. She has worked in the classical music industry since 2005 in New York, London, and Oslo, and is also active as a freelance translator. She lives in Zurich.

URSULA PHILLIPS is a British translator. Her translation of Zofia Nałkowska's 1927 novel *Choucas* (Northern Illinois University Press, 2014) won the Found in Translation Award 2015, while Nałkowska's *Boundary* appeared in May 2016 (also from NIUP). Other translations include Maria Wirtemberska (*Malvina, or The Heart's Intuition*), Narcyza Żmichowska (*The Heathen*), and Wiesław Myśliwski (*The Palace*).

TEGAN RALEIGH is a PhD candidate in Comparative Literature at UC Santa Barbara. She has translated works of both fiction and non-fiction from French and German into English, for which she has received awards that include the PEN/Heim Translation Fund Grant and a fellowship from the American Literary Translators Association.

JAMIE RICHARDS is the translator of several works from Italian and Spanish, including Giovanni Orelli's *Walaschek's Dream* and Serena Vitale's interviews with Viktor Shklovsky, *Witness to an Era*. She holds an MFA in Literary Translation from the University of Iowa and a PhD in Comparative Literature from the University of Oregon.

BRENDAN RILEY is an ATA Certified Translator of Spanish to English. He holds degrees in English from Santa Clara University and Rutgers University and certificates in Translation Studies from UC Berkeley and the University of Illinois. His translations include Álvaro Enrigue's *Hypothermia*, Juan Filloy's *Caterva*, and Carlos Fuentes's *The Great Latin American Novel*.

DOUGLAS ROBINSON has been translating from Finnish since 1975, including entries in BEF 2010 and BEF 2015. His most recent translation is of Aleksis Kivi's great 1870 novel *Seitsemän veljestä*, which he has translated as "The Brothers Seven." He is Chair Professor of English at HKBU in Hong Kong.

ANGELA RODEL is a literary translator living in Bulgaria. She received a 2014 NEA Translation Grant for Georgi Gospodinov's novel *The Physics of Sorrow*. The novel was also shortlisted for the 2016 PEN Translation Award. Six novels in her translation have been published by US and UK publishers. Her translations have appeared in literary magazines and anthologies, including *McSweeney's*, *Little Star*, *Granta*, *Two Lines*, *The White Review*, and *Words Without Borders*.

PETRA ŠLOSEL is a translator and art historian, holding a double MA in Translation Studies and Art History from the University of Zagreb. Currently working on a research project for the Croatian Association of Visual Artists, she is simultaneously pursuing her interest in literary translation. She lives and works in Zagreb, Croatia.

JAN STEYN is a literary translator and critic who works on modern and contemporary texts written in Afrikaans, Dutch, English, and French. His literary translations include *Newspaper*, *Works*, and *Suicide* by Edouard Levé; *Orphans* by Hadrien Laroche; and *Alix's Journal* by Alix Cléo Roubaud.

KAREN VAN DYCK directs Hellenic Studies at Columbia University. Her recent translations include The Scattered Papers of Penelope (Graywolf, 2009), a Lannan selection, The Greek Poets: Homer to the Present (Norton, 2009), and the Guardian Poetry Book of the Month Austerity Measures: The New Greek Poetry (Penguin 2016).

# ACKNOWLEDGMENTS

DIRECÇÃO-GERAL
DO LIVRO E DAS
BIBLIOTECAS

FÉDÉRATION
WALLONIE-BRUXELLES

ILLINOIS
**ARTS**
COUNCIL
AGENCY

ISTITUTO
*italiano*
DI CULTURA
CHICAGO

STYRELSEN
DANISH AGENCY FOR CULTURE

AMT FÜR KULTUR

NORLA
NORWEGIAN LITERATURE ABROAD

POLISH CULTURAL
INSTITUTE
LONDON

swiss arts council
**prohelvetia**

SLOVENIAN
BOOK
AGENCY

CYNGOR LLYFRAU CYMRU
WELSH BOOKS COUNCIL

PUBLICATION OF BEST EUROPEAN FICTION 2017 was made possible by generous support from the following cultural agencies and embassies:

DGLB—The General Directorate for Books and Libraries / Portugal

Etxepare Basque Institute

Fédération Wallonie-Bruxelles

Illinois Arts Council

Italian Cultural Institute of Chicago

Kulturstyrelsen—Danish Agency for Culture

Lichtensteinische Landesverwaltung

Norwegian Literature Abroad

Polish Cultural Institute

Pro Helvetia, Swiss Arts Council

Slovenian Book Agency

Welsh Books Council

# RIGHTS AND PERMISSIONS